BLOOD PASSAGE

ALSO BY HEATHER DEMETRIOS

Exquisite Captive
BOOK ONE OF THE DARK CARAVAN CYCLE

BLOOD PASSAGE

BOOK TWO

of the

DARK CARAVAN CYCLE

HEATHER DEMETRIOS

BALZER + BRAY

An Imprint of HarperCollinsPublishers

Balzer + Bray is an imprint of HarperCollins Publishers.

Blood Passage

www.epicreads.com

Library of Congress Cataloging-in-Publication Data
Demetrios, Heather.
  Blood passage / Heather Demetrios. — First edition.
      pages   cm (Dark caravan cycle ; book 2)
  Summary: "Nalia and her comrades travel to Morocco to
search for Solomon's sigil" — Provided by publisher.
  ISBN 978-0-06-231859-6 (hardback)
  [1. Genies—Fiction.   2. Magic—Fiction.   3. Wishes—
Fiction.   4. Morocco—Fiction.]   I. Title.
PZ7.D3923Blo   2015
[Fic]—dc23
                                                           2014048045
                                                           CIP
                                                           AC

Typography by Torborg Davern
Map art © 2014 by Jordan Saia
15 16 17 18 19   LP/RRDH   10 9 8 7 6 5 4 3 2 1

❖

First Edition

For my siblings Meghan, Jake, and Luke

The Arjinnan Castes

THE GHAN AISOURI: Once the highest caste and beloved of the gods. All but annihilated, the members of this female race have violet eyes and smoke. They are the only jinn who can access the power of all four elements: air, earth, water, and fire.

THE SHAITAN: The Shaitan gain power from air and have golden eyes and smoke. They are scholars, mages, artists, and the overlords who once controlled the provinces.

THE DJAN: The largest caste and the peasant serfs of Arjinna's valleys. They have emerald eyes and smoke, and their power comes from earth—the sacred soil of Arjinnan land. They are manual laborers, denied education or advancement.

THE MARID: Caretakers of the Arjinnan Sea and fishing folk, these serfs draw their power from water. Their eyes and smoke are blue. They are the peasants of the coast, as uneducated as the Djan and subjected to equally brutal labor.

THE IFRIT: Long despised throughout the realm, the Ifrit have crimson eyes and smoke. Their power comes from fire, and they use its energy for dark magic. They are soldiers and sorcerers.

The Jinn Gods and Goddesses*

GRATHALI: Goddess of air, worshipped by the Shaitan

TIRGAN: God of earth, worshipped by the Djan

LATHOR: Goddess of water, worshipped by the Marid

RAVNIR: God of fire, worshipped by the Ifrit

* *Because the Ghan Aisouri can draw power from all four elements, they worship every god, though individual Aisouri have their favorites.*

BLOOD PASSAGE

MARRAKECH, MOROCCO

SHE'D BURIED HIM ALIVE.

The surrounding darkness was a black, writhing worm—hungry. It twisted around his body, tightening its grip. Malek finally understood what those hours, days, *months* in the bottle had cost Nalia. Her betrayal, why she couldn't love him: that all made sense now. How could she ever forgive him for *this*?

What little air remained inside the metal box the Ifrit had stuffed him into stank of iron as Malek's blood continued to gush out of his nose, his mouth, his ears. His body was folded into the steamer trunk like a contortionist's: knees hitting forehead, the curved bones of his spine digging into the trunk's side. Each round with the psychic jinni pushed him past his threshold of pain into a whole new universe of agony. She'd been going through the contents of his brain like it was a drawer full of junk, throwing whatever wasn't of use to her to the side. He didn't know how much he was losing or what would be left when she was through with him.

If she would ever be through with him.

"Where is she, *pardjinn?*" his captor asked once again. Her muffled voice came to him from above. Malek knew the bitch was standing over the trunk in the icy room her soldiers had thrown him into, waiting for him to break. She'd already assured him several times that he would.

Malek tried to conjure Nalia's face in the darkness: the cinnamon skin, those eyes that always held a secret, the curve of her lips he'd hardly gotten to kiss. He hoped to God he never saw her again. If he did, it would mean his captor had won.

It would mean Nalia would die right there in front of him.

PART ONE

Conquer fear and you conquer yourself.
Conquer yourself and you conquer the world.

—Ghan Aisouri Mantra

1

SEVENTEEN HOURS EARLIER

RAIF WONDERED HOW MANY TIMES YOU COULD CHEAT death before it wised up.

Any minute now, he expected to hear the harsh cry of an Ifrit soldier cutting through the laughter, singing, and buoyant voices that filled the Djemaa el-Fna, Marrakech's main square. He gripped Nalia's hand as he scoured the crowded expanse for the crimson glow of Ifrit eyes. He was taking the name of the square seriously: Assembly of the Dead. Malek had told them how, not so long ago, the square had been used for public executions. As soon as Raif had stepped out of the taxi that had brought them into town from the airport, he'd felt the malicious presence of the jinn who hunted them. Ifrit *chiaan* made the air heavy, covering the energy of the bustling North African city like lava. Hot and destructive, Ifrit magic would incinerate everything if it could.

"I thought you said you knew where this place was," Raif said.

Malek shot him an annoyed look. "I said my *driver* knew where it was. Usually when I come to Marrakech, I don't have jinn babysitters who think it's a good idea to throw my cell phone out of a *moving plane*."

Raif forced himself to keep his temper in check. It would only give Malek more excuses to point out Raif's comparative youth. He'd had enough of the *pardjinn's* snide commentary on the plane. All that mattered was that Raif got Solomon's sigil before Malek did. Otherwise, Nalia's former master would have a ring that would allow him to control every jinni on Earth—including Nalia, Raif, and Zanari.

"Don't be so dramatic, Malek," Nalia said. "The plane was still on the runway and we couldn't risk anyone being able to track us."

"I hardly think the Ifrit know how to use advanced GPS technology," Malek snapped.

"Wanna keep it down, *pardjinn*?" Zanari said. "I was hoping to avoid capture until we at least got some dinner."

Malek ignored her, pushing through the throng of people that crowded the square.

"This place is nothing like your angel city," Raif said to Nalia. Morocco wasn't just a different country—it felt like an entirely new realm. And yet it was full of wishmaker humans and dirt in the sky and iron that made him sick.

"Los Angeles," she corrected, smiling. "I prefer Morocco. It's more like home."

"We'll be in Arjinna soon," he said, squeezing her hand. *First the ring, then home.* The words had become a prayer, a mantra, a shot in the dark.

Nalia tightened her hold on him. "I hope so."

The square was all shadows and smoke, the inky night kept at bay with small lanterns set on the cobblestones. Smoke from hundreds of food stalls filled the night air, mixing with the incessant beat from the drum circles that lay scattered around the Djemaa el-Fna. Storytellers cast spells and magicians passed around hats after each trick, hoping for a few dirhams for their trouble. The souks bordered the northeast end of the square, a huge swath of labyrinthine alleyways filled with shops selling everything from love potions to rusted scimitars. Most of the Djemaa's perimeter was taken up by restaurants where diners lounged at tables laden with pots of sweet Moroccan mint tea and tagines, the famous Moroccan crockery.

Raif's stomach growled as the scent of lamb and spices wafted over from a nearby table under one of the food tents in the center of the square. He couldn't remember the last time he'd eaten. Dinner didn't sound like such a bad idea, but he wanted it in the privacy of the *riad*, where he could finally relax. He was still drained from the unbinding ceremony he'd performed to free Nalia from her bottle, less than twenty-four hours before. Being in those horrible human planes hadn't helped much, either. It was unnatural, spending so many hours in the sky.

"Nalia, does that street look familiar?" Malek asked. He pointed to an alleyway leading away from the Djemaa.

"I'm afraid I can't help you, Malek," she said, her voice cold.

"Whenever you brought me here, I was in a bottle around your neck."

"Nice, sister," Zanari said. She gave Nalia an appreciative nod and Malek cursed under his breath in Arabic.

Raif fell back as Nalia and Malek continued to bicker about which direction the guesthouse was in. "Anything?" Raif asked Zanari.

She shook her head. "A lot of Ifrit are searching for Nalia—my *voiqhif* told me that much. But nobody knows where she is yet."

Having a sister with the ability to psychically view any place or person in the realms was incredibly useful . . . when it was accurate, anyway.

"Do they know what she looks like?" Raif asked.

"They know about the birthmark," Zanari said. "That's all I can see."

Nalia had already made sure to glamour her eyes, turning them Shaitan gold instead of the telltale Ghan Aisouri violet that would get them all killed. Likewise, the tattoos snaking over her hands and arms had been covered, although those would not have been so out of place in Marrakech. Already, several women had called out to her and Zanari from behind the veils covering their faces, waving around cards with henna designs that looked very much like the tattoos hiding under Nalia's glamour. But the birthmark on her cheek was something she wouldn't disguise; it wasn't the best time, Nalia reasoned, to offend the gods by covering up a sign of their favor.

Raif frowned. "I'll feel a lot better once we stop moving."

"No chance of that anytime soon," Zanari said, with a nod at Malek.

The *pardjinn* had promised that the *riad* he was taking them to was safe—a discreet hotel with only eight rooms, hidden in the folds of the medina's confusion of narrow alleyways and streets. The ancient sector of Marrakech was the perfect hiding place for them, but what made it ideal was also the thing that was keeping them from finding their way around it themselves. They'd been in the square for only fifteen minutes, but that was long enough to be ambushed by the enemy.

"I can tell you this much," Zanari continued. "Calar wants Nalia to disappear. I don't think we should expect an all-out battle. She'll want to do this quietly."

The Ifrit empress had her very best killers scouring Earth. But after killing Haran, Nalia had proven that highly skilled assassins—even ghouls with dark powers—weren't enough to take down the last of the royal Ghan Aisouri.

"This place is crawling with Ifrit," Raif said.

Zanari nodded. "Can't see any, though."

"Probably disguised. But if we feel them, they feel us."

Raif's eyes swept the crowded square. Nobody seemed to be paying Nalia any attention, but it would take only one mistake to alert the Ifrit.

As Malek turned to say something to her, Nalia's head scarf slipped down. His hand reached out to adjust it. In seconds, he'd secured the scarf so that it twisted around Nalia's neck and head like those of the Moroccan women in the square.

"He's a man of many talents, isn't he?" Zanari said wryly.

"Half the time, I don't even think Malek's touching her on purpose," Raif said. "He's just so used to doing what he wants with her."

It bothered him that sometimes Nalia didn't seem to notice Malek's closeness. The way they moved in tandem, how she always came when he called: Raif wondered how long it would take for her to realize she wasn't Malek's slave anymore.

Raif quickened his steps and threaded his fingers through Nalia's, rubbing his thumb against the scar around her wrist, where Malek's shackles had once been. She raised her other hand to the head scarf, self-conscious.

"I look silly, don't I?" she asked.

It was a lucky thing the women in this part of the world wore such clothing—it allowed Nalia to hide the identifying birthmark on her cheek that had helped Haran find her. The ghoul had killed six jinn before he got to Nalia, including her best friend, Leilan. He'd nearly killed Nalia herself.

Raif shook his head. "Not silly at all. Beautiful as always." He leaned in to kiss her, but Malek's voice stopped him.

"PDA isn't approved of in Morocco," he said. "You kiss her out here and you'll attract way more attention than you want."

"PDA?" Raif asked.

Nalia shot Malek a glare. "Human thing," she said, turning back to Raif. *Later*, she mouthed with a tiny, secretive smile. His breath caught a little as he thought of the room they'd share, just the two of them.

Raif pulled his eyes away from her mouth and cleared his

throat. He had to stay focused. "No luck?" he asked, nodding at the street Malek was dragging them toward.

Nalia shook her head. "I don't know what's safer—staying in the square or walking through the medina. At least here it's open. Gods, why did the sigil have to be in the Crossroads?"

To jinn, Morocco was known as the Crossroads, the country on Earth with the highest concentration of jinn and the location of the portal between the human realm and Arjinna. Full of refugees, slaves on the dark caravan, and expatriates, the city was a hub of jinn activity. Raif knew it would be difficult to blend in with the human population. He was too recognizable as the face of the Arjinnan revolution, and no doubt word had spread that the Ifrit had increased their efforts to capture him. The sooner they got out of here, the better.

"This would be a good time to say, once again, what a terrible idea it was to take all my guns from me," Malek said.

Nalia had emptied the plane of Malek's firearms by throwing them onto the tarmac before taking off from Los Angeles—a necessary precaution after Malek hypersuaded Zanari, controlling her mind so that she put a gun to her own head. Raif wasn't sure what had kept Malek from killing Zanari that night; he'd just seen Raif kiss Nalia and help free her from the bottle. To say Malek was enraged would be an understatement. Emerald *chiaan* sparked at Raif's fingertips and he closed his fists over it, stanching the flow of magic. There'd be time enough to make the *pardjinn's* life miserable.

"Malek, I trust you about as much as the Ifrit looking for me," Nalia said. "And I certainly would never arm one of them."

Malek placed his hand against his heart. "You wound me."

Nalia ignored him, pulling Raif toward the circle nearest them, which had formed around a band of musicians. Drums and tambourines accompanied the high lilt of an old man dressed in a traditional kaftan, a robe of homespun cloth with a pointed hood that lay flat against his back. The music conjured thoughts of campfires in open fields, women dancing barefoot in rich Arjinnan soil, and the feel of his *tavrai* around him. A pang of homesickness hit Raif as the words of the song became clear to him: *so long, so long, so long have I journeyed.* He glanced at Nalia and saw his longing reflected in her own eyes. Gods willing, they'd be there soon, restoring their ravaged homeland together.

"If we had my cell, we'd be there by now," Malek muttered to Nalia as he stared at the map in his hand for the hundredth time.

"You control the CEOs of every Fortune 500 company," Nalia said, her eyes never leaving the weathered faces of the musicians. "I'm sure you can manage to read a map."

"I haven't had to read a map in seventy-five years," Malek said. Though Malek didn't look much older than Raif, he'd been alive for over a century. Being half-jinn, Nalia's former master aged incredibly slowly, much like his full-jinn counterparts.

Malek crumpled the map and threw it to the ground. Raif closed his eyes and took a breath. He wished he could discipline Malek like he would a *tavrai*: extra guard duty or a few rounds in the training ring with his most brutal fighters. But Raif wasn't in the Forest of Sighs and Malek certainly wasn't under his command.

"Nalia, you know Earth better than I do—what are our options?" he asked, drawing her away from Malek and Zanari.

"Get out of the Djemaa right away, for one. I can feel the Ifrit, but I can't—" Nalia stiffened. "There," she whispered.

She inclined her head slightly to the left, and Raif's eyes slid to where an Ifrit soldier was making his way through the crowd. He was dressed in a kaftan, the hood up, but even from here Raif could see the glow of the jinni's scarlet eyes. Raif turned away—he'd be recognized in an instant.

"Is it just the one?" he asked.

"I think so," she said. Nalia pretended to drop something, and when she stood, Raif noticed the glint of her jade dagger in her hand.

"I'll try to be quick, but be ready, just in case," she said.

There was no question who would fight—Nalia was four times stronger than he was, the only surviving member of a royal knighthood, with access to all the elements instead of just one, like most jinn. It wasn't time to be proud. Raif caught Zanari's eye and she nodded. She'd seen the Ifrit, too.

Just as the Ifrit neared them, his eyes narrowing as he took in Nalia's face, Zanari bolted toward Nalia. "There you are!" she said loudly.

Nalia turned, startled. Zanari wrapped her arms around her and pressed her lips to Nalia's. Raif's eyes widened. He hadn't been expecting that, but then, neither had the Ifrit. The jinni stopped just a foot away, confused.

Zanari pulled away. "I thought I'd lost you," she said, her voice soft and seductive. She'd turned more than a few heads, but all that mattered were those precious seconds that distracted the Ifrit.

Nalia swallowed. "N-no. I'm . . . here." She smiled and dipped her head toward Zanari, whispering something in her ear.

His sister laughed, but from where Raif was standing, he saw her flex her fingers, ready to use her *chiaan*. Nalia dove to her left, the jade dagger winking as it sliced into the Ifrit's skin. One cut of the charmed blade and he was paralyzed. The humans nearby screamed. Zanari manifested a shadowy barrier around them to put some distance between the humans and the body on the ground.

"So much for flying under the radar," Malek said.

"You need to get us out of here," Raif ordered. "I don't care how, but make it happen, *pardjinn*." He rushed over to where Nalia kneeled over the Ifrit. The jinni's eyes were wide with terror.

She held the blade over the Ifrit's chest, her face pale. Raif took the knife out of her hand and drove it into the jinni's heart, pulled the blade out, then wiped the blood on his pant leg before giving it back to her.

"Let's go," Raif said. He pulled Nalia up with him.

"They're coming." Zanari was clutching at her head. "They don't know it's us, but they know something happened here."

They raced toward the dark, twisting streets of the medina. Malek grabbed a Moroccan man who stood on the fringes of a circle surrounding a cobra that swayed back and forth to his charmer's hypnotic tune.

"I'll give you five hundred dirhams to take me to Riad Mel-houn," he said in rapid-fire Arabic.

"Eight hundred," the man responded, his eyes no doubt taking in the cut of Malek's wool coat and the expensive watch on his wrist.

Malek glared. "Seven hundred. That's too damn much and you know it."

"This isn't exactly the time to be bargaining, Malek," Nalia growled.

"*Yalla,*" the man said, waving his hand with weary resignation. *Let's go.*

Raif grabbed Malek's arm. "Why didn't we do this from the start?"

"I hate being cheated" was Malek's reply. He shrugged off Raif's hand and followed the guide.

"Humans," Raif muttered.

They plunged into the medina as the square behind them filled with the sound of police sirens.

THEIR GUIDE LED THE WAY OUT OF THE SQUARE, WITH
Malek on his heels. Raif motioned for Nalia and Zanari to walk
ahead of him while he took up the rear. He glanced over his
shoulder every few minutes. Someone was following them—he
could feel it. The skin on the back of his neck prickled and the
air shivered with the unmistakable pulse of jinn energy. But every
time his eyes passed over the faces surrounding them, all he saw
were humans.

They turned into one of the narrow streets off the square,
hardly wide enough for the motorbikes that zipped through
them. Women in colorful head scarves and men on rickety bicycles crowded the neighborhood. A blast of sound behind him sent
Raif halfway into one of the tiny shops selling supple leather slippers dyed every color of the rainbow. A motorcyclist wove in and

2

out of the crowd thronging up and down the street, shouting for people to get out of his way. The space was barely wide enough for two people to walk abreast, yet the driver somehow managed not to hit anyone.

Raif shook his head. "Fire and blood."

"Bonjour! Ça va?" said the owner of the shoe shop.

"Oui, ça va," Raif muttered. The jinn ability to understand all languages was the only advantage he seemed to have tonight. His magic couldn't make their hotel instantly appear or root out whoever was following them, but random pleasantries were easy enough.

There it was again—that prickle.

He turned, his eyes sharpening as he shifted from prey to predator. The medina was full of shadowed alcoves and tiny, hidden alleyways, and in the chaos of people, stray cats, donkey carts, and motorbikes, it was all too easy for a jinni to remain out of reach. He heard a familiar, piercing whistle up ahead—two high notes and one low—an old signal he and Zanari had come up with when they were children in order to find each other in the dense Forest of Sighs. He whistled back, then stepped into the street. He had to get this jinni off their trail or they'd lead him right to the *riad* that was supposed to act as a safe house.

Zanari and the others were already half a block away. Nalia looked over her shoulder and Raif's breath caught as lamps of every shape and size from a nearby shop bathed her in a momentary glow. Just then, with the light painting her skin, she seemed paper thin, a fantasy wrought in light and shadow. A creature from the legends his mother used to tell him after a long day of working in their overlord's field. Nalia's eyes grew anxious and he stepped into her sightline. The worry slipped from her face as he hurried to catch up.

"Raif, someone's following—"

"I know," he said. He put his arm around Nalia, drawing her close to him. Even though there was no one in all the realms who could protect Nalia as well as she could protect herself, he still couldn't shake that endless night of calling her back from the shadowlands. After her battle with Haran, the only thing that had kept her in the land of the living was his refusal to let her go.

"I need to deal with this jinni behind us," Raif said. "I'll meet you at the *riad*—Zanari will tell me where it is." Only his sister and his mother knew his true name, which allowed them to contact him any time of the day or night, communicating in images. Once Zanari reached the *riad*, she'd be able to show him how to navigate the tricky medina streets using *hahm'alah*, the magic of true names.

"No," Nalia said.

He bristled at the tinge of authority in her voice, that bit of Ghan Aisouri that would always be a part of her. *She cares about you, that's all*, he told himself.

"It's too dangerous," she added.

He jumped aside as another motorbike zipped through the crowd. "No more than walking through this street," he said. "I'll be fine. Stay close to Zan."

Before she could say anything else, he pressed his lips against her forehead and slipped out of the flow of pedestrians into an empty alley. Signs in Arabic, French, and English advertised

Moroccan wares, but the shop fronts were closed here, their metal gates pulled down except for a lone tailor who sat in the fluorescent light of his cramped closet of a shop, sewing kaftans as he watched a soccer game on an old television. The sport was similar to the jinn game of *hado*, only in *hado*, the ball was made of fire and players could evanesce across the field.

Other than the tailor, the street was empty, dark except for puddles of wan light from a few streetlamps. Raif glanced up at the low roofs. All he could see was a patch of black sky and the distant light of Earth's stars, pale imitations of Arjinna's chartreuse constellations.

Footsteps—close. Boots scuffing across cobblestones, a heavy tread. Raif suddenly wondered if Haran was the only ghoul who had been in Calar's employment. Muscles tense, he stepped into the nearest patch of light, his eyes piercing the shadows. Waiting.

"Let's stop the games, brother," Raif called as the steps got closer. He raised his hands, palms out, ready. Green *chiaan* poured from them, a cascade of energy.

"*Kajastriya vidim, tavrai,*" called a voice from the darkness.

Light to the revolution: the Arjinnan resistance's traditional greeting.

"My soldiers do not hide in the shadows when challenged," Raif said.

An unfamiliar Marid stepped into the light. He wore human clothes: jeans, those hooded short robes they called sweatshirts. "We have not had the honor to meet, sir," the jinni said as he placed a fist over his heart in the revolutionary twist on the jinn greeting.

"Your name?" Raif kept his hands raised.

"Elorou, sir. I was born on Earth and my parents head the resistance cell here in Marrakech," he said.

"Come into the light."

The boy stepped forward. There hadn't been much time for Raif to learn how to lead from his father. Those first years of the resistance were a blur of whispered conversations and late-night meetings at which Dthar Djan'Urbi would meet with his most trusted friends to plot an end to the feudal system that had been in place for thousands of years. Raif had witnessed a few skirmishes, but his first real battle had been the one his father had died in. Just days later, Raif was named his successor. One thing Dthar said had never left him, though: *If a jinni won't look you in the eye, he's not worth the piss in the bottom of a latrine.*

This jinni looked him in the eye. Raif lowered his hands.

"I thought you were an Ifrit tracker," Raif said. "A bad one—I knew you were following me the whole time."

The boy reddened. "You were not alone, sir. My orders—"

"Don't call me sir." Raif wasn't stupid: he knew it was impossible to avoid all power structures entirely. But he'd had to call his overlord 'sir,' and Raif would be damned if he'd make anyone do the same for him.

"Oh. Uh. Right." Elorou coughed slightly. "My orders were to speak to you and you only. I didn't want to draw needless attention. As you know, the Ifrit are being especially systematic in their search for you. They've more than tripled their presence in Marrakech alone."

"How did you find me?" If this boy could track Raif so easily, there wasn't any hope for evading the Ifrit.

"I'm stationed at the airport, so my parents told me to keep an eye out for you. My usual job is to intercept the slave traders. Sometimes they try to ship bottles overseas."

Raif shook his head, disgusted. That had been Nalia three years ago. Only fifteen summers old, drugged so she couldn't use her powers to defend herself or escape, then sold to Malek.

"What do you do when you find bottles?" he asked.

"I take them and free the jinn inside. If they don't have a master yet, it's easy enough. If they have a master traveling with them, I kill the master, then free the jinni."

Yet another child forced to kill because of the Ifrit and their ruthless hold over the jinn.

"Do you kill the traders, too?"

"When I can. They're very good at running away. Cowards." Elorou spit on the ground.

Raif nodded, satisfied. "All right. What's your message?"

"We've captured Jordif Mahar, sir."

Finally some good news.

Raif smiled. "Excellent. How are things on Earth's side of the portal? Safe enough for a meet there?"

Elorou nodded. "Huge battles on the Arjinnan side and Ifrit coming through to Earth all the time. But we control Earth's side for now. It's safest on the western portion—the Ifrit can't spare enough soldiers to guard the whole thing."

The politics of the portal were complicated, in large part because the territory between the two realms resembled a border more than a portal. Jordif had found a way to navigate the delicate balance between the government in Arjinna and the free jinn on Earth, but that had included turning a blind eye while thousands of jinn were trafficked on the dark caravan and sold to human masters in exchange for human weapons. Slaves for arms. Now the resistance had taken over Jordif's responsibilities and cut ties with the traders. And thanks to Nalia's negotiations with one of the human leaders of the slave trade ring, it would be nearly impossible for the Ifrit to continue receiving arms in payment for their slaves.

"Bring him to our post on the west portal at dawn. I'll get there when I can." Raif started walking back toward the main street, then stopped. "Until then, show him the hospitality of the *tavrai*."

"Sir? I don't understand. Um. I mean, being from Earth and all."

"No food. No water. Iron shackles. Use a whip if necessary. But I want him alive when I see him tomorrow. *Jahal'alund.*"

Elorou paled, but quickly recovered as he placed a fist over his heart. "*Jahal'alund.*"

In seconds the young revolutionary was gone, leaving nothing behind but a few wisps of sapphire evanescence.

ZANARI FOLLOWED NALIA AS THE GUIDE PUSHED DEEPER into the medina, where the streets were empty, every door shut tight against the darkness. Other than the occasional stray cat and the drunken man who followed them for a few blocks singing love songs in Arabic and French, Zanari and her companions were alone. After fifteen minutes of walking, Raif's sister was well and truly lost. She had no idea what direction they were going in or where they'd come from. She'd tried to pay attention, but the serpentine streets made it impossible to keep a map of the neighborhood in her head. Finally, the Moroccan leading them stopped in front of an ornate wooden door cut into a nondescript mud-brick wall. Like so many of the doorways in Morocco, it was surrounded by colorful tiles and inlaid with brass flourishes.

"Shukran," Nalia said, thanking the man in Arabic.

A tiny plaque on the wall read RIAD MELHOUN. After traipsing through the deserted, narrow streets of the medina, Zanari hadn't expected much from their *riad*. Still, after seeing Malek's lavish mansion, she was surprised the *pardjinn* deigned to stay at such a humble establishment.

Malek reached into his pocket and pulled out a wad of dirhams. He handed over the money, then waved the guide away. Walking into the darkness, the man whispered, *"Bismillah."*

Immediately, Zanari's body contracted and she clutched at her throat as it began closing up. Her *chiaan* froze, as though it had been dipped in a vat of ice water. Beside her, Nalia fell against the wall, gasping. Malek stared at them for a moment, and then understanding dawned in his eyes.

"Oh. Right," he said, looking from Nalia to Zanari. "The *bis*—well. It'll pass."

Almost as soon as the pain had Zanari in its grip, it was gone. "What in all hells *was* that?" Zanari said.

In those few terrifying seconds, Zanari felt like she understood what the slaves on the dark caravan went through, being stuffed into bottles by traders and masters. She glanced at Nalia. The other jinni was leaning over, hands on her knees, face pale.

"That word our illustrious guide said when he walked away is a powerful protective spell," Malek said. "It keeps humans safe from jinn, but it can't hurt you permanently."

He reached for Nalia, as though to comfort her, but she jerked away. Malek's hand fell to his thigh and his jaw tightened.

"Was that human a mage?" Nalia asked.

"No," Malek said. "He was simply a Muslim whose belief in

the word was real. It's quite effective, isn't it?"

"It doesn't bother you?" Zanari asked.

"I've built up a bit of a tolerance for it—I grew up hearing the word all my life. It's very common for people in cultures like mine to utter it as a prayer before any kind of journey, especially at night or in deserted places." A cold smile played on his face. "In this case, being a *pardjinn* does have its advantages."

Malek grasped the brass door knocker and banged it against the door. It swung open to reveal a small man in a sweater vest and pressed slacks. He gave them a wide smile.

"Monsieur Alzahabi! Madame Alzahabi! What a pleasant surprise—we weren't expecting you."

"*Salam aleikum*, Fareed." Malek stepped out of the deserted street and Zanari murmured under her breath, "*Madame Alza-habi?*"

Nalia shook her head. "My passport has Malek's last name. He tells people I'm his wife when we're traveling because it makes things less complicated."

"Oh, my brother's gonna *love* that," Zanari said.

The door shut behind them and Zanari stood in the foyer, staring. It was like entering another world. There had been no hint of the opulence that hid behind the dirty, cracked walls in the alleyway. The *riad* was built in the traditional Moroccan style with smooth-as-porcelain *tadelekt* walls and an inner court-yard with a central splash pool, its ceiling open to the stars. The balcony overlooking the courtyard was covered with swaths of linen that guests could pull across the railing for more privacy. Potted palms stood beside marble columns carved in a repeating teardrop motif and lamps like metal balls of lace hung in shallow alcoves, their delicate designs reflected on the floors and walls.

"Like it?" Malek asked.

Zanari nodded, turning to Nalia. "Is this what the palace is like?"

"A little." She paused, blushing. "This would be the servant's quarters, though."

"Well, I'm just a simple country girl. This place is amazing," Zanari said. The arches surrounding the courtyard curved in keyhole shapes and the doors to the first-floor rooms had been painted in intricate detail.

"Malek doesn't have many good qualities, but I can never argue with his taste in hotels," Nalia said.

"Thank you, darling," Malek purred. "Your vote of confidence means so much."

"Did you not hear the part where I said you don't have many good qualities?" Nalia said.

"*Not many* is a far cry from *none*."

Malek ignored her scowl as, up ahead, Fareed ushered them through one of the keyhole-shaped arches into a private alcove that acted as a small sitting room. The night had grown cold, but a fire crackled in a fireplace and a pot of mint tea sat on a tray beside an assortment of cookies.

"There will be four of us in total, Fareed," Malek said. "How many rooms do you have?"

The manager's face fell. "Just two, *monsieur*. I'm terribly sorry, if I'd known—"

"That's fine," Malek said. "My wife and I will take one and you can put her brother and sister in the other."

Zanari felt Nalia stiffen beside her. "Maybe I should stay with . . . my sister," Nalia said, glancing at Zanari. "Make it a girl's night."

Malek smiled and drew her close to him. "You can have a girl's night some other time."

Then he kissed her.

It wasn't a kiss for polite company: it looked hungry and a little punishing. With Fareed looking on, Zanari knew Nalia was helpless. She couldn't afford to make a scene, not when they were pretending to be humans on holiday.

Nalia gently pushed Malek away. "My *dear husband*, let's not be rude now."

Malek chuckled and gave Fareed a wink. "How can I resist?" he said.

Fareed gave a small bow. "How indeed?" He gestured toward the velvet couches in the alcove. "Please. Sit. Refresh yourselves while I have the rooms prepared."

As soon as Fareed was out of sight, Nalia turned to Malek. "Don't you *ever* do that to me again, you bastard."

"Now, is that any way to talk to your husband?" he said.

Nalia turned away from him as wisps of *chiaan* slipped past her fingertips.

"I'm going to find the restroom, Zanari," she said, her body shaking with anger. "Don't look in his eyes."

Zanari nodded, motioning for Nalia to leave. It wouldn't

be so easy for Malek to hypersuade her again. "I can handle the *pardjinn*, sister. I learned my lesson with him the hard way. You go . . . take a breather."

Nalia hurried across the courtyard, and Malek watched her for a moment before reaching into his pocket and pulling out a box of clove cigarettes. He lit one, and the ember glowed in the dim light from the colorful lamp that hung above them. It was in the shape of a top, the body made of tiny glass panes that had been fused together. Malek blew the smoke up toward the ceiling, a self-satisfied smirk on his face.

"You really are a piece of work, you know that?" Zanari said.

"When you've been around as long as I have, you'll understand a bit more," Malek said as he tapped the cigarette against the rim of a gold ashtray on a side table. "How old are you, anyway?"

"Twenty-one summers."

Malek nodded. "But your brother is younger. I wonder, why are you so eager to play Follow the Leader with him?"

Zanari picked up the teapot and poured some of the fragrant brew into a delicate red glass. It was a question she was only too happy to ignore.

"Ah, I've hit a nerve, I see." Malek gestured toward the tea with his hand. "I recommend two sugars. Pairs well with the mint."

"My brother is an excellent leader," she said. One sugar. She wanted two, but it was the little victories that counted.

"Really? Because I get the feeling things are a bit dire over in your utopian headquarters. Seems like a problem with the management to me."

Zanari hadn't lied; she supported nearly everything Raif did and she believed he was the best jinni to lead the jinn to freedom. Better than she would have been, if only because he enjoyed the fight. But sometimes she had to ask herself: was she fighting for her brother, or Arjinna? The longer she spent on Earth, away from the conflict in her realm, the more Zanari began to have questions she'd never thought to ask. Meeting Nalia had shown her that some of the truths she'd clung to her whole life were wrong. Not *all* the Ghan Aisouri had been evil, just most of them. And seeing the way Nalia fought, the enormity of her powers, had gotten Zanari wondering: if Nalia wasn't supposed to rule, why had the gods given her such power?

"Your attempt at sabotage is pretty obvious," Zanari said. "Divide and conquer, right? It's not going to work, *pardjinn.*"

She hated that there was a kernel of truth to what Malek was saying; was it possible that she and her brother had been just as brainwashed as Nalia? No one had ever asked Zanari if she wanted to fight, to have a life controlled by hatred.

Malek leaned forward and poured himself a glass of tea, then slowly stirred in his two cubes of sugar with a small silver spoon.

"I'm merely making conversation," he said mildly.

"I prefer silence."

Zanari felt a tug—*habm'alah.* She crossed to the other end of the alcove and held up her hand. A puff of jade smoke slipped out of her palm and she saw her brother's face. She sent him an image of the alcove so that he'd be able to picture it and evanesce directly inside. Moments later, Raif was standing near the fireplace.

"What'd I miss?" he said.

"Apparently Nalia and Malek are married," Zanari said. "And you should have two sugars in your mint tea."

NALIA LEANED AGAINST ONE OF THE MARBLE COLUMNS in the courtyard, gazing at the splash pool. It was a shallow rectangle of water, inlaid with blue, yellow, and red tiles in the popular *zillij* pattern of overlapping eight-pointed stars. The shape was everywhere in Morocco; it was as though the whole country were part of one vast constellation.

Somewhere inside its borders lay Solomon's sigil, buried deep in the Sahara. Nalia ran her finger over the tattoo on her forearm, just one of the many Ghan Aisouri symbols that covered her hands and arms. Her skin held the memory of her mother pressing the needle into it:

"You are now old enough to keep our greatest secret," her mother says as she cuts the star's lines into Nalia's skin. Drops

of blood slip out of the points like tears. "This is how you will find Solomon's sigil if the gods forbid, we are ever in need of its power. The Aisouri are the only thing standing between that ring and the enslavement of our race. We can only use it if our very existence is threatened." Nalia grits her teeth against the pain. If she cries, her mother will press harder. "Vasalo celique," Mehrdal Aisouri'Taifyeh says. "That's all you need to know. Follow the stars."

Nalia thinks she will never need to trace Antharoe's path beneath Earth's sandy floor, where her ancestor left stars as clues. Who is more powerful than the Ghan Aisouri? When her mother finally puts the needle away, Nalia shivers as the weight of the mark on her skin settles over her. If she wanted, Nalia could take the ring for herself. Make her mother bow before her. As if Mehrdal can hear her thoughts, she takes Nalia's chin in her hand, her fingers squeezing. "The gods will punish you if seek out the sigil for any reason other than to save our race," she says. "Do you understand?" Nalia nods, then backs out of the room as soon as her mother loosens her grip. Once dismissed, Nalia runs to the temple. She will make the vous required of her now that this secret is in her blood. She will not break them, not for anything.

Vasalo celique, she repeated to herself. Follow the stars. Much easier said than done.

Nalia looked up. The sky was clear and the stars shone brightly overhead. If she hadn't been here before, she never would have guessed that such loveliness lay within the medina's darkened streets. It was one of the things she'd always liked when she'd visited Morocco with Malek: the whole city was a treasure map of wonders.

Malek. That forced kiss of his still burned, nothing like the searching gentleness of Raif's. Malek's kiss wanted to possess, consume. They hated her a little, those lips. She could feel Malek's *chiaan*, the fire of it. Even now it boiled inside her.

Godsdamn him.

Her eyes strayed to the red and pink rose petals that floated on the pool's surface, and she took a deep breath of the amber-scented air. The oil burned nearby, the rich smoke wafting throughout the courtyard. It made her think of the palace, and the ripple effect of remembering the loss of her home turned Nalia's mind to the greatest loss of all: Bashil. She shouldn't care about Malek's mind games when her brother's life hung by such a thin thread.

Nalia lifted her hand and whispered Bashil's true name into the smoke that appeared on her palm. No matter how many times she called him, the smoke refused to show her his face. She pressed her hand against the marble column beside her and rested her head against the stone. Her lips moved in a silent prayer, one to each of the gods: *Please let him be alive. Please let me go home soon.*

She had to stop letting Malek control her emotions—his power over her was limited to her obligation to grant his wish. That was all. She had to stay focused for Bashil's sake.

The door to the *riad* opened and Nalia turned, expectant. But instead of Raif, a well-dressed couple stepped through the foyer. Fear began to bloom in her stomach. She should never have let Raif go off on his own. Nalia hurried back to the alcove, intent on suggesting Zanari go with her in search of him, when she heard Raif's voice—Zanari must have sent him their location.

"There's no way you're sharing a room with her," Raif was saying as she neared the private room. "Nice try, though."

Nalia slipped through the doorway and Raif immediately reached for her. She gave him a chaste hug, then stepped away. "The staff thinks you're my brother," she said softly.

"Yes, these displays would be a little too Luke Skywalker and Princess Leia, wouldn't they?" Malek set his empty tea glass on the table, which now held four covered tagines. The scent of lamb and cardamom filled the room.

"Princess who?" Raif looked to Nalia and she sighed.

"*Star Wars*. Human thing. Don't worry about it."

Fareed poked his head through the archway. "A small surprise for my honored guests." He motioned for Nalia, Raif, and Zanari to be seated. All Nalia wanted to do was sleep, but this was not how things were done in Morocco. A guest must feel welcome, and, in North Africa, welcoming took time.

When they were settled on the couches, two musicians strode through the archway and took up positions on cushions in the far corner of the large alcove. As the drummer began to play, two women wearing sheer harem pants and tight bodices that ended well above their hips slinked into the room. The gold coin belts wrapped around their waists made a soft tinkling noise as their hips swayed in time to the sound of the tabla. Their movements were snakelike—darting, then slow and sensual.

But their eyes were unfocused, glazed over in a way that was sickeningly familiar to Nalia. Though their bodies were present, the women weren't there. A memory slithered through her: the small, smoky room in Istanbul. A slave auctioneer. Standing under a spotlight in nothing but a chemise, the drugs that weakened her power pumping through Nalia's veins. Malek, sitting in a dark corner, watching her with hungry eyes.

Nalia didn't realize she was trembling until Raif put a hand on her knee and leaned close.

"What's wrong?" he whispered.

She shook her head. One word, one look at him, and she'd fall apart. Nalia could feel herself slipping out of her own grasp, like sand clutched in a palm. The past was too present, with Malek in this room, his wish hanging over her head.

"Fareed, we're not damn tourists. Send them away," Malek said, oblivious.

Nalia's eyes flew to the girls' hands as they rose above their heads to brush the air. They each wore thick silver cuffs on both wrists.

"Ah, but these are not just any belly dancers. Please, enjoy." Fareed closed a curtain across the alcove's entryway and as soon as he did, the dancing changed. Slowly, the dancers' bodies began to evanesce, but not in any way Nalia had ever seen. Their smoke began at their feet—Marid sapphire and Djan emerald—and wound around their bodies like vines. As the tempo of the music behind them quickened, the smoke swirled more rapidly until their dance could only be seen between wisps of evanescence: a hand, gracefully flicking the air, the curve between ribs and hip, gold coins, scars on whipped backs.

"Enough," Nalia said in Kada. The musicians' hands slid

from their instruments and they stared at her, shocked. They hadn't known she was a jinni until she spoke in the jinn tongue. Immediately, the smoke cleared and the belly-dancing jinn stood in the center of the room, a light sheen of sweat covering their bodies.

Nalia stood, crossing to the girls. "Is Fareed your master?"

The jinn looked at one another, fear slipping and sliding across their features. Nalia knew how hard it was to process things in that state: the blur of it all, that hummingbird heartbeat, the disorienting sensation of being disconnected from your *chiaan*. Human drugs did not mix well with jinn energy. Nalia pushed up her sleeves and showed them the scars on her bare wrists.

"You're among friends," she said softly.

Malek stood. "Nalia, move."

She turned. "Stop ordering me around. You're not my—"

"Master," he snapped. "I'm aware of that fact. But unless you want them telling our Ifrit friends about this little encounter, you'll let me handle this." Malek looked at the musicians. "You two. Over here. Now."

The belly dancers shrank at the authority in Malek's voice and the musicians scrambled to their feet.

"Sir," the Djan dancer said, "I'm not sure how we've upset you, but our master, he'll . . . What I mean to say is, I'm sure there's . . . something we can do to bring pleasure to your evening." She trailed a hand down Malek's arm, her lips curling suggestively.

Nalia's heart broke and she reached for the girl. "That's not necessary."

Unthinking, she touched the girl's bare skin and the jinni gasped. "Ghan Aisouri," she breathed.

"Jesus Christ," Malek said. "Nalia, you're as bad as the boy wonder over there. What part of *incognito* do you jinn not understand?"

But Nalia wasn't hearing him. All she could feel was the poison in the jinni's blood, a sick-making sludge that strangled the girl's *chiaan*. The jinni pulled away from Nalia, her face filling with shame.

"He commands us," she said, so that only Nalia could hear. "There's a needle three times a day . . ."

Nalia turned to Malek. "Your *friend* Fareed is drugging them," she spat. "Did you know about this?"

"No," he said. "But what he does with his slaves is his business. Sometimes it's the only way to . . . maintain control."

Nalia's *chiaan* reared up inside her, ready to attack. "You disgust me," she said.

There was a pause, then, pregnant with all the things she wanted to say.

"Sometimes I do, yes," he finally said. His eyes bore into hers. "But not always."

"Did you do this to Nalia?" Raif asked. Quiet. Dangerous.

"No," Malek said. He had the gall to appear offended.

"He didn't have to," she whispered.

The spotlight, so hot on Nalia's skin. She can't feel her chiaan, the poison the trader told her was medicine is eating her blood, scraping her bones and she's so thirsty. The wishmakers raise their hands and call out prices, but each time the man in the corner with the clove cigarettes bids higher.

"Going . . . going . . . gone," the auctioneer says. "Sold to Malek Alzababi for . . ."

The belly dancers moved toward the door. "I think it's best if we leave," the Marid said.

Malek turned to the slaves. "Look at me." The jinn's eyes locked onto Malek's, which burned scarlet as his *chiaan* pulsed with his dark power. Nalia made no move to stop Malek from hypersuading the jinn. He had no choice. The slaves knew who she was.

"You're happy because the human tourists gave you a large tip." Malek's voice slipped into its hypnotic tone: a warm tropical beach, rich red wine, silk sheets. "You want to go to bed now. It's late and you're tired."

The jinn nodded and Malek slipped a few large bills in the top of the prettiest jinni's bodice. He patted her cheek.

"Now be a good girl and get the hell out of here," he said.

The jinn left.

Malek dusted his hands, as though he'd been engaged in an unpleasant task, then sat down. "Speaking of . . . we need to make our plans for tomorrow. I know someone in the city who can help us."

Nalia stared after the jinn. She was desperate to go home and save her brother and yet every part of her ached to steal those girls' bottles and set them free.

But she couldn't do both.

Raif narrowed his eyes. "You know 'someone.' I'm not sure we want to work with the kinds of contacts you have, Malek. And now's a good time to remind you that there's *us*"—he pointed to himself, Zanari, and Nalia—"and then there's you. Dead weight: that's all you are."

Nalia felt a stab of guilt. She knew Raif was only here because he didn't want her to face the Ifrit alone. If it weren't for her, he'd be at the cave already, searching for the sigil. She'd given him the map—an enchanted tattoo of an eight-pointed star that matched her own—and a bottle filled with her blood, necessary for passage through the cave. But he'd refused.

Malek lit a fresh cigarette and took a long drag, then set it on an ashtray before digging into the fragrant tagine. "I suggest an attitude adjustment on your part, boy." He nodded toward the archway the slaves had exited through. "You've seen what I can do."

"Yes," Raif said, "I have." He leaned forward. "But a dark power isn't necessary to manipulate people, and anyone can pull a trigger. So I'm wondering, Malek, what am I supposed to be so scared of? I'm a full-fledged *jinni*—you're a human with one magic trick up your sleeve."

"Then you're a fool," Malek said quietly. "Nalia's the most powerful creature in this room and she's bound to *me*, to grant *my* wish. It's not me you'll be up against when we get to that sigil: it'll be her."

"Enough," Nalia said. Her voice rang with quiet authority. Malek and Raif both looked to her, silent. She focused on Malek, eyes blazing. "You should know that I'll be doing everything in my power to ensure that Raif gets that ring."

He smiled. "No, Nalia, I'm afraid you won't. In this case, your power is spoken for."

Was it? She wouldn't know until they were standing in front of the sigil just how long the wish bound her to Malek.

"Your wish only requires me to take you to the *location* of Solomon's sigil. Once we're there, you'll be outnumbered by three jinn trained since birth to fight," she said. "This journey is nothing more than a sightseeing trip for you, Malek."

"We'll see," he said softly.

Zanari clapped her hands. "Okay, I don't know about you guys, but I'm exhausted. We need to eat, then sleep. So, tomorrow: what's happening?"

Raif gestured for Nalia to sit beside him and she sank into the couch, feeling unbearably selfish for not working harder to convince him to get the sigil without her. She resolved to try again tomorrow—as much as she wanted Raif close, Malek was right: when it came down to it, the magic of the wish only worked in her former master's favor. Protecting Nalia from the Ifrit wasn't as important as Arjinna's fate.

"The voice of reason—thank you, Zanari." Malek took a bite of his couscous, ignoring Zanari's glare. "I know a jinni in Marrakech who can get us a guide while we're in the desert. It'd be easy enough to find a Berber to help us through the Sahara—plenty of Moroccan nomads about—but for our purposes, I think a Dhoma is best. We'll be in their territory and those jinn don't take kindly to strangers."

Dhoma: the forgotten.

"Absolutely not," Nalia said. "We have enough problems as it is."

It was said the Dhoma were wild, trickster jinn who lived without rules and haunted the desolate landscape of the Sahara with no one to keep them company but the Berber nomads who roamed the lonely dunes. Though their magical ability was vast, they chose to live simply and rejected modernity.

Malek snorted. "And you say *I'm* intolerant."

"They're more like criminals, really," Raif said. "My *tavrai* have been held up several times by the Dhoma on their way through the desert. They're insanely protective of their territory and demand tolls from anyone who steps past their invisible borders."

"All the more reason for a Dhoma guide," Malek said, smug.

It was his fault they were being forced to cross the godsforsaken desert in the first place—though he was a *pardjinn*, Malek couldn't evanesce. If he hadn't made that third wish, Nalia, Raif, and Zanari could have evanesced directly to the cave's entrance from Los Angeles.

"What happens if they discover I'm a Ghan Aisouri?" she said.

"They hate my caste. My ancestors refused to help the Dhoma when Solomon enslaved them."

The Ghan Aisouri had seen it as a just punishment for abandoning Arjinna. *Let them rot in that wishmaker realm, since they think it's so much better than ours.* Nalia wasn't sure if those were her ancestors' exact words, but it was what her mother would have said. Not long after Solomon put on the ring, the Ghan Aisouri began using Earth as a penal colony; any jinni who committed a crime stood a chance at being banished from Arjinna forever and enslaved to the Master King. Nalia never ceased to wonder at the cruelty of her caste.

"You jinn need to bury the hatchet," Malek said. "This all happened three thousand years ago."

"You forget how long we live, Malek." Raif stood and began pacing the room. "It wasn't so long ago for *us*. We're talking about our grandparents, great-grandparents. I'm telling you, the Dhoma are not going to help."

Malek crossed to the fireplace and let out a contented sigh as his skin got as close to the flames as possible without burning. Because Malek was a *pardjinn*, he needed to be around his element nearly as much as a full jinni.

"Listen," he said, "you're going to have to set aside whatever issues you have with the Dhoma. Raif's description of the lightning storm above where the sigil's hidden is at the precise spot of the Dhoma's most sacred site, *Erg Al-Barq*—the Lightning Dune. There's no way we're getting near there without the Dhoma's permission."

"And if they refuse?" Nalia asked.

"They won't. Trust me," Malek said. Nalia raised her eyebrows and he sighed. "I have every confidence that my contact will help us. She just . . . might need a little convincing."

"I've seen how you convince people, Malek," Nalia said. "I'm not hurting anybody and I'm not letting you hypersuade your way through Morocco."

"I think when you meet my contact, you'll understand that hypersuasion would be ill advised."

"I still think it's too risky," Nalia said. "All it takes is one traitor like Jordif and we'll have Calar's whole army on us in seconds. A human guide won't be able to betray us to the Ifrit."

"Well, you've got me there," Malek said. "You jinn are quite the experts at betrayal."

Nalia held his gaze for a long moment, long enough to see hurt replace anger. Just a few days ago he'd held her in his arms, happier than she'd ever seen him. *I love you . . . more than anything else in the world*, he'd said. Malek had been willing to give up his search for the sigil, but her betrayal—every bit of which he deserved—had put an end to that resolve.

Malek looked away and lit another cigarette, his lips pulled down.

Raif nudged her. "Eat," he said softly. "It's been hours since you put anything in your stomach."

Nalia took the cover off the ceramic dish, unleashing a cloud of steam and mouth-watering aromas. The food looked delicious, but she wasn't hungry, not anymore. Even so, Nalia picked up a fork and forced herself to eat. For Bashil. For the chance to see her homeland again.

Home. Bashil. That had to get her through whatever tomorrow would bring.

"As much as I'm enjoying the company, I think it's time to call it a night," Malek said. "Big day tomorrow." He glanced at Nalia as he threw his coat over his arm. "I'll keep the bed warm, Madame Alzahabi."

He was gone before Nalia could spit in his face or kick him or do any number of violent things to his person. Gods, he was infuriating.

"Sister, how did you *live* with him for three years?" Zanari said.

Nalia speared a piece of lamb with her fork harder than was necessary. "I slept with a knife under my pillow."

Zanari turned to her brother. "I hate to admit it, but I think Nalia has to stay with Malek."

"Are you kidding me?" Raif growled.

"Well, you and I certainly can't, unless we want to be hypersuaded like those jinn," Zanari said.

"Then the three of us will share a room," Raif said. "I'll sleep on the floor."

Nalia shook her head. "If Fareed is a slave owner, that means he has Ifrit contacts. We can't do anything to arouse his suspicion. We have to play along for now." She sighed. "*Malek* will be sleeping on the floor tonight."

Nalia leaned toward Raif and brushed his cheek with her lips.

"It's only for a night. I'll see you in the morning."

"Have I mentioned today that I hate Malek?" Raif asked.

Nalia smiled. "Maybe once or twice."

A MINUTE LATER, NALIA WAS STEPPING INTO THE ROOM she shared with Malek, her eyes immediately going to the bed that sat beneath a delicate canopy. It was empty. She could hear the shower running in the bathroom, and some of the tension inside her loosened. Like the rest of the *riad*, it was a beautiful room, decorated in rich gold, red, and purple tones. Thick Berber rugs covered the tiled floor and a large metal lamp hung from the ceiling, casting a delicate pattern over the plum walls. It was unbearably romantic.

Nalia crossed to the bed and threw a pillow onto the floor, the smack of it hitting the tile only nominally satisfying, then quickly manifested a pair of shorts and a loose-fitting T-shirt. She changed, then slipped into bed and turned off the light, her back to the bathroom.

A few minutes later, the door opened and steam poured into

the room, carrying Malek's scent: sweet pine, like a dark forest.

"I know you're awake, Nalia," Malek said.

"There's a knife under my pillow and I'd be more than happy to acquaint you with it," she replied.

The bed sagged with Malek's weight and in less than a second, her Ghan Aisouri dagger was at his throat. The razor-sharp jade glinted in the moonlight that drifted in through the sheer curtains that covered the window. He wore nothing but a thick towel wrapped around his waist, and drops of water dripped down his neck from the wet hair that curled just above his ears.

He looked down at her palm pressing against his bare chest, ignoring the knife. Nalia tried to stop the flow of *chiaan* between them, but it was impossible with their skin touching. He burned, as always, and her eyes shifted to the amulet she'd carved over his heart years ago.

"You're forgetting something," Malek said.

"What's that?"

"The wish. I imagine you're not allowed to do anything that would prevent you from granting it. Seriously injuring me would definitely set us back, wouldn't you say?"

"Why don't we find out?"

Nalia pressed the blade to his throat and Malek held her eyes with infuriating calm as it refused to come in contact with his skin. She growled as she threw it into the wall, where it stuck halfway to the hilt, then she reached back and slapped him as hard as she could. At least the wish didn't protect him from that. Malek stared, his eyes wide with shock, then he laughed, utterly delighted.

"Damned if I don't love you more like this," he said.

"You don't even know what love is," she snarled.

Malek's lips tightened and Nalia felt the tiniest jolt of satisfaction upon seeing the pain that lashed his face. It was gone in an instant, but she knew her words had hit their mark.

"I guess we'll have to disagree on that, won't we?"

Malek lunged forward, knocking Nalia onto her back. His onyx eyes roved over her face. She lay very still, staring at him. He leaned toward her, the heat of his bare skin on her own, scorching. His lips, so close. She shivered and he smiled.

"Is this how you imagined it would be, Malek?" Nalia asked softly, just as his lips were about to fall on her own. "You, having your way with me while I lay on my back, hating you and wishing you were Raif?"

His jaw twitched and he shoved himself off her. "Your ability to lie to yourself is impressive, Nalia. If I didn't know better, I'd almost believe you'd hate every second of making love to me. Except." He gave her a velvet smile. "I can read your body like a map. And when you shivered just now—it wasn't because you were cold."

Malek crossed the room, grabbing a pair of silk pajamas that were lying over the back of a chair.

"Good night, Nalia." He shut the bathroom door behind him.

Nalia crawled under the covers and stared at the useless dagger pinned to the wall. As soon as she granted Malek's wish, she was going to plunge the blade into his chest. It wouldn't kill him, but she wanted to cut his heart out, anyway.

Malek ignored the call to prayer.

He had promised himself long ago that he would never bow to anyone again, not even a god. The familiar sound of his childhood broke the predawn quiet of the city, shattering the peace that had lain over it like a soft blanket.

Allahu Akbar. God is great.

As the muezzin's voice traveled from the nearby mosque, rising and falling over the roofs of sleeping Marrakech, Malek checked to make sure the gun's barrel was full, then tucked the small firearm he'd gotten from Fareed into his belt, where it would be concealed by his suit coat. He couldn't be too careful in Morocco, especially not when the city was crawling with Ifrit.

Allahu Akbar. Allahu Akbar. Allahu Akbar.

He looked at the girl in the middle of the bed, the way the lavender dawn slid over her face. He wished he could hate her. Kill her right now in her sleep. It was humiliating, how desperately he wanted to crawl across the bed and take Nalia in his arms. Even after her betrayal. Even after seeing the way she looked at Raif, nothing but a hotheaded boy with a laborer's tan and soldier's manners.

I'll never love you, she'd said.

Her *never* was his *always*, and Malek needed to change that, to stop this crushing desire and affection that was turning him into a shell of himself. How could he have let things go so far, given her so much power over him? His hand moved, unconsciously, to his bare neck. He still panicked a little every time his fingers brushed nothing but his own soft flesh. The bottle was gone, but it had only been two days since he'd watched Nalia grind it under her foot. It had felt like a heart attack, like a knife in the gut: real physical pain that he could still feel the echoes of.

I'll never love you, she'd said.

The muezzin's voice pushed against him, part balm, part burn. He couldn't remember the last time he'd prayed.

As-salatu khayrun minan-nawm. Prayer is better than sleep.

He is seven years old, kneeling on a worn prayer rug, his eyes full of sleep and his limbs heavy. Amir is beside him, swaying on his feet. Malek reaches over to hold his brother's elbow, keeping his eyes on his uncle and cousins. They will beat Amir if he falls asleep during prayer again. Amir looks up and shoots his twin a grateful smile. Shukran, he mouths. Thank you. Malek nods once, then turns away from the face that is almost identical to his own and begins his prayers.

The sky lightened and the rooftop patios began to fill with half-awake Moroccans who set their prayer rugs beside satellite dishes and clotheslines. Malek watched as they went through the familiar motions, that dance of submission he swore off long ago.

La ilaha illa Allah. There is no god except the One God.

Nalia stirred and Malek gazed at her a little longer, then pulled his eyes away, back to the window that overlooked the city's rooftops. Their adventure last night reinforced for Malek how it was all too easy to get lost in the city and equally easy to stay hidden within its storied walls. He'd have to be careful today:

49

they couldn't afford to waste time, not while the Ifrit were on the hunt.

There was a strangled gasp from the bed and he whirled around, forgetting, for a moment, his careful nonchalance.

"Bashil!" Nalia screamed. She was sitting up, clutching the sheets to her chest, her eyes scanning the empty room.

"Just a dream," he said, turning away before she could see his concern. He'd overheard her speaking to Raif about her brother. In all likelihood the child was dead, though Nalia had said she couldn't be sure. A good thing Malek hadn't allowed her to go rescue the boy when she'd asked, else Nalia would probably be dead, too.

There was a rustle of sheets and then he felt her move past him without a word. She shut the bathroom door behind her, the click of the lock the only greeting Nalia would deign to give him. His hand slipped into his pocket and he took out the necklace he'd been carrying with him since Nalia had torn it off her neck and thrown it at his feet. A gold pendant inlaid with the lapis lazuli of Arjinna's Qaf Mountains. He'd never forget the thrill of seeing Nalia's reaction to the necklace: a surprised delight that he wanted to give her over and over. Malek shoved it back in his pocket.

I could have made her happy, he thought.

This jinn revolution he'd heard Nalia and the others speak of was doomed, Malek knew that much. And if Nalia wasn't killed trying a foolish rescue of a child in a heavily guarded prison camp, then that dolt of a boy who slobbered over her would manage to somehow get the job done himself.

Malek sighed and threw on his coat as the last of the morning's prayer rose to the skies. December in Morocco was cold, sometimes cruelly so. But a little fresh air would do him good. He started toward the door, hesitated, then crossed to the bed and rested his hand on the warm pillow. Then he left, shutting the door softly behind him.

A boy was in the hall, carrying a tray loaded with mint tea and glasses. He smiled when he saw Malek.

"*Sbah el kheyr*, Monsieur Alzahabi," he said.

"Morning," Malek replied.

"Your wife—she is awake also? I can bring tea to the room if you would like."

Your wife. The little lie had been worth seeing the look on Raif's face when he found out.

"Yes, she is. But don't bother with tea—she'll come down if she wants some," Malek said. The boy nodded his head and continued down the hall.

Malek glanced at the elegant courtyard below, wishing he were there with Nalia under different circumstances. *Wish.* He hated the word.

No matter. Solomon's sigil was closer than ever and once it was on his finger, Nalia—and every jinni that ever stepped foot on Earth—would be under his control.

6

HUNDREDS OF MILES FROM THE *RIAD*, RAIF WAS SCAN-
ning the flat expanse of desert, empty but for a few flat-topped
trees, a line of low, rocky hills, and the occasional tuft of desert grass. The portal to Arjinna was a few feet away, invisible to
human eyes. It looked as though a piece of sky had been ripped
from the air and placed just above the sand, a jagged oval shimmering like the surface of an opal. Raif knew that if he walked
through that border, all he would see was suffering. And yet it
called to him, a magnetic pull that almost hurt to ignore. It didn't
matter how bad things were in Arjinna, it was home. Where he
belonged.

"*Jabal'alund, tavrai,*" a jinni said, placing a fisted hand over
her heart. "It is an honor to finally meet you."

Raif waved away the jinni's formal manner. "We're all in this mess together. The honor's mine, *tavrai*. Now, let me see this *skag*."

The jinni hesitated, then gave a curt nod, her body still in the rigid pose of a soldier before a commander. "As you wish."

Raif followed the *tavrai* along something resembling a path. The desert winds made the improvised walkway hard to find, but the cairns all over the sand helped him navigate the desert floor. Each one of the small piles of white stones represented a jinni who had died on the crossing. It was a memorial of sorts. Nobody knew how it began, only that the cairns seemed to multiply every year. Some were slaves on the dark caravan who'd been so brutally abused and drugged before the portal crossing that they'd died as soon as they evanesced from the bottle—or never evanesced at all, the bottle nothing more than a coffin. Others were refugees who'd been injured during the crossing, either by an Ifrit guard or the treacherous passes in the Qaf Mountains.

This is why I fight, he thought, gazing at the endless rows of cairns.

It was almost dawn and the Sahara was cloaked in early-morning quiet. A cool wind blew fine grains of sand around his scuffed boots, and the last stars were fading from the sky. Just twenty-four hours ago he'd been unbinding Nalia from the bottle and now here he was, overseeing an execution.

"So where is he?" Raif asked, when the jinni stopped.

She pointed to a small, black hole cut into the face of the nearby hills—a cave. "In there, *tavrai*."

Raif took in the nervous soldier before him. Though she

wasn't much younger than Raif, she seemed a child. "Where'd you find him?"

"Hiding like the rat he is. We tracked him to Argentina—one of Earth's countries—and captured him before he could evanesce. It was a good thing you warned us about Jordif when you did; we were able to intercept a delivery of bottles for the dark caravan just last night."

Raif nodded. "Excellent work." That would make Nalia happy—or infinitely more sad.

The jinni gave a quick bow. "Thank you."

Raif didn't bother to correct his soldier a second time. No matter how hard he tried to make everyone in the revolution equal, they still insisted on strict military protocol, complete with bows and "sirs" and the like.

"Bring him out."

It made Raif sick that the jinni who'd once been his father's friend had become a central player in the dark caravan. Thanks to Jordif, the jinn slave trade had claimed thousands of lives. He imagined Nalia, drugged and afraid while Jordif helped sell her to Malek. "We'll hang him beside the portal so all who enter Earth will see what happens to jinn who help the Ifrit."

Uncertainty flashed across the soldier's face, but one cool look from Raif and she placed her fist over her heart in a parting salute, then left for the cave in a cloud of Marid blue evanescence.

"Still got the magic touch, I see," said a low female voice behind him.

He'd know that voice anywhere. Raif turned, grinning.

"Shirin!"

He'd been so preoccupied with Jordif that he hadn't felt her presence; that, and she was one of the stealthiest jinn he knew. The *tavrai* didn't call Shirin his wolf for nothing.

His second-in-command's face broke out in a smile and she threw her arms around his neck and pulled him into a crushing hug. Then she stepped back and punched him as hard as she could in the stomach.

Raif cursed, doubling over. "Fire and blood, what'd you do that for?"

Shirin looked down at him, nostrils flaring, hands on her hips. "I thought you were dead, you *skag*! Didn't you think it'd be a good idea to check in with your second every now and then?"

She looked the same as always: hair pulled back in one long braid, a face with the deep tan of a laborer. Her revolutionary uniform was faded and dusty: black shirt and pants with a white armband to symbolize an Arjinna free of castes, where the color of your eyes and smoke didn't determine the course of your life. Her hands and arms were covered in bruises and scabs and she had dark circles under her eyes. Raif was pretty sure the bloodstain on her pants wasn't hers.

He groaned as he straightened up. "I've been a little busy."

At first, his time on Earth had been about trying to force Nalia to agree to a trade: he'd free her from Malek if she took him to the location of Solomon's sigil. But there were a few things he hadn't counted on, the largest one being Nalia herself. Falling for her had been like his first battle with the Ifrit, when he'd rushed headlong into the fray, praying to the gods he wouldn't die, so scared he thought he'd shit his pants, so happy he never wanted the battle to end. Helping Nalia kill a ghoul, trying to keep her alive, and unbinding her from the bottle paled in comparison to the sheer terror of loving her—and losing her. But he couldn't tell Shirin any of this, and not just because she'd recently made no secret of her feelings for him. She had enough on her plate right now, and Raif falling for the enemy was something he still wasn't sure how to explain.

Shirin crossed her arms, her dark green eyes flashing. "*Too busy*? You couldn't have taken a second to get a message to me? Maybe let me know the humans hadn't killed you in some barbaric way, with their metal wagons—"

"Cars."

She narrowed her eyes. "Whatever."

"They're actually quite civilized," he said. "The humans, that is." She glared. "I mean, civilized compared to the Ifrit."

Raif was stalling, he knew that. But things had been . . . complicated between them ever since she'd kissed him. He hadn't done anything about it. Though it had happened just days before he came to Earth in search of Nalia, it felt like centuries ago that Shirin had pressed her lips against his. He'd only had a handful of lovers in his life—male or female *tavrai* who'd helped him forget the war for a night or two. He'd never felt anything more than passing desire. It had been the same when Shirin kissed him. Nalia was different. In just a few days of knowing her, she'd become—for better or worse—his second element. As essential as the earth he needed for his *chiaan.*

Shirin gave him a long look, frowning. "Something's up. You're acting weird. Are you high?"

Raif rolled his eyes. "Yes, Shirin, I came to Earth so I could vacation in a cloud of *gaujuri*." The potent drug was a cross between a hallucinogenic and a tall glass of *savri*, Arjinna's spiced wine. A look of hurt passed across Shirin's face and he lightly punched her in the arm. "Hey. I know I left you at a crappy time. I swear to the gods I have to be here doing what I'm doing."

"On this super-secret mission you don't trust me enough to tell me about?"

"Shirin, if the Ifrit capture you——"

She pursed her lips and gave one curt nod. She was family to him, this girl, and he felt terrible about keeping her out of the loop. But it was safer this way. No one else could know about the ring. No one.

"So what brought you out here?" he asked. "Need a change of scenery?"

Traveling through the portal was dangerous in the best of times. It was heavily guarded by the Ifrit on the Arjinnan side and crawling with their spies on Earth's side. It had taken over two hours for his soldiers to secure this section and several of his fighters were holding back the Ifrit on the Arjinnan side, buying Raif the time he needed.

"I got word you were holding a meet at the portal," Shirin said. "I was killing Ifrit just down the mountain, so I thought I'd stop by."

He snorted. "What's your tally this week?"

"Eleven and counting."

"Nice."

"You?"

"Just one." He shrugged. "Actually, I can't claim the kill—I assisted. But you'll never guess who it was."

"I wish you'd say it was Calar."

"If I'd killed the Ifrit empress, do you think I'd be wasting my time with the execution of one of her puppets?"

"Fair enough. Who, then?"

"Haran."

"*No.*"

His lips turned up at the shock on Shirin's face. "Yes. By the way, he's a ghoul and it was a Ghan Aisouri who killed him."

"Are you sure you're not high?"

"*Shirin.*"

"Okay, brother, you're gonna need to start from the beginning."

He filled her in on Haran's gruesome trek through Earth as he searched for Nalia, a cannibalistic killing spree that had ended with Nalia's jade Ghan Aisouri dagger in his heart.

"Are you telling me there's really a Ghan Aisouri hiding out on Earth?"

He nodded. "The rumors are true, yes."

"Why aren't we hanging her *salfit* ass alongside this traitor Marid? Plenty of room for another noose."

Raif winced. He knew it would be like this with the *tavrai*—they didn't know Nalia like he did. All they would see at first were her purple eyes and the proud tilt to her chin. They'd assume she was like the rest of her now extinct race—a bloodthirsty tyrant who believed in the slavery of the Djan and Marid castes.

"It's not like that, Shirin. She's good. *Really* good. She killed

Haran, she's trying to help the revolution—"

"Raif, are you hearing yourself at all?" Shirin stepped closer, jabbing her finger at him for emphasis. "The best thing we could do is execute her *as soon as possible.* Better yet, let's bring her through the portal and do it somewhere public, so everyone can see who the real leader of Arjinna is."

Raif cocked his head to the side. "And who's that?"

"*You,* idiot."

"No. *The people*—"

"The people need a leader. And as long as this Ghan Aisouri's alive, she's the heir to the throne, right? The empress by default because she's a 'daughter of the gods' and the Ifrit killed her whole race during the coup so she's the last royal blah blah blah."

"She doesn't want to be empress," Raif said. "She just wants to go home." He left out the part about Nalia wanting to save her brother from a work camp in Ithkar—it would only endanger Bashil.

Shirin stepped closer to him. "Did she tell you that?"

"*Yes.*"

"Of course she did. She doesn't want you to kill her, right? Mark my words, *tavrai,* if that bitch gets into Arjinna alive—"

"Shirin. Stop. Just stop, okay?" His voice was too loud, gods, he was shaking with anger.

She stared at him, and when her eyes dimmed, he knew Shirin had seen beyond his flimsy attempts to hide what he felt for Nalia. "No. *No.* Please tell me you haven't—"

Raif could feel his face reddening, and Shirin's hands flew to her mouth, her expression horrified. "Oh, fire and blood, are you

59

serious? You fell for a Ghan Aisouri?

The air filled with green and blue smoke, and before Raif could say anything, Jordif Mahar was standing a few feet away, flanked by two revolutionary guards. Raif sent a silent prayer of thanks up to the gods—he had no idea what he would have said to Shirin. He strode across the sand in Jordif's direction, doing what he always did when things were too much: he took the conversation with Shirin and put it away, where he wouldn't have to deal with it until he had time. This was how he'd dealt with the pressure of leading an army since his father died, since Kir had disappeared into the palace's dungeon. Box it up, put it away.

"For your involvement in the dark caravan and for crimes against the people of Arjinna, you've been sentenced to death," Raif said. He'd always dispensed with small talk, the flattery of the court. His was a blood, sweat, and tears war; he had no time for pleasantry.

"On whose authority?" Jordif snapped. His once jaunty handlebar mustache had fallen to a pathetic droop and his usually immaculate clothing was dirty and stained. He looked nothing like the magnanimous jinni who'd hosted Raif and Zanari when they first came to Earth a little over a week ago.

"Mine," Raif said.

Jordif raised his eyebrows as Raif walked into his line of sight. "Thought you were all bark and no bite, a pup trying to take his papa's place. I guess I had you pegged wrong."

"Clearly," Raif gestured to the gallows a few feet away and Jordif's breath caught.

"A traitor's death, I assume?" Jordif said.

Raif wouldn't be able to undo the three years Nalia had endured on the dark caravan, but killing Jordif was a start. This was the jinni who'd made it possible for Nalia's slave trader to smuggle her through the portal. Maybe he'd even stood by as the trader went through, clutching the tiny bottle Nalia had been trapped inside.

"Yes. A traitor's death."

Jordif's hands would be cut off before he was hung, to prevent him from using his *chiaan* to make an escape. They'd leave the body hanging, foregoing the ritual burning of the dead. Soon, Jordif would be nothing more than a snack for the vultures, his spirit forever barred from the godlands.

Raif pointed to the gloves on Jordif's hands. They were made of solid iron, painful and highly effective. It kept him from accessing his *chiaan* and had the added side effect of intense nausea.

"Those gloves," Raif said, "are *nothing* compared to what the jinn on the dark caravan deal with. Stuffed into bottles lined with iron, drugged, raped—gods know what else happens to them. Do you know how many jinn die on the journey through the portal alone?"

Young jinn were especially sensitive to iron. Many of the children sold on the dark caravan didn't have the strength to evanesce out of the bottle when their masters summoned them. They remained in their tiny prisons, slowly starving to death.

"And the ones who do survive—you might as well be running a prostitution ring," Raif continued, his anger rising. How could he have overlooked the dark caravan all this time? It had taken falling in love with one of its victims to open his eyes to just how bad things were. "Have you heard of what their masters do to them?" he said.

He thought of the way Malek looked at Nalia, like she was a meal he wanted to savor.

Jordif's eyes grew hard. "You're just a *boy*, you know nothing about what it takes to survive centuries of Ifrit and Ghan Aisouri oppression." Jordif struggled forward, but Raif's soldiers held him back. "I did what I had to do to save the few jinn who'd managed to escape. If I hadn't, there'd be nowhere to run. The Ifrit wanted control of Earth; I convinced them to let it remain free. Everything has a price among us, you know that. Someone had to pay it. So go ahead and kill me, you little *skag*. But all you're doing is unleashing total Ifrit control on Earth."

Jordif hurled a wad of spit in Raif's direction, but it landed short. Raif turned to one of the jinn holding on to Jordif and gave a slight nod. The jinni's fist landed on Jordif's nose, breaking it. Jordif cried out as blood gushed down his face.

"String him up," Raif said.

"No trial, huh?" Shirin murmured as the *tavrai* pulled Jordif toward the gallows.

"Fuck it."

Shirin gave him a sidelong glance. "Missed you," she said, an approving smile on her face. "Thought all this Ghan Aisouri business had made you soft."

"I have my priorities."

But this thing with Jordif was personal and he knew it. A shred of doubt crept in and for a second, as his soldiers placed the noose over Jordif's neck, Raif wondered if he'd made the wrong decision. Was he making life worse for the jinn who'd sought Earth as a refuge?

Then he thought of Nalia, huddled inside a bottle Malek had worn around his neck so that he could carry her with him like some exotic pet. Nalia, taken from her home, her brother.

"You've become the monsters you're fighting," Jordif gasped. "Your father would be ashamed of you, Raif Djan'Urbi. *Ashamed.*"

"My father believed in justice," Raif said, his face expressionless. "This is the people's justice." Hatred, hot and thick, ran through him, taking over his senses, drowning his *chiaan*. "May the gods never forgive you."

His resolve hardened, strong enough for him to watch as his soldiers cut off the older jinni's hands. Jordif screamed, his eyes never leaving Raif's.

One of the *tavrai* stepped forward. "It's time for the last words."

Jordif opened his mouth to speak, but Raif stepped forward and kicked the stool out from under the traitor's feet.

"That's a privilege he doesn't deserve," Raif said.

They'd tied the rope so that Jordif's neck wouldn't break right away. Raif watched as the dying jinni struggled against the rope, his bloodied stumps splattering the soft sand below him. There were the gurgling, choking sounds of death, the bulging eyes that Raif forced himself to look into. Then it was over.

Jordif's body swayed under the flat-topped tree just as the sun broke over the surrounding sand dunes, bathing the desert in golden light. Raif let out the breath he'd been holding and looked away, to where the glowing orange disk burst into the sky.

You've become the monsters you're fighting. Was it true? It couldn't be, not if Nalia loved him. But the words had burrowed under his skin.

"Breakfast?" Shirin asked brightly.

NALIA WALKED ALONG THE BALCONY THAT BORDERED the second-floor rooms, one hand skimming the smooth wooden railing. Down below, a small group of tourists ate breakfast, chattering in various languages. Nalia eyed the buffet table set up near the splash pool: Moroccan crepes, fried and thick, fresh yogurt with pomegranate seeds, and an assortment of cheese and olives. Her stomach growled, but she ignored the hunger. First, she had to assure Raif that she'd survived her night with Malek unscathed. She shivered and rubbed at the goose bumps on her flesh, angry all over again about her body's betrayal last night. Malek's words, taunting: *when you shivered just now—it wasn't because you were cold.* She didn't want Malek, and the idea that he thought she did sickened her. After a lifetime of not being touched, her body was hungry for affection and it didn't care

7

where that came from. But Nalia cared. She wanted Raif's skin against her own, *his* hands on her body. No one else's.

But she was a murderer. Maybe all she deserved was the touch of Malek's equally bloody hands.

You have to tell him, Nalia thought. The knowledge that she'd killed Raif's best friend weighed heavily on her. She'd made the connection on the tarmac, just as they were about to leave LA. The Kir her mother had forced her to kill was the Kir that had been like a brother to Raif. It was all she'd thought about on the flight to Morocco, but they hadn't had a chance to be alone and it wasn't a conversation Nalia wanted an audience for. She knew it would be smart to wait until they'd gotten the sigil, but she couldn't bear to have this between them. Every time she was near Raif, Nalia felt like she was lying to him. She didn't deserve the tender look he gave her when no one was looking or the unspoken promises that lay beneath all their conversations.

Now she stood before the door to his room, suddenly nervous. Except for a few stolen moments in Malek's mansion as they were preparing to flee the oncoming Ifrit, Nalia hadn't been alone with Raif since before she stole her bottle from Malek. So much had happened since then—the unbinding, their flight to Morocco, killing an Ifrit in the Djemaa.

Before she could knock, the door swung open and Zanari motioned her inside.

"How long were you going to stand there?" Zanari asked.

"I was testing your psychic powers."

"Uh-huh."

Zanari was a remote viewer; she could see things happening

thousands of miles away, so it wasn't hard for her to know some-one was standing outside her door. Nalia was glad Zanari couldn't read minds, especially now, when her confession about Kir was all Nalia could think about.

"Where's Raif?" Nalia asked, glancing around the room. It was similar to the one she shared with Malek, steeped in the lush elegance of Moroccan decor: bright, handwoven carpets, carved bedposts, and colorful lamps.

Zanari nodded toward the closed bathroom door. "He just got back from his meeting and now he's in the shower. Should be finished soon."

"His meeting?"

Zanari sat on one of the unmade beds as she tied the laces on her boots. "Revolution stuff. I asked, but he didn't want to talk about it." She grasped the velvet pouch around her neck and held it open as she waved her hand over a circle of earth on the room's wooden floor. The dirt shot into the pouch, a rainbow of earth.

In order to best access her *voiqhif*, Zanari sat in a *chiaan*-infused circle of earth that magnified her ability to follow the signal lines connecting her to her targets. For Zanari, it was as though the universe were composed of intersecting highways that her psyche could travel along, stopping whenever she saw some-one or something of interest.

"See any movement from the Ifrit?" Nalia asked.

"There are several still in Los Angeles—they've posted a guard at Malek's house, much good it will do them. There are definitely soldiers in Morocco who are focused on finding you, but nobody seems to have any leads, thank the gods. They have a picture of you in their minds, but it's an old one, from before the coup. They're mostly looking for a jinni with your birthmark—just like Haran."

Nalia glanced at the bathroom door. Raif had refused to consider going on ahead, but maybe Zanari would listen to reason.

"You guys have to leave us—get the sigil. It's probably only a matter of time before they find me. And the longer Raif stays in Marrakech, the more likely it is he'll be recognized. We can't fight off the whole Ifrit army."

Zanari sighed. "Honestly? I totally agree with you. I mean, don't get me wrong, I'd feel terrible leaving you alone with Malek, but the thought of him getting the sigil instead of Raif . . ."

"I know. What Malek said last night—it's true," Nalia said. "The wish's magic is in *his* favor, not Raif's. I honestly have no idea what will happen in that cave."

"Gods. I keep picturing them both running toward the damn thing," Zanari said.

"Please tell me you two have some kind of plan." Nalia held up her hand. "*Don't* tell me the plan. Just tell me you have one."

Zanari grimaced. "Um. We're working on that. It involves running and hitting."

Nalia closed her eyes. "Why is he so godsdamned stubborn?"

"I think my brother's afraid that if he leaves you now, he'll never see you again. I think that would kill him."

Nalia wanted to deny it, but all she could do was nod. Nothing was guaranteed. She'd be lucky to get out of Morocco alive. Zanari stood and grabbed her room key, then turned toward the door. "I'm going downstairs to get some food—want any-thing?"

Nalia's eyes flicked to the closed bathroom door, panicked. "I'll come with you. I hardly ate any dinner."

Coward, she thought. If she was alone with Raif, she'd have to tell him about Kir. And she couldn't bear to have him look at her with disgust or hatred. Nalia wasn't ready for that. Not ever, but especially not now, when everything in her life was so uncertain.

Zanari rolled her eyes. "Sister, you don't have to play the blushing maiden, okay? When you and Raif are ready, come find me." She gave Nalia a wave and was out the door without another word.

Nalia sat on the edge of Zanari's bed, staring at the bathroom door. *Raif*. Tendrils of steam snuck out from beneath it, like the tentacles of a jellyfish. A war raged inside her: tell him, don't tell him. She didn't know what to do. She longed for Thatur, her gry-phon, who had always counseled her.

She stood, restless, and crossed to the window that looked onto the street below. Children on bicycles clattered over the cobblestones, women clothed in bright kaftans carried shopping bags heavy with fresh bread. Shopkeepers began raising the metal shutters that covered their stores, where Nalia caught a peek of bolts of cloth and mannequins wearing head scarves. A little boy skipped by, singing a song in Arabic. His smile reminded her of Bashil, and the hole inside her grew wider, deeper.

The bathroom door opened, and the room filled with the scent of the *riad*'s rich musk soap. Nalia could feel Raif behind her, his heat and energy whispering to her in a wordless language only they knew. She was suddenly terrified to turn around. If she looked at him, she wouldn't be able to say what she needed to.

I killed your best friend, she thought. *I killed Kir. No. I was forced to kill—*

"I was going crazy last night, imagining him in that room with you," Raif whispered, his lips against her neck. His hands slid down her arms and Nalia leaned into him, even though she knew she shouldn't. Her confession retreated as his *chiaan* connected to hers, electric. Raif turned her around so that she was facing him. He made no effort to disguise the want in his eyes.

Nalia rested her hands on Raif's bare chest, a thrill running through her as she felt his heart beating fast and sure under her skin.

"Raif, nothing happened."

"What if he'd tried—"

Nalia reached up and pressed a finger against his lips. "I've got a pretty good uppercut. You never need to worry about me around him." She had a flash of Malek pushing her onto her back, his lips a breath from her own. "Now that he's not my master, Malek is nothing but a *pardjinn* I owe a wish to."

It was true that she was stronger than Malek, but her former master didn't fight like other people; he fought the mind and heart. He would use the worst parts of Nalia against herself, like he had last night.

Now, she thought. She'd tell Raif the truth and he'd hate her for it but at least it'd finally be out in the open.

"Raif—"

"They found Jordif," he said softly.

She stiffened. "Where?"

"Someplace called South America," he said. "We executed him this morning."

Nalia's eyes widened. "That fast?"

Raif nodded. She let that sink in for a moment. It was something like justice, but it didn't satisfy. She wasn't sure if anything would.

"You know what an evil part of me wishes?" she said.

The Ifrit part, she thought to herself. As the only jinni left that had access to all four elements, it meant that Nalia shared the fire her enemies drew strength from.

"Hmm?" Raif tucked a piece of her hair behind her ear, his rough fingers grazing her cheek.

She looked at the scars around her wrists, reminders of her slavery that would never go away. "I wish you had put him on the dark caravan. Made him a slave to someone like Sergei Federov. *That's* what he deserves. Death is too easy."

How many times had she wished for her own death? Haunted by the massacre of her people, forced to obey Malek's every whim and subject to the torture of the bottle—death had always seemed kind. A black-cloaked angel of mercy.

"Who's Sergei Federov?"

"One of Malek's business partners. He's . . ." She shivered. Eyes like the Taiga in winter, soul like the bottom of a deep well.

Yes, she thought, *that would be justice.*

"Jordif received a traitor's death," Raif said. "His punishment will never end."

Nalia's breath caught. To have your body pecked at by birds, to forever roam the shadowlands, deprived of the ritual burning that set your soul free . . . she almost felt sorry for Jordif. But then she thought of the horror of slavery, of the bottle, and of all the masters who took advantage of their jinn. Nalia had been one of the only jinn she knew whose master hadn't forced her to sleep with him—in that, at least, she'd been lucky. Malek could be cruel, but he wasn't a rapist. Though last night, she hadn't been so sure, not at first.

Laerta," Raif whispered. *Come here.*

He drew her to him so that her heart pressed against his chest. He smelled like the Forest of Sighs, where the revolutionaries made their home: grass and trees and good, clean dirt.

"I'm so tired of everything," she said. "I just want to get my brother."

"I know," he whispered against her hair.

"I wish . . ." Nalia sighed. Not even she could get herself out of having to fulfill Malek's wish.

She felt Raif's *chiaan* wrap around her like a soft blanket, a bright, restless energy that had begun to feel like home. Nalia pressed closer to him, all too aware that they were finally alone. He gasped a little as her *chiaan* slid into him and he tightened his arms around her.

She'd never forget the moment when they first exchanged energy. At the time, Nalia had thought the intensity of feeling him inside her was because she'd spent so many of her years on Earth trying not to touch any jinn. The texture of her *chiaan*, so different from the other castes, would have instantly marked her as a Ghan Aisouri, as it had the night before, with Fareed's slave. The only reason Nalia had been able to avoid being killed by the Ifrit during her three years of captivity on Earth was because Calar had thought all the Ghan Aisouri were dead. When Raif's *chiaan* had surged through her, exploring, it felt like she'd peeled back the layers of her skin to show him what was underneath. But now she knew she hadn't just been responding to the sensation of another jinni's *chiaan* mingling with her own; it was encountering Raif himself, the force of him, that had been so disorienting.

Still was.

"I don't know if I'm ever going to get used to this," he said, a smile in his voice.

"What about this?" she whispered, brushing her lips against his.

"Definitely not."

He returned her kiss and when he opened his mouth, she tasted the sweet mint of Moroccan tea, felt the warm earthiness of his *chiaan* collide with her own. His kiss enveloped her in warmth, his want matching perfectly with her own. Raif was a rule meant to be broken, a promise made in starlight and darkness.

She forgot about Kir. She forgot about everything.

They tumbled onto one of the beds and the room melted away as Raif's whole being seeped into her. He'd risked everything for Nalia—the revolution, his life. He'd offered himself up like a sacrifice to a fierce and lovely goddess and she had let him.

You don't deserve this, she thought as his hands snaked under her shirt. *You don't deserve* him.

Nalia grabbed his hands. "We have to go soon," she whispered. "To meet Malek's contact, remember?"

Raif's hair was still damp from his shower, a dark halo around his face as he looked down at her, like the images of Tirgan, the god of earth that graced the palace's temple. "Zan won't come in, you don't have to worry about that," he said.

How could she explain without explaining? She had no right to take any more from him than she already had.

I killed your best friend.

Coward. Tell him the truth. TELL HIM.

"It's just . . . everything's so complicated right now—"

"It's actually pretty simple: I love you," he said. She sucked in her breath. "And you love me." Raif trailed a finger along her jaw. "Right?"

She nodded. *So so much.* Nalia pulled away.

"What's wrong?" he murmured, his breath hot against her neck.

"Nothing," she lied.

He traced her collarbone, a thoughtful expression on his face as he looked down at her. "Did I tell you about my home in Arjinna?"

She shook her head and he shifted to his side, propping himself up on an elbow. "It's in the middle of a *widr* tree, built right into the branches, a little ways away from the other *ludeen.* There's a pond nearby and honeysuckle grows beneath the windows year round. You'll love it."

She tried to imagine it: waking up beside Raif every morning, smelling the sweet Arjinnan air. Falling asleep beside him each night. They'd never had time to discuss what would happen in Arjinna. There had simply been that promise, when they were still enemies: they wouldn't kill one another when they reached their native land, and Nalia wouldn't try to steal the ring, nor could Raif use it against her. That was all.

But so much had changed since then.

It hurt, this love he had for her. Soon it would be gone. Once he found out the truth, he'd never look at her like this again.

"Raif—"

He stopped her words with a soft kiss. "Just for the next few minutes, can we pretend we're there already?" he said. "We have the rest of the day to deal with Malek and fight Ifrit and get to the cave. I want you to myself before I have to share you."

The space between hope and reality was growing wider, a chasm they wouldn't be able to bridge for long. Anything but right now, this moment, felt like a hazy, half-remembered dream. She wanted to hold on to it a little longer before it wasn't real anymore.

"So if we were in your *ludeen*, what would be doing?" she asked, suddenly distracted by his finger as it traveled down her neck and settled on the top button of her shirt. She stopped breathing, her entire being concentrating on where his finger rested.

Raif smiled. "Relaxing." He undid the button, his eyes never leaving hers. "Last night I was thinking about how worried you've been about everything, how you can never get out of your head."

Another button.

"Uh-huh," she whispered.

His eyes were filled with a secret kind of knowing. "And I thought maybe you'd feel better if you could just . . . let go."

Another button. His hair fell forward, brushing against her cheek, and her *chiaan* vibrated—she actually felt it *tremble*—as though Raif's closeness had struck a chord inside her, one that kept playing the same sweet note over and over and over.

"I . . . um . . . I'm not sure . . . let go?"

Another button.

Raif lay his palm against her stomach and Nalia felt his *chiaan* push through her skin, right into the knot he was unraveling inside her.

"Right now," he murmured, "there's nothing in the whole world but you and me."

The last button.

Nalia reached her hands up, her fingertips skimming the scarred surface of his chest, where Ifrit bullets and Shaitan whips had cut into his flesh. He closed his eyes as she touched him. Rays of sunlight peeked through a lattice screen, creating a golden pattern against his skin.

He leaned down and brought his mouth to her chest, taking a leisurely path to her stomach. Her hands gripped his shoulders, his hair. Dust motes swirled around them, a motorcycle went by on the street below, someone in the hotel was playing Arabic love songs. Her breathing quickened the lower he got, and she could feel Raif smile against her belly. It was becoming impossible to hold the magic inside her, to keep herself in check. Control: it was all she knew, all she had.

"Just let go," he whispered.

"Raif . . ."

But it was a weak protest, her hands grasping his hair as his lips seared her skin. His fingers undid the drawstring of the loose-fitting pants she wore.

"What?" he said, his lips turning up at the shocked expression on her face. "This isn't how they do things at the palace?"

She shook her head. She couldn't speak, couldn't think.

"I might be a good guy, Nalia," he said. "But I never claimed to be well behaved."

He pulled the fabric down and smiled—a devilish upturn of the mouth that made Nalia bite her lip. He laughed softly, then brought his mouth back down to her skin. Faint wisps of *chiaan* slipped from her fingers, coating Raif in liquid gold. He shuddered as her power seeped into him and then there was just warmth, gods so much warmth, and light and breath and she let go of everything except the delicious release that was pulsing through her, this unexpected grace of weightlessness.

Nalia gasped, her body filling with light. Raif's fingers twined with hers and his lips moved to her inner thigh, then her knee. She looked down at him, eyes wide, and he laughed softly against her skin.

"Feel better?" he asked.

All she could do was nod. Raif crawled over the blankets and lay beside her, then pulled her to him.

There was a soft knock on the door. "You guys?" Zanari called. "I hate to do this, but the car's outside waiting for us. Time to go."

Raif groaned. "Five minutes," he called.

His eyes traveled down Nalia's body. She dropped her forehead to his chest and kissed the skin over his heart. She wanted this dream to be her reality, to pretend the past didn't matter.

To pretend she deserved him.

8

MALEK SAT IN THE FRONT SEAT OF THE RANGE ROVER, directing the driver to get as close to the souks outside the Djemaa el-Fna as the narrow streets would allow. They'd have to go on foot the rest of the way, but luckily he could make it to Saranya's shop in his sleep. His jinni contact had been practicing her magic in the same location for hundreds of years. Malek couldn't count how many times he'd been in her home, drinking mint tea and talking for hours. But it'd been a while since he'd had the guts to knock on her door.

He stared out the window, frowning. The streets were filled with peddlers selling spices, elaborately embroidered slippers, and cone-shaped tagines. Ancient palaces and souks surrounded the Djemaa like the petals of a tightly packed rose. Malek held an unlit cigarette between his fingers, tapping out a nervous beat against his knee. Going to Saranya was a terrible idea, he knew, but there was no one else who could help them. Even if there were, he wouldn't know if he could trust another jinni. Saranya would help, whether she wanted to or not.

Three years, he thought. It was hard to believe it'd already been that long. Every morning he woke up and the remembering would happen right away, the wound still fresh. Malek had told himself he'd never go back—how could he, after the terrible choice he'd made?—but he couldn't risk losing his chance at the ring, and the sooner they got out of Marrakech and into the desert, the better.

But that wasn't the truth, not really. He could lie to himself all he wanted, but the real reason he was willing to endure Saranya was that even now, after everything she'd done to him, he couldn't bear the thought of Nalia being captured by the Ifrit. They would kill her and Malek wasn't sure he wanted to live in a world where Nalia didn't exist. After she'd betrayed him, he'd told himself Nalia deserved to suffer, that he would *make* her suffer. But after sitting up all night watching her toss and turn in her sleep, having one nightmare after the other, the resolve to punish her had crumbled.

Khatem l-hekma, he chanted to himself. *Khatem l-hekma*. It was what the Moroccans called Solomon's sigil, a ring described time and again in their ancient texts, most of which filled the shelves of the study in his Hollywood Hills mansion. Though he'd combed Earth in search of the ring, Malek had always believed it would be somewhere in Morocco. The place seemed to draw the jinn, whether they were conscious of it or not, and it wasn't just because the portal to Arjinna was located within Morocco's borders. There was something else, a dash of magic in the air, like a seductive mystery just waiting to be solved.

"Arrêtez ici," Malek said to his driver as they neared their destination. *Stop here.* Moroccans moved between French and Arabic as seamlessly as if they were the same language. Sometimes it was easier for Malek to speak French here than the perfect Saudi Arabic he was so accustomed to. Moroccan Arabic was like a dance he'd learned long ago, the steps both familiar and strange.

"Oui, monsieur." The driver stopped and Malek turned around.

"Ladies, follow me. You," he said, looking at Raif, "stay out of sight."

Much to Raif's frustration and Malek's delight, they'd decided that it would be impossible for Raif to join them on their meeting with the guide. He was far too recognizable. He'd insisted on waiting for them in the car, hidden behind the tinted windows. Raif whispered something in Nalia's ear and she laughed softly.

Malek slipped out of the car without so much as a backward glance at the others. They'd catch up.

Business in the Djemaa was well under way, thick with late morning crowds. Malek pushed into the river of women in head scarves, tourists, and donkeys, barely sparing a glance for the treasure trove of goods that spilled out of shop fronts. Every detail reminded Malek of years past when he and Amir would get lost for hours, people watching and stealing sweets off the carts pulled by old men. A sudden stab of longing for his twin hit Malek—it was to be expected, here of all places. But it wasn't welcome.

At a tiny wooden sign tacked high on a wall that read souk

D'ÉPICES, Malek swung right. Huge cones of spices came into view outside shops with walls taken over by glass jars containing mysterious powders and herbs. The air was full of the scent of musk, frankincense, and sandalwood.

"So who is this jinni contact of yours, exactly?" Zanari asked as she and Nalia caught up with him.

"An old friend," he said.

She frowned. "How do we know we can trust this jinni? If they work with you, they can't possibly be someone with our best interests in mind."

Zanari's Medusa-like braids spilled over her shoulders, and her eyes were lined with dark kohl. She wore human clothes: a sweater, jeans, and tennis shoes. But there was something about her that remained exotic—the glint in her eye, maybe. She wasn't half-bad looking, a young Cleopatra, but her eyes were too like Raif's.

Despite how infuriating it was to have the Djan'Urbis around, Malek couldn't deny how useful Zanari's psychic gifts were. Already, her ability had made it fairly easy for them to evade Ifrit detection.

"I trust her with Nalia's life," he said.

Nalia looked up at the sound of her name. Malek's eyes settled on her golden ones, as light as his were dark. "Is that enough assurance for you?" he asked, directing the question to Nalia.

"I suppose it will have to be."

"Of course," he added, the hurt surfacing, "the value of your life depreciates considerably once I have that ring. You're a means to an end."

Nalia paled, then gave him a small smile. "As were you, Malek."

Her words were a door slammed in his face. Malek shoved his hands in his pockets and fingered the lapis lazuli necklace.

They kept walking, through keyhole-shaped arches, the twists and turns painfully familiar. Malek kept expecting to see Amir around each corner, biting into a fig or bargaining for the spices his wife wanted. A phantom brother, come back to haunt him.

They left the spice souk behind and turned into a dim alleyway. It was cold here, and quiet. The only sounds were their footsteps and the flutter of pigeons' wings. The air smelled of the musty dampness of drying wool and the amber oil that burned in lamps all over the city. The doors they passed here were bolted shut, faded and peeling as though they hadn't been opened for centuries, markers on this journey he had taken so many times.

Malek made a left after the last of the closed-up shops, onto a dead-end street. The closer he got to their destination, the more he regretted coming to the souk. It would be all too easy for Nalia to learn about the very darkest part of him, the incomprehensible depth of his depravity. Even he couldn't understand it. Couldn't forgive it.

Zanari's voice slashed the silence. "Where in all hells are we going, *pardjinn*?"

Malek said nothing as he neared the door built into the peach *tadelakt* wall at the far end of the deserted street. No more beautiful than the rest of Marrakech's wondrous entrances, the door nevertheless demanded one's attention. An arch composed of the ubiquitous eight-pointed star *zillij* tiles bordered the door with symbols representing the four elements carved into the stone above the arch. Each symbol was inlaid with lapis lazuli, the distinctive blue stone of the Qaf Mountains of Arjinna. A brass knocker in the shape of a *hamsa* sat in its center, an outward-facing palm that seemed to bar their entrance. It was a distinctive shape, with the three middle fingers fused together, while the stylized pinkie and thumb pointed outward. Intricate swirls and flowers wrought into the metal made up its surface.

Nalia pointed to the hand. "What's that? I keep seeing it everywhere."

"It's a powerful ancient symbol that humans use for protection," Malek said. "It creates a kind of shield around them that's impossible for a jinni to break through."

"So you've taken us to a door that won't open for jinn? Great, Malek," Zanari said.

He made a big show of raising his hand and placing his palm over the door knocker so that his fingers lined up with those of the *hamsa*.

"This particular hand won't harm us. The real *hamsas*—the ones human mages have put spells on—are priceless heirlooms, passed down by Moroccans from generation to generation. This one *is* magical, though: it can sense whether or not the hand touching it belongs to a jinni. If it does . . ."

He waited until he felt the slight tingling of the magic as it latched onto his *chiaan*—he didn't possess as much as a full jinni, but it was enough to gain entrance. The door fell away as though it had never been there. Malek stepped through the stone arch.

"Welcome to the jinn souk."

It was the closest to Arjinna Nalia had been since she was stolen from her homeland.

The souk spread out before her, as far as the eye could see. At first glance, it looked like the human souk they had left behind: narrow cobblestone streets lined by tiny stalls that crowded against one another, huddling like beggars in the cold as their occupants cried out to passersby. But what the stalls held had no place in the human markets. Goods overflowed into the tiny pathways: baskets of dried *widr* leaves, known to cure all manner of small ills, boxes of dried sugarberries, yards of sea silk, a glossy, infinitely soft fabric made from deep-sea plants that Marid jinn gathered and wove. Chunks of volcanic rock from Ithkar used for dark magic sat beside bundles of *gaujuri*, the hallucinogenic herb smoked with water pipes. The air smelled of Morocco, but also of home—essence of vixen rose and the spicy scent of elder pines found deep in the Forest of Sighs.

A jinni burst out of his stall, holding up bottles of cloudy water. Nalia stifled a laugh as he called out, "Sacred oasis water—good for strengthening Marid *chiaan*. Try it, you'll see!"

"People don't actually *believe* him, do they?" she whispered to Zanari. "A *sacred oasis*?"

She shrugged. "Arjinnans are desperate. They're not buying dirty water—they're buying hope."

Malek wove through the stalls as though he were on autopilot, pushing them deeper into the souk.

"Trick the humans and protect yourself from slavery! Fake shackles, one size fits all!"

"How did I not know about this?" Nalia said. Neither Malek nor Zanari heard her above the clatter of the buy and sell.

"Come in, come in, a pretty *sawala* for a pretty jinni."

Nalia stepped forward and ran her hands over the fabric of the *sawala*. Gold and deep blue, almost purple, the clothing she'd worn every day in court seemed suddenly . . . foreign. The tunic had two high slits on either side and came with wide-legged pants made of fine, thin sea silk that caught the light like the scales of a fish. She could almost remember the feel of those pants against her skin, a caress. It had always been a welcome change from the Ghan Aisouri leathers and heavy cape she'd worn outside the palace.

"You like, yes?" an old jinni said to her. He wore the square cap of a tailor, the tassel swinging beside his cheek. "I give you good price—democratic price."

"Oh, it's lovely. But I can't. Thank you, I—"

The jinni pressed a belt made of antique jinn coins into her hand. "Seven thousand dirhams, sister. Or, twenty-one thousand *nibas*—give or take."

Nibas. Of course Arjinnan currency would be used here—it was the only coin that could not be manifested, and was thus of true value to the jinn.

"Forget it, grandfather. She's not buying." Zanari pulled Nalia away from the tailor.

"He would have kept you there all afternoon, if you'd let him," she said once they were further down the crowded lane. Nalia smiled. "Thanks. I don't have much practice with this sort of thing."

"Let me guess: the Ghan Aisouri didn't do much of their own shopping,"

"I didn't touch money until Malek explained American dollars to me," Nalia confessed.

Zanari rolled her eyes. "When we get home, I'm sending you out to the markets."

When we get home.

There were still so many *ifs*. *If* they got home. *If* she could rescue Bashil. *If* Raif's *tavrai* didn't convince him to hate her. *If* he could forgive her, once he learned about Kir.

"We'll see," was all she said.

Malek turned down a dark corridor off the main road and, moments later, stopped in front of a small shop. Unlike the stalls they'd been passing, this shop had a proper door and windows, both of which were closed. A star-shaped lamp made of multi-colored glass panes hung above the door, though, and its light emanated a cheerful glow. A sign on the door in Kada read: POTIONS AND SPELLS: INQUIRE WITHIN.

Malek raised his hand and knocked on the door. After a few moments, it swung open, and a jinni with glossy black curls that fell to the waist of her blue embroidered kaftan stared at him, her golden Shaitan eyes wide with shock. Then she shook her head, as though waking from a dream.

"Well, if it isn't my long-lost brother-in-law," the jinni said.

NALIA STARED. "BROTHER-IN-LAW?"

"So, what," the jinni said, ignoring Nalia and pushing her finger into Malek's chest, "you think it's okay to just disappear, right when we need you the most?"

Malek frowned. "Saranya." The name sounded familiar, but Nalia wasn't sure why.

"It wasn't like I was here all the time, before . . ." Malek trailed off, his eyes looking anywhere but at his sister-in-law. "It's been hard for me, too, you know."

Saranya snorted. "Oh, I'm sure it has."

"We'd make good coin selling tickets to this show," Zanari said under her breath.

Nalia bit back a smile. It wasn't often she got to see someone give Malek a dressing-down. She rather liked seeing him scramble to defend himself.

"Well?" Saranya said to Malek. "Are you just going to stand on the street?"

She turned and started into the house.

"Lovely to see you, too," he called after her. He turned to Nalia and Zanari, gesturing for them to follow him inside. *"Yalla."*

Let's go.

Nalia stepped through the doorway, thankful to be once removed from the icy conversation that immediately started up between her former master and his sister-in-law. They spoke in a mixture of rapid-fire French and Arabic, Saranya listing her grievances and Malek trying unsuccessfully to defend himself. Clearly it'd been a while since Malek had visited. He ran a hand through his hair, crossed his arms—small tells that he was agitated.

"What in all hells is going on?" Zanari muttered.

Nalia shrugged. "I have no idea." It was a whispered argument that she could only catch snatches of.

Malek had never mentioned a sibling to her. Nalia's mind reeled as she tried to make sense of what this meant, that there might actually be people in the world who loved Malek.

"We should leave," she murmured to Zanari as Malek and Saranya continued their argument, oblivious to the two jinn that hovered near the front door. "We're putting this woman in danger by being here."

Zanari leaned against the doorframe and crossed her arms. "I don't know. This is the most fun I've had in days."

"Saranya, this is Nalia," Malek said, motioning toward her.

"My—" He stopped, and Saranya raised her eyebrows.

"*Your* nothing," Nalia said, glaring at Malek. Three years was enough time to suffer Malek's proprietary air. She placed her right hand over her heart and bowed her head.

"*Ghar lahim*," she said, the Kada equivalent of *nice to meet you*. "I used to be Malek's slave, but circumstances, thank the gods, have recently changed."

Malek winced and Saranya whirled around. "Your *slave*?" she yelled at him. "Amir would be *sick* if he heard that. You know how involved he was in my work. How could you have a slave when he spent his life fighting against everything the dark caravan stands for?" She shook her head. "He'd be so ashamed of you."

A look of pain shot through Malek's eyes, but it quickly disappeared, replaced with his usual detached amusement. "That wouldn't have been anything new, now would it?"

Amir—his brother?

The hurt and anger in Saranya's eyes deepened. "Unbelievable." She turned to Nalia and Zanari. "*Jahal'alund*," she said. "*Batai vita sonouq*."

It had been so long since Nalia had heard those words: *My home is yours.*

Nalia and Zanari touched their palms to their hearts.

"Forgive me for my rudeness," Saranya said, motioning for them to follow her. "I wasn't expecting . . ." She waved her hand in the air. "Well, you know how he is, I guess."

"Unfortunately, yes," Nalia said.

Malek grunted, but Nalia ignored him as she followed

Saranya into a spacious sitting room decorated with Moroccan textiles, ceramics, and overstuffed sofas covered with vibrant pillows. A young girl, not much more than ten summers old, sat in the corner. At the sight of the three strangers, she jumped up, a book of jinn poetry slipping to the floor and landing face up. An illustrated dragon hovered above the pages, its flames spilling over the spelled paper. The little jinni's eyes filled with fear, and Saranya crossed to her, wrapping her thick arms around the child.

"It's all right, sweet one," she whispered. Saranya looked up. "This is Maywir," she said as she turned to Malek, her eyes cold. "She's staying with me while we find a permanent home that is suitable for a child rescued from the dark caravan."

"But she's so young!" Zanari cried out. She looked at Maywir, horrified.

Now Nalia knew where she'd heard that name before. "Saranya," she said. "I've met jinn that you've sheltered." Nalia bowed low. "You honor the slaves with your selfless sacrifice."

Nalia had learned of the underground caravan two years ago, after meeting a young jinni at Habibi, the jinn club once run by Jordif Mahar. With the increase in trafficking, a network of jinn had grown all over the world to shelter slaves who had been rescued before they could be sold to a human master. The jinn who cared for them were risking their lives. The slave traders and the Ifrit weren't known for letting their "cargo" slip away without a fight, not to mention the humans who had a vested interest in the multibillion-dollar industry.

"Yes, my *Dhoma* sister-in-law is quite the humanitarian,"

Malek said, his mouth turning up in a smirk for Nalia's benefit. "Or in this instance, would we say *jinnitarian?*"

Nalia reddened at his emphasis on the word *Dhoma*. She hoped he wouldn't bring up their conversation in the *riad*. How could she have been so certain she couldn't trust them? Here was this jinni, risking her life to save jinn just like Nalia. Every day she spent on Earth showed Nalia just how flawed the Ghan Aisouri teachings had been.

Saranya gestured for Nalia and Zanari to sit on a couch pushed against one of the green *tadelakt* walls. It was a colorful room, cozy and lived in. It wasn't a shop so much as a home: not the kind of place Nalia expected any relatives of Malek Alzahabi to have. His mansion had been extravagant, yes, but cold, like a catalogue display. This place felt lived in. Love existed there, and happiness. Sadness, too, but Nalia couldn't figure out where that came from, other than the dark caravan refugees who passed through Saranya's doors.

"Please," Saranya said. "Make yourselves comfortable. I'll be right back with tea." She turned to Mayvir, who stared at them with wide, shy eyes. "Come, sweet one."

Before they could say anything else, Saranya slipped out of the room, through a beaded curtain that led to what Nalia guessed was the kitchen.

"In Morocco, it's customary to discuss business over mint tea," Malek said. "Things move more slowly here than where we're from."

"*We* are not from the same place," Nalia said. Malek frowned but before he could say anything, the front door opened and a teenage boy walked through, a leather book bag thrown over his shoulder. When he caught sight of Malek, the boy let out a cry of joy.

"Uncle!" He threw his arms around Malek, beaming.

Nalia stared. The resemblance between them was so close it was uncanny. Stranger still, Malek's whole face lit up as he returned the boy's crushing hug.

"Tariq!" he said, holding the boy against him. He closed his eyes and Nalia looked away. The moment felt too private and it confused her, seeing Malek like this.

Saranya entered the room carrying a tray with an elaborate silver tea service and several delicate glasses. "Tariq, let him breathe."

Her voice was soft as she set the tray down on a low table in the center of the room and her eyes glazed over, wet.

Tariq let go of Malek. "But, Uncle, what are you doing here? We called so many times . . ."

Malek looked away from the boy's eager eyes. "It's complicated, Tari, I've been . . . busy." He glanced at the boy's satchel. "What are you doing home so early?"

"It's nearly lunch," Tariq said. "You're staying, right?" Without waiting for Malek's answer, he turned to his mother. "Mama, can he——"

Saranya held up her hand. "We'll see. Why don't you tell your uncle about the prize you won in school?"

Tariq launched into the story, his words tumbling over one another in their haste to get out. As Saranya prepared the tea, Nalia watched the Dhoma jinni. She seemed . . . kind. Nothing like the people Malek associated with on a regular basis. Nalia wondered what had made this woman decide to marry his brother, a *pardjinn* with limited powers who would stain the bloodline. She wondered what Malek's brother was like. They obviously weren't close if Malek's being a master came as a surprise. Saranya set the glasses in a semicircle on the tray and began pouring the tea in Moroccan fashion, from several inches above the glasses.

Once she'd finished pouring the tea, Saranya glanced at Malek. "I'm assuming you're not simply here to introduce me to your friends," she said.

Malek glanced at Tariq. "It's a delicate matter. Perhaps . . ."

Saranya looked at her son and he started to protest. "Into the kitchen with you, *gharoof*," Saranya said. "Maywir needs help with the salads, anyway."

Nalia's breath caught. How many times had she called Bashil *gharoof*—little rabbit?

Tariq gave a dramatic sigh as he turned to Malek. "You're not leaving again, are you?"

Malek hesitated, and the boy's face fell. "I have something very important to do," Malek said, his voice surprisingly gentle. "You'll take good care of your mother, yes?"

His nephew nodded, glum, then trudged into the kitchen. Malek watched him for a moment, a wistful expression on his face, and when he turned back and saw Nalia staring at him, he coughed uncomfortably.

"This doesn't have anything to do with all the Ifrit coming through the portal yesterday, does it?" Saranya asked.

She put two sugars in a glass and handed it to Nalia with a small spoon.

"It's safer if you don't know the details," Nalia said. She accepted the glass Saranya handed her, then stirred in the sugar until the water absorbed the crystals. Nalia sighed as the scent of mint and sugar wafted up to her, and she drank gratefully.

"What is it you need from me?" Saranya asked, once everyone had a glass of tea.

"A guide," Nalia said. "One who knows the desert as well as his own face. One who is discreet and loyal. Malek believes you may know someone like this."

"You are going to a specific place?"

Nalia nodded. "Yes. But because Malek can't evanesce, we need to travel the human way." She glared at her former master. "It's his third wish, the place we're going. I won't be free of him until I grant it."

Malek's eyes hardened at *free of him.*

Saranya gave Nalia a long look. "And this thing Malek has wished for—this is why the Ifrit have sent half an army to Earth?"

"The Ifrit have nothing to do with the wish," Malek said.

"So they want *you,*" Saranya said, her eyes still on Nalia.

Nalia nodded slowly. "Yes."

"Do you know someone who can help us?" Zanari asked, clearly tired of the vague conversation. She sat on the couch, legs spread and a scimitar strapped to her back, a soldier unaccustomed to elaborate tea rituals and sitting in pretty living rooms.

Saranya took a sip of her tea and slowly set it back on the table. "This is the wrong question to ask," she said. "The question is, *why* would I help you? If it's true that the Ifrit are looking for Nalia, then I'd be placing my life and my son's life in far more danger than usual." Saranya pursed her lips. "Tariq has already lost his father. What would he do if I were gone, as well? And Maywir and the others like her that live with me, where would they go?"

Nalia looked from Malek to Saranya. "I'm sorry, I didn't know about your husband. *Hifä lä'azi vi.* *My heart breaks for you.*"

Saranya nodded her head in thanks at the simple words of condolence shared among the jinn.

Is that why Malek had never spoken of his brother? Nalia's eyes trailed to Malek and he stood, turning his back to the room.

"I've lost people I love, too," Nalia said. "The jinni who's after me—she killed nearly my entire family."

Because Nalia continued to hide behind the disguise of Shaitan eyes, Malek's sister-in-law had no way of knowing Nalia meant the Ghan Aisouri. Though Nalia's loss was catastrophic, she wasn't the only jinni who had suffered under the brutal Ifrit regime.

Saranya remained silent, staring into her glass of tea as though it were an oracle.

"Thank you for your hospitality," Nalia said, standing. "I appreciate you taking the time to listen to our request."

Malek turned, a protest forming on his lips, but Zanari followed Nalia's lead and stood as well. Nalia knew there was only one way she could convince this woman to help her. As she moved toward the exit, she reached out and covered Saranya's hand with her own. As her *chiaan* connected with Saranya's, the other jinni looked up, startled.

"I need your help, Saranya," Nalia said. "But I won't beg you for it. Nor will I ask you to endanger your life without knowing fully what you're getting yourself into."

"So *you* are the Ghan Aisouri I hear whispers about."

Nalia inclined her chin, but gave no response.

"She's the only chance we have of stopping the Ifrit," Zanari said quietly.

I just want to go home, Nalia was tempted to say. *I want my brother. I want my land.* But it seemed so selfish, those thoughts, in light of what was happening in her realm. It didn't matter what she wanted; it never had.

Malek and Saranya shared a long look. Nalia didn't know what their silent conversation was about, but at the end of it, Saranya sighed.

"Your guide will meet you here tomorrow morning, after the first prayer."

"We need to leave *now*," Malek said. "The longer we stay—"

"You want the best, am I right?" Saranya asked.

"Yes," Nalia said.

"Well, the best is in Libya right now picking up a jinni who ran away from her slave trader. He won't be able to return until morning."

The midday call to prayer sounded then, the muezzin's voice from the human part of the souk cutting through the tension in the room.

"Now if you'll excuse me," Saranya said, "I must pray."

"But this song is for the human god," Zanari said.

"The jinn gods have never heard the cries of their people

on Earth." Saranya looked at Nalia as she said this. Nalia could almost feel those shackles on her wrists again. The weight of them. The shame. "How many more jinn need to be on the dark caravan or executed before people start to see the truth?" Saranya continued. "The gods of Arjinna don't care about any of us. Maybe they never have."

For so long Nalia had forced herself to kill such thoughts: the gods were the gods and that was that. But more and more she found herself wondering: maybe it was true—maybe they didn't care one bit.

10

ZANARI TRAILED BEHIND NALIA AND MALEK, HER HANDS at her sides, fingers tense and ready to channel *chiaan*, if need be. Earth confused her. It was so big, each place vastly different from the next. In the city where Nalia had lived, there were roads in the sky and people bought food in large, cold buildings. In Morocco, donkeys crowded the roads and skinned animals hung from hooks outside butchers' stalls, flies buzzing around the meat.

Earth had its problems, she knew: Zanari could see them in the beggars on the streets and the thin children in dirty clothing. But something about it called to her, made Zanari feel a sense of possibility. It buzzed inside her, heedless of her responsibilities to the *tavrai* and their cause. Zanari savored the sensation, a live thing, wild and exhilarating. What was the point of staying in Arjinna and dying for a lost cause? *Maybe the Dhoma have the right idea,* Zanari thought. She wondered what it would be like to stay on Earth and build a life far from the Ifrit. Then she immediately felt guilty. How could she even consider abandoning the dream her father had died for?

She shook her head, scanned her surroundings. Now was not the time for idle thoughts.

They were heading back to the human souk now, with nothing left to do but return to their *riad* and wait. Zanari didn't know where or what Libya was, but she was having a hard time believing there hadn't been another guide to help them get through the desert. She hated having to rely on so many strangers for help. She wondered if Raif would have been as trusting of one of Malek's relatives. Saranya might be helping jinn on the dark caravan, but Jordif had helped a lot of jinn, too.

There was a commotion up ahead and Zanari arched her neck to see what the jinn were shouting about. Moments later, a massive horse pulling a cart pushed past the crowd. The horse's owner struggled to maintain control as the animal whinnied, straining against the reins. A little boy, not much older than five summers, was standing in the horse's path, transfixed. The horse reared its forelegs, its hooves inches above the boy's head. Someone screamed and then Zanari saw it—a burst of golden *chiaan* that shoved the boy out of the horse's path, just as its hooves came crashing down on the cobblestone street.

Nalia's head scarf slipped down, her birthmark plainly visible as she bent to help the child. A shopkeeper across the street stared intently at Nalia's face. The jinni walked a few paces away and sent a stream of *chiaan* in the air: red. An Ifrit signal.

"Nalia!" Zanari shouted. She pointed to the signal in the sky. Malek was by Nalia's side at once, pulling her into a side street. Zanari followed and they hurtled through the souk, not stopping until they found a lonely archway far from the main road.

"I'm sorry, I'm so sorry," Nalia was saying when Zanari caught up with them.

"You should have let me help you put the damn thing on," Malek said. Nalia's scarf fell to the cobblestones at their feet.

The air shifted, as though it were a dragon awaking from its nap.

"Did you feel that?" Zanari murmured.

"Fire and blood." Nalia flexed her fingers. "Well, I guess they know we're in Morocco."

The energy was scalding and everywhere all at once.

"Do we have a plan?" Zanari asked.

"Yes," Nalia said. "Kill as many as you can."

"Winner buys drinks?"

"Definitely." For a second, it was like being back at home, just before a skirmish.

Maybe Nalia could fit in with the tavrai.

Around the corner, Zanari could see jinn fleeing in all directions. The vibrant market filled with shouts and the cries of young children. Tables laden with Arjinnan spices, spelled amulets, and bolts of sea silk crashed to the ground as the panicked crowd surged toward exits and doorways. The air became thick with rainbow clouds of evanescence as Djan, Shaitan, and Marid jinn evanesced from the souk. Most of them, Zanari guessed, had heard the stories of the carnage the Ifrit left behind, or they had witnessed it firsthand.

The evanescence nearest them materialized into the body of an Ifrit soldier who was twice the size of the horse Nalia had just saved the child from. His eyes lit up as he recognized her.

The Ifrit gave them a mock salute. "Got an order to capture or kill," he said. His voice was gravel and the sound of things crushing. "I like to kill."

Nalia raised her hands, palms out. "So do we."

The Ifrit sent a ball of flame toward them before charging. Out of the corner of her eye, Zanari caught a blur of motion. Nalia.

In seconds she was behind the Ifrit, lacerating his back with razor-thin bursts of *chiaan*. Her face glowed from the magic within her. It was the first time Zanari had seen Nalia in action. *No wonder the Ghan Aisouri were able to rule us so easily.*

The Ifrit soldier didn't stand a chance. He screamed and as he toppled forward, Nalia drove the point of her dagger into the beast's neck. First flesh, then bone, gave way.

Nalia grimaced as the blood poured out, but Zanari kicked the soldier for good measure as she pulled the knife out of the body. She wiped the blood on her pants and handed it to Nalia; one less monster to kill the *tavrai*.

Malek was staring at Nalia as though he'd never seen her before. And it was true: he'd never seen *this* Nalia before.

"Lucky for you she granted that amulet," Zanari said to him. She had no doubt Nalia would have made short work of Malek if she could.

Malek ignored her and moved toward Nalia. He'd noticed

what Zanari hadn't—Nalia's pale face as she looked down at the dead Ifrit. "Are you all right?"

This was a different Malek, softer—kind, even. *Gods, he really cares for her,* Zanari thought with disgust.

At the sound of his voice, Nalia thrust her dagger back into its holster and gave a toss of her head. "I'm fine."

Up ahead, a wall of crimson smoke descended on the souk.

"We need to evanesce," Zanari said. The Ifrit were closing in, more than even Nalia would be able to handle—they had to get back to the human section of the medina.

"I can't." Nalia gestured to Malek, who stood just behind her. "You go ahead. I'll catch up."

"I know the city," Malek said. "I'll be fine. Distract them so I can get away and I'll meet you back at the *riad.*"

Nalia glanced from Malek to the Ifrit, then nodded. "Wait until we've got them running before you head back." She turned to Zanari. "Ready to piss off some Ifrit?"

Zanari manifested a second scimitar so that she held one in each hand. "That's what I was born for."

Malek leaned against the wall and lit a cigarette as though he could care less that highly trained killers were a block away.

Nalia rolled her eyes. "Let's go."

They evanesced so that they stood on the opposite side of the street, just steps away from a trio of Ifrit.

"Looking for us?" Nalia called to the nearest soldier.

As expected, he gave chase. Zanari knew Malek was slipping down a side street, safe, while she and Nalia sprinted down a narrow cobblestoned alley, sending painful rays of magic over their shoulders every few seconds at the Ifrit who pursued them.

"I can't believe we're trying to save his *pardjinn* ass," Zanari said.

Fire rained down as the Ifrit closed in on their prey. Nalia directed her *chiaan* into a well and the water flew out, creating a protective curtain that doused the flames.

"Nice," she said, taking in the wall of water. Zanari shook her head in awe—to have the power to channel every element!

"I need more access to the wind," Nalia said, motioning to a nearby roof. She evanesced, her body dissolving into the air just as an Ifrit charged through her wall of water. Zanari sent a stream of *chiaan* into the beast's chest, an instant kill, then she shifted her body into a cloud of jade smoke and joined Nalia on the roof.

"Well, you've made this easy," a voice behind them said.

Zanari turned. A group of Ifrit had assembled on the roof, and they hadn't come alone.

Goose bumps scattered across Zanari's skin as she took in the beast that strained on the soldier's leash. "Shit," she muttered.

The *sárawq* were hideous creatures, half cobra, half scorpion, and the size of a lion. One bite could kill, and a lash from its tail could cut a jinni in half. The monster hissed, exposing needle-thin teeth framed by a thick, reptilian hood. Beside her, Zanari felt Nalia go very still.

Rather than backing away from the beast, Nalia began moving toward it, her eyes locked on the creature while she mimicked its swaying movement. The Ifrit let go of the leash and the *sárawq* snapped its neck back, then darted forward in a lightning-quick movement.

But Nalia was faster.

She launched into the air, slicing her dagger clean across the beast's throat. As the *s'arawq*'s head detached from its body, Nalia landed beside its Ifrit caretaker and pushed him off the roof with a burst of *chiaan*. His scream ended with an abrupt thud. In seconds, she was beside Zanari. The other two Ifrit were still staring at her, dumbstruck.

"Let's get out of here," Nalia said.

She leaped over the gap between the roof they were on and the one beside it, her body floating through the air before landing gracefully on the other side. Zanari took a running start, catapulting to where Nalia stood waiting for her. As soon as she felt solid ground beneath her feet, Zanari started to run, following Nalia across the flat roofs of Marrakech. They ducked beneath clothing lines and jumped over chairs and strange discs that Nalia had once said were satellite dishes, whatever that meant, all the while dodging the bullets of *chiaan* the Ifrit sent their way.

The Atlas Mountains loomed in the distance and the sun was high and in Zanari's face, making it difficult to see. The city became a sea of flat roofs with occasional rectangular minarets that stood between them, like strange buoys. As soon as they could, they jumped back down, into the bustle of the human souk, heading toward the *riad*.

"I think we lost them," Nalia said. She glanced at Zanari, her eyes bright and a carefree grin on her face. "Why didn't you tell me you could fight like that?"

Zanari returned the smile. "Sister, you never asked."

MALEK HURRIED THROUGH THE JINN SOUK, PAST CLOUDS of red smoke and screaming women who held their babies tightly to their breasts. The arrival of so many Ifrit had created utter chaos in the crowded market. The shopkeepers' banter and touting had been replaced by angry shouts and bursts of defensive *chiaan*. A table stacked with bottles of *savri* had been tipped over in the shoppers' need to find cover, and the wine from the broken bottles made it seem as though the streets ran with blood. Everywhere jinn were evanescing. Some corridors were so thick with their smoke that Malek could barely see in front of him. When he finally came upon the souk's entrance, he stumbled through it, coughing as he retraced his steps through the human markets. Though it was true the Ifrit were searching for Nalia, they knew he was her master. From what Malek had heard, they still had guards posted at his mansion in Hollywood. It would be best to get out of sight, and fast.

Soon he was back in the throng of Moroccans and tourists that filled the streets surrounding the Djemaa. The day had grown cold and Malek pulled his cashmere scarf more tightly around his neck.

It's not grief I see on your face . . . it's guilt, Saranya had told him before he left the house. The others had been too far away to hear, thank God.

But Saranya was wrong about that—there *was* grief. Mountains of it. Malek just hadn't allowed himself to feel anything for so long. The problem with falling in love with Nalia wasn't just that she didn't return his feelings; it was that, for the first time in years, Malek was letting his heart be more than an organ that kept him alive. That wasn't his first mistake where Nalia was concerned, but it would be his last. He'd wanted Nalia for a few months. The sigil? He'd wanted *that* for a lifetime. If nothing else, Malek Alzahabi knew what his priorities were.

He turned down a deserted street, where the only sound was an old man in a kaftan speaking softly to his donkey. Then: crimson smoke everywhere, a heavy, sulphuric fog that made it impossible to see. There was a roar and, before he could register what was happening, someone was shoving Malek from behind toward a sleek black SUV that materialized out of thin air, barely wide enough to navigate the souk's streets.

"What the fu—"

Malek struggled against his captors, trying to reach for the gun tucked into his waistband. One of them said something to him in the language Nalia sometimes spoke with Raif and Zanari—Kada. He didn't understand, but the harshness of the voice and the burn of the rope one of his captors was tying around his wrists told Malek everything he needed to know.

As he was being pushed into the backseat, he caught a glimpse of red eyes and a sneering mouth before rough hands pulled a black sack over his head. There was the slam of the car door being shut and then Malek fell back against the seat as they sped off. The only sound was heavy breathing and the thrum of the engine. There were so many turns, he had no idea where they were, but the slow speed suggested they were still in the cramped quarters of the medina.

"This is unnecessary," Malek said, his voice calm. Pinpricks of light filtered in through the sack's fabric, but that was all he could see. "I'm one of your arms distributors, for Christ's sake. And I have ample resources—whatever you need on Earth, it's yours. I promise I'll cooperate."

And he would—until he got the sigil and could muster a team of jinn to track down and kill whoever was holding him captive.

A cool voice spoke from the front seat, female. Amused. "Ample resources? I highly doubt you can tempt me with anything Earth has to offer, *pardjinn*."

"I assure you, I can."

She laughed then, a sultry, strangely ominous sound. "We'll see."

It was hours before Malek's captors took the sack off his head, well after the third call to prayer had come and gone. The first thing he saw was an ancient courtyard, empty but for a few birds that drank from the rectangular splash pool cut into the stone floor. He'd been expecting something more sinister, an abandoned warehouse or basement, but the Ali ben Youssef Medersa was one of Marrakech's most popular tourist attractions. Since it was after business hours, the fourteenth-century school was deserted. He glanced up as his Ifrit guards shoved him into the airy, elegant space. The sun had nearly set and the sky was a bruised peach, soft and darkening. He wondered if he'd ever see it again.

The dying sunlight cut across the *zillij* tiles that covered the imposing pillars that bordered the courtyard, a starburst of geometric shapes and colors that repeated on the portico walls behind them. It was Solomon's seal, winking back at him. It taunted Malek, this symbol. It was as if Morocco were holding the sigil just out of his reach, no matter how fast he ran toward it. The dusty orange stone that made up most of the walls was covered in dense Arabic script, carved into it centuries ago. Malek wasn't a religious man, but the medersa made him want to be—at the moment, anyway.

It would be nice, he thought, *to have a shred of peace. Just a shred. To pray and think that someone would listen.*

His eyes scanned the tiny arches that overlooked the courtyard from the second story. Each one contained an Ifrit guard that stared down at him with menace in his eyes. Malek's guards pulled him away from the courtyard and into the halls of what used to be the school's dormitories on the second floor. They pushed him toward one and he ducked through the thick wooden doorway and into the tiny, dank cell. It was nothing more than four whitewashed walls and a rickety wooden chair. There wasn't a light, but a small window near the ceiling showed a patch of sky through wrought-iron bars.

One of the guards pointed gruffly to the chair in the corner.

Malek sat, if only because the ceiling was so low it brushed the top of his head. The door to his cell slammed shut. It was a medieval thing, with steel studs and an iron handle.

"Hell," he muttered.

The medersa was at the very edge of the central souk, in a quiet, fairly abandoned quarter. He'd already seen how well guarded it was and even if he screamed his head off, who would help him? He wasn't sure if Nalia would ever find him here, or if she'd even bother to look. He certainly hadn't given her much incentive. Though she was under an obligation to grant his third wish, she couldn't very well be blamed for not granting it if he was nowhere to be found.

The mosques began their battling calls to prayer: the fourth of the day. *Maghrib:* sunset. The words rolled over him, for once soothing. Tonight he felt the muezzin's plaintive wail to the heavens as it throbbed against the sky. He needed a miracle, a power beyond his to intervene. It'd been a long time since he'd felt that way. Nalia worshipped her gods with reverent devotion. Malek envied her that simple belief. For him, Allah had always been a question mark. A faceless uncertainty that never heard his cry for help. Why would tonight be any different?

Malek unrolls his prayer mat. His body bends in supplication, but his will refuses to submit. Amir whispers the words beside him.

They press their foreheads to the ground. Malek keeps his eyes open.

The minutes ticked by as the room descended into velvet darkness, and soon the only light came from a sliver of moon that shone through the bars. When the fifth and final call to prayer sounded, Malek closed his eyes and went through the motions of the prayer in his head, his lips forming the words in silence. It brought no comfort, and as the last note of the muezzin's song faded away, he stood and began pacing the room, sneering at the darkness.

Finally the cell's door opened and a female jinni walked through it, followed by an Ifrit carrying an old-fashioned steamer trunk that he placed in the center of the room. The female formed a sphere of crimson *chiaan* between her hands, then tossed it toward the ceiling. It lay suspended above them, a glowing coal that cast the room in an eerie bloody wash. She wore a form-fitting red gown covered with a simple black cloak. A bit formal for the surroundings, but Malek never pretended to understand the jinn.

"Leave us," she said to the guard. Malek recognized the voice—the jinni from the car. "I'll call when I have need of you."

The proud tilt of her chin, the straightened spine, and the way the Ifrit backed out of the room before closing the door behind him told Malek enough: here was the jinni who'd ordered his capture.

Malek waited until the guards left the room, then pulled his gun out from where he'd tucked it into his waistband. They hadn't bothered to search him.

Amateurs, he thought. He might not have been a full jinni, but he was Malek Fucking Alzahabi and no one kidnapped him and got away with it.

"Who are you?" he said, pointing the gun at her.

The jinni laughed, the sound surprisingly rich for such a tiny creature. She gave a toss of her blond hair before narrowing her eyes at him. "I'll forgive your rudeness just this once. However, point a weapon in my face again and I'll have it shoved down your throat."

"My dear, you have no idea who you're dealing with," he said softly. There was a faint *click* as he turned off the gun's safety.

The jinni's eyes glinted, a predator with an invisible net. "Neither do you."

And then the world exploded and there was just red and blinding light and pain, pain, pain.

It was as if an ice pick had been shoved into the back of Malek's skull. All that existed was this excruciating sensation, an endless flood of agony, and then her voice in his head: *Let me properly introduce myself. I am Calar, empress of Arjinna and leader of the Ifrit.*

It felt as if there were an actual presence in his brain, a slithering evil that hunted through the secret caverns of his mind. Pushing, pushing, but never finding what it was looking for.

Malek cried out, clutching at his head, shaking it. He'd take a hammer to it if he could: anything, *anything* to get her out.

Then, just as suddenly as it had arrived, the pain vanished, and Malek was once again in control of his senses. When he opened his eyes, he saw that he'd fallen to his knees, an unwilling supplicant to the cruel mistress before him. His gun lay in a corner and there was a dull throb behind his eyes. He looked at her, unbelieving.

She was young: Nalia's age or not much older. He'd always imagined Calar as a towering Ifrit who'd spent centuries plotting the demise of the Ghan Aisouri, ancient and consumed with bitterness. Yet the crimes Calar had ordered were all the more chilling because of her youth; if she was like this now, what would her reign look like when she grew in her abilities?

Nalia. He had to get to her, warn her somehow. There was no other reason why Calar would deign to meet with him.

"I don't understand," Calar said to herself. She stood looking down at him with the emotional detachment of a scientist. "Did someone train you to do that?"

"Do what?"

"Protect your thoughts. It's like a fortress, that mind of yours. And you're only a *pardjinn*."

"Sorry to disappoint," he said.

Malek closed his eyes for a moment, then rose to his feet in one single, graceful movement. He frowned at his dirtied hands and pulled a handkerchief out of his pocket, dusting them off before throwing the square of linen to the floor. He'd lived too long and dealt with too many adversaries to show just how terrified he was, but there was only the thinnest veneer hiding the panic that had bloomed in his gut. She'd been in his *head*. How the hell had she done that?

"I want Nalia," Calar said, her voice hard. "You're going to summon her. Now."

"I'm afraid I can't do that." Malek spread his hands, a mock apology. "She's a free agent now. No more shackles. No more bottle."

For a moment, Calar looked taken aback, but she rallied quickly, one eyebrow raised. "Then you will bring *me* to *her*."

"Perhaps if you asked nicely," Malek said. Arrogance was his default and though he didn't want another demonstration of Calar's psychic power, he wasn't ready to admit defeat. He stepped closer, the pain in his skull so great that the room seemed to flicker in and out, like a flashing light bulb. "You may be empress of Arjinna, but this is *my* realm. *My* kingdom."

Malek fixed his eye on the empress's. Would his hypersuasion work on her? It'd be risky to try, but he might have to.

Before he had the chance to call forth his power, Calar smiled and waved her index finger with a *tsk-tsk*. "I wouldn't, if I were you."

"I thought you couldn't read my mind."

"I can't. But I have a few hypersuaders in my employ and I know the look they get, just before they're about to use their power. It won't work on me, anyway."

He wondered if jinn with psychic abilities were as rare as Nalia had thought.

"I like you, Malek Alzahabi." Calar drew closer, her voice low and playful. "I imagine we're not so very different." She smelled like a campfire and something else—a dark, sinful scent, dangerously intoxicating.

"That might be a bit of a stretch." He tilted his head to the side, studying her. "You're quite something, I'll give you that."

A year ago, he might have been tempted by her pale skin and dark red lips. The way her eyes glinted like rubies and fresh blood. He used to like bad girls, the ones with the cruel smiles and rough kisses. But not anymore.

Her lips turned up, a carnal invitation. "You have no idea."

Calar reached out and before he could do anything, her hands were pressing against his temples. Malek jolted at the unexpected sensation of the empress's skin, a burning energy he'd never encountered before. The only jinni he'd ever physically interacted with was Nalia—the feel of her skin against his own had been pure, unadulterated pleasure, something inside him calling to something inside her, satiating a hunger neither of them knew they'd had. But Calar was an entirely different matter. Her *chiaan* was like being thrown into a volcano, a deluge of malicious energy pulsing into him, igniting his Ifrit nature. Under her skin the worst of him unfurled until all he felt was the anger and the hate and the pleasure that came with winning, no matter the cost. Calar crushed her lips against his. She tasted like the middle of the night, when he couldn't sleep and anything, *anyone*, would do.

She laughed as her poison-apple lips pulled away. As the

connection broke, Malek came back to himself. He stumbled, falling against the wall, drunk with *chiaan*, his body shaking from the overdose of energy.

"Where is she?" Calar purred. She walked slowly toward him, feline. Her eyes glinted with a manic light. What the hell had just happened to him?

"This is absurd," Malek said. What was Calar's game? "You're a jinni, an empress. Surely you can find one girl?"

"I'm sure you'll agree that she's remarkably good at keeping herself hidden."

"I'm afraid none of your jinn squabbles concern me."

"I could just kill you," Calar said softly. "But I hate breaking pretty things."

Malek shook his head. "Death threats aren't an effective way to persuade me."

Calar leaned close to him, her lips inches from his own. "You've felt what I can do."

"The answer will always be no," he said. "I'll never take you to her. Besides," he added, "I've never liked blondes."

Understanding dawned in her eyes. "Love." She said the word with scorn as she turned away from him. "How very boring. I expected better from you."

Bravery wasn't something he'd needed much of in his lifetime, not with his powers and his general aptitude for cunning. But he was going to need it now.

Malek shrugged. "I seem to be disappointing the women in my life a lot lately." He turned to go, absurdly impossible, yes, but he wasn't going to just stand there. "Now, if you'll excuse me——"

She threw her *chiaan* against him, its force throwing Malek across the room. He hit the wall before slumping to the ground. The agony came even quicker this time, a hot poker pressing into his skull. His animal scream was a distant roar and he clutched at his head as the lacerating pain intensified until the world turned black and fell away completely. When he came to, Calar was reclining on a velvet settee she'd manifested, a thoughtful expression on her face. The pain was still present, just down enough notches for him to remain conscious.

"I rather thought that would end you," she said.

"I'm pretty hard to kill."

Calar stood then, her hands bleeding *chiaan*. "Usually, I have to be . . . gentle . . . in order to keep my prisoners alive. But you."

She smiled. "I don't need to be gentle, do I?"

Malek spit out the blood pooling in his mouth, then grinned.

"Just how I like it."

It was a game of chicken. He wanted to be the one that didn't swerve.

NALIA STOOD AT THE TINY WINDOW IN RAIF AND ZANARI'S room, looking down onto the darkened street below. Malek should have arrived hours ago, but it was too dangerous to go looking for him. They couldn't risk leading the Ifrit to Saranya's home, and with soldiers all over the city, the likelihood of finding him without being discovered was small. She and Zanari had managed to fight off the Ifrit in the souk, but they might not be so lucky next time.

Raif's sister had already tried to find Malek with her *voighif*, but all she could see was a wooden door, white walls, and a trunk of some kind.

"He and Saranya are probably just reminiscing over old times," Zanari said. She was lying on one of the beds, throwing a ball of *chiaan* up and then stretching it like taffy when it came down.

"I doubt that." The tension in Saranya's home had been thick enough to cut with her jade dagger. "Something was off with them," Nalia said. "Obviously Malek hasn't visited in a while, but there was something else. I don't know. We're just lucky she's going to give us that guide."

"True," Zanari said. "The sooner we get that ring, the better."

The light went out of her eyes. Nalia didn't have to ask why; she knew Zanari was constantly checking in on the *tavrai*, who, from the sound of things, were barely holding on to their headquarters in the Forest of Sighs. Things were getting worse in Arjinna by the minute. If Raif didn't return soon with the ring, he and Zanari may as well not return at all. Nalia didn't think any good could come of the ring, and, yet, it seemed like the Djan'Urbis had no other option.

Zanari's stomach growled. "Gods, where is my good-for-nothing brother? I'm starving,"

They could have manifested their dinner, but Fareed kept a close eye on his guests' comfort and he had no idea any of Malek's companions were jinn. Nalia needed to keep it that way.

"I just hope Raif can figure out how to pay with human money," she said.

A tug.

Nalia gasped.

"Nal? What is it?"

A tingling, burning tug on her chest. Someone was calling

Nalia, using her true name. And only one person knew it now that her mother was dead.

"Bashil!" Nalia cried out. Her hands flew to her chest and she leaned over, tears slipping down her cheeks.

Zanari shot off the bed. "Are you okay?"

"More than okay," Nalia said. The weight of her fear now momentarily suspended, it was as if she'd suddenly become a wisp of cloud, a swirl of evanescence. Laughter bubbled up inside her, a spring, then a geyser. "My brother—he's alive. Alive, Zan. He just used *bahm'dlah!*"

Zanari clapped her hands and crowed. "Who says the gods don't listen to us on Earth?"

Nalia lifted her hand and in a puff of golden smoke she saw Bashil's face in some kind of jail cell. Then it was gone. She tried to connect with him again, but there was nothing.

"I don't understand . . . Where'd he go?" she said, panic rising once again. "Fire and blood." Nalia balled her fist, disappointment covering her joy like a cloud crossing the sun. *He's alive*, she reminded herself. That was all that mattered right now.

"Listen, sister. Now that he's awake, I have a better chance of seeing how he is," Zanari said. "I'll use my *voiqhif*, okay?"

Zanari had tried to find Bashil several times before, but all she'd seen was darkness, an impenetrable wall that had been impossible to break through. Nalia had refused to believe he was dead. Unconscious, maybe. But not dead.

And she'd been right.

Zanari sat on the floor, then pulled off the pouch of earth from around her neck. She opened it, then swung it in an arc over her head. The dirt hovered in the air, then settled on the floor in a perfect circle, with Zanari in its center. She held out her hand as she muttered under her breath. Seconds later, a pad of paper and a pencil appeared on her palm. Then she closed her eyes.

Nalia watched as Zanari's eyelids flickered, like the delicate petals of a flower caught in a slight breeze. Her breathing became deeper as she settled into a trance state. Nalia imagined the lines of information Zanari traveled as an enormous set of underground freeways, each one leading to a specific person, place, or event. She hoped Zanari would be able to find Bashil among the millions of psychic roadways.

Zanari's pencil began to fly across the paper in her hand. Nalia couldn't see what she was drawing; the movements were too quick, too agitated. After a few seconds, Zanari's eyes flew open. She stared, unseeing, her gaze outside the room's walls. She took one shuddering breath and then it was over.

"I have no idea why this came up when I searched for your brother," Zanari said. She held the pad of paper up for her to see. Nalia stopped breathing, her mind clear of every thought, her body suddenly cold. The face drawn with Zanari's quick, sure hand had invaded Nalia's nightmares for over three years.

She'd never forget the Ifrit jinni she'd saved from more of her mother's torture and the certain death that would follow. This was the jinni who had betrayed Nalia's kindness by leading the Ifrit army through the same secret passage beneath the Qaf Mountains that Nalia had shown her.

"That's the one," Nalia whispered.

"The one what?"

"She's the Ifrit I told you about—the one I snuck out of the palace. The mind reader. I saved her and she . . . ," Nalia tore her eyes from the beautiful face with the proud tilt to her chin. Though she looked different without the bruises and cut lip she'd had in the dungeon, Nalia would recognize the jinni anywhere.

Zanari's eyes went wide, her face suddenly ashen. "Nalia . . . how can you not know who she *is*?"

"The prisoner wouldn't talk during the interrogations. At all. We never learned her name."

Fear bloomed in Nalia's stomach, a thorny terror pushing up, past her ribs and into her chest, her throat. And she knew—before Zanari said a word—she suddenly knew who the prisoner was.

"Calar," Zanari said, her eyes drifting to the sketch. "That's her name."

The silence in the room became a roar in Nalia's ears. The walls seemed to close in, like hunters surrounding a kill.

Calar. Calar. Calar.

She might as well have killed the Ghan Aisouri empress herself and handed the Amethyst Crown to the Ifrit.

"But . . ." Nalia stared at Zanari, eyes pleading, *Undo it*, they begged her. *Let me not know this.*

"When I looked for your brother, I hit that black wall for a second—the thing that's been there since I started looking for him. Then I could suddenly push through. Everything was blurry, I saw Calar's face. A dark room. That's all."

Nalia gripped at her hair, pulling until the pain focused her. "My father. Calar might have questioned him. He's Shaitan. If he's alive, I'm sure he's been forced to serve the Ifrit at the palace.

He's a scholar, a mage. He could have . . . fire and blood, he might have *told* her Bashil was alive . . . and if she knows he's my brother—oh, *gods*."

"Whoa. Nalia, you're jumping to some conclusions here. Remember, my gift isn't one hundred percent. The lines are really focused on you right now so since you're looking for Bashil and Calar's looking for you, it's all coming at me in the same way. And me seeing Calar doesn't mean Calar herself, necessarily— you have to remember that. It could mean she gave an order about all the work camps in Ithkar and because this affects Bashil that's why we're seeing her face. It could be a million things."

Nalia hugged herself. "But what if it's not a million things? What if he's in the palace dungeon? He looked like he was alone in a cell, not with all the prisoners in Ithkar like he usually is."

The door opened and Raif stepped inside, balancing cartons of food and bottles of water.

"There should be enough," he said. "I got everything Fareed suggested . . ." He trailed off as Nalia turned toward him.

"What happened?" He set the food down on the nearest table and crossed to her.

"I think Calar has my brother."

"*What?*"

Zanari threw up her hands. "Nalia, don't take this the wrong way, but I seriously doubt Calar has time to go looking through all of Ithkar for your kid brother. Even if she wanted him, it'd be almost impossible to find him so quickly. There are *thousands* of prisoners in the camps, most of them children that look just like him."

"But if she has him, if she's hurt him, then maybe that's why the *haḥmidah* isn't working right. He doesn't have the strength to—" Her voice broke and she covered her mouth. "I just need to be alone right now."

Raif reached for her. "Nalia, you have to eat."

"I'm not hungry."

It was too much—knowing Bashil was alive, but unsure if Calar had him locked up in the palace dungeon; knowing that *Calar* was the Ifrit she had saved, that Nalia had practically given the kingdom away to the usurper empress . . .

The game of cat and mouse they were playing wasn't simply Calar trying to secure the throne.

This was personal.

She'd buried him alive.

The surrounding darkness was a black, writhing worm—hungry. It twisted around his body, tightening its grip. Malek finally understood what those hours, days, *months* in the bottle had cost Nalia. Her betrayal, why she couldn't love him; that all made sense now. How could she ever forgive him for *this*?

What little air remained inside the metal box the Ifrit had stuffed him into stank of iron as Malek's blood continued to gush out of his nose, his mouth, his ears. His body was folded into the steamer trunk like a contortionist's: knees hitting forehead, the curved bones of his spine digging into the trunk's side. Each round with the psychic jinni pushed him past his threshold of pain into a whole new universe of agony. She'd been going through the contents of his brain like it was a drawer full of junk, throwing whatever wasn't of use to her to the side. He didn't know how much he was losing or what would be left when she was through with him.

If she would ever be through with him.

I deserve this, he thought. And not just because of Nalia. Malek had been the shadow that lurked in the corner of so many people's lives, but Amir . . . he'd been nothing but light.

Amir stares at the piles of American dollars as Malek throws them on the bed. "Brother, I don't understand."

Malek beams. He's never felt so proud in his life. "I got it for us. I used my power, and the banker, he just gave it to me."

Amir's eyes darken. "But none of it's yours."

"It is now."

"Take it back," Amir says. "At once. This isn't who you are. Who we are. And what will we tell Mother?"

"We'll tell her the truth: that our jinn father left us with one good thing that will help us survive." Malek threw the empty bag across the room. "If you want to keep begging on the street, be my guest. I'm buying us passage to America and you can come with us or go to hell, for all I care."

"Where is she, *pardjinn?*" his captor asked once again. Her muffled voice came to him from above. Malek knew the bitch was standing over the trunk in the icy room her soldiers had thrown him into, waiting for him to break. She'd already assured him several times that he would.

Malek tried to conjure Nalia's face in the darkness: the cinnamon skin, those eyes that always held a secret, the curve of her lips he'd hardly gotten to kiss. He hoped to God he never saw her again. If he did, it would mean his captor had won.

It would mean Nalia would die right there in front of him.

"My dear, I admire your tenacity, truly I do," Malek said through clenched teeth. "But I can assure you that there is no way in hell I'm helping you find her."

The spinning started again and the box shot off the ground, whirling faster and faster until all Malek could do was scream. It was a primal howl heard by no one but the cruel jinni who had thrown him into this unending vortex. He heard her laugh then, a delighted trill that was far more terrifying than the box they'd put him in.

Finally, the trunk lay still. The lid flew open and once again Malek stared into the crimson eyes of his torturer.

"Do you remember where she is now?" Calar asked.

"I can't say that I do, no." He spit out the words, and drops of blood landed on the stone floor.

Fiery ripples of *chiaan* slipped from her fingers and wound around Malek's head, pushing underneath the skin. He cried out as the blood vessels popped, as his brain became a sponge.

Malek bit back the whimper that clawed up his throat and closed his eyes. Nalia, descending the staircase in his mansion, her eyes meeting his across the crowded room. Nalia, pressing her lips to his in an empty movie theater. Nalia, saying, *I'll never love you.*

Calar smiled. "Let's try this again, shall we?"

Malek needed to catch his breath, find that reserve of strength inside him that had been reduced to Nalia's face, her smell. If he could just keep holding on to that, he could stand whatever Calar threw at him, he was sure of it. He sat up slowly, his body screaming.

"A . . . question . . . if I may." *Just a few minutes of peace,* he silently prayed.

The corner of Calar's mouth turned up. "An answer, if I wish."

"You're the empress of Arjinna. You have an army. Why are you bothering with me at all?"

"My army is in the middle of a civil war," Calar said. "They don't have time to run around Earth chasing one girl."

"But you do?"

"She's an old acquaintance of mine. I'm doing her a courtesy."

It was a good act, but Malek wasn't buying it.

"You're afraid of her," he said softly.

Of course. Calar's power was terrifying, but Nalia's was greater, if what he'd learned of the Ghan Aisouri were true. What would happen if Nalia came back to Arjinna and fought for the throne?

"Let me tell you a story," Calar said, her voice low and dangerous. "Once upon a time there were two girls in a dungeon. One was the prisoner, one was the guard. The prisoner *wanted* to be there. It was her choice, part of a much larger plan. She let the royal knights beat her and cut her. She let them think they had broken her will. But she was just waiting for the right moment to use her power. The guard . . . she didn't want to be there. She was weak and scared. Her mind was filled with pretty magic, the face of a little boy. She did not have a warrior's mind. The prisoner was *not* afraid of her."

Calar walked toward the tiny window, set high in the wall. Moonlight glinted off the metal bars.

"That being said, she's unaccountably good at evading attacks," she continued. "It was a stroke of luck that we were able to capture you. To be fair, I thought your mind would be more yielding, but no matter. I'll just move on to the next plan of attack. This way's a bit more complicated, but since you've proven to be rather useless, I'll just have to exert myself."

Calar turned around and rapped on the cell door twice. It opened immediately. "Bring the boy," she said to the Ifrit standing guard outside.

Moments later, a child stumbled through the doorway. He was dirty, thin, as though he'd been plucked out of a coal mine. Sick, too, from the looks of him.

"Is this supposed to mean something?" Malek asked, gesturing toward the child.

Calar smiled and the boy looked up for the first time. Golden eyes with the slightest curve at the edges. Eyes that could break him in seconds. Nalia's eyes.

Malek stared. There was only one jinni who could possibly look like Nalia.

"Bashil?"

13

RAIF STARED AT THE CEILING, LISTENING TO NALIA'S deep, even breaths as she lay beside him. He'd slipped into her room well past midnight, once it was clear Malek wasn't coming back anytime soon. In the light from the hallway, he'd found Nalia curled up in the middle of the bed, blankets twisted around her legs. Sleeping, it was almost easy to forget she was a fierce warrior with a price on her head, an empress in hiding.

Wide awake, Raif gave himself over to the images he'd received from his mother through *habm'alah* a few hours before. Details of the war in Arjinna had become a sandstorm spinning ceaselessly through his mind: whole villages burning to the ground, executions of political prisoners. The Ifrit were fighting the *tavrai* in earnest now, intent on eradicating them from the land entirely. If the guide Saranya had promised to provide fell through, Raif didn't know how much longer he could afford to wait for Nalia. The ring was like the nuclear weapons humans so loved: once it was in his possession, Calar would have no choice but to leave Arjinna and take the Ifrit with her . . . or else Raif would make them. He'd promised Nalia he would never wear the ring and he would try to keep that promise. But the truth was, Calar wouldn't go down without a fight. Raif knew Nalia would never forgive him if he put that ring on his finger. And yet, it might be the only way to save Arjinna.

Raif sighed and lifted his arm, tracing the lines of the tattoo Nalia had burned into him with her *chiaan*. It had only been a few nights since they'd huddled together in Malek's conservatory while the storm Nalia had manifested thundered against the glass. She'd given him the tattoo, an exact replica of the one on her arm, so that he could locate the sigil on his own. But at the last minute, he'd decided to stay, refusing to let her accept death at the hands of a flesh-eating ghoul. She was in as much danger of dying now as she was then. Even though Haran could never hurt Nalia again, Calar had more than just a ghoul assassin to do her dirty work. Today was just a taste of what the Ifrit empress could throw their way. What would have happened if Zanari hadn't been there, fighting by Nalia's side? Yet it was becoming increasingly clear that the choice to stay with Nalia was also the choice to let more *tavrai* and innocent jinn die. Raif's conscience hadn't been clean for a long time, but he wasn't sure if he'd ever be able to forgive himself for that. And neither would Zanari. She'd taken one look at their mother's message and left the room, the door slamming behind her. She didn't have to say it; they needed to leave. *Now.* Yesterday.

Raif sat up, the sheets pooling at his waist. Gods, it was too much—he didn't know what the hell to do. Raif was a fool to travel with Nalia to the cave. If the wish protected Malek right up until the moment he picked up the ring, there was a good chance Raif would have to fight her in order to get the sigil. He was no match for a Ghan Aisouri's power, and Nalia was powerless against the wish. When it came to the sigil, Malek had an edge. Raif's only plan was to run faster than him, hit harder, and use every ounce of brutality he'd learned on the battlefield. But it might not be enough. Raif was quickly running out of excuses to stay—but he couldn't quite make himself go.

I choose her. Every time. And it shamed him.

Nalia mumbled something and turned over. Raif lay down and wrapped his arms around her. He breathed in the scent of amber that always clung to her, amazed that her smell had already begun to feel like home to him.

"No," she said, her voice muffled by the pillow. "I don't want . . ."

"Nal?" he whispered.

She whimpered, then mumbled something else, her breathing becoming rapid, irregular. Raif wasn't sure whether he should wake her from the nightmare she was having or hold her through it until the dream fell away. He pressed his lips to her hair and tightened his arms around her.

Shalinta, Shalinta, she whispered.

Forgive me.

Nalia screamed. Raif sat up and gently shook her awake.

"Nal, it's just a dream," he said. Her eyes opened and she startled at his touch. "It's me—you're okay. It was just a dream."

She stared at him as she sat up, something dark and uncertain brewing in her eyes. He reached across the bed and turned on the small lamp beside his pillow. She blinked at the light as though it pained her.

"Nal, you're safe." He reached for her, but she shrank away.

"It wasn't just a dream," she whispered.

Rohifsa, you—

"Don't call me that," she said. "You're just making it worse."

Song of my heart. Soul mate. Don't call her that?

Raif ran his hands over his face, as though he could rub away the exhaustion. "Okay . . . what do you want? Something to drink? Maybe you need to eat, you didn't have any dinner—"

"I killed him, Raif."

"I know you did." He wondered if Haran would always be a little alive, lurking in the dark corners of Nalia's mind. "And he's gone forever and can never hurt you again."

She shook her head. "I'm not talking about Haran." She took a breath. He'd never seen her like this—nervous and uncertain.

"Kir," she said softly.

"What about Kir?" he said. Had he told her about him? Raif couldn't remember. There hadn't been much time for conversations about the past.

"I . . ." Nalia bit her lip. Her eyes rose to meet his. "I killed him."

Raif stared at her as the words hung in the air between them. At first, he didn't understand—it was as though she'd told him a riddle, and he'd never been very good at solving those. But then the words crystalized and they were sharp and cruel, instruments fashioned to torture him. He stumbled out of bed, struggling to stand, as though the floor were the bottom of a swiftly sinking boat. The water was getting higher.

"That's . . . no . . . but . . ." Words—they wouldn't come; and breath, that wouldn't come either.

She hadn't said that, hadn't meant it. Raif had heard her wrong. He was dead tired. Obviously he'd misunderstood her. Nalia had begun taking on the sins of the Aisouri, as though she herself had committed each and every crime of her race. That was it, that's what Nalia had meant: she believed that being a member of the royal caste automatically made her complicit in Kir's death. The realization was like a last-minute pardon when he'd expected to be executed. Raif sat on the edge of the bed, as close to her as she would allow.

"Gods, Nal. Don't do that to me." He pressed his lips to her forehead, delirious with relief. Her eyes were just as confused as his had been a moment before, and he gave her a small smile. When would she ever forgive herself for things that had been beyond her control?

"I thought you meant . . . never mind," he said. "Listen, I know it feels that way." She looked down, clasping her hands together. "When I lead my *tavrai* in battle and some of them die, I always feel like I'm the one who killed them. Like it's my fault." He rested a hand on her knee. Nalia didn't flinch this time, but he could feel her trembling beneath him. "Just because a Ghan Aisouri killed Kir doesn't mean you're his murderer." He shook his head. "I never thought I'd say this to a royal, but . . . I know his blood isn't on your hands." He scooted closer to her. "Nalia, you're good. Your heart is so good and I know—"

"Stop," Nalia whispered. She looked up at him then, her golden eyes filled with tears, two shimmering suns that called to him. Promised warmth, a glow to bask in.

"Raif." She took in a shuddering breath. "I really killed him.

I . . . it was me."

He went still.

Kir, running ahead of Raif, through the maze of trees in the Forest of Sighs.

Kir, sneaking a bottle of savri from his father's secret stash. "Do you think we'll get drunk?" Raif asks. Kir grins. "I hope so."

Kir, sticking out his tongue to catch the first drops of a rainstorm.

Kir, asking the prettiest jinni to dance at the harvest festival—his body moves with an unexpected grace.

Kir, pushing Raif away as the Ghan Aisouri close in on him.

Kir, falling, falling, falling to the bloody mud as they drag him away.

Raif could feel himself detaching, becoming the jinni who looked down at captured prisoners and informed them they were sentenced to die. He stood as *chiaan* rushed to his hands.

"Tell me everything." The words were short, clipped. A general's order.

Raif made himself look at her, this living, breathing reminder of what happens when you lose your focus, when you forget what you're fighting for. Death was the cost of war. He knew that better than anyone else. But the way Nalia was looking at him now, this was a whole new kind of death. There would be no one but them to mourn what was lost.

"She made me! Raif, it was an order. My mother was my commanding officer and I had to obey, I *had to*." She stood then, a dancer waiting for the next beat. He watched her, silent, as she came toward him with tentative steps. "I didn't want to, I swear to all the gods in all the worlds, there was no choice—"

"There's *always* a choice!"

His shout seemed to reverberate off the walls, magnifying the pain underneath all the anger. Raif grabbed his shirt off a nearby chair and threw it over his head. "Were you ever going to tell me? If you hadn't had this dream—would you have just gone on pretending it had been someone else?"

She was sobbing now, the tears coming out in great, heaving gulps. But for the first time since he'd met her, he didn't care. There was not one single part of him that wanted to comfort her, to take her pain away.

"I've tried . . . but I . . ." She took in a shuddering breath. "Yes, I was going to. Everything's been so crazy and I was just waiting until I don't know I . . . gods Raif, I'm sorry, I'm so sorry."

"You're sorry," he said, his voice flat.

"I know it doesn't mean anything, me saying that."

He started toward the door, not really sure where he was going, just knowing he couldn't be here with her.

"He would have died no matter what, Raif," Nalia said, her

voice thick with tears. "My mother said if I didn't do it, she'd make it worse and so I was quick, so quick, and afterward—"

"Shut up," he said.

Nalia fell to the bed as if he'd slapped her. For a moment, they stared at one another in the dim light of the room, hope crackling, then burning between them, like a love letter held above an open flame.

For once, the choice was obvious: he was going.

"I never want to see you again." The words came out of his mouth, but he wasn't here anymore, not really.

Going.

"I love you," she whispered.

"No," he said, "I don't think you do. That's not possible for your kind—I'd forgotten that."

Gone.

NALIA OPENED HER EYES AS THE FIRST *ADHAN* SOUNDED.

The dawn call to prayer dipped and swooped over Marrakech like a newly awakened bird. She'd been sitting on the hotel floor staring at nothing since Raif and Zanari had left the *riad*, hours ago. Malek had never showed and she had to assume the worst—he'd been captured by the Ifrit. She wasn't sure what that meant for his wish. Didn't care.

She closed her eyes again as the longing in the muezzin's voice tore through her.

As-salatu khayrun minan-naum. Prayer is better than sleep.

Maybe she'd been praying to the wrong gods all along.

But then: a tug on her heart, insistent.

"Bashil," she whispered.

Nalia lifted her hand and waited for her brother to send her an image. Seconds later, it came, a puzzle she'd have to put together.

First, his face.

Nalia smiled as tears dripped down her cheeks. She sent him an image of the broken bottle and her bare wrists. She hoped he would understand that she was coming soon.

The next images from Bashil came in quick succession: the portal between Earth and Arjinna, a desert, palm trees, the Dje-maa-el-Fna.

"What?" she said aloud, forgetting for a moment that he couldn't hear her.

Bashil was in Morocco.

For the moment, Nalia didn't care how or why, she just had to see him. She sent him a picture of a compass and he responded with a picture of an intricately carved door. The sign above read MEDERSSA BEN YOUSSEF and below that, in Arabic: YOU WHO ENTER MY DOOR, MAY YOUR HIGHEST HOPES BE EXCEEDED.

Nalia pressed her forehead to the ground, sobbing out her thanks to the gods she had begun to doubt. She sprang to her feet and changed into jeans and a sweater, then slipped on a pair of tennis shoes. She considered writing a note for Malek, but dismissed the idea as soon as it came to her head; it was a courtesy he didn't deserve.

Nalia stood in the center of the room and closed her eyes, holding the image of the door in her mind. Her body began to unfurl, skin and bones transitioning to smoke. The scent of amber, then the minty coolness of evanescence overtook her, a slight chill that wrapped around her like an autumn wind. Seconds later, she was standing in front of the door. Nalia looked up and down the deserted street. It was early, the dawn call to prayer having only just finished. It felt as if the entire souk was still asleep.

She put her hand against the ancient door, hesitating. Nalia had no idea who Bashil was with—a slave trader? How else would he have made it through the portal and onto Earth? It was possible that the darkness Zanari had come up against had been the bottle Bashil was being transported in. There wasn't much time, then. The trader would want to sell her brother as quickly as possible so that he could return to Arjinna and collect more "cargo." But there was also the chance that he had somehow escaped and this was a safe house on Saranya's underground caravan.

She didn't want to think of the last possibility—that Zanari had been wrong and that Bashil had been identified and taken prisoner by Calar. But this didn't make sense, not anymore. Bashil would have conveyed that danger to her somehow, and he hadn't. Still, she'd probably have to fight their way out of this.

Nalia slipped her dagger into her right hand. She could almost hear her mother's voice as she thought, *Everyone is an enemy until proven otherwise.* The Ghan Aisouri mantra had always served her well. Turned out most jinn *were* her enemies. Even the ones she had fallen in love with. There was no doubt she and Raif weren't on the same side anymore. Would he issue an order to have her killed?

"Stop it," she whispered. Raif was gone, but the gods were giving her Bashil. It was a trade she'd make any day.

Nalia pressed against the door. It gave way, swinging inward, silent. She quickly stepped inside and shut it behind her, stealthy as a hunting gryphon. There was no sign of life, but she knew Bashil was here, somewhere. She wished there'd been more time for her to know exactly what she was getting into. She wished Raif and Zanari were here to back her up.

Wish. What a terrible little word.

It appeared as though Nalia were in some kind of historical building, now used for tourism. There was a small window to her left with a list of admission prices and guides in several languages. She hugged the wall and crept toward the huge double doors that led to a mesmerizing courtyard. It was too open, with a dozen windows looking down on it from the second story. A quick sweep of the area with her eyes told Nalia that Bashil wasn't there. She retraced her steps, back to a stairway she'd passed that likely led to the second floor.

Almost as soon as she reached the top, Nalia heard a moan from behind a closed doorway. The door was locked from the outside and Nalia slid the bolt back, then peeked into the dim room, her dagger pointed out. Something—*someone*—was heaped in a corner, a pile of dirty clothes speckled with blood. But she recognized the expensive Italian shoes.

Nalia gasped. "Malek?"

His only response was a soft groan. Nalia closed the door behind her and sheathed her dagger, then rushed over and gently moved Malek onto his back. His eyes remained closed, but a pitiful whimper slipped past his lips.

Nalia stared. It was painful to look at him. It appeared as if the beating he'd undergone had been reserved exclusively for Malek's head and face: there were deep bruises on his temples and dried blood like tear tracks crawled down his cheeks. Draega's Amulet would keep Malek alive, but she didn't know what kind of permanent damage he would sustain from the torture he'd been subjected to.

It scared Nalia, seeing Malek like this. The violence was so crude, so intentional. His skin was a collage of purples, his nose bloodied and broken, his lips swollen, shirt torn. It brought her no joy to see Malek suffer. Maybe a few weeks ago she could have left him to fend for himself, but not now. Not after everything she'd begun to understand about her former master. She didn't love him, didn't even like him, but she couldn't leave him here, at the mercy of whoever had done this to him.

"Malek, wake up," she whispered.

She had to get to Bashil, didn't have time to carry around Malek's dead weight. She could feel time running out, as though it were a tangible thing that could slip through her fingers.

"Malek, *esb'a*," she said in Arabic.

Wake up.

"*Hayati*," he groaned. *My life.*

It was the first time Malek had used that term of endearment for her since she betrayed him. Nalia couldn't tell if he knew she was there or was calling out to her from that gray land she had traveled to the night Haran almost killed her.

"Nalia." He said her name like a prayer he didn't expect to be answered. "Nalia."

She didn't have to come when he called anymore. So why was she staying by his side? She should let Malek think he was alone in that dark place. She'd been there before, too. Because of him.

"I'm here," she whispered, close to his ear. "Malek, I'm here." His eyes opened, or tried to. His hands reached for her, clumsy. She looked down and saw that they were tied together with thick cords.

"*Hayati*. Go. She's coming for you."

"Who? Who's coming for me?"

But he cried out and was lost again to the ocean of pain that had swallowed him up.

"Malek?" His fingers loosened where he'd grabbed her arm and his breathing dipped; he was unconscious again.

She pressed her fingers against his neck; she barely felt his *chiaan*—he was as close to death as the amulet would allow him to be. There was only one way she could revive him.

Nalia sliced the cords off his hands with her dagger, then twined her fingers with his. She closed her eyes, pouring her *chiaan* into him. She barely felt him at first, a faint whisper in her veins, nothing more. But then he gasped, his *chiaan* suddenly awake, surging through him. She opened her eyes. He was still unconscious.

"Come on," she whispered. "We have to go. Wake up. Wake the hell up."

His eyes snapped open and his grip on her hands became firm. "Nalia? What are you—"

"No time. I have to get my brother. Have you seen him?"

"Yes, but Nalia, she—"

"I'll be back. Don't go anywhere."

She dropped his hands and stood. A glint of metal caught her eye—a gun, abandoned in a corner of the cell. She grabbed it and pressed it into his hands. "Use this if you need to."

"She's here."

But Nalia wasn't listening as she slipped through the door and closed it behind her. She had to get to Bashil. Gods, what if he was in the same shape? Panic tore through Nalia and it was all she could do not to scream his name.

There were ten doorways on the second floor, all of them opening into empty cells. She was about to go downstairs when she saw one more door, tucked around a corner.

Please be in there.

Nalia slid back the iron bolt on the door, cursing as it singed her bare skin. She pressed her palm against the rough wood and the door swung open. It was too easy and yet . . . her head whipped to the right as she heard something scurry across the floor. There, hiding behind a chair, was a small boy. Bright golden eyes stared at her. As she came further into the room, he stood.

"Nalia-*jai*?" It had been so long since someone had used the familial suffix with her.

"How did you find me?"

"*Gharoof.* My little rabbit," she whispered. He was so thin, *gods*—she fell to her knees and held out her arms.

His face broke open—relief, joy, everything Nalia was feeling. Bashil started toward her, then froze, his eyes wide.

Nalia turned.

"It's been a long time, Ghan Aisouri."

Blond hair, piercing ruby eyes. That stubborn tilt to the chin.

"Calar."

How did you find me? Bashil had asked.

Nalia vaulted to her feet. "It was you contacting me. You took my true name out of his head!"

"It was just sitting there, out in the open."

Calar looked past Nalia, her eyes narrowing. Bashil screamed, a terrible agonized cry that cut Nalia in two. She ran to her brother, shielding him with her body, but whatever was hurting him was faster than her. Bashil was clutching his head with his hands, his body convulsing as he fell to the stone floor. Blood was pouring out of his ears, his eyes, his nose.

"What are you doing to him?" Nalia screamed. She threw a hand up, sending a flood of *chiaan* toward Calar. The empress ducked and the room echoed with her cruel laughter and still Bashil screamed. Nalia launched herself at Calar, and their bodies clashed in a cloud of red and gold *chiaan*. She barely felt the pain of Calar's magic as it lacerated her skin.

"Let's see how good you are at keeping me out of your head now, *salfit*." Calar's eyes glowed a fierce, blinding red, but before Nalia felt a thing, a gun went off and Calar stumbled back. As she turned around, her feet caught on her long gown and she fell to the floor, hitting her head on the corner of a table. Malek stood behind her, the gun toppling to the ground as he leaned against the doorway for support. "I don't think I . . . She's still . . ." He trailed off as his eyes caught sight of Bashil. He'd stopped moving.

A strangled cry broke from Nalia's lips and she stumbled toward her brother. "Wake up, *gharoof*, wake up," she pleaded as she pulled him onto her lap. His body was so light, skin and bones.

"If you wake up, I'll let you eat as many sugarberries as you want." Her voice caught. She gripped his tiny hands, pressing her lips against the dirty fingers. "And we'll go dragon hunting, just me and you."

His eyes fluttered open. The gold of them had turned a dull yellow, like late winter sun. They locked on hers, the bloody tears slipping down his cheeks. His body convulsed once, twice.

She was dimly aware of the gun going off again. Again. Again.

"Keep your eyes open," she whispered. She held him tightly. "You're okay, we're together now. You're okay."

"Nalia, I can't keep them off forever," Malek said. "There are soldiers everywhere. We need to go *now*."

More shots.

Nalia pressed her palm against his heart—gods, his skin was freezing—and pushed her *chiaan* into him. But there was nothing for her magic to hold on to: it was like filling a broken glass with water. The *chiaan* slipped out of his skin and onto the floor.

"No!" She spoke to him in rapid Kada, trying to keep him conscious—

Gods, pleasepleaseplease—

"Bashil, stay awake, stay awake." His *chiaan* had always felt like a playful house cat, jumping and tumbling and bright, but she couldn't feel it anymore—

His eyes closed. "Bashil, *no*! Listen to me . . . I'll bring you back. I can bring you back." Raif had done it for her, held her while she wandered the in-between.

Pleasepleaseplease—

His blood: everywhere. His body still, his body *still*—

"Bashil," she cried. Tears and blood everywhere, everywhere—

Please—

Bashil sighed once and then she felt it, just as it had been with Kir: a going. It was as if a tiny bird had taken flight, leaving behind a shivering bough.

A shroud of pale gold *chiaan* slipped from Bashil's skin, covering him for a moment before dissolving in the air, as though his soul had evanesced, leaving his body behind.

"NALIA." MALEK WRAPPED HIS ARMS AROUND HER. "*Hayati*, we have to go. Come."

It was as if she couldn't hear him at all. The fierce girl who'd intimidated his drug lord clients and the presidents of corrupt governments had disappeared. This Nalia clutched at her brother's body, her cries deep and guttural. She stared at Bashil's face, begging him to wake up, fingers gently tracing his lips, cheeks, closed eyelids.

It broke his heart.

"We have to go," he whispered again. "To Saranya's. We'll be safe there. Please, Nalia."

His own brother's face came to mind, unbidden. Had Amir been alone when it happened? Was there anyone to hold him, as Nalia held her brother? Malek pushed the thought away. He didn't deserve to grieve, to feel the ocean of sadness inside him.

"Give me the boy," he commanded.

Her only response was to hug Bashil tight against her. Malek tried to pry him from her arms, but her limbs had turned to stone and he was in no state to fight her; he could barely stand as it was.

There were screams outside from the humans in the souk. The Ifrit had arrived. Malek grabbed her chin and held it. Gods, if he could only hypersuade her. She'd learned some Ghan Aisouri mind trick as a child, though. Strong enough to keep him out.

His fingers pressed into her skin. "Look at me. Calar's soldiers are here. We are leaving. Now."

She nodded and he helped her stand.

"It's rude to leave the empress's presence without her dismissal," said a voice behind him.

Malek turned. Calar was leaning against the table that had knocked her out, a self-satisfied smirk on her face. "Should have killed me, *pardjinn*. Look where love gets you."

So fast he barely registered it, Nalia grabbed the gun out of his hand and pointed it at Calar. With one arm still wrapped around Bashil, she pulled the trigger, but it missed Calar's heart, only hitting the Ifrit's arm. Nalia aimed for her head, but Calar was faster than the bullet. Her crimson smoke filled the room and then she was gone, the bullet lodged in the plaster wall.

Nalia's hand shook and the gun clattered to the floor. Malek picked it up. She'd used the last bullet, so he shoved it into his waistband, then wrapped an arm around her shoulders.

"Don't worry," he said. "We'll kill that bitch first chance we get."

Nalia just stared at him with dead eyes.

"Come," he said softly. He pulled her down the hallway, glancing out one of the arches at the courtyard below. Dead Ifrit littered the stone floor. Swirling plumes of crimson smoke blanketed the sky above the medersa's courtyard, like a red sandstorm.

He led Nalia down a narrow stairway and searched until he found a back door. Nalia moved as though she were in a trance, barely conscious of her surroundings. Malek put an arm around her, leading her out of the medersa and down a side street that wasn't far from Saranya's home in the jinn souk. That was his only bit of luck, that Calar had chosen a prison just a few blocks from the only place in Morocco that would open its door to a *pardjinn*, a dead child, and the jinni at the top of Arjinna's Most Wanted list.

"We'll be there soon, *hayati*," he whispered as he placed his hand on the *hamsa* of one of the three entrances to the jinn souk. His hand warmed as red *chiaan* poured from his palm and the *hamsa* glowed. When the door disappeared, revealing the souk beyond, he pulled Nalia through the entrance. She stumbled and the child nearly slipped from her arms.

"Give him to me."

She stood in the middle of the street, sobbing as she clutched her brother. "Bashil," she said, over and over again—a question, a prayer, a mourning cry.

Malek reached out his arms. "Let me carry him. I need you to be able to use your *chaan* if we get surrounded."

She shook her head. "I . . . can't . . ."

"Is this how it all ends?" he said. "You want to give that sadistic jinni the satisfaction of watching the last royal die in the mud of the jinn souk?"

There it was—a small spark in her eyes.

"No," he said softly. "What you want is to kill her, yes?"

Nalia nodded.

"Then live long enough to do it." He held out his arms again and this time, she let him take the boy.

Malek dragged Nalia further into the souk, past already bustling teahouses and bakeries selling freshly manifested sweetbreads. He stole two kaftans from a display in front of a tailor's shop, then drew her into an alcove.

"Put it on," he said.

Her shirt was covered in blood, as was his. She obeyed, numb. The garment was too big for her, but there was nothing to be done for it. He handed Bashil to Nalia while he pulled the homespun kaftan over his head. He kept the pointed hood up, hoping it would cover some of the wounds on his face. When he looked over at her, Nalia was gently rocking Bashil, her lips moving in a soundless song.

Saranya's door was in sight. Malek grabbed Nalia's elbow and led her closer to the main street. He waited in the shadows until a squad of Ifrit passed, then stepped into the light. He forced himself to walk slowly toward the familiar door of his brother's home, as though he were simply out for a stroll with his family.

No one gave them a second look. He rapped on Saranya's door three times, waited a beat, then knocked twice more. The old signal from when Amir was alive.

It opened immediately. Saranya stared at them, sucking in her breath as her eyes fell on the dead child.

"We need your help."

MALEK STOOD AS SARANYA CAME OUT OF HER BEDROOM.
The living room stank of the cigarettes he'd chain-smoked, waiting as his sister-in-law attended Nalia. As the door closed behind
her, he saw Bashil's body laid out on a high table. He was naked
from the waist up, rib bones sticking out like a gutted fish. Nalia
stood beside him, a wet cloth in her hand. She looked up, her face
ravaged by grief. The door closed.

Saranya had already explained the ritual to him. When a
jinni died, the family washed the body in scented water and special oils. A priest of the jinni's caste would often come and say the
prayers of the dead, though in this case, that wouldn't be possible.
Not with Calar and her soldiers combing the souk for a dead boy
and his Ghan Aisouri sister.

"How is she?" he asked as Saranya drew closer. He already

knew the answer, but he had to fill the heavy air. It was pressing against him, all this death and despair. Waking up his memories.

"Her brother is dead, Malek. How do you think she feels?"

The look she gave him, the one that said *you should know*, cut him. Malek stared at the worn rug at his feet and gripped the lighter in his fist as though it were a *hamsa* that could protect him from the truth.

"How did it happen?" The question was past his lips before he knew he was asking it.

Saranya's eyes became a darker shade of gold, like sand at sunset. "With Amir?"

He nodded. The room was closing in. Why was he doing this to himself, now, when he needed his strength more than ever? He'd spent three years avoiding the thought of his brother's death.

"For my first wish," Malek says, *"I'll have Draega's Amulet."*

The jinni's eyes widen, but she says nothing.

"*I know what it is, child*," he says. "*Furthermore, I know you can do it.*"

"*First, my name is Nalia. Second, I'm not a child—I'm fifteen summers old. And, no, I can't give you the amulet. That magic is far too powerful for me.*" *But even as she says the words, her body begins to contract. She cries out in pain.*

Malek smiles. "*You are new to granting, new to Earth. Perhaps you aren't yet aware of the rules. If it's in your power to grant a wish, you have no choice. Need I remind you that you're mine? My slave. And you will do as you're told.*"

A defiant blush blooms across the girl's cheeks. She is lovely, his little slave. But young and foolish. Stubborn. He'd had to break her, like the Arabian horse he'd recently won in a card game with a Saudi prince in Monaco. She'd been wild, too.

Malek pulls the bottle out of his pocket. He'd have to get a chain for it soon, wear it around his neck. "In you go, then." Nalia swallows, then shakes her head. "No. I can do it." Malek raises his eyebrows. "I'm sorry, I don't think I heard you right. I can do it . . ."

"Master," she finishes. She spits the word out, as if it is meat that has been left in the sun to spoil. "I can do it, Master." Then she smiles, a wicked little upturn of the mouth. "But you must pay the price. This wish is not for free."

"He was sitting in that chair." Saranya pointed to a carved wooden chair near the kitchen. "He was laughing about something Tariq had said and then suddenly he just . . ." Saranya took in a shaking breath. "There was no blood. No anything. It was as if his soul had run away."

"So he wasn't alone?"

She shook her head.

Malek turned away, ashamed—afraid—of the unexpected wetness in his eyes. "Alhamdulillah."

Thank God.

"But we were," she said softly, with a glance at the closed doors the dark caravan refugees slept behind. "Tariq and I."

Again, they'd reached an impasse. For years he and Saranya had been traveling on this road: her, asking the same questions. Him, gliding past them, searching for the curve up ahead.

But it always came to this: why had Amir's death made Malek a stranger?

Saranya crossed to the window and looked through the curtains at the bustling street outside. It was the lunch hour, and jinn were on their way to the teahouses or their homes for the afternoon meal.

"As soon as she's finished, you two need to move on. It's not safe for any of us with you here."

"I know." He slipped his hand into his pocket and gripped Nalia's necklace, the metal warm beneath his skin. "What about the child?"

"She needs to burn the body. You'll have to take him with you into the desert. There's nowhere to do it here. Nowhere the Ifrit won't see."

"We're not dragging a corpse around the Sahara," Malek hissed. "There has to be another way to take care of this—the boy. To take care of the boy." He frowned, glancing at the door. "Can't we leave him with a jinn priest or something?"

Saranya brought her face close to Malek's. "First of all, I'm not an undertaker. Second, this is her *brother*. You think she's just going to leave his body behind so you can get whatever wish you've forced her into granting?"

"The wish is irrelevant," Malek said.

"Knowing you, Malek, I doubt that very much."

"Goddammit, Saranya, I've spent the past twenty-four hours being tortured and watching Nalia . . . watching . . ." Malek turned away, wiping at his eyes. "Fucking hell."

The room was silent, but if he listened closely, he could hear

Nalia's voice through the closed door. Singing. From the soft lilt of the song, he knew it was a lullaby, even though he didn't understand a word of it. He'd never been able to learn Kada. Never cared before now.

"You really love her." Saranya's voice was full of wonder.

Malek kept his back to his sister-in-law when he answered. "Irrelevant."

She sighed and held out her hand. "Give me that shirt."

"What?"

"Your shirt. It's covered in blood. You're the same size as Tariq—you can wear something of his while I wash this."

He'd forgotten about the blood. It had dried hours ago. He undid the buttons, cursing his shaking hands. What was wrong with him?

It took a while, but he finally got the shirt off. He turned around and held it out to Saranya—the most idiotic thing he'd ever done.

She stared at the amulet on his chest. To a human, it would simply look like an intricate tattoo over his heart, a combination of Celtic knots and script in ancient Kada. He'd told the women he'd taken to bed—before he started sleeping alone, his thoughts on Nalia—all manner of exotic stories about how and where he'd gotten the tattoo, what it meant. But Saranya was a jinni. She knew better.

"Draega's Amulet," she breathed.

He could see her do the math: forehead creasing, biting her lip. Then he looked into her eyes: flashing gold, drenched in fury, betrayal, and then a deep sadness that was all too familiar.

"How could you?" Her voice was low, cold as the snow atop the Atlas Mountains. "He was your brother. Your *twin* brother. He had a son—" Saranya's voice broke.

"I know the price. Now grant the wish."

"Are you sure you're capable of love?" Nalia asks. "The gods will know if you're lying. You must give them that which you love the most."

"When I want commentary, I'll ask for it. Now grant the damn thing."

She sighs, a deep regretful sound that tears at the resolve in his chest.

"As you wish," she whispers.

This was why he'd stayed away, why he drank too much and smoked too much and never slept a whole night through. The amulet seemed to burn his skin, scratch at the heart underneath it. The heart that had been protected by a thick wall of ice until Nalia burned through it with her *chiaan* and her smile and the way she felt in his arms.

Saranya stared at Malek, silent, her hands clutching the long sleeves of her kaftan. Her *chiaan* sparked, then golden tendrils of magic twined around her fists like loving eels. Malek knew it wasn't words she was at a loss for. She needed a knife, a gun, a flaming torch she could shove down his throat. But no matter what she did to him, he wouldn't die. Not unless he wanted to.

A sob broke the silence and they turned as one to the door that Nalia mourned behind. The midday call to prayer began outside, the muezzin's voice from a nearby mosque as full of longing as Nalia's cries. The front door opened and Tariq stepped through, his school bag slung over his shoulder. He looked around, expectant, and when he saw Malek he turned into an excited, bouncing thing, all smiles and brightness. He'd left for school just after Malek had arrived with Nalia, Saranya rushing him out before he knew what had happened.

"You're still here!" His eyes landed on the amulet. Malek turned from the boy's curious stare, terrified he'd ask about it.

Saranya threw Malek's bloodied shirt on the floor. "Your uncle and his friend will be leaving soon. You should say your good-byes." She stalked out of the room.

Tariq looked at the shirt, then back at the closed door. "What happened?"

I killed your father.

It was like looking into a mirror and seeing a younger, softer version of himself. Malek and his brother had been identical twins, but there'd been small differences. Tariq had Amir's full lips and wide fawn eyes, that guileless expression that had frustrated Malek to no end. He had Amir's good heart and large, strong hands that made beautiful things.

Malek stepped toward his nephew. "Tariq," he began. "I . . . you should know that . . ."

What to say to the boy? Malek knew, without a doubt, that he would never see him again. Even if Saranya never told him the truth, there was no way she'd allow the man who'd murdered her husband to be in her son's presence. He couldn't remember why he'd ever thought the amulet was worth the price.

Saranya swept back into the room. Her eyes were red, but she was otherwise composed.

"Lunch is in the kitchen," she said.

"Can I—?" Tariq began, but one stern look from his mother silenced the boy.

Tariq rolled his eyes and shuffled into the kitchen. Outside, an engine revved and honked once, then twice.

"The guide is here," Saranya said. "Tariq can give you some clothes and then I want you gone." She stepped closer to Malek.

"Never show your face here again."

"Why are you helping?"

"I'm not helping you." Saranya pointed to the door. "I'm helping *her*. Now get the hell out of my house."

The door opens. Just a slight push against the thick rug that covers the bedroom floor, but Nalia hears it. In seconds, she's awake, her jade dagger clutched in her hand. The Three Widows beam their moonlight into the room so that it's bright enough to see the shadow near the door.

"I am awake and I am not afraid to kill," Nalia says.

This is a lie. She has just had to kill a boy and it has unmade her. She no longer knows who she is. Who the Aisouri are. But the intruder doesn't need to know this. The elder Aisouri have turned the palace into a fortress since one of the servants slit his Aisouri lover's throat in the middle of the night. Most likely a tavrai carrying out orders from the child general

Raif Djan'Urbi. Nalia hasn't slept well since.

"Nalia-jai?" Bashil. His voice catches, as though he's trying hard not to cry.

She drops the dagger and pulls back her covers. "Laerta, gharoof. Laerta."

Come here, little rabbit.

He pushes the door shut and walks slowly to her bed, sheepish. His tear-stained cheeks glimmer in the Three Widows' light.

"What happened?"

She reaches down and helps him onto the bed. He is five summers old and is supposed to sleep in the dormitory with the other kefuhm. Nalia hates the word: *blood waste*. As if Bashil is worth nothing because he was not born a girl. As though any jinni not born a Ghan Aisouri is a waste of good royal blood and effort.

"It happened again," he says. Then promptly bursts into tears.

"Shhhh." Nalia holds him against her while he cries.

He was dreaming of fire, of the flames the resistance touched to their father's home and lands. He is dreaming of almost dying.

"Gharoof, no one can hurt you here. That's why you and Father have come to court. It's the safest place in all of Arjinna."

He looks up at her, his eyes fountains that leak tiny streams. "Will you kill them, Nalia-jai? All the bad jinn—will you?"

Nalia swallows. "I will kill anyone who tries to hurt you."

This is not a lie. She is afraid to kill, but not afraid to protect her brother.

She reaches across him to the small table beside her bed and hands him the stone Thatur had given her years ago, when she, too, was a small, scared child. The calming spell worked into the stone was a subtle, yet effective, magic that had gotten her through the many trials of growing up Aisouri.

"I think it's time you had this," she says.

Bashil's eyes grow wide. "Your worry stone? Really?"

It is a flat piece of polished lapis lazuli from the Qaf Mountains, the size of a large coin. A groove has been worn into its center, large enough to rub his thumb over.

"Yes," she says. "It helped me so much that I don't need it anymore. It will help you, too, I promise."

He rubs his tiny fingers over the gold-flecked stone.

"Whenever you're scared or worried," she continues, "just rub this with your thumb and, I promise, you'll feel a little better."

"I'll keep it with me always," Bashil says. He hides it in a little, defiant fist.

"As you should." Nalia smiles. "Now go to sleep. I'll wake you before the dawn bell so Mother doesn't find out you slept in here again."

Mehndal Aisouri'Taifyeh thinks Bashil makes her daughter soft, that love is a weakness. She is wrong. Nalia knows that love is strength. Her mother has never loved, so she doesn't know this.

Bashil kisses his sister's cheek, then nestles against her, burrowing under the thick bedclothes. His skin is warm and smells of sugarberry soap.

Nalia whispers a prayer over him as he falls asleep, asking Grathali, the Shaitan patron goddess, to protect her little golden-eyed brother. She falls asleep to the sound of his even breaths.

"I DIDN'T AGREE TO THIS."

Moustafa, their Dhoma guide, glared at the shrouded body Nalia had placed in the back of the battered SUV that would take them into the Sahara. He had the thick beard of the Dhoma men, but wore Western dress—a black leather jacket and Ray-Bans.

Malek stepped closer to the guide and fixed his eyes on the jinni's crimson ones. Though Moustafa was of the Ifrit caste, being a Dhoma meant that his allegiance was to his tribe, not his race. He knew that the guide would honor Saranya's order to keep Nalia protected.

"You *will* take us into the Sahara with this body and you won't say another word about it." He motioned to the driver's-side door. "*Yalla.*"

Let's go.

Moustafa blinked once, his eyes cloudy, then he nodded amiably and said in passable Arabic, "We should leave soon, my friend. Lots of traffic at this hour."

It was only early afternoon, but it was already the longest day of Malek's life.

Saranya was standing near the back door of the house with Nalia. She looked from Moustafa to Malek, eyes narrowed. She shook her head slightly, then hugged Nalia, whispering into her ear. Nalia nodded at whatever his sister-in-law said, then slipped into the backseat of the SUV. Beside her were bags of food and cases of water.

"Buckle up, *hayati*. People don't drive here as they do in Los Angeles."

She didn't say a word. It was as though her body were a prison, hiding the Nalia he'd known in a cell so far away, so deep, that she might never resurface. He reached across her with the seatbelt and locked it into place. Then he gently tucked a blanket around her, to ward off the chill that the afternoon sun couldn't dispel. She wore dark gray harem pants and a loose gray sweater: her mourning garments, the color of ash, as was the custom among the jinn.

As he closed her door, Malek told himself he needed Nalia alive so that he could get the sigil. He tried to bring back the rage her betrayal had woken in him. But his wish seemed far away, a mirage on a distant horizon, and he couldn't summon the anger. After Calar, it seemed silly to look too far ahead. What she had done to both of them made everything before seem petty, small. There was only now, only this.

He turned to Saranya. "Thank you."

She pointed to the tinted window Nalia sat behind. "If it weren't for her, I'd call the Ifrit myself." A cold wind whipped up the street, howling. "And don't hypersuade my driver again. He risks his life every day to help the jinn on the dark caravan. The last thing he needs is you in his head."

"Give me a little credit. I'm trying to save the last Ghan Aisouri's life."

"Only because her life suits your needs." Saranya stepped closer. "She doesn't love you. Never will. Did it ever occur to you, Malek, that you can live forever and yet you have nothing to live for?"

Malek watched his sister-in-law walk up the steps to her home, open the door, and close it to him forever.

He stood there for a moment, staring at his brother's home. Then he turned on his heel and got into the front seat of the SUV.

"*Bismillah*," Moustafa said, as he started the car.

Instead of the pain he would normally feel at the word, Malek felt nothing. He checked the rearview mirror—Nalia hadn't reacted at all. Strange. But perhaps because the word was used as a blessing for the trip and not to ward off jinn, it didn't have the same effect as when the man in Marrakech had used it. This was a word where intention was everything. Malek had forgotten that many of the Dhoma had abandoned the jinn gods in favor of Morocco's Allah. He wondered if Moustafa was religious, or had simply adopted the Moroccan culture. With Dhoma, it was hard to tell. Either way, he was able to utter a *bismillah* without feeling pain or causing it to his fellow jinn.

"Drive," Malek said.

It wasn't long before they left the jinn souk behind and were speeding along the highway outside the medina's thick wall, past pale yellow taxis and men riding donkeys. Before Malek and Nalia reached their destination, they had a mountain range to pass through and hundreds of miles of desert.

And a body to burn.

Malek glanced in the rearview mirror. "Nalia. Now might be a good time to elaborate a bit on what happened to Raif and Zanari."

"They're gone." Though her voice was dull, he saw the glint of pain in her eyes. There was clearly a story there.

"Yes, I—I can see that. What I mean is, are they at the cave already?"

"I don't know."

He sighed. "Is there a way to find out if—"

"Don't worry, Malek, my brother might be dead, but you'll get your precious fucking sigil."

He stopped asking questions after that.

They sped past kasbahs and textile shops and tiny farms. Then through the winding Atlas Mountains, where Berber villages nestled against the steep mountainside. Patches of snow clung to the terrain and made the journey treacherous. At times they slowed to a crawl on the two-lane road, stuck behind a slow truck or one of the tourist vans. Twice, Moustafa stopped the car at one of the roadside cafes, where they'd get food and glasses of *café au lait*. Nalia stayed in the car.

Evening fell as they entered the lush Drâa Valley, with its

forests of palm trees harvested for dates, now just mere shadows caught in the SUV's headlights. The occasional mosque or mud-brick home broke up the density of trees, but the roads were empty of people, save for the few bicyclists who hugged the sides.

"We stop for the night," Moustafa said, once they'd reached M'Hamid a few hours later, a small desert town nestled against the Sahara's shore.

It'd be no use pushing him. Malek knew the sand dunes would be impossible to navigate by night. He nodded.

"You have a safe place for us to stay?" he asked.

"Yes, but . . ." Moustafa's eyes traveled to the back of the SUV, where Bashil's body still lay. Nalia looked up.

"He will be buried at sunset tomorrow," she said. "It is our way. Do the Dhoma not keep the sacred rites?" Nalia's voice had risen, each word drenched in grief. "Do you throw your dead to the dogs, then? Force their spirits to find the godlands on their own?"

"Do as she says," Malek said, his voice quiet.

Moustafa sighed. "Shalinta," he said. Forgive me. "Only it is not safe to draw attention to ourselves. The slave traders send their spies through these villages, looking for runaways from the dark caravan. They notice anything suspicious."

"I'll worry about logistics," Malek said. He could feel the gun in his waistband, once again full of bullets. "You drive. That's what you're paid for."

Moustafa sighed again, muttering to himself in Kada. His Arabic was good enough, but it was clear it was the driver's second language. Like all jinn, Moustafa could speak each of Earth's languages, but some—like Nalia—were better at it than others.

A half hour later, they were ushered into a *riad* devoid of the elegance of their Marrakech lodgings. It catered to human travelers backpacking through the Sahara, adventurers ready to spend days under the harsh sun, then sleep beneath the stars. The rustic inn had an open-air plan, not much more than a collection of rooms that faced out onto a patio with a fire pit. Several people sat around the blaze, laughing and drinking mint tea. Malek noticed two jinn sitting among the humans, recognizable by their striking eyes. One male, one female. They had green eyes, like Raif and Zanari. Djan, then. They hugged their knees, their shoulders hunched forward, as if by curling their bodies they could protect themselves from the slave traders and their runners who scoured Earth, looking for escaped jinn. Their wrists were still bare, but the fear in their faces told their secret. Not his problem. One of them looked up, locking eyes with Malek. He looked away before the jinni could memorize his face.

Still, Malek couldn't shake the unease that had begun to settle into him. What would have happened between him and Nalia if he had freed her, been gentle?

She would have run away.

"Separate rooms," Nalia said.

Malek spoke in rapid Arabic to a turbaned man standing near the fire. As soon as their rooms were made available, Nalia brought Bashil inside, Malek shielding her with his body. She shut the door behind her without a word or glance in his direction.

Malek didn't know much about jinn death ceremonies, but

167

he'd once been around when one of Saranya's relatives had died. In addition to the ritual washing, one person had been chosen to sit by the deceased's bedside, to, as they believed, keep the spirit company while they waited for the ceremony that would usher them into the godlands. Superstitious nonsense was what Malek thought it all was, but it'd been hard for him, knowing that Saranya had sat beside his brother as he made that journey. *Enough*, he thought. He had to rein in these thoughts of Amir before they drove him crazy. Usually he'd get drunk, but alcohol was difficult to find in Morocco, as were women he could spend the night with and easily discard the next morning.

His stomach growled as he eyed the tagines in the small dining room nearby: mounds of couscous, vegetables, and meat in clay dishes. Malek signaled for the inn's owner to bring him one, then pushed open the door of his own room. He only had a few hours until they needed to be back on the road, though he doubted sleep would come. Not this night.

Malek thought he would feel relief—a sick relief, but relief nonetheless—if Saranya ever discovered the truth surrounding Amir's death. But all he felt was a deep sadness and regret. Amir had been the only person who had given a damn about him.

And I killed him.

It had been a desperate arithmetic: as Malek's power on Earth increased, so did his enemies. At the time, it had seemed like he'd had no choice. Pay the price for the amulet or face death, and soon. He'd bought Nalia from her slave trader just days after Amir had told Malek he never wanted to see him again. The rage Malek had felt at being abandoned after everything he'd done for his brother consumed his thoughts. Malek gave his Ifrit nature free reign, no longer bothering to control his darkest impulses. Still, almost as soon as Nalia granted him the amulet, Malek regretted it. But he couldn't take it back. Not ten minutes after making the wish, Saranya called. He'd been too much of a coward to answer his phone. Deleted the message without listening to it, ignored every call, then finally changed his phone number.

Now, all Malek had left was the sigil and the hope of what it could bring him. If he failed to get the ring before Raif, Malek didn't know what he would do. He'd been banking on Nalia being forced to fight Raif, but she was certainly in no state to do that now. So what was his plan? Raif was probably in the cave this very minute, the ring as good as his. Saranya had been right: without the sigil, Malek had nothing to live for. With it, he could have everything he wanted. Even Nalia. He'd never force her to be with him, but she'd come around eventually. All he needed was time, and Malek had plenty of that.

But there was no longer a thrill to the hunt. Just a bone-deep weariness and an ache that wouldn't go away.

Nalia sat in a hard-backed chair beside the bed where Bashil lay. She could imagine his face under the shroud, clean of the blood that had spilled from his eyes when Calar attacked him. Clean and pale and lifeless. The room smelled of frankincense, the scent of those hours in Saranya's home, bathing Bashil's body to prepare it for its final journey.

She thought about nothing. Just stared at the tiny bundle of cloth that lay before her. Her thumb slid against the worry stone that she'd discovered in Bashil's pocket, just before she bathed him.

I'll keep it with me always, Bashil had said.

"I'm so sorry, *gharoof*," she whispered. She imagined him waiting in that shadowy place, alone and frightened. "Don't be scared, little one. I'm here." Tears streamed down her face. "You'll be in the godlands soon."

I failed you, she thought.

She rubbed the stone until her skin bled. Blood, blood, blood on her hands. The gods would never forgive her. She would never forgive herself.

When the room turned from black to gray and the wail of the first prayer poured over her from a nearby mosque, Nalia rose from her chair and stepped outside. She knocked twice on Malek's door. He opened it immediately.

"Get Moustafa. It's time," she said.

The drive into the desert was miserable. There was no road, no markers. Just endless sand. The SUV pushed over the dunes in jolting stops and starts that threw her body up every time they sped over a ridge. Nalia kept one hand on the door, one on Bashil. It was sick-making and the car was beginning to fill with a rotting, musty scent that reminded her of Haran.

Moustafa jerked the wheel to the right, driving around a dune too steep for the SUV to roll over. He shifted into a lower gear and the wheels spun for a moment before finding purchase in the powdery sand.

She turned around, her hands hovering above the shroud. Flowers. That was what Bashil needed. Nalia closed her eyes, but there was no answer in her body as she tried to summon her *chiaan*. She clenched her fists, unclenched them. Waited. It was as if she had been hollowed out, gutted so that every bit of *chiaan* had leaked away. Panic bloomed in her chest and Nalia tried to recall the last time she'd used her magic. All she could remember was pouring every ounce of her energy into Bashil and seeing her *chiaan* spill from his body onto the cold stone floor of the cell he'd been imprisoned in. Tears pricked her eyes.

Nalia turned around. "Stop the car."

Moustafa looked to Malek, who gave a slight nod. "Do as she says."

He stopped at the top of a low dune. "This way," he said, "we have momentum, yes? Being stuck in desert not so good, my friends."

Nalia pushed open the car door and stumbled out. She fell to the sand, pressing her palms against the earth. Its warmth was all she felt—not magic, simply the heat of the sun. She closed her eyes, tried to find that quiet place within her. But it was only sand and skin, nothing more. She couldn't feel the energy of the world around her, couldn't sense the currents of magic that were usually hers for the taking.

"*Hayati*—what is it?" She hadn't noticed Malek kneeling beside her.

"It's gone," she whispered. She looked up, hating the concern in his eyes, hating how grateful she was for it. "My *chiaan*. Malek, it's *gone*."

"That's impossible."

She held out her hands. "See for yourself."

Malek twined his fingers through hers so that their palms pressed together. After a moment he frowned, then gently squeezed her hands. Usually when he touched her, the fire inside Malek threatened to obliterate Nalia. Now she couldn't feel a thing. He looked down, then raised her hands to his lips, kissing her fingers.

"You just need to rest," he said gruffly, letting go. "Come."

He helped her back into the car and she fell against the seat, silent tears streaming down her face.

"You're a Ghan Aisouri," he said quietly in her ear as he pulled the seatbelt over her body. "Don't forget that."

Without *chiaan*, Nalia might as well be dead.

"How can you stand it?" she heard Malek ask Moustafa when he returned to the front seat. He gestured toward the dunes.

In every direction there was nothing but sand, great rolling hills of it, broken up only by the occasional shrublike tree or cairn.

"The desert can change you," Moustafa said, above the roar of the engine. "Some people, they go crazy seeing all this sand. Others find Allah. Make no mistake, my friend, the desert wants you for itself. Either way, it will not let you go easily. You'll see."

"Well, that's damn ominous," Malek muttered.

Moustafa laughed. "*Inshallah*, we arrive safely at your destination and you can decide for yourself how long you want to stay."

Hours later, the sun dipping toward the horizon, Nalia saw a herd of wild camels making their slow way over the dunes. The sun cast their long shadows on the sand so that they created an undulating tableau. There were no such creatures in Arjinna and she could imagine how much Bashil would have liked to see them. She almost smiled. He would have insisted on riding one.

It seemed like a sign.

"Stop here," she said. Nalia pointed to a flat-topped tree surrounded by dunes, not far from where the camels plodded toward a destination known only to them. "I'm taking him there."

Bashil would not have a Shaitan funeral; that required a mountaintop, and it had been too treacherous to take him to the top of the Atlas range in the middle of the night. The breeze blew strong and steady here, though, and she liked the idea of him being carried away by Grathali, returning to Arjinna in the arms of the goddess of air.

Malek got out of the car and followed her to the rear of the SUV. "Let me help."

She pulled open the hatch and gently lifted Bashil's body. "You've done enough."

He hadn't killed Bashil, but he'd kept her from rescuing him for three years. In Nalia's eyes, he was as much to blame as Calar.

"Moustafa. I need your fire," she said to the driver in Kada.

The Ifrit Dhoma would think nothing of her request—her golden eyes marked her as a Shaitan, a jinni whose element was air, not fire. The guide nodded, his eyes somber, and followed Nalia.

She pushed past Malek and carried Bashil over the dune, out of sight. When she reached the tree, she lay him beneath its spindly boughs. It was a strange specimen, the tree, more an overgrown shrub than anything else, but it felt like a marker of some kind. More permanent than the ever-changing dunes around her, Nalia longed to manifest a pyre of sweet-smelling cedar to lay Bashil's body on and fistfuls of flowers to cushion his head and drape over his body. He deserved so much.

"Are you ready?" Moustafa asked. He stood quietly beside her, gazing down at the shrouded figure at their feet.

Nalia nodded.

Moustafa lit one match, then placed it on the palm of his hand. His crimson *chiaan* covered the flame and it burst between his palms. He knelt, then gently lay the fire on top of Bashil, near his heart. Moustafa's hands moved quickly over the flames, intricate movements Nalia didn't understand. When he stood, she saw the kindness he had done her. Covering Bashil's body was a flaming lotus, the color of a precious garnet.

"*Shundai,*" Nalia whispered.

Moustafa waved away her thanks. "*Hif la'azi vi.*" *My heart breaks for you.* It had been just yesterday that she'd spoken those same words of condolence to Saranya. The guide parted her shoulder, then left her alone.

The sun fell through the sky, a blazing disk of fire that spilled tangerine rays over the dunes before disappearing completely. Nalia watched as the lotus flames licked Bashil's body, thirsty. There was no smoke. The jinn had been created from smokeless fire and to smokeless fire they must return in order to enter the godlands. Nalia began whispering the prayer of the dead.

Hala shaktai hundeer. Ashanai sok vidim. Ishma capoula orgai. Hala shaktai hundeer. Gods receive his soul. Fill it with grace and light. Grant entrance to your eternal temples. Gods receive his soul.

Nalia said the prayer again and again as the fire had its fill of her brother's body. Moustafa's Ifrit fire was like no other flame. It consumed Bashil in less than an hour, burning brighter as time passed. In the gloaming, all that remained of him was a pile of cool ash. The lotus blazed once more, brighter than ever, then faded entirely.

She raised her head, rubbing the ash into her forehead, mixing it with her tears in the Shaitan way. A furious gust of wind swept past her, and what was left of Bashil flew into the air in a sudden funnel, a swirl of dead evanescence in the arms of the Shaitan goddess. Nalia cried out as the last of her brother blew away.

Then there was sand everywhere, raining down on her, drenching. Nalia turned, shading her eyes. A wall of sand was pushing across the desert, blocking out the sliver of moon that had crept into the sky. She stood still. Waiting.

"Nalia!" Malek sprinted down the dune behind her, pointing at the sand that hurtled toward her. She watched Malek run, saw the look of terror on his face. He was a curious thing, this *pardjinn* who couldn't die.

"Sandstorm!" he shouted as he got closer.

She faced the wall of swirling, hurtling earth. There was no *chiaan* quickening in her veins, no rush of power. She smiled at it, this merciful giant that would make everything stop.

Nalia cried out as Malek threw himself over her, pushing her to the ground and shielding her from the storm with his body. She felt his palm against her mouth, meagre protection against the desert's onslaught.

The sand hit, a wave of shattered earth that crashed over them, wind everywhere, roaring like an ancient beast finally freed from its subterranean prison.

"Bismillah." Malek whispered his god's word for protection over and over. *"Bismillah."*

It was the first time Nalia had heard Malek pray. She closed her eyes, hoping the sand would bury them both.

18

LIGHTNING.

It burst from the night sky and stabbed the sand dunes below, over and over, like a crazed murderer.

"Fire and blood," Raif muttered.

Beside him, Zanari grunted her assent. They'd been sitting on a low sand dune across from the cave for hours, waiting for the lightning storm to let up.

They'd spent the previous day combing the area surrounding the cave, moving out in ever widening circles, like ripples in a pond. There'd been nothing but sand, as though the whole world were covered in fine, shifting grains that whispered with each gust of wind. It wasn't like Raif had been expecting a door he could simply walk through. But he thought there'd be *something*.

"There's a reason this cave's been hidden for thousands of

years," Zanari said. "I mean, think about it: Malek knew this place existed. He'd considered it as a possible site for the sigil, but the lightning made it impossible for him to check it out."

"But we have a Ghan Aisouri's blood," Raif said, holding up the small bottle of Nalia's blood that she'd given him in Los Angeles. "And he's nothing but a *pardjinn* with too high an opinion of himself. Why in all hells can't we get in there?" he fumed.

He'd wasted precious drops of Nalia's blood as he'd run his fingers through the sand, hoping the entrance to the cave would present itself. Nothing.

They'd finally concluded that the entrance must be directly below the lightning storm. He and Zanari had spent the past twenty-four hours waiting for a break in the barrage of electric light, taking turns sleeping.

Zanari counted under her breath. "Three seconds between lightning strikes. That's all we get. Nalia's blood won't even help us—we'll be dead before we can open the bottle."

Raif's mouth tightened. Hearing her name hurt more than it had a right to. He stood up and began hiking up the moonlit dune, more a soft-boned mountain than a gentle rise in the sand.

"Then I'll have to be quick," he said.

He was tired of waiting and the longer they stayed outside the cave, the more likely it would be that Nalia and Malek would arrive. The thought of going through the cave with her was worse than the very real possibility of being struck by lightning.

"Raif Djan'Urbi, you stop right where you are," Zanari shouted. "Have you lost your mind?"

Yes.

He turned around. His sister stood below him, the lightning cutting into her fierce expression. With her head of braids, she looked like the statues of Grathali, goddess of air, that he'd seen in Shaitan temples. Strangely formidable.

"Either I try to get in that cave or we go home with nothing," he said. "It's suicide either way."

"She already killed Kir." The words hit him like an avalanche, rocks sliding down, into his heart, his lungs. "You walk into that lightning, then you're letting her kill you, too."

"What's that supposed to mean?" Raif glared at his sister as the rocks continued to fall, weighing him down.

"You've always taken risks, but this?" Zanari shook her head.

"It's an easy way out."

"Fuck you."

Like he'd kill himself over a Ghan Aisouri.

Zanari stared at him. "Really?"

He turned away from her, ashamed.

"See what she's done to you?" Zanari said. "Before you met Nalia, all you cared about was the revolution. And that worried me, so when you started to have feelings for her, I thought maybe that could be a good thing, you know? I wanted you to have a life, to have something to look forward to each day. But we were wrong about her. I thought she was different, that she was my . . . my *friend*. But Nalia's just another *salfit* Aisouri—a killer, a liar. If you walk up that dune, you're letting her win. You're letting them all win."

Raif stared at the lightning. It blinded him, made it so all he could see were endless bursts of light. For once, night lost the battle; every time a bolt hit the earth, a new day dawned.

He heard shuffling and panting and then his sister was beside him. "I'm sorry," he said. How could he have spoken to her like that?

She took his hand. "When Malek hypersuaded me, when he made me put that gun to my head, a part of me knew what was happening. But I couldn't stop it. I was screaming inside, but my body wouldn't listen. Love can be like that, too."

"Love is a gun to the head." He snorted. "Yeah, sounds about right."

Zanari sighed. "We need to regroup. Okay? Find another way in."

"Zan, there is no other way."

"Then we wait for her. She has to let you in, she made a vow."

That was the moment. The vow. He'd never felt closer to another jinni in all his life. At the time, he'd refused to acknowledge that he was falling for Nalia. But a part of him had known. When another person makes you feel whole—even though you didn't know you weren't—that changes you.

He pushed up the dune, closer to the lightning than he'd ever been before. He could see the surface of the sand just above the fiery bolts: a perfect circle burned black, smoking.

There was a gust of wind, so strong it nearly blew him down the dune. Raif dug his heels into the sand and laid a hand on the ridge. It was warm, as though he weren't standing on sand but a large, sleeping giant.

"Raif?"

He turned. Zanari had slipped down the dune and was

struggling toward him. Every time the lightning flashed, twin bolts were reflected in her large, sad eyes.

He couldn't go back to the *tavrai* empty-handed. He couldn't. But to wait for Nalia . . . Raif took another step toward the top of the dune. He could do this. He just had to throw the blood on the sand.

"If you die, it's over," Zanari said. "No more second chances for the revolution. You said so yourself, when you insisted we come here in the first place." She drew closer, her voice soft. He had to lean in, to hear her over the wind. It was gusting all around them now, pushing the sand into the air. "I'm sorry we were wrong about her, but you've got to buck up, little brother. Love sucks. Dying sucks more."

It'd been almost forty-eight hours since the moment Nalia told him she'd murdered his best friend. Before that, everything had been clear: he would choose Nalia, every time. No questions asked. Maybe the gods were punishing him for putting his desires before the revolution.

Maybe the gods don't give a damn. Weren't they the ones that had given the Ghan Aisouri their power in the first place?

"One more day," he said, relenting. His sister was right: they had to wait a little longer. "Then I have to try. With or without Nalia. I can't go home until I have the ring, Zan. It's our last hope."

"I'll take what I can get." She clapped him on the back and started down the dune, then turned around after she'd gone a few steps. "Hungry?" Surprisingly, he was. Raif nodded.

"How about I manifest us some of those cheeseburger things

the humans were making in Los Angeles? I've been practicing—I think I might have it down."

He tried to smile. "Sounds good."

As Zanari started toward the small camp they'd set up, Raif grabbed a handful of sand and threw it at the spot the lightning kept striking. It had barely settled when the next bolt crashed into the dune again. He didn't stand a chance. Raif turned to follow his sister when the earth began to tremble. The dune shifted, the sand suddenly rolling like an ocean in a storm.

Zanari looked back at him, calling his name in a panicked shout. Raif hurried toward her as the ground beneath his feet heaved. He reached out, grabbing at the air for balance. He went down, rolling head over foot, Zanari just ahead of him. Raif squeezed his eyes shut tight as sand rained down on him. If he didn't get up soon, he'd be buried alive.

They reached the bottom of the dune just as the sand behind them crested, a tidal wave with the weight of an entire desert behind it. He grabbed Zanari's hand and they sprinted across the sand, pushing their feet through the soft earth as the wave gained momentum. Raif realized with a sinking heart that it would be impossible to outrun it.

"We have to evanesce," Zanari shouted.

But the sand would swallow them up before they could get airborne, their atoms pulling apart and entombed in a desert grave forever.

He tried to answer, but sand filled his mouth. They dove to the side as the wave of fine sand crashed beside them.

The grains began to take form, somehow conscious . . . *aware*.

It looked like . . .

"Oh, gods," he whispered.

The sand morphed into bodies that clawed their way out of the bowels of the desert, onto its surface. An arm, a leg, then a chest, the suggestion of a face.

An army, shifting with the wind.

Each flash of lightning brought out new details wrought in sand: ancient armor, spears, shields, horses made of sand that pawed at the ground. It reminded Raif of long days on the shore of the Arjinnan Sea, when he and Zanari and Kir used to make sand palaces. Each body, each weapon and horse was carved with expert precision, real in every way except material.

It was an army that couldn't bleed.

The sound of each soldier emerging from the dunes was an unsheathed sword, the sand swirling into breastplates and spears and thick limbs. The soldiers moved forward, closing ranks. Their eyes were dark holes, their mouths open in a perpetual scream. They didn't speak so much as roar, their voice the wind that gusted across the Sahara.

Zanari cried out as one aimed its spear at her heart. She dove and the weapon soared past her. It dissolved into a harmless handful of sand as soon as it hit a dune, but its speed alone could have torn a hole through her flesh. Raif reached out and hauled her up while his other hand sparked with emerald *chiaan*.

The soldier nearest Raif lunged and Raif stumbled back as a stream of *chiaan* shot from his hand. The soldier raised a sand shield, and the earth absorbed the magic. Indestructible.

Raif pressed his palms to the sand, calling forth as much *chiaan* as he could from the earth. He didn't know if Tirgan, patron god of the Djan, gave a shit that two of his jinn were about to die on Earth. Raif hoped so.

The sand soldier pulled a scimitar out of its sheath and swung it once above its head before slashing at Raif's chest. Raif ducked just before the weapon met its mark, then sent his *chiaan* across the sand, throwing the grains into the sky. A joyful battle cry escaped his lips as the sand rained down, burying the creature.

"Nice, little brother!" Zanari shouted. She was wielding *chiaan* whips like a dragon hunter, her eyes gleaming in the jade light of her magic. The whips flicked against the soldiers, lobbing off body parts. It wasn't killing the things, but it slowed them down.

The ranks continued to rise from the sand, at least fifty fighters in all. Above, a bird cried out, then two, then more. The insistent caws of a small group of birds filled the air as they flew in a circle, gathering speed before spreading out to cover the circumference of the army below. The sand soldiers looked up, roaring as one. The birds shrieked in response, a musical war cry. The army shot arrows of sand at the sky, but the creatures above plunged and dipped and swerved, moving targets that were impossible to hit.

"What are they?" Zanari asked.

"I have no idea."

They were huge: a cross between a crow and an eagle, with a

shock of bright color on their breasts. The one with white feathers turned its head and stared at Raif, its eyes intelligent and a familiar bright blue. Marid blue.

The flock darted toward the army below. Raif and Zanari were forgotten as the birds swooped through the ranks, disorienting the sand soldiers. Soon the army became a muddled sandstorm as the soldiers ran blindly through the dunes, their bodies reduced to gusts that pummeled the jinn in their midst. Sand flew into Raif's eyes, nearly blinding him. He tried to cover his nose and mouth, but the sand got through, suffocating.

Beside him, Zanari coughed as she fell to her knees and covered her head. He joined her, shielding her body with his own. The sand was a furious beast that kicked and bit, but Raif gritted his teeth and prayed they wouldn't be covered by a dune. And then, just as suddenly as it came, the storm was over. The sand settled and the only sound was the strike, strike, strike of the lightning.

Raif opened his eyes. The desert had shifted so that where once there had been gently rolling dunes there were now towering piles of sand. He and Zanari were in the middle of a valley that hadn't existed just minutes ago. Before him, standing in a line across the top of a dune, perched seven birds. The moonlight caught the ebony sheen of their feathers, their massive beaks and jinn eyes.

Fawzel: shape shifters.

"Zanari . . ." he whispered.

"I see, little brother."

The Dhoma had found them.

Raif planted his feet and held his hands at his sides, ready. He didn't know why the Dhoma had helped them, but it'd be foolish to assume they meant no harm. One of the *fauzel* unfurled its massive wings and flew toward Raif and Zanari while the others continued to perch on the sand dune, motionless sentries. Even from this distance, Raif could feel their collective gaze.

Just before the bird reached them, it shot higher into the air and hung for a moment, suspended. Then it began to fall, slowly at first, then faster, spinning with the grace of a dancer. Evanescence began to swirl around its outstretched body, a tornado of Marid blue that hid the bird's form as it drew closer to the little valley where Raif and Zanari stood. Moments later, the evanescence cleared and a Marid jinni stood before them, his blue eyes piercing. Raif caught the familiar scent of the sea: salt and the fishing villages of Arjinna. He wondered how a Marid fared in one of the driest places in the worlds.

It was the same bird that had looked Raif in the eye during the battle: just like the feathers that covered the jinni's body when he was a bird, his dark hair contained one white stripe that ran along his cheek and well past his shoulders. He was a large jinni and, like all male Dhoma, had a thick beard and wore his hair long.

"Jahal'alund," Raif said as he placed his hand against his heart in the traditional greeting.

"Likewise," the *fauzel* said. "What brings you to our land, wanderers?"

Raif frowned, uncertain. He understood the jinni, but his Kada had strange inflections and, like the humans in Morocco, incorporated Arabic and French.

"My sister and I mean no harm," Raif said. "We're new to Earth and we're exploring its wonders. We thank you for assisting us with those . . . creatures."

Raif couldn't risk the truth. Not now, not after they'd come so far. The Dhoma could easily turn him and Zanari over to Calar if they wanted to. The reclusive tribe was known for being unpredictable, especially if they felt threatened.

The Dhoma cocked his head to the side, a birdlike gesture. "Several things tell me you're lying. Shall I elaborate?"

Raif raised his chin. "By all means."

For a split second, Raif considered fighting his way out of this. But the jinni before him was clearly powerful and he had six of his friends ready to swoop in and assist if necessary. If their performance earlier was any indication, they were more than up to the task. Already the birds on the dune were rustling their feathers, preparing for flight.

The Dhoma pointed to Raif's arm. "That symbol there—this is old magic. Powerful. It is said that the only jinn who have such markings are Ghan Aisouri and yet you, my friend, are most certainly *not* an Aisouri. There is a story there, yes?"

Raif stared into the jinni's eyes. Being cagey had never served him well. That first lie was a mistake.

"Yes, there's a story there."

The Dhoma inclined his head. "Next, I find it odd that your journeys with your sister should bring you to such a precise spot.

The *Sakhim* don't attack unless provoked. My guess is that you got very close to where the lightning struck. You weren't, by any chance, looking for something . . . specific . . . were you?"

He knows, Raif thought. *How could he have learned the Ghan Aisouri's best-kept secret?*

"We might have gotten off on the wrong foot," Raif said.

The Dhoma's smile wasn't kind. "I agree."

Keeping his eyes on Raif and Zanari, he whistled, a sharp order by the sounds of it. Immediately, the flock of shape-shifting Dhoma surged into the air. In seconds, they had Raif and Zanari surrounded, jinn spilling out of evanescence: Marid blue, Shaitan gold, Ifrit red, Djan green.

"I'm thinking this is a bad thing," Zanari said under her breath.

"Yeah." Raif angled his body so that he was shielding his sister. "Any ideas?"

"Nope."

The jinn all wore human clothing Raif had seen in Marrakech: long, colorful robes, with expertly tied turbans that wound around their heads, then swept across their mouths so that only their eyes showed. He couldn't tell which ones were male or female.

"You will come with us, Raif Djan'Urbi," the Dhoma leader said.

Zanari snorted. "What did I say, little brother? I can't take you anywhere."

Even here, they knew his face.

"And if we refuse?"

"It will be an uncomfortable journey," the Dhoma said.

In other words, there was no choice. They were clearly outnumbered. Raif glanced once more at the *Erg Al-Barq*. He'd been so close.

"What do I call you?" Raif asked the jinni before him. "Only fair I know your name if you know mine."

"You may call me Samar, should you have a chance to call me anything."

"That doesn't bode well," Zanari said.

Samar ignored her and raised his hands. Two coils of thick iron rope suddenly hovered over his palms. He looked at Raif and Zanari over the improvised shackles. "A necessary precaution, I'm afraid."

Raif held out his wrists and Zanari did the same. The rope tied itself, burning their flesh. If it stayed on for long, the iron would weaken him and Zanari considerably, possibly even kill them.

"I hope this is just a temporary solution," Raif said.

"That depends entirely on you." Samar nodded to one of the Dhoma, who immediately evanesced.

Raif watched the Ifrit red of the jinni's smoke as it spilled into the sky. That color had always been a harbinger of death and despair. He hoped it didn't mean the same here in the depths of the desert.

"I'm sure my people will be anxious to meet the jinn who dare to disturb our ancestors," Samar continued.

"Hold on right there, brother," Zanari said. "We have nothing to do with your ancestors. We're here for the revolution—we have no quarrel with the Dhoma."

Samar raised his eyebrows. "You expect me to believe you didn't know you were disturbing a mass grave?"

"What mass grave?" Raif said.

Samar pointed to the *Erg Al-Barq*, "That is the site of thousands of jinn slaves, buried alive by their master, King Solomon."

Before Raif could respond, Samar gestured for them to follow him.

"Come," he said. "We sail."

19

THE STORM STOPPED ALMOST AS SUDDENLY AS IT BEGAN. and yet it seemed to go on for an eternity as Malek sheltered Nalia's body with his own. The desert threatened to entomb them, but there was nothing he could do but wait out the punishing winds.

When the sand finally settled around them and the desert was calm once more, Malek wasn't superstitious enough to think the *bismillah* had actually worked. But then again, he wasn't going to rule it out.

"There are more things in heaven and earth, Horatio, than are dreamt of in your philosophy,'" he whispered as he sat up and took in the landscape.

Nalia remained lying on the sand with her arms covering her head. Malek reached down and gently helped her sit up. She coughed, then turned away from him and spat into the sand.

"Are you all right?" he asked.

"I thought I would die." She sounded disappointed.

"I wasn't going to let you," Malek said as he stood.

"Because you want the sigil!"

"That's not why, Nalia. And I think you know that."

She looked up at him with empty eyes, silent. He left her sitting there, unable to bear her brokenness. Saranya was right. She would never love him.

The dunes had shifted so that they seemed to be in an entirely new desert. Malek turned in a slow circle, looking for the SUV. It was disorienting, this endless sea of sand.

"Moustafa!" he called.

The tree Nalia had burned Bashil under had been to Malek's left when he'd run over the dune. Just the top of the tree was visible now and the dune beside it had disappeared.

So had the SUV.

"Shit." Malek stalked across the sand to where Moustafa should have been. There was nothing there but sand, no hint that a vehicle filled with all their supplies and their driver lay under it.

He heard Nalia gasp behind him.

"Maybe the bastard evanesced," he said. "Left us here to die."

Nalia shook her head. "Even if he had, that storm would have blown him apart."

Malek kicked at the sand, cursing.

"Stop it," Nalia said, her voice sharp. "You dishonor him."

She knelt on the sand. "Go."

He threw up his hands and headed back to the tree, the only marker for miles. A few moments later he heard Nalia's voice as if she were standing beside him. He turned. Here, in the calm after the storm, the desert had no secrets. Her voice echoed clearly, the words of the prayer cutting into him, the same one she had said for Bashil. Malek didn't know what the words meant, but he felt the lament as though it were his own.

They were alone in the middle of the Sahara Desert without food, water, shelter, or transporation. He didn't have a cell phone—not that he'd have any service—and he'd left his gun in the car. It wouldn't be much help against the Ifrit, anyway.

Nalia hadn't eaten in nearly two days. She was barely standing after the sandstorm. If they didn't get help soon, she'd die.

"Bismillah," he whispered.

Nalia expected to drown in this desert. Soon, she would sink below its sandy waters, free of Malek's pointless exercise in survival. The stars above were distant beacons, the lights of celestial ships that crossed the dark waves of the Saharan night. She and Malek were adrift and there was no hope of rescue.

Nalia was fine with that.

It was cold and the bitter wind cut through her thin clothing. She walked on and on, with no direction, no thought other than to follow where Malek led. He'd given up trying to talk, this shadow of hers. But she felt Malek's resolve to keep watch over her. He wouldn't let her go, no matter how much she begged him to leave her.

Night claimed her grief like a prize, reveling in it, spoils from a bloody war. Sometimes the pain would hit Nalia all over again, as though she were hearing for the first time that Bashil was dead, and she would sink down to the sand, where her tears would water its unforgiving soil. She clutched it in handfuls or fell into it, curled up like a child for minutes, hours.

After climbing their highest dune yet, Nalia collapsed. "I'm done," she said.

"I know."

A violent gust of wind swept past them and Malek, unthinking, pulled Nalia to him, taking the brunt of the wind's temper. She buried her face in his chest as the sand swirled around them like angry ghosts. She could feel his heart speeding up, as though it wanted to finish the conversation it had started with hers long ago.

Nalia pulled away from him just as another gust of freezing wind sliced into her. Malek slipped off his jacket and set it over her shoulders. She'd refused it before, but was too cold now to care. It was warm and smelled like him, a little bit spicy and all too familiar.

"What happened with the others?" he asked again.

"The others?" she said, her voice far away. She sank into the warmth of his jacket.

"You know who I mean: Raif and Zanari."

Nalia lay on the sand, curled into a fetal position. "I killed Raif's best friend. He found out."

"Well, I'm sure you had your reasons."

Nalia closed her eyes. "I did. They weren't good ones."

The coat was warm and she didn't care that Malek sat close

because he shielded her from the cutting wind.

"I'd love to clarify this situation—it's not quite making sense," Malek said. "Raif left you in Marrakech, a city occupied by an army that wants to kill you."

"Yes."

"But you still love him."

"Yes."

Malek struck a match and the scent of cloves filled the air.

"For the record, I'm fine with you killing whomever you wish," Malek said.

She pressed her forehead into the sand and sobbed. For Bashil. For Raif. For Kir. How was it possible to have tears left to cry? She had left a trail of them behind her, a salty river that gouged the sand with her sorrow.

Nalia didn't protest when Malek pulled her onto his lap. She was a rag doll. He held her and spoke in a low voice, a monologue of old poems in Arabic. Once whispered in lush, ancient courtyard gardens, they were saffron words dipped in honey and cream.

"My brother," she kept saying, over and over. *My brother.*

The night wore on, endless and cold, but there was warmth in the shelter of Malek's arms. For once, he was the safe harbor, not the storm.

RAIF HAD NEVER SEEN ANYTHING LIKE IT.

When Samar had said *we sail*, Raif had assumed the Dhoma leader was fond of metaphors.

Not so.

First, the soft rustle of sand, then the snap of heavy fabric in the wind.

Surging over the highest dune, a ship appeared, sailing the Sahara as though it were an ocean. It was massive, as big as one of the galleys the Marid used for fishing in the depths of the Arjinnan Sea. The wooden ship was exquisitely carved and had an alarmingly lifelike ghoul as its masthead. Her mouth had been fashioned into a perpetual, hungry *O* so that every time the fore of the ship plunged toward the sand, the ghoul seemed to tear into the desert's grainy flesh.

A crew of turbaned Dhoma were scattered about the ship, attending to duties or staring out at the desert expanse.

"After you," Samar said.

Raif had never been on a ship before, but after only a few moments on the Saharan sea, he could see why his Marid compatriots never liked to be far from their vessels. The wind, the speed, the feel of the wood rocking underneath his feet—it did him good. Cleared his head.

The *Sun Chaser* cut through the night, navigating the sands without effort. Instead of the splash of waves against the hull, there was the hiss of sand on wood. The wind carried soft desert scents instead of the salty tang of the ocean. Raif drank deeply.

"I'm a little less bitter about being taken captive," Zanari said as they stood at the railing.

"Sure beats the palace dungeon," Raif said, laughing. "The Marid *tavrai* would love this."

So would Nalia. The thought came, unbidden, and Raif gripped the railing as the fury and love and despair tore through him. It would pass. It would *have* to pass.

Too soon, the Dhoma camp came into view. The *Sun Chaser* pierced through a thick *bisabm* as it neared the patch of light in the middle of the desert's inky darkness. The thick shield shuddered, invisible except for a slight iridescent glint in the moonlight. It was a good shield, nearly as strong as the one Raif and his *tavrai* had created over the Forest of Sighs, the resistance's Arjinnan headquarters. It wouldn't keep out the Ifrit army, though.

The ship glided to a stop in a natural sandy harbor filled with skiffs. From the bow, Raif had a good view of the Dhoma camp.

Nomad tents spread across the sand, hundreds of elaborate structures of improbable height that only the jinn could have devised. Delicate glass Moroccan lamps hung from poles outside the tents' entrances, colorful bursts of light that painted the sand. Fires crackled throughout the Dhoma camp and the smell of roasted lamb filled the air. A rapid-fire percussion of African beats with Arabic flair came from a nearby circle of Gnawa musicians. Raif had seen performers like this in the Djemaa—he only knew these ones were jinn because of the unique sound of their instruments.

Samar gestured to the gangplank. "Follow me."

Raif turned to his sister. "You okay back there?"

"I'm fine." Zanari frowned at the Dhoma who held her elbow. "I can walk by myself, brother, thanks."

"All right, whatever you say." The jinni let go as his body faded until it disappeared completely.

"What in all hells?" Zanari turned in a circle as the invisible Dhoma laughed.

Raif stared. Between the shape shifting and invisibility, he had no doubt that the rumors were true about the Dhoma possessing powers Arjinnans had yet to discover. Raif suspected that in his realm there were many jinn who, like Zanari, were afraid their powers would be used for ill by the ruling castes. It was a beautiful thing, to see free jinn express themselves so openly.

"Noqril, show our guests some basic courtesy, please," Samar said.

The jinni reappeared a breath away from Zanari, closer than before. Not only was he invisible, but the braided strip of orange hair swinging over his shoulder marked him as a *fawzel*. A formidable opponent, that one.

That didn't keep Zanari from shoving him away from her. "You're not my type."

Noqril raised his eyebrows, leering. "We'll see."

Raif laughed. "Good luck with that, brother."

As they walked through the improvised village, the Dhoma stopped what they were doing to watch the new arrivals. Their clothing was strange, Moroccan Berber with a jinn twist. The men wore embroidered kaftans over loose linen pants. The women wore thick leggings or wide cotton pants under layers of shawls and tight-fitting tunics covered with thick strands of amber necklaces. From what he could see of their hands in the lamplight, they were covered in henna, much like Nalia's Ghan Aisouri tattoos. Most of the males and females wore turbans or loose head scarves, the ends of which they moved over their faces when Raif and Zanari passed.

"What, do they think we're Ifrit spies or something?" Zanari asked.

"I think they're just really private," he said.

Samar stopped before a large tent in the center of the village, and the jinni standing guard reached over and pulled open the flap. Raif and Zanari followed Samar inside. Thick rugs covered the sandy floor. Samar slipped off his leather slippers and motioned for Raif and Zanari to do the same before venturing further into the tent.

"This is our council room," he said. "The representatives of the Dhoma will be joining us shortly. They will have many questions for you and I suggest you answer them honestly. If not, I promise it won't go well for you or your sister."

Raif nodded. "You've made that clear."

Raif and Zanari sat on two of the thick cushions scattered around a low wooden table. A chandelier hung above it with dozens of candles that shivered in the wintry breeze that blew through the open flap.

Raif raised his wrists. "I don't suppose you could take them off of us?"

Already the iron from the rope was entering his system, weakening his *chiaan* and making his head throb. The nausea would set in soon.

"I will, as a courtesy," Samar said. "For now. You should know that this tent is spelled so that no one can evanesce into or out of it. I wouldn't recommend attempting an escape."

He nodded to another Dhoma guard who stood just inside the tent flap. The jinni sheathed his scimitar and crossed to where Raif and Zanari sat. His hands hovered over the ropes and after a moment they began to unravel.

Raif let out a sigh and rubbed his wrists as the rope fell to the table. His skin was bright red, as though he'd been branded.

"You sure know how to make a girl feel welcome," his sister said, as she inspected her own wrists.

The guard ignored her as he made his way back to his post and Samar left the tent without a word.

Zanari stretched her arms above her head and moved her neck in a slow circle. "Fire and blood, I'm sore. What in all hells was that sand army?"

"I have no idea," Raif said, "but I'm really not looking forward to dealing with them again. I'm guessing the *Sakhim* are Solomon's security system."

Worry gnawed at him. He hated what Nalia had done, but he knew it'd be nearly impossible for her to fight that army on her own. Malek would be of no help. Raif didn't want to see or speak to her again—but he didn't want her to die, either.

He turned to his sister. "Where's Nalia now? If we can give the Dhoma an idea of how close she and Malek are, they might be more willing to listen."

Her eyes narrowed, suspicious. "This has nothing to do with a broken heart, does it? Because the sooner you forget about her—"

"Zan. Malek stands a good chance of getting that sigil. We need to know what kind of progress he's making."

"All right, all right, give me a minute. That iron rope really did a number on my *chiaan*. I don't think I'll get much, but we'll see."

Zanari closed her eyes and her breath turned shallow. She leaned forward, as though she were trying to see something better, something far beyond the room they sat in. It was several moments before she spoke.

"Cold. Really, really cold." Zanari gripped the edge of the table. "She's in the desert. I see . . . sand . . . it smells like . . . cloves. Malek's smoking."

So they got out of Marrakech. He wondered where Malek had disappeared to and how Nalia had found him.

"Nalia's lying on the sand. Malek's trying to wake her up but she won't, she can't . . . something's wrong, he's upset . . . He's shaking her, but she's . . ."

Zanari opened her eyes. "I can't get any more. I'm sorry." She swayed a little and Raif put an arm over her shoulders.

It was just like last week, when Raif was certain he was going to leave Nalia, but then Zanari had a vision of Haran in Nalia's house. That night, standing on Jordif's roof in LA, Raif was evanescing before he was even conscious of leaving. *I choose her. Every time.*

But not this time. He couldn't. And it was killing him. She'd murdered his best friend, but the thought of her lying in the middle of the Sahara, sick, with no one but a slave master to watch over her . . .

Zanari waved her hand over the table in front of them and a bottle of wine and two earthen mugs appeared. She poured Raif a glass and pushed it into his hand.

"Drink up," she said. "You look like hell."

He was so transparent. Gods, was it that obvious, how completely Nalia affected him? He sighed. "How sick is she?"

Zanari downed her glass and poured another. "I couldn't tell. It was strange. I could sense Malek—even though he's a *pardjinn*, his *chiaan* is strong enough. But I only felt him—not her. If I hadn't seen her, I would have thought Malek was alone."

"How is that possible? If anything, Nalia has more *chiaan* than she can handle."

Her skin under his. *Just let go.* Nalia's hands gripping his hair. The taste of her. Golden *chiaan* drenching his body.

"Fire and blood," he growled.

Zanari jumped. "What?"

He waved his hand, swatting at the air. "Nothing."

There was the sound of raised voices outside the tent, then Samar ducked through the flap. The room quickly filled as ten Dhoma took their places around the table, Samar among them. Behind them, Raif recognized the shape shifters, four women and two men. There was something different about them, a hawklike intensity to their gaze, their shoulders thrust back as though some part of them was still in flight. Each of them had a thick, colorful strip of hair that contrasted with the rest of their long locks, just like the feathers of their bird forms.

Once everyone was seated, a tray with a large silver teapot appeared before an old jinni sitting opposite Raif and Zanari. He began pouring the tea into small, colorful glasses as Samar spoke.

"Before we ask you any questions, Raif Djan'Urbi, the council would like to hear why you've trespassed onto our land and, more specifically, why you and your sister were attempting to enter the *Erg Al-Barq*."

Raif looked at Zanari and she nodded. "We are here to retrieve Solomon's sigil so that we can dethrone Calar and bring peace to our land and equality for all jinn," Raif said. He leaned back in his chair, soaking up the silence.

"Not one to mince words, are we?" Zanari murmured.

The old jinni pouring the mint tea froze. "The *khatem l-hekma?*" he asked, his voice hushed.

Raif furrowed his brow. "I don't know these words."

"The ring of wisdom. It is what the Moroccans call Solomon's Seal—the sigil you speak of," Samar said. He leaned forward. "You came to our land and risked your life for something that's been hidden for three thousand years? The greatest mages on

Earth—jinn and human—have not been able to find it. What makes you think you can?"

Raif pointed to the tattoo of the eight-pointed star on his arm. "You were right. This *is* old magic: Ghan Aisouri magic. It led me here, to the *Erg Al-Barq*. You said there's a mass grave of your ancestors under the lightning—that may be true, but it's more than a burial ground. It's the City of Brass spoken of in the stories. And somewhere in there is the sigil."

"The Ghan Aisouri are dead," the jinni beside Raif said. She was his mother's age, handsome, with wide Marid eyes. "Even if what you say is true, they are the only ones who have enough power to get inside it."

"That's where our story gets really interesting," Zanari said.

"I'll put this in the simplest terms," Raif began. "There is one Aisouri who lives. She's the jinni who gave me this tattoo, which brought me to the *Erg Al-Barq*. Though she's promised to lead me to the sigil once we're inside the cave, she owes her *pardjinn* master his third wish, which, unfortunately, is that she take him to the sigil as well. She is with him as we speak. Without her, we cannot enter the cave."

"A *Ghan Aisouri* was on the dark caravan?" a jinni across the table asked, shocked.

"She was the only survivor of the coup and a slave trader rescued her," Raif said. "He pretended to help her and took advantage of her weakened condition. That was how he was able to get her into a bottle in the first place."

"And you were able to free her?" Samar asked.

Raif paused, remembering that night in the canyon. "I think, in the end, she freed herself," he said quietly. He'd never forget the terror of Nalia slipping back into the bottle and the despair when his spell failed to work.

"Where exactly is this Ghan Aisouri?" The jinni who spoke waved his hand, as though Raif had conjured Nalia out of thin air. Sometimes he wished he had. Then he wouldn't have to love her.

"In the desert."

"The desert is very big," said a jinni with dark skin and bright emerald eyes. She had a strip of gold hair, similar to Samar's: a *fawzel*, then.

"It is," Raif agreed. He turned to the shape shifters. "I'm sure you'd be able to find them. We believe they might be lost."

"I see no problem with that," the same jinni said, her eyes flashing.

"What I think my wife, Yezhud, is trying to say," Samar began, gesturing to the jinni who'd spoken, "is that we see no reason why our ancestors' graves should be disturbed. Your problem has nothing to do with us. We Dhoma keep to ourselves. Surely you know that."

Raif bristled. "Trust me, the last thing you want is for this *pardjinn* to get ahold of the sigil. He's an evil man and will bring suffering to every jinni on Earth. If I don't get the ring, he will. She has to grant his wish. If Malek Alzahabi puts on that ring, this will have plenty to do with you."

Samar sat up straighter. "Malek Alzahabi?"

Raif nodded. "Do I have your attention now?"

The jinn were silent, but from their worried expressions he

could tell that they knew exactly who Malek was and what he was capable of.

"You can stop the act, brother," Raif said. "You wanted honesty and I gave you honesty. I expect the same from you. We both know you at least have an idea of what's in that cave. Otherwise you wouldn't have called this meeting."

The Dhoma leader looked at the jinni beside him, a wizened man with a hunched back and arthritic hands. The elderly jinni nodded.

"What do you know of the sigil?" Samar asked.

"It's a powerful ring, worn by the human king Solomon," Raif said. "Anyone who wears it will be able to control all the jinn in his or her realm. Solomon wore it for many years, and the jinn under his rule built his temples and palaces, fought his wars, and obeyed his every command."

"Before the Ghan Aisouri were killed in the coup, we learned from one of our spies in the palace that the legend of Antharoe is true," Zanari said. "*She* was the one who took the ring off Solomon's finger when he died. Then she brought it to the City of Brass and hid it, protecting it in a cave beneath the city so that no one but a Ghan Aisouri could enter."

"And burying our ancestors forever!" cried one of the council members.

"You see," Samar said, "there's a bit more to the story than what you know. It is true that Solomon wore the ring and enslaved all the jinn on Earth. But some of them rebelled. As punishment, he sent thousands of his jinn from Jerusalem to the land we live in now. He wanted them to build a great city in the west—the

Medina al-Nouhas, the City of Brass. On the day the city was finished, the jinn disappeared. No one has seen them since. Some say they are imprisoned inside the city, in brass bottles."

"*Gods*," Zanari said.

Samar leaned forward. "This is why we are called the Dhoma—*the forgotten*: because when our ancestors cried out to Arjinna, begging the Ghan Aisouri to help us find our brethren, they refused. They said it was our fault we left Arjinna and that this was what happened to jinn who chose Earth. By the time Solomon died and the remaining jinn on Earth were free to find their loved ones imprisoned in the City of Brass, it had already been covered by a great sandstorm, unlike any Earth has ever seen. We've tried to move the sand around the dune, but no matter how many Djan pour their *chiaan* into it, not a grain will move."

Raif knew exactly what had happened—a great sandstorm? No way. It was Antharoe, the Ghan Aisouri protectoress of the ring, who'd seen fit to cover the city with the *Erg Al-Barq*. The lightning dune. Brilliant. *Evil*, he thought, *but brilliant*.

"And then, of course, there are the *Sakhim*," Samar continued, "put there as a punishment by Solomon to be the eternal guardians of his city. They were a group of human soldiers led by a man named Sakhr who stole the ring and wore it for a short time before Solomon managed to retrieve it. We've lost many Dhoma in the attempt to rescue our ancestors because of those cursed humans."

"The Ifrit are no better," Raif said. "They are just as cruel as the Ghan Aisouri, crueler even. They love nothing more than to spill innocent blood. They even use ghouls. If we can get the sigil—"

"And what?" a council member across the table asked. "Then *you* can wear the ring?"

"I wouldn't wear it," Raif said. *Not unless I have to.* "If Calar knows it's in my possession, she'll have no choice but to return to Ithkar with her soldiers."

"But she'll be back—or some other enemy will take the Ifrit's place," Samar said. "This is the way of jinn nature—human nature, too. The ring—"

"You don't know what it's like over there!" Raif roared. He stood, glaring down at the Dhoma before him. The guards in the back moved forward, their scimitars gleaming in the candlelight. Raif paid them no mind. "The people of Arjinna are nothing more than frightened mice hiding in whatever hole they can find. The Ifrit have already exterminated one race and they won't hesitate to get rid of the rest of us. My *tavrai* can't hold on any longer. It's the end."

"Then come to Earth," one of the jinn sitting at the council table said. Raif turned. She was young and wore the robes of a healer. A Shaitan, with almond eyes and chestnut skin. "This is why our ancestors left Arjinna in the first place, when the Ghan Aisouri gained control. They refused to swear allegiance and were given a choice: death or banishment. They chose Earth." She swept her arm out, toward the entrance to the tent. "As you can see, we are a safe and happy people now. Join us."

"You have to hide in the middle of a desert, living in a village protected by a *bisahm*," Raif said. "I have it on good authority that the Ifrit regularly raid your Dhoma camps, looking for slaves on the dark caravan, even stealing some of your own jinn to sell to human masters. You're in this war, whether you like it or not. Help the revolution so that we can all go home."

It was silent, save for the patter of sand blowing against the tent.

"He speaks truth," said the old jinni. "Our peace has been shattered many times in recent years. Our way of life is dying. Maybe it is time, as the young jinni warrior says, to return to the land of our gods."

There was an uproar as every voice in the room battled to be heard.

"I'd say this is going well," Zanari said under her breath.

"As well as can be expected."

Samar stood, towering over the table. "*Silence!*" Immediately, the room quieted. He turned to Raif. "This Ghan Aisouri. She is certain she can enter the cave?"

Raif nodded. "Yes."

The council members looked at one another. Despite being Dhoma, this meant something to them. Raif needed to capitalize on that somehow.

"Why is this Ghan Aisouri willing to help you?" Yezhud, the jinni with the Djan eyes and dark skin, asked. She wasn't on the council, but that didn't seem to stop her from speaking, most likely because she was Samar's wife and was accustomed to having her voice heard.

"We made a deal," Raif said. "I agreed to help free her from her *pardjinn* master in exchange for the sigil."

"It seems to me," a jinni near the end of the table said, "that what our focus should be is on keeping this Ghan Aisouri *out of* the cave."

"I think you're not seeing something, brother," Raif said, an idea suddenly forming. "If we get into the cave, then your ancestors—the ones in the bottles—we can free them."

"They're long dead," said one of the council members. "No one can survive a bottle that long."

"Not if the bottles weren't lined with iron," Samar said, his voice becoming excited. "Bottle magic is complicated, but I know this much: a jinni stops aging the moment they're placed in a bottle. They can live in there indefinitely. It's the iron that kills them."

"You're saying that you think we can go into that cave and I'll be able to find my *great-grandfather* as a young jinni, with his whole life ahead of him?" one of the council members asked.

Raif nodded. "That's exactly what he's saying. But if we don't hurry, that Ghan Aisouri I was telling you about? She's sick and if she doesn't get help soon, none of us are getting into that cave."

21

MALEK HELD NALIA IN HIS ARMS AS THE SUN ROSE OVER the dunes. Ripples of sand surrounded them, as though they were stranded in the middle of a golden sea, the last two living creatures on Earth.

"Wake up, *hayati*, please," he whispered.

He'd been saying that for hours. She wouldn't. Sometime in the frigid night she'd fallen asleep curled against him, then retreated into some hidden place within herself that he couldn't reach.

He watched the sunlight spread across her pale face. She looked at peace and there was really no point in waking her. If she opened her eyes, he'd have nothing to offer: no food, no water, no shelter. Maybe it was better this way. The last time he'd watched Nalia sleep was after she'd had a nightmare about Haran, the ghoul that had nearly killed her. Strange that after living so long the happiest night of his life had only been a week ago. He'd believed that she wanted him, needed him. All lies, he knew that now. But it had felt so real. For nearly an hour, he'd watched her, breathless and terrified because no one had ever had such an effect on him. He'd known it was foolish, to let himself feel that way, but he'd been powerless against the pull of her *chiaan*. The feel of her in his arms.

Their only hope was that someone other than the Ifrit would find them, and soon. A Berber nomad, one of the Dhoma. Unless, by some miracle, Nalia woke and her *chiaan* returned, there was nothing to be done. It was pointless to walk. Though he had a vague sense of direction based on the sun, he could only carry her for so long.

A shadow swept across the sand and Malek looked up—a flock of strange desert birds. They circled over him, like vultures spying carrion.

"Off with you!" Malek shouted. He grabbed a fistful of sand and threw it at the creatures, but they swooped out of range, then settled on the ridge of a nearby dune. Seven birds. One of them flew off, in the opposite direction of the sun. It was eerie, these huge black beasts that stared him down. As if he needed any more problems.

Once the sun crested over the horizon, Malek picked Nalia up and carefully descended the dune they'd hiked up to late the night before. He found some shade, then lay against the dune, holding her to his chest. He pulled off the kaffiyeh that had been twisted around his neck and draped the checkered scarf over them. It was meager protection against the elements, but it was all he had. Malek closed his eyes and waited for sleep, focusing on the beat of Nalia's heart and her faint breath on his neck.

Zanari stood over the sleeping couple. She was glad Raif wasn't here to see this: Malek holding Nalia, her head on his chest. Samar had insisted on one of the Djan'Urbis staying at the camp as insurance against escape. Raif had been more than happy to let Zanari be the one to go, though she could tell by his restlessness that he was worried. Nalia had killed his best friend but it was eating him up, not knowing if she would be okay.

The salfit and the slave owner, she thought. *They deserve each other.* Zanari lifted her foot and sent the toe of her boot into Malek's ribs.

He jolted up with a shouted curse in Arabic, the kaffiyeh slipping from his face. Nalia fell to the sand, her eyes remaining closed. Zanari couldn't tell what was wrong with her. She didn't look injured.

"Get up," she said. She wore a pair of sunglasses the Dhoma had given her, in order to more easily avoid any chance of Malek making use of his hypersuasion again.

"Where the hell have you *been*?" he growled. His voice was raspy, his lips chapped. He wore dirty jeans and a torn T-shirt. She'd never seen him look like anything less than the most powerful human in the world.

"Oh, I'm sorry," Zanari said. "I had no idea you'd miss us,

what with you trying to kill me and all."

Malek looked down at Nalia and gently lifted her into his arms. She hung, limp and lifeless.

"What's wrong with her?" Zanari said.

Just a few days ago she and Nalia had been fighting side by side. Willing to bleed for one another. But Nalia had broken Raif's heart and killed someone Zanari had loved. There was no going back from that. So why did it hurt to see Nalia like this?

"I'm not saying another word until you give me water," Malek said. "A lot of it."

Zanari turned and motioned for him to follow her to the *Sun Chaser.*

"A *ship*?" Malek said as they neared the lowered gangplank.

"I thought you weren't saying another word until you had water. I liked that policy."

"Enjoy your little power trip while it lasts, Zanari. I assure you it'll be short lived."

Zanari turned and flicked her thumb across the tip of her nose, the jinn version of flipping someone off.

"I always thought you Djan were a classy bunch," Malek said.

She was surprised he knew what the gesture meant. Then again, it wasn't hard to imagine Malek giving the jinn he encountered cause to do the same.

"It's a Dhoma sand ship," she said. "I'm taking you to their camp. There's a healer there, and you'll be safe from the Ifrit until Nalia recovers."

"You're guests of the Dhoma?"

"That's one way of looking at it," she said.

Samar leaned over the railing of the ship. "What's wrong with her?" he asked.

Malek sighed. "Water. Then I'll explain."

They set sail immediately. The Shaitan Dhoma on the crew raised their hands to the sky, their palms turning the color of burnished gold as they called for the power of air. A steady gale whipped over the desert and as the sails caught the wind, Zanari leaned against the mast, using it to keep her balance as the ship navigated the dunes.

Malek drank as much water as the Marid jinn on the ship would manifest for him, then poured it over his face and head. Nalia lay on a pile of blankets beside him, still and lifeless.

"Thought you'd be in the cave by now," Malek said, once he'd finally finished.

"Turned out to be a little more difficult to get inside than we thought," Zanari said. "Don't think that gives you an advantage, *pardjinn.*"

He raised his eyebrows. "I always have the advantage."

"Really? Sitting in the middle of the Sahara, waiting to die?"

"I can't die." He smiled and pointed his index finger at her.

"That's an advantage, wouldn't you say?"

Zanari snorted. "Your arrogance knows absolutely no bounds. One of these days, the gods are gonna catch up with you."

"Then they'll have to be a lot faster than they've been thus far."

Zanari shook her head. "Okay, you've had enough time to blaspheme the gods and drink a lake's worth of water. Now tell me what happened. You're supposed to have a Dhoma guide and a functioning Nalia, and I see neither," she said.

Malek counted off on his fingers, his eyes darkening as he described each new horror. "Calar spent the better part of a day torturing me—lovely woman, I can see why your realm is doing so well right now. Apparently, she's a bit like you."

"Like me? What the hell's *that* supposed to mean?"

"A *voighif* of sorts. Has some mental magic. Basically she can get in your head and fuck it all up to hell."

Zanari stared. "I knew she could read minds after Nalia recognized her in my drawing, but . . . fire and blood."

"Well, blood and a little bit of fire, later on, but I'm getting ahead of myself," Malek continued. His voice was tight, like he was stretched thin, ready to break. All the calm and swagger was gone, leaving only a man on the verge of a breakdown. "Nalia's brother paid a visit to my cell."

"Wait. *Bashil* is in Morocco?"

"*Was*, not *is*."

As Malek narrated the events of the past day in a brief, strained monologue, Zanari finally understood why Nalia wasn't waking up.

"What can I say?" he finished. "It's been a pretty shitty twenty-four hours, Zanari."

Zanari closed her eyes. She hated how much it hurt, hearing what had happened to Nalia. She wanted to think it was fair, that somehow the gods had seen fit to dole out their own form of justice, linking Kir and Bashil. But the cruel, gruesome death of an innocent boy was never something to feel satisfaction over. Gods, if she'd lost Raif that way . . .

They passed the rest of the journey in an uneasy silence as the *Sun Chaser* glided across the Sahara. The *fawzel* flew in two formations: one ahead of the ship and one behind. Zanari hoped they could make it to the Dhoma camp before any Ifrit patrolling the desert caught sight of them.

The peaks of the Dhoma's tents came into view, a burst of life and color on the barren landscape. Zanari still had trouble believing the structures were made of canvas. Some were two or three stories and leaned like drunken men. Many had smoke from cooking fires coming out of the roofs or jinn calling to one another from their windows. And over it all, the shimmering *bisahm*.

"We're here," Zanari said.

"Will your brother be gracing us with his presence?" Malek asked.

Zanari glanced at Nalia. *He's going to lose his mind.*

"Unfortunately, yes," she said.

The Shaitan sailors calmed the wind, and Samar threw an anchor over the side of the ship. At the bottom of the gangplank stood the jinni from the council room who'd worn the white robes of a healer.

"I'm told we have a Ghan Aisouri in need of care," she said. Her raven hair was pulled back in a loose bun and she reached out a hand as Malek neared with Nalia.

"The injury is in her mind, I think," Zanari said. "She lost her brother."

"I'll do what I can." The healer's golden eyes caught on Zanari's, and Zanari blushed, suddenly breathless. "I'm Phara, by the way," the healer said.

Zanari placed her hand over her heart in greeting. "Zanari. Um. Djan'Urbi."

"I know." Phara smiled once more, then turned to Malek, frowning. All the Dhoma knew he'd been a slave owner. Their camp was a stop on the underground caravan, so this didn't sit well with them. "Follow me."

Zanari walked behind them, dazed. She didn't need this kind of distraction, a jinni who made her light-headed just by looking at her. Besides, it never ended well. Male, female, it didn't matter. Anyone Zanari thought she'd had a connection with turned out to want her brother and his power more.

She scanned the village for Raif. She found him sitting in their tent, his head in his hands.

"Hey, little brother."

He looked up, his eyes bloodshot. "How is she?"

Zanari sat on the floor opposite him. "I'll tell you, but I want you to promise me something."

"Zanari—"

"Listen. I know you still love her. Of course you do, love doesn't just go away like that." She snapped her fingers. "But you can't forget who she is and what she's done."

"How. Is. She?"

"It's bad." She took his hand. "Her brother. Calar killed him in front of Nalia. It was really awful, Raif. She's alive, but . . . she hasn't woken up. Malek says her *chiaan* has disappeared."

She could feel Raif's own *chiaan* plummet, as though some-one had cut him, bleeding the magic out.

"I shouldn't have left," he whispered. "Why did I—"

"Because *she's a murderer*. Because you need to be the leader of the revolution now, not a lovesick boy." Zanari stood up, suddenly enraged. She was tired of Nalia, tired of the power she had over Zanari's family. "Her brother died. *All* your brothers are dying,"

She swept past him, out of the tent, and across the camp. She didn't stop until she reached the lake, that impossible body of fresh water nestled between two mountain-high dunes.

It had always been like this, their whole lives: Zanari keeping her brother sane, Zanari doing whatever her brother wanted, Zanari cleaning up his messes.

She was the eldest Djan'Urbi child. But the *tavrai* hadn't given a second thought to passing over Zanari, not to mention her mother. Raif had only been fifteen summers old when Dthar Djan'Urbi died, but he was chosen as the next leader without question. He'd always felt everything too much, had never been comfortable in their father's shoes. Every day he was trying to impress a ghost.

It didn't matter that Zanari had a power few jinn possessed. It didn't matter that she was far more levelheaded or a better strategizer or the only one in her family capable of making the tough choices. What mattered was that she wasn't a son. The Djan had always been patriarchal—even the barbaric Ifrit had no qualm choosing a young female to lead them in the bloodiest stage of the war yet.

She thought about what Phara, the healer, had said in the council meeting the night before: *Join us.*

The Dhoma were free jinn, living in relative peace. What was stopping Zanari from leaving Arjinna forever, just as they had? She wasn't sure she knew anymore.

RAIF WAITED UNTIL THE SUN HAD SET TO SEE HER.

Zanari's words had stung, but they were no surprise. Nobody understood what Nalia was to him, least of all himself. As the sun moved through the sky and day turned to dusk, Raif fought a war in that tent, his heart battling reason.

She killed Kir. Then, *I love her.* Then, *But she killed your best friend.* Then, *I still love her.*

Finally, he stood up and left the tent, no closer to a resolution than he'd been since he'd heard she was sick. He didn't know what he'd say or what it meant that he kept being drawn to her side against both of their wills. He wondered if there'd always be this push-pull with Nalia and if he'd simply have to learn to live with it, like the scars from the uprisings.

The healer's tent was at the edge of the camp, set against a dune and far from the noise of the fires and communal tables. A glass lamp in the shape of a red star hung from a pole near the entrance. The flap moved to the side, and someone exited the tent. It was dark and it took a moment for Raif to recognize Malek. He wore Dhoma clothing, a kaftan over linen pants, with the fabric for a turban wound loosely around his neck. He held a cigarette to his lips, but lowered it as Raif stepped into the moonlight. They stared at one another for a long moment, then Malek threw down the cigarette and strode toward him.

"She needed you," Malek said, his voice low and dangerous. It was the last thing Raif had expected him to say. "She needed you and you abandoned her. You left her to *Calar*. Do you know how close Nalia was to dying? And you—you could have saved them both, but instead there was just my gun and not enough time. And now she's gone and I don't know if she's ever coming back."

Each word was a perfectly executed punch, hitting him right where it would hurt. For once, everything Malek said was true.

"Get out of my way, *skag*."

Raif started forward, but Malek pulled back his right arm and swung, his fist landing squarely on Raif's jaw.

Raif's hands flew in front of him, his emerald *chiaan* twisting around Malek so that the *pardjinn* flew back, then fell to the ground, hard. Raif heard something crack and the sound was deeply satisfying. The *skag* would need a healer for that one. Malek cursed, struggling to his feet, but Raif kicked his legs out from under him so that Malek was on his stomach, defenseless.

Then Raif pressed his boot against Malek's spine, pushing harder when he grunted in pain.

"So help me gods, Malek, I know I can't kill you, but I will get as close as possible. Now, I am going into that tent. I suggest you find somewhere else to occupy your time."

He lifted his foot and Malek got to his knees, then slowly stood. Sand clung to his stubble and he ran the back of his hand across his mouth, then turned to the side and spit.

"I've always accepted Nalia for who she is," Malek said. "She's darkness and light. Always will be. You can't tame her."

"I would never try to *tame* her," Raif said. "She's not an animal to be trained."

"My feelings for Nalia and my method of expressing them may not have your nobility, but they're what kept her alive. So go in there, convince the girl lying in a coma that abandoning her was the right thing to do. *Inshallah*, she will see you for the coward you are." He paused. "If she ever wakes up."

Malek lit another cigarette as he strolled toward the outskirts of the camp. Raif watched him go, seething. The bastard was right. He *was* a coward. Letting Nalia go had been a relief. Without her, he wouldn't have to disappoint his *tavrai*, he wouldn't have to forgive her, or live with this love that was so big it threatened to crush him.

Raif slowly turned toward the tent. Could he forgive her? Could he *really* choose her every time?

He took a breath and walked inside.

As Raif entered the tent Phara stood, ghostlike in her white healer's robes. It was warm, too warm, and completely silent. A pot of herbs burned on a small table: desert sage, sandalwood, and a host of other scents Raif couldn't place. Nalia's bed was in a dark corner. In the dim light from the few candles that lit the room, he saw that she lay beneath a purple striped blanket, her dark hair splayed across a white pillow. The only color in her face was the black curve of her eyebrows and the soft lashes that brushed the dark circles under her eyes.

"On Earth, they say purple is the color of healing," the jinni said as she crossed to him. "And, of course, she's a Ghan Aisouri. They say she has purple eyes."

Raif nodded. Swallowed. "Yes. They're . . . they're beautiful. When they're open." He gestured to the bed. "Can I . . . ?"

"Of course. Talk to her, let her know you're there. It helps."

"When will she wake up?"

Faqua celique. *Only the stars know.* The jinni smiled and moved toward the tent flap. "Will you be here for a while?"

"Until she wakes up."

"Then I will let you be."

Raif moved toward the bed in a daze. Zanari had called him a lovesick boy, and he was.

I choose her. Every time.

He sat in the chair beside the bed and reached under the blanket for Nalia's hand. He remembered what Zanari had said, about Nalia's *chiaan* disappearing, but this . . . Raif hadn't expected the shock of feeling nothing when he touched her. It was wrong, absurd. Like touching a human—no hint of magic under that skin, nothing but the dim beat of her pulse. This was a girl who had more power than any jinni he'd ever known, a girl whose *chiaan* had gotten inside him and burned down every wall he'd ever built. That first night when he'd danced with her, it was as if he'd taken a drug, so overwhelming was the feel of her inside him.

And now there was nothing.

It was as if Haran had tried to kill her all over again. Raif couldn't bear it if this time the darkness won. He kicked off his boots and pulled back the blanket, then lay beside her, his hands gripping both of her own.

"I love you," he whispered. "I love you and I will never leave you again."

Nalia smelled like the desert, her hair drenched in the healer's herbs. Fine grains of Saharan sand still clung to her skin and he gently brushed them away. He pressed his lips to her cheeks, her neck, and then poured his *chiaan* into her, just as he had done the night Nalia stole the bottle. He felt a tiny flicker, a faint echo of the power he knew Nalia had locked away inside her. His heart quickened and he tried to latch onto her *chiaan*, to join them, but it retreated, like a frightened creature.

"You're not alone, *rohifsa*," he said, his lips against her skin. "I'll be right here when you're ready to come back."

He held her, eventually falling asleep. When he awoke, she still lay there, suspended between life and death.

Phara was sitting across the room, carefully mixing a poultice. "It's time for her medicines," she said.

Raif sat up. "What do they do?"

"They keep her alive while she decides if she wants to go to the godlands or not." She picked up a small vial filled with an orange liquid. "Do you want to help?"

That night, when they were alone in the tent, Raif told Nalia about the life they would have one day, when the war was over. He described the house he would manifest for them in detail, imagined the faces of their children.

"We'll laugh every day and at night we'll make love in our field, under the light of the Three Widows. We'll swim in the Infinite Lake and climb the Qaf Mountains. Wake up, *rohifsa*. We can start over. We can start now."

Nothing.

He told Arjinnan tales he'd heard around fires and stories from his mother's lips. He sang the love songs of his people. He whispered prayers to the gods. He gave her his *chiaan* as though it were a tonic.

She remained empty, her *chiaan* hidden away.

It hurt to look at her, and Raif stared at the canvas ceiling of the tent, focusing on the shadows the candlelight threw against the fabric. He reached up a hand and used the slight trickle of *chiaan* left in him to turn the shadows into constellations, an old trick of his from childhood, when he couldn't fall asleep: *B'alai Om*, the Great Cauldron, Tatarun, the mage who'd traveled to the godlands to learn the secrets of alchemy.

"You forgot Piquir's sword."

Raif's hand fell and he turned, his breath catching. Her eyes were open. They stared not at him, but at the ceiling above her.

"*Nalia.*"

She turned to look at him. She didn't smile and her violet eyes had turned a dull gray. Raif was afraid to touch her, afraid to send her back to wherever she'd been hiding.

"Did I get what I deserved?" she whispered.

"No." Raif pulled her to him, his eyes damp. "Oh, no, my love, don't think that way." He pressed his lips against her hair. "I'm sorry, *rohifsa*. I'm so sorry. For all of it. Everything."

She went still against him and he held her face in his hands.

"I love you," he said. "I love you so godsdamn much."

He leaned closer, his lips longing for hers, but Nalia slid away from him, clutching the blankets to her chest. He stared at her, bewildered.

"Nal?"

"You should have let me die."

TEARS SLIPPED DOWN NALIA'S FACE AS SHE TRIED TO run the brush through her hair. It was a stupid thing, really. Just a tangle of knots left over from the sandstorm, nothing to get upset over. Yet somehow her inability to perform this one simple task threatened to break her. Bashil, Raif, her dead *chiaan*, the awful wish she still had to grant—

Nalia grabbed a hunk of hair and forced the brush through it with vicious strokes. Her scalp throbbed and strands came out in snarled chunks and still her head was a mess of knots. She growled and tried again. The bristles caught, the tears came thick and fast. She tore the brush out of her hair and threw it across the room. It hit the soft tent wall, impotent.

She snatched a pillow off her bed and screamed into it. It felt good to burn her throat, to sound the rage that had been building inside her from the moment she'd woken up. She threw the pillow down. Took a breath. Then she crossed to the table where Phara kept her medical supplies. Sitting beside a ceramic washbasin was a large pair of silver shears. Nalia picked them up. It was a satisfying sound, this soft kiss of metal against hair. The long tresses that Raif had once curled around his fingers fell to the thick rug that covered the desert floor.

"For you, Nalia-jai." Bashil hands her a vixen rose. She takes it from his chubby fingers and breaths in its heady scent.

"Shundai, gharoof. It's beautiful. What shall I do with it?"

He motions for her to kneel and she does. They are eye to eye. She kisses his baby cheek, quick, before their mother can see.

Bashil holds out his hand and Nalia returns the flower.

He reaches up and threads the stem through the long braid that encircles her head. He bites his lip in concentration, so serious.

"There," he says proudly. He runs his fingers across the braid, making sure the rose is secure.

Nalia looks at her reflection in the fountain beside them.

"More beautiful than a jewel," she says.

Nalia set down the shears with shaking hands, then stood before a small mirror near her bed. If it hadn't been for the birthmark that bled onto her cheek below her right ear, she might not have recognized herself at first glance. She reached up and ran her fingers through the short, boyish cut. She felt lighter, like she could float away.

Phara came through the flap. "It's almost time for . . ." The words died on her lips as she stared at Nalia.

"I didn't want to brush it anymore," Nalia said. She crossed to the shelf where a bottle of wine sat and poured herself a glass. It was thick and sweet, the way jinn liked it.

"Actually, it becomes you," Phara said.

Nalia raised the bottle and the healer smiled. "Just a small glass. Can't have you drinking alone."

Nalia poured the wine and they drank in silence. The healer was the only person she'd allowed in the tent since she'd woken up the night before. The jinni's cool voice and calm demeanor demanded nothing of her. She didn't know anything about Nalia, had no access to her dark past and bleak future. To Phara, Nalia was a patient. No more, no less.

Phara finished her glass, then stood up. The hair on the ground disappeared with a sweep of Phara's palm. Nalia watched her. How much more of herself would she leave behind in this desert?

The healer crossed to the small table where the shears lay. "Let's just . . . get this a little more presentable, shall we?"

"It doesn't matter to me," Nalia said, her voice hollow.

"Well, one of my hobbies is beauty magic, so indulge me."

For the next few minutes, Phara fussed over Nalia's hair. It was a relief to be touched without *chiaan*. Nalia never thought she'd feel that way, but it was true. She didn't have to read Phara or worry that too much of herself was being revealed to the other jinni. There was only the feel of gentle fingers moving through her hair, cutting away the evidence of Nalia's grief.

"I wonder what Raif will think," Phara said softly.

Nalia said nothing. *Bashil. Bashil. Bashil.* Her mind empty but for that one word that gutted her.

"Come," Phara said. "The council is waiting."

Phara had already told Nalia the new plan for getting past the lightning over the *Erg Al-Barq.* The Dhoma had decided that as soon as Nalia's *chiaan* returned, she would lead Raif, Malek, Zanari, and a small group of Dhoma into the cave. In exchange for allowing Nalia and the others onto their sacred ancestral land, Raif would help free the imprisoned Dhoma.

Nalia took a deep breath of fresh air as she stepped outside the tent for the first time since waking up. It was hot, the intense heat of the day burning off the nighttime chill. The sun felt good and Nalia curled into herself, guilty. She didn't deserve to feel pleasure.

"How do they know Solomon's Dhoma are even in these bor-tles?" Nalia asked as Phara ducked out of the tent behind her. She wondered if the healer could tell that Nalia was going through the motions of being alive, having a conversation only because that was what was expected of her. Inside there was only: *Bashil, Bashil, Bashil.*

"The stories are how they know." Nalia turned at the familiar voice. Malek stood beside the tent, a cigarette in one hand and an ancient copy of *The Arabian Nights* in the other. "Welcome back, Nalia. Nice hair, by the way—it's quite fetching."

She wasn't fooled by his casual greeting. He looked at her hungrily, unable to mask the feeling in his eyes.

She let out a breath. "Malek. What are you doing outside my tent?"

"We have an agreement, you and I. Third wish and all. I have to protect my investment."

He was thin, gaunt even, and he'd abandoned the sleek perfection that had once been as much a part of him as breathing. Clothed in the garb of the Dhoma, Malek looked nothing like himself. And yet, there was still that arrogant half-smile.

Nalia looked away and followed Phara toward the large tent in the center of the camp. Malek kept pace.

"So, these jinn. We just find the bottles and . . . open them?" Nalia said to Phara. It was a nice thought, freeing thousands of slaves. Bringing life back into the world. For a moment, she felt something like hope stir in her chest.

"It's likely the bottles were inscribed with the same seal on Solomon's sigil," Malek said. "That way, only Solomon himself could release his prisoners. According to my research—which is vast, I assure you—the sigil has enormous magical properties. Controlling jinn is probably just the beginning. Solomon was a master alchemist, one of the wisest humans that ever lived. No doubt he learned every secret of the jinn he could. It will take ages to discover all that the ring can do."

"You know what, Malek? I don't care about the ring," Nalia said. Her head was pounding and she wanted her brother and why couldn't they all see that she was a walking corpse? "I don't care about what it can do. I don't care who gets it." Her voice rose, flitting on the edge of sanity. "I don't care, I don't care, I don't care."

"What about Raif?" he said quietly.

"I. Don't. Care."

Malek raised an eyebrow. "Well, that changes things."

"No it doesn't."

Love is a weakness, her mother had said. It turned out, Mehndal Aisouri'Taifyeh had been right. Calar had found that weakness in Nalia and used it for all it was worth. She'd done better than kill Nalia: she'd left her alive so she could feel Bashil's loss over and over, knowing it was her fault he was dead.

They reached the tent, and a large jinni standing guard pulled the flap back. Phara slipped off her shoes before stepping inside and Nalia followed suit. Malek hovered near the entrance, but the guard stepped in front of him.

"I'm part of this expedition," Malek said.

"They don't want you in here, slaver," the guard growled.

Malek stalked off with a muttered curse.

Eleven jinn, including Raif and Zanari, were seated at a large wooden table in the center of the room. About a dozen other jinn stood around the perimeter. A chandelier filled with candles and the sunlight from the open tent flap provided the only light. Raif's emerald eyes met Nalia's in a silent plea. She looked away. He didn't understand and she couldn't begin to explain.

I'm dead inside, she wanted to say.

A jinni with a dark beard and a thick stripe of white in his long hair stood and gestured to the empty cushion on the floor at the head of the table.

"Welcome, Nalia Aisouri'Taifyeh. We have heard much

about you and thank the gods for your recovery. I am Samar, one of the council members."

Nalia settled on the cushion, while Phara took the last empty seat at the table. "Thank you for your hospitality."

"We understand that your *chiaan* has yet to return," said an older woman to Nalia's left.

"Yes, unfortunately that's true."

Nalia slipped her hands into the wide pockets of the Dhoma pants she'd been given to wear. Without her *chiaan*, her hands were nothing more than minimally useful appendages. She wondered if human soldiers felt this way, when they fought their wars and came home without legs or arms. Her fingers brushed against Bashil's worry stone and she gripped it.

"Phara?" Samar looked to Nalia's healer.

"We've tried many things," Phara said. "So far, Nalia has been unable to replenish her *chiaan*." She cast a sympathetic look in her direction. "She's still weak from her illness, though. She just needs time."

Nalia wasn't so sure. She'd heard of this happening, of jinn losing all connection with the elements. Sometimes it was because of grief or illness. Sometimes black magic, a curse. There was no cure. Either the jinni recovered her *chiaan*, or she didn't.

"Time is not something we have a lot of," Zanari said. "The Ifrit offensive has decimated our troops. Our *tavrai* report that they're barely holding on to our headquarters in the Forest of Sighs. We need the sigil and we need it now."

She looked at Nalia, her face a collage of anger and hurt,

sadness, Nalia didn't have to guess why Zanari looked at her with such distaste: Nalia had killed Kir and had broken Raif's heart several times over. She doubted his sister could ever forgive her. It hurt, this loss of a sister-friend. First Leilan, then Zanari.

"What about the *pardjinn*?" asked an elderly jinni seated near Raif.

"I don't think we need to worry about him," Raif said. "It's true that Nalia must grant his wish, but I believe I'll be able to secure the ring without a problem. I'm a full jinni and trained soldier. Malek's nothing more than a violent aristocrat."

Nalia wondered if she was the only one who heard the uncertainty in his voice. Her eyes shifted to Raif, but darted away when he looked at her. She hoped for all of their sakes that Raif had a plan to ensure he was the one with the ring. Maybe he was just bluffing, hoping to secure the Dhoma's permission to trespass on sacred land.

"Why do we continue to discuss this?" said a female council member. "The presence of these jinn endangers our people. The Ifrit are rounding up Dhoma in Marrakech—why are their lives less valuable than these Arjinnan swine?" She swept her hand around the table to indicate Raif, Zanari, and Nalia.

"Do you believe we should allow our ancestors' punishment to continue for an eternity?" Samar asked, his voice cutting.

The jinni he spoke to looked down, chastened.

The Dhoma leader folded his hands and continued. "So the question remains: how will we get inside the cave if Nalia's *chiaan* doesn't return?"

"There's only one way to find out," Nalia said.

Raif stared at her. "That's a death wish." As soon as the words left his mouth, understanding dawned on his face. He turned to Samar, his voice panicked. "She's incapable of thinking clearly right now. Her brother's death——"

"——is not the issue," Nalia said. "If the Ifrit are already targeting Dhoma in Marrakech, they will come here next. Staying here risks everyone's life. I can't evanesce. I have no *chiaan* to fight with. Where would I go that they wouldn't find me right away? Zanari's right. We're running out of time."

"The lightning will *kill you*, Nalia," Raif said. "Right now you're as vulnerable as a human."

"My only value to anyone here is my ability to open the entrance to the cave," she said. "If I can't do that, then there is no point to me being alive, anyway." She paused. "I'd rather die trying to open the cave then die at the hands of the Ifrit."

Raif stood. "Her soul is on your conscience if you consent to this," he said to the council.

The jinn around the table remained silent. Raif turned to Nalia, his eyes burning into hers. She forced herself to meet his gaze. Raif threw the council a look of contempt and stalked out of the tent. "*Ma'aj yaqif-la.*"

I wash my hands of it.

"All those who believe the Aisouri should lead the mission tomorrow, show your favor," Samar said.

Of the ten Dhoma on the council, eight placed a hand on the table, palm up.

Samar nodded. "*Jahal'alund*, then, Nalia Aisouri'Taifyeh. We will journey at dawn."

Nalia bowed her head slightly, then stood. She couldn't tell if the look on Zanari's face was satisfaction or pity.

Nalia walked out of the meeting tent and didn't stop until the camp was a distant speck. She searched until she found what she was looking for: a flat stretch of sand atop one of the dunes. She didn't care about the ring; didn't care about much of anything anymore—except Raif and Zanari. She had to make sure they got that sigil. Otherwise, then coming to Earth and Raif risking his life for her—it would have meant absolutely nothing.

She placed her palms on the sand, every inch of her searching for the electric connection between the natural world and her body. Bashil's face came to mind, but she pushed it away. She couldn't give in to her grief, not now. In the earth's silence, she tried to recreate that fusion of self and element in her memory—the tingling heat, the rightness of it. Willing it to manifest inside her.

Nothing.

Please, she begged. It was the only prayer she could manage.

Please.

Nothing.

Nalia stood and slipped off her shoes, then stepped into the first pose of *Sha'a Rho*, Dawn Greeter. The Ghan Aisouri martial art was intended to strengthen *chiaan*; she hoped the poses could also bring it back.

Nalia closed her eyes, calling up the scent of the Ghan Aisouri training room in the palace. Sweat, incense, the oiled wood of the floor. The gryphons, the wooden sticks that hit her limbs into alignment, the sound of the Aisouri moving as one. She raised her arms as her right leg sliced the air behind her in a vertical arabesque, the pose executed with the precision and control that had been beaten into Nalia since childhood. One breath. She launched into Dancing Crow, an impossible pose without *chiaan*, as it required Nalia to pull herself into the sky. Her chest tightened, despair threatening as she abandoned the pose. She inhaled, grasping for the focus she'd had just moments before, then moved to the third pose, Leaping Gazelle.

Breathe. Align. Stretch. Bend. Kick. Flip. Crouch. Breathe. Center. Breathe. Focus.

Each pose of *Sha'a Rho* was a struggle, a fight with her body. It was no longer a dance with the universe; it was a death march. Nalia's eyes blurred, the desert turning soft and watery. She pushed on, the wall between Nalia and her magic growing thicker, taller. How could she ever climb it?

Pose 378: Dragon's Claw. Impossible. Breathe. Breathe. Breathe. Pose 439: Windstorm—without evanescence, it was nothing more than a whirling dervish's desperate prayer. Pose 524: Battle Cry. Nalia shot into the air, but she listed to the side and lost her balance, pinwheeling her arms like a wounded bird as she tumbled to the ground.

And she knew. The gods had turned their faces from Nalia and thrown the remaining minutes of her life into an hourglass. She could almost see the grains of sand pouring down.

"Please!" she shouted at the sky.

"I doubt they're listening."

Nalia turned her tear-soaked face to the girl behind her.

"Zanari."

The last person she thought would seek her out. There was so much she wanted to say to Raif's sister, but Nalia could tell from the stony expression on her face that it would only fall on deaf ears.

"Thank you for backing me up in there," Zanari said, jutting her chin toward the Dhoma camp.

"You were right. We've run out of time."

There was a long pause, awkward without their once-easy camaraderie. "What the two of you have—it's reckless," Zanari said softly. "How many people need to suffer before you see that?"

"This isn't about anyone else," Nalia said.

But as soon as the words were out of her mouth, Nalia knew they weren't true. She'd battled the ghosts of her past to be with Raif and he'd had to go against everything he believed, betraying his *tavrai*'s trust, to be with her. Their relationship had never belonged entirely to them.

"Do you remember what I told you, the day after Haran died?" Zanari finally said.

Zanari had been washing Nalia's hair, helping her bathe since she was still weak from Haran's dark magic. Nalia could smell the soap, feel the surprise in her chest as the words that would change everything tumbled out of her mouth: *I love Raif.*

Just don't make a fool of him, Zanari had said.

"Yes," Nalia said softly. "I remember."

"I think we can both agree that you didn't keep your promise." Zanari's bright green eyes flashed and, for the first time, Nalia realized what an intimidating figure Raif's sister cut with the scimitar strapped to her back and the kindness absent from her face. "At first, I thought maybe you guys could make it work. Somehow. But now . . . Do you have any idea what the *tavrai* will think of Raif if they find out you killed Kir and he wants to be with you anyway? Or that he's risked his life and the revolution several times over just to protect you? Not to mention you're a *Ghan Aisouri!* They would hang him, Nalia."

Everything between Nalia and Raif had happened so fast. She'd known him for two weeks. *Two weeks.* And yet what they had felt ancient, like it could shatter the world if it wanted to. There hadn't been time to think about how selfish they were being, or how many lives they were putting in danger simply by loving one another.

"The *tavrai* will never know about us," Nalia said. "That's all over now." *You should have let me die,* she'd told him.

"I don't think my brother is aware of that," Zanari said. "You're his *rohifsa* and he won't hear otherwise. Not even from you."

Nalia's eyes settled on the desert that surrounded her. The dunes rose and fell in endless waves. They looked almost pink in the sunlight. So beautiful. Part of her wondered if she should just start walking. Start walking and not stop until she collapsed.

"It doesn't matter," Nalia said. "I'll be dead the minute that lightning strikes me." She had a sudden, sickening realization. "It's why you pushed the council to vote the way they did—to leave before I have my *chiaan* back. Isn't it?"

Zanari shook her head, stricken. "No—Nalia, that's not true. I'll never forgive you for what you did to Kir, and how you lied to Raif about it, but I don't want you to *die*. I told Raif we should go home and forget the ring, but he refuses to leave you. I pushed to go tomorrow because the longer we wait around, the more *tavrai* die. The more likely it is that the Ifrit will find us. My vote had nothing to do with you."

For a moment, Zanari's face seized up in something like grief, and she looked away. When she turned back to Nalia, her eyes were glistening.

"What Calar did to your brother—that's nothing compared to what she'll do to Raif when she gets her hands on him. And the closer he is to you, the easier it will be for her to capture him. You can't protect Raif anymore, not without your *chiaan*. He's just one Djan. Raif doesn't stand a chance if the Ifrit catch up with us."

Nalia reached out a hand, but Zanari shrank away, as though the touch would burn her. Nalia ignored the hurt.

"I'm going on that dune tomorrow for him," Nalia whispered.

And for you.

"What about Malek's wish?"

"It doesn't have any control over me without my *chiaan*."

Zanari was quiet for a moment. "Well, you're the most powerful jinni in all the worlds. If anyone can survive that lightning, it's you." She sighed. "I'm sorry about what happened to Bashil. I'd never wish that on you."

"I know. Thank you."

"He was an innocent kid and I know how much you loved him," Zanari continued. "I know because that's how much I love *my* brother. I'm his big sister and I have to . . . I can't let him die, Nalia. I know you understand that."

Nalia nodded. If she'd been given the choice, Nalia would have let every single living creature in all the worlds perish before she'd give up Bashil.

Raif's sister turned and walked away without another word. When she reached the bottom of the dune, jade evanescence swirled around her body. In seconds she was gone, leaving behind the faint scent of sandalwood.

For the first time in her life, Nalia had nothing left to lose.

A ROUGH HAND SHOOK RAIF'S SHOULDER. HE SAT BOLT upright, disoriented. The night clung to him like an ill-fitting cloak.

"Wake up, Djan'Urbi." Samar. In the dark of the tent, he could hardly see anything, but he recognized the Dhoma leader's gravelly voice.

"What's going on?" he said, instantly awake.

"Ifrit. The *fauzel* scouts report red evanescence half a kilometer from here. A lot of it."

Raif threw back the covers and felt around in the darkness for his pants. When he stepped outside, Zanari was waiting for him. It was pouring rain, the drops hard and cold. In seconds, Raif was soaked.

"It's over, little brother," she said. "We tried. We failed. We need to get back to the portal before the Ifrit arrive."

Raif was already heading toward the healer's tent. "I have to get Nalia. Get as far away as possible."

"And go where, Raif?" Zanari growled.

"There's nowhere to run in this desert, my friend, and she can't evanesce," Samar said. "Your Ghan Aisouri's only hope is to get inside the cave before the Ifrit find her."

"She'll die. We've been over this. The lightning—"

"There is a reason the Aisouri are called daughters of the gods," Samar said. "She may survive."

"Being an Aisouri means nothing if she doesn't have any *chiaan*," Raif said.

He kept seeing Nalia's eyes, gray and dim. Without her magic, she was defenseless.

Samar took in the wakening camp. "Then I have no choice but to give her to the Ifrit. I won't risk my people's lives unless it's to save those of my ancestors."

"They'll kill her," Raif said, incredulous.

"Yes," Samar said. "I imagine they will."

Raif had never wanted to murder someone so badly in his life.

"Hey." Zanari put her hand on his arm just as Raif reached for the scimitar strapped to his waist. "*We* can still leave. You need to get home and get back in the fight. If we stay here we'll die."

"Zan, you're delusional. Get back in the fight?" he spat. "We are being *wiped out* over there. If we go back to Arjinna without the ring, without Nalia, we're done. She is our *only chance*."

"Are you saying that as the leader of the revolution or as her lover?"

Raif's eyes flashed. "I'm not leaving her. And I'm done with this conversation."

"What about the *tavrai*?" Zanari said, grabbing him before he could turn away. "What about *me* and Mama?"

Raif put his hands on Zanari's shoulders. "Go, Zan. Get to the portal. Tell the *tavrai*—"

"Tell them *what*, Raif?" Zanari was furious, practically spitting. "That you'd rather die a pointless death trying to save a Ghan Aisouri than come home to fight a battle you can actually win?"

The rain was coming down harder now, pummeling him. He leaned forward, his lips close to his sister's ear. "Tell them there's hope for our future when a Djan is willing to die for a Ghan Aisouri. Tell them the old ways are dead."

"Raif, please don't do this," she begged as he let go of her.

Thunder boomed, a shout from the gods.

"I'm not leaving her." Her squeezed his sister's hand. "Don't waste time. Get to the portal."

Samar nodded. "Meet me at the lake after you have the Ghan Aisouri. Tell the healer it's time. I will bring the others."

Raif grabbed his sister in a fierce hug before she could argue, then ran to the healer's tent. He wouldn't let himself think that he might never see her again.

Seconds later, he stood outside the tent, his hand against the soaked flap, waiting. His love was nothing more than a wooden sword waved before a fire-breathing dragon. But he wasn't just protecting the jinni he loved; he was protecting the future of his realm.

He stepped inside and crossed silently to her bed. Phara slept across the room, oblivious. He leaned down and pressed his lips to Nalia's short hair.

"Wake up, *rohifsa*," he whispered.

Nalia's eyes snapped open and her free hand immediately reached under the pillow for her jade dagger.

"It's me!" he said, backing away, hands raised.

"Raif? What are you——"

"They're here. Hurry."

He didn't have to tell her who *they* were. In seconds she was out of bed. She crossed to Phara and gently shook the healer awake.

"Sister, it's time."

"Fire and blood," she said, groggy. "No common courtesy, these Ifrit."

Phara stumbled out of bed and began throwing medical supplies into a leather bag. Raif turned around as they changed their clothes. He peeked out of the tent flap. The camp was still dark and silent, but he could see shadows moving around as the Dhoma took up defensive positions around the perimeter.

"We're ready," Nalia whispered.

He led them into the storm, toward the lake, but she stopped and grabbed his arm. "Malek."

In his fear for Nalia, he'd forgotten all about the *pardjinn*.

"So?" Raif tightened his hold on his scimitar. "Leave him as a present for the Ifrit."

"If my *chiaan* returns, it'll make me come back for him before I go into the cave. We have to take him with us."

Raif cursed under his breath and motioned for her to follow him. Malek's tent was near the back of the camp, near the latrines. A small punishment from the Dhoma.

Nalia made to go inside, but Raif held up a hand. "Let me. For all we know, he sleeps in the nude."

A tiny smile sneaked across Nalia's face. He latched onto it, a piece of bread thrown to a starving man.

"I hate to disappoint either of you," Malek said as he came out of the tent and stood underneath the tiny awning over its entrance, "but I am neither nude nor asleep. Bit of an insomniac these days. What's going on?"

"Ifrit," Raif said. "We're leaving."

"Excellent. I was tiring of this little desert retreat, anyway. Do we have a plan?"

"No," Raif said. "Let's go."

The *bisahm* shivered above them. He could see red *chiaan* in the distance.

"It's not going to last much longer," Phara said, pointing to the shield that protected the camp.

"By the time they get through we'll be gone," Raif said. A jinni stalked toward him in the rain, the braids in her hair swirling around her like tentacles.

"What are you still doing here?" Raif hissed as Zanari drew closer.

"You have a message for the *tavrai*? Then deliver it your own damn self," she said. Zanari glanced at Nalia and a look passed between them. Nalia nodded and his sister turned on her heel and started for the lake, where Samar and the other Dohma waited.

"What was that about?" he said.

"The minute I die, you better evanesce with her to the portal," Nalia said, ignoring his question. "I have enough death on my conscience as it is."

The minute I die. Not if I die.

There was nothing he could say that hadn't already been said, and she knew it. As Raif watched Nalia follow his sister, only two thoughts remained: save their lives or die trying. That was all that mattered. The sigil could rot for all he cared.

When they reached the lake, Samar was waiting with the Dhoma who had volunteered to journey into the cave. They stood in the rain, silent. There was his wife, Yezhud, the *fawzel* who had been so against Raif in that first council meeting. Beside her stood the lecherous jinni from the *Sun Chaser* who had flirted with Zanari: Noqril, if Raif remembered correctly. Having an invisible jinni in the cave with him wasn't something Raif was looking forward to, but he had no say in which Dhoma would accompany them.

"This is Umbek," Samar said, gesturing toward a giant of a Marid with striking blue eyes. Raif nodded a greeting and Umbek grunted in response. "Anso," Samar said as he pointed to a wiry Shaitan. Her skin had a sickly yellowish tinge and she was so thin he could see the outline of her bones.

There was another burst of bright crimson *chiaan*, closer now. The Ifrit would be at the camp any moment.

"All right, brother, we need to get the hell out of here," Raif said.

Samar nodded. "Follow me."

They skirted the lake and climbed over the large dune bordering it. There, docked in the middle of a valley, was the *Sun Chaser.*

"This storm is a good omen," Samar said as they hurried to the ship. His Marid eyes drank in the pouring rain that lashed their faces. "It happens so rarely in our desert. It is a blessing from Lathor."

Raif followed Nalia with his eyes as she ascended the gangplank. "We need Ravnir's help tonight, not Lathor's."

"The god of fire isn't known for his mercy," Noqril said, sidling up to Zanari. "Being an Ifrit, though, I'll put in a good word for you." He winked.

"You do that," Zanari said as she pointedly moved as far away from Noqril as possible.

"Give it up," Raif said. His sister generally preferred females, but that wasn't why Noqril didn't stand a chance with her. The Ifrit laughed as he joined the other *fawzel* who stood at the bow of the ship in their jinn forms, silent.

"They will assist us with the *Sakhim,*" Phara said, nodding toward the *fawzel.*

Raif wasn't looking forward to facing the cursed sand soldiers again, but he was grateful the Dhoma were willing to help fight them.

They boarded the *Sun Chaser,* and the Shaitan crew ran around it, drawing wind from the sky to make the sails taut. The Marid kept the rain from touching the ship so that it was a dry oasis in the middle of a drenched desert. The other jinn set to work casting a thick *bisahm* over the ship. It wouldn't keep the

Ifrit out for long, but some protection was better than none.

Raif pulled Malek roughly aside. "I need your help," he said quietly. It killed him to say it, but he had no choice.

Malek raised his eyebrows. "*You* need *my* help? This should be interesting."

"You love her," Raif said. "In some twisted *pardjinn* way I can't begin to understand, but I know you do. Help me keep her off that dune."

Malek looked across the ship to where Nalia stood against the railing, gazing at the lightning storm in the distance.

"I've known her a lot longer than you," Malek said. "One thing you don't seem to understand about Nalia is that she's going to do what she *wants* to do."

Raif grabbed a fistful of Malek's shirt and shook him. "Why don't you just tell the truth for once? You'd rather Nalia risk her life than lose your chance at the sigil."

"The last time I chose her instead of the sigil, it didn't work out very well for me." Malek pushed Raif off him, then smoothed his shirt. "And you can stop with the noble lover routine. The truth is, Nalia's the best weapon you have in your arsenal. Lose her, you'll lose your war. So tell me, *tavrai*: are you intent on saving Nalia because you love her, or because you don't want to go home empty-handed?"

Malek walked away, hands shoved into his wet pockets.

"Bastard," Raif muttered.

Raif had never been one for strategy. He led on guts, instinct. Until very recently Nalia had been a means to an end. Not anymore. Still, he couldn't totally deny what Malek had said and it bothered him: Nalia *was* the best weapon in his arsenal. It suddenly occurred to Raif that he had no idea what Nalia planned to do, now that her brother was dead. How would he feel if she decided not to fight, as he'd assumed she would?

Raif crossed the deck and stood beside her. Nalia's hand gripped the railing, knuckles white. He hesitated, then put his hand over hers. It felt like a small victory when she didn't pull away. And in that moment, it was all that mattered, his skin touching hers.

"Noqril, it's time," Samar said from his perch on the quarterdeck.

The Ifrit nodded as he set his palm against the ship's thick mast. In seconds, he was invisible.

Nalia stared. "Raif . . ."

"Yeah, he does that."

As the ship began moving across the dunes, it shimmered and then disappeared entirely. Nalia gripped Raif's arm and his eyes slid to hers. It made him unaccountably happy, that extra bit of contact, even if the familiar sensation of her *chiaan* was missing.

"Everyone, make sure you're touching the ship!" Noqril's disembodied voice commanded. "As long as you maintain contact, the Ifrit won't see you."

The dunes were black in the storm and it was slow going, the *Sun Chaser* no longer skimming easily over the earth. The wet sand dragged at the ship's hull, and the rain made it difficult for the sailors to navigate the Sahara's rolling surface.

The ship slid down a dune and Zanari clamped a hand over her mouth. "Gods, I have to get off this thing."

Phara leaned close to her. "May I?"

Zanari nodded and Phara pressed her palm to his sister's forehead. Her golden *chiaan* shimmered over Zanari's skin, returning the color to her cheeks.

"Better?" the healer asked, her voice soft.

Zanari stared into the other jinni's eyes. "Yeah. Um. Much."

Behind them, there was a burst of light, then a billow of smoke and flame. The Dhoma crew stared at their camp, stricken.

Yezhud came to stand beside Nalia. "Having you on this ship is an act of war," she said. "If you can't get my husband in that cave, all those Dhoma suffering right now—it's for nothing. Samar seems to think you are worth this sacrifice. I hope he's right."

Raif pointed at the camp. "The *Ifrit* are the enemy. Not her."

"I'm not so certain." Yezhud's eyes were filled with grief and she turned away, trailing her hand along the ship's railing as she headed toward where Samar stood at the bow, shouting instructions to the crew.

"You don't have to do this, Nalia," Raif said again.

"Yes I do."

Lightning blazed in the distance, an electric sword that plunged into the earth.

"*Erg Al-Barq,*" Malek whispered, coming to stand beside them. "Finally."

NALIA GAZED ACROSS THE FLAT EXPANSE OF SAND AS the crew of the *Sun Chaser* fanned around her, their vessel docked between two dunes. The *fawzel* flew in slow circles, their wings fighting the downpour.

Lightning crackled as it cut through the sky.

"*Kajastriya vidim,*" Zanari said to Raif, who stood just a few feet behind Nalia. *Light to the revolution.* "I never thought I'd mean that so literally."

"*Kajastriya vidim,*" he whispered. Nalia couldn't feel his *chiaan* anymore, but she heard the despair in Raif's voice, as though he were already grieving Nalia's death.

Zanari punched him lightly on the arm. "See you out there, little brother."

Nalia swallowed the lump in her throat as Raif grabbed his sister in a crushing hug. She wouldn't let them lose one another.

Zanari let go and moved further down the dune, joining the Dhoma who waited for the *Sakhim* to rise. She didn't say good-bye to Nalia—didn't even glance in her direction. Whatever friendship they'd had was gone now. Nalia watched her go, hurt. She'd never wanted any of this: slavery to Malek, the ring, even her heritage as a Ghan Aisouri. All of it had been forced on Nalia by the gods and the slave trader who'd stolen her. Not for the first time, Nalia wished she'd died in the palace with the other Ghan Aisouri. What had been the point of surviving?

"Look at it," Malek breathed. He stared at the dune in wonder, his eyes alight. Nalia had never seen something capti-vate him so completely. He was usually impossible to impress. "To think that just under that dune is the greatest treasure on Earth . . ." He laughed quietly. "That's a damn fine security system."

"Why is it so important to you?" Nalia asked.

"You know what it is to feel powerless," he said softly. "Do I really need to explain?"

Power. It was something she'd never coveted. All her life, Nalia had simply wanted to get through. To survive. First, the grueling practices and training of the Ghan Aisouri. Then, her enslavement to Malek. Nalia had been happy to fade into the background at court, to sneak away to play with her little brother, or roam the wild Qaf range with Thatur, his gryphon wings carrying them far above the peaks. She had never wanted to be the one an army protected.

Samar came to her side. "The *Sakhrim* will rise as soon as you get close to the dune. Don't try to fight them. We will guard you. Just get to the top as fast as you can."

It will all be over soon, she thought as she began to walk. Either she would die and be with Bashil and the rest of her caste or she would succeed and have another chance to kill Calar. Nalia didn't really care what happened, so long as the waiting was over. So long as no one else died in her place. The rain poured and she held her hands out, palms up, as she lifted up a soundless prayer to Lathor, goddess of water. The wind howled and she turned her face to its fierce kiss and prayed to Grathali, goddess of air. The ground began to shake and she sank her knees into it as the *Sakhrim* rose from their desert tomb, sending her prayers to Tirgan, god of earth. The *fauzel's* assault on the sand soldiers began. The air filled with the sound of Dhoma battle cries, harsh, guttural songs of war.

Nalia stared at the lightning. It was time to honor Ravnir and hope he smiled on her as he had on Antharoe. He'd given her ancestor the lightning; would he take it away for Nalia?

She pushed across the field, Raif and Malek a breath away, on either side of her. The thin leather slippers Phara had given her sank into the wet sand, and the gauzy fabric of her Dhoma clothing clung to Nalia's skin. The earth bucked and swayed as the *Sakhrim* materialized, but Nalia kept her balance. The years of *Sha'a Rho* made this walk through the monsters' den easier than it should have been. A beast of a soldier with a gaping black hole for a mouth burst out of the sand to her left. The thing was at least eight feet tall and the sound of its roar put thunder to shame. The jade dagger that never left her side would be useless. Nalia turned away, following Samar's advice, her eyes on the lightning. A *fawzel* swooped down and pecked out the *Sakhim*'s rocky eyes and the creature stumbled, then crashed onto the desert floor, dissolving into the Sahara once more.

All around Nalia, sand flew into the sky, deadly geysers that pushed against the falling rain. The *fawzel* cried out to one another in their bird language, gathering into formations, then breaking apart with astounding speed. A sand spear whistled across the battlefield toward her, and Nalia flipped over it in a graceful arc.

"Still got the magic, I see," Malek said, coming up beside her as she landed on her feet. He was panting heavily and his shirt was torn, his clothing covered in wet sand. She pushed him to the ground as an arrow made of hard-packed sand sped toward his heart.

"Not the kind that will help me up there," she said.

It was slow going, a journey spent crawling on her knees as much as running for her life from a cursed army whose only command seemed to have been *destroy*. Malek stayed close, but Raif kept his distance, focused on the fighting. Nalia snuck a look behind her. Seeing Raif in action was a thing of beauty. He had a rough grace as he fought, agile and quick. Efficient.

The scent of battle threatened to overwhelm Nalia with a barrage of memories: the bitter tang of defensive *chiaan*, scorched earth, the stench of blood. And the primal roar of it all—death and life and now now *now*.

Nalia reached the dune as the battle continued to rage behind her. It had been like running through a mine field. Her limbs shook, weak from illness and the loss of her *chiaan*. Malek lay against the sand, panting.

"If it's all the same to you," he said, "I say we stop running."

Nalia rested her knees on the dune, staring up at its peak.

"No more running," she agreed.

Raif was still on the field, his back to her, hands outstretched. His *chiaan* surged from his fingers and he dug his heels into the sand, as though he were trying to keep hold of a wild beast that strained upon its leash. But the beast was inside him and it wanted out. He let go and the *chiaan* landed on the cursed soldiers, turning several to piles of sand. Raif stumbled back, his shoulders sagging. Nalia wanted to wrap her skin around him, hide him in the stars—anything to strop the death screaming toward him from all sides.

"You ready?" Malek asked.

"It doesn't matter whether I am or not," Nalia said. "I don't have a choice." She pointed to the battle below, where the *Sakhim* continued their hellish punishment of protecting the cave. "And neither do they."

Nalia stood and crossed to where Raif crouched on the sand, replenishing his *chiaan*. Scrapes from *Sakhim* arrows crisscrossed his arms, and he had a cut over his right eye. She could feel the energy flowing around him, not *chiaan* but a blood lust she'd never had, a fierceness forged in his earliest years. This was the Raif Djan'Urbi Nalia had secretly observed on the battlefield during the last uprising, standing on a pile of rubble with a defiant fist raised to the sky while the Ghan Aisouri cut down his father.

"I'm going up," she said. *Chiaan* of every color lanced the air, electric rainbows of light meant to kill an enemy that couldn't die. It was beautiful and terrible.

Raif stood, his hands dripping *chiaan*, and angled his body toward Nalia, still keeping an eye on the battle below. He gripped her hand. "You can still change your mind." His voice broke. "Nal. *Change your mind.*"

"It might work," she whispered.

"It might not."

Nalia leaned her forehead against his, just for a moment. "I love you, Raif Djan'Urbi."

Then she headed toward the light.

The sand at the top of the dune was black. Thick tendrils of steam rose up from its surface as the heat of the electric storm made contact with the wet earth. The air was stifling, unbearably hot. Nalia stood just outside the lightning's range, waiting.

"Where does lightning come from, Nalia-jai?" Bashil is sitting with her on the palace roof, staring at a storm far away, over the Arjinnan Sea.

"From the gods, *gharoof*," she said as the battle raged below. It was as if he were beside her, right now.

"When I get big, I'm going to chase the lightning," he says. She hugs him closer, her arm around his shoulder.

"And what will you do with it?" Rain pounded Nalia's skin and she slipped out of her shoes and dug her toes into the earth.

"I'll eat it!"

She had chased the lightning across three continents, an ocean, and a desert. She had chased the lightning through the land of the dead, through the fog of grief that had taken over her senses. Running, running and for what?

For Bashil, she thought, as sudden certainty swept through her. Because his death had to mean more than a vendetta. Because even though he would never see it, her brother deserved a world where he wasn't considered a *kefuhm*. A world where a Ghan Aisouri could love a Djan without fear. *For Raif*. So that he could survive the war and build the utopia he dreamed of. *For me*. This last realization surprised her, but it was true. She'd been chasing lightning for years, straining toward a freedom she never thought would be possible. Lightning was fleeting, true, but when it struck, it could burn through anything.

Even grief.

Nalia peeled off the wet layers of her clothing. The air seared her skin, as though she were on the surface of the sun. She reached down and gripped handfuls of wet sand and spread it over her body—water and earth together. She drank in the wind and as it filled her lungs, Nalia dove inside herself, pushing deeper, past the surface fear and grief and into the depths. She grabbed hold of the part of her that had broken the bottle and she didn't let go as she rose to the surface, casting aside the despair she'd been drowning in. The elements would speak to her again. The gods would listen. She'd *make* them.

I am Ghan Aisouri, she thought. Her mother's words came back to her: *Conquer fear and you conquer yourself. Conquer yourself and you conquer the world.*

Nalia was not afraid.

"*You can't eat lightning, gharoof!*"

"*You can too!*" Bashil jumps out of Nalia's arms, and his chiaan flits around him as he stabs the air with little bolts of magic. "*I bet dragons do it all the time. I bet it tastes like spicy peppers.*"

She waited for a break in the lightning; then she stepped into the center of the blackened circle.

Nalia Aisouri'Taifyeh looked up and smiled. She opened her mouth.

Bashil was right.

Spicy peppers and fire, liquid, popping, bright
Burning inside and out
A rush of energy, the earth tipping on its axis, sand everywhere
Light, incandescent, startling, end-of-the-world bright, white
and nothing nothing nothing
Death and awakening in the center of everything
Light as air, hard as stone, breath of sky, tongue of flame
A rush of self, returning, molding, exploring
Yes yes yes
More and more, so much, not enough, too much
A burning boy, a lover's lips, just let go just let go
Blood on a stone wall, black teeth, teeth of eels
Scars on wrists, burning, endless caravan of horrors
A face in dreams, heart in hands, shalinta, Kir, shalinta
Purple eyes, purple smoke, sandalwood and honey and amber
Gods, gods, filling every place inside her
Power, unstoppable
A coronation of blood

An empress is born.

26

RAIF CRIED OUT AS THE LIGHTNING TORE INTO NALIA. Thunder shook the earth, a sound like the end of the worlds. Her body became the flash of blinding light cast down from the sky. There was no Nalia, just the light, everywhere the light.

The bolt froze, suspended between sky and earth. Steam blanketed the dune's crest, covering the place where Nalia had been. Raif scrambled up the dune, flinching as a wave of wet heat rolled toward him.

"Nalia!"

He screamed her name, over and over. His feet slipped on the sand and he clawed at the dune, his arms propelling him up the slope. The heat was a wall and he could go no further. He waited while she burned, helpless. Terrified he'd smell the smoked-meat stench of dying flesh. The rain stopped. And—

Silence.

Complete, as though the universe were holding its breath. Raif turned. The battle below was over. The *Sakhim* stood, impotent, staring up at the place where Nalia had been just moments before, their faces a mixture of failure and relief. A gust of wind tore through their ranks and their bodies disintegrated, swept across the Sahara by Grathali's fists of air.

The Dhoma stood in a line, waiting. Zanari and Malek stared at the top of the dune in horror and awe as the lightning disappeared from the sky.

Raif caught the musky sweetness of amber on the wind. Not so long ago, that scent meant death and terror. It meant the Ghan Aisouri were near, scimitars in hand. But now it just meant home.

Raif's head whipped back to where Nalia had been standing only moments before, smiling up at the deadly sky. The steam on top of *Erg Al-Barq* cleared and a spear of violet light burst from a cloud of purple smoke. The light shifted and pulsed in the plumes of amber-scented evanescence, then dimmed until all that remained was the glint of skin in the milky light of a desert moon.

He sprinted over the dune's ledge. Nalia lay in the center of an eight-pointed star burned into the sand, her naked body curled in a fetal position. He couldn't tell if she was alive. Her body was so still. But whole. Unburned. Luminescent.

"Nalia?"

His *rohifsa*, the song of his heart, turned her head. Raif fell to his knees as she opened her violet eyes.

PART TWO

You cannot have the moon without the night. Its light needs the darkness to kiss. Who else can hold it but the shadows? What else can make it shine?

—The Sadranishta

27

BY THE TIME MALEK AND THE OTHERS REACHED THE top of *Erg Al-Barq*, Nalia was standing beside Raif, once again wearing the Dhoma rags she'd discarded. In all his years on Earth, he'd never seen anything more lovely than the sight of Nalia's naked body cloaked in lightning.

For a moment, Malek stood on the lip of the dune, drinking in her violet eyes and the rosy blush that graced her cheeks. Nalia was alive. Impossibly. More alive than he'd ever seen her. He wanted to bend the knee, swear his fealty. There was no doubt that he was in the presence of royalty.

"*Rohifsa*," Raif was whispering, his lips against Nalia's newly shorn hair as he held her against him.

Rohifsa. Malek hated the word. Hated that it had come out of

Raif's lips. He'd heard it before, a term of endearment between Amir and Saranya.

The stain of his brother's blood seemed darker now. After so many years of ignoring it, Malek couldn't stop thinking about what he'd done. What he'd taken away. It was as if Bashil's death had killed Amir all over again, only this time Malek couldn't stop *feeling* it.

Feeling hurt like a bitch. No wonder he'd avoided it all these years.

"The lightning is strong, no?" Samar said as he joined the circle forming around Nalia.

"That's a bit of an understatement," Malek said.

Phara swept past Malek, her healer's robes billowing in the breeze behind her. "Nalia. What can I do?"

Nalia smiled. "Nothing." Her eyes filled as she held out her hand. Phara gasped when she touched Nalia's skin.

"So *that's* a Ghan Aisouri's *chiaan*," Phara said.

Nalia squeezed the healer's hand, then crossed the blackened circle, no longer the site of an endless lightning storm, and stood before Samar.

"*Shundai*," she said. "I owe you my life."

Samar pressed his hand to his heart in reply. "The lives of my ancestors are payment enough." He paused, searching Nalia's eyes. "You really are a daughter of the gods."

"I'm not sure that's such a good thing," she said. But she didn't deny it. That, Malek thought, was interesting. More than interesting.

"What was it like?" Anso asked. Malek couldn't put his finger on it, but there was something wrong with that jinni, with her sallow skin and eyes too big for her face.

A small smiled played on Nalia's lips. "It tasted like spicy peppers."

Raif laughed.

Malek's eyes traveled to the shape on the sand. "I'll be damned." He knelt down and ran his hand along the nearest point of the star. "The *khatem l-hekma*," he said, shaking his head. It was suddenly real, this ring he had dreamed of for so long. This ring he needed on his finger.

A *fawzel* cried out in the sky and as it dove toward the dune, its body beginning to swirl in a flutter of ebony feathers and green evanescence. Moments later, Yezhud stepped onto the sand. Malek stared. It was the first time he'd seen the shape shifters change form.

"Of course," he whispered, suddenly understanding one of the *Arabian Nights'* mysteries. "Solomon spoke the language of the birds." Shape shifters. Solomon didn't speak a magical bird language—he simply spoke to the birds as he would any of his jinn.

The *fawzel* hurried across the sand and stopped before Samar. "The Ifrit are headed this way. One of their scouts must have seen the *Sun Chaser*."

"How are our people?" asked Samar.

Yezhud shook her head. "They fight. *Inshallah* the Ifrit will leave once they see that the Aisouri and her companions are not in the camp."

The Dhoma around the circle were silent. Samar clapped his hands once. "Those coming with me, stay here. The rest of you, back to the camp. *Jabal'alund.*" He turned to his wife and spoke quietly to her.

"No!" she said, her eyes flashing.

"You must," Samar said. "The *fauzel* need you."

"I need you," Yezhud whispered, her bottom lip trembling.

Samar drew his wife away and after a short, whispered conversation, he brushed the tears from her cheeks and kissed her forehead. Moments later, she was an ebony bird with a golden breast, rising into the sky.

Malek studied the remaining jinn. There were five Dhoma, Raif, Zanari, and Nalia. Including himself, that made nine.

"I'm sorry, brother," Raif said as the *Sun Chaser* departed, its carved-ghoul masthead feasting on the sand.

"I must protect her. She'll be fighting, but at least outside the cave she can fly away. Escape." Samar glanced at Nalia. "I'm sure you understand."

Raif nodded. "I do."

Malek turned away. *He* was the one who had saved Nalia's life in Marrakech and, later, in the desert. It had been *his* body that never gave in to Calar's torture, *his* arms that had protected Nalia from a sandstorm that would have buried her alive. But to all of them—the Dhoma, Raif, even Nalia—Malek was nothing but a slave owner. No one on Earth would ever believe that Malek Alzahabi understood what it meant to bleed for someone he loved. Or that he wanted to do it again. For her. Always for her. How else to atone for enslaving the person he cared most about in the world? How else to earn her forgiveness . . . her love?

He scanned the top of the dune. All he could see was a patch of blackened sand that had been struck by lightning for thousands of years.

"Where's the entrance to the cave?" he asked.

Malek wasn't sure what he'd been expecting, but certainly more than this. The stories spoke of twenty-five gates made of obsidian and brass pillars that, from a distance, looked like twin flames.

Nalia held up her left arm. It had the similar henna-like tattoos that were on her right arm and hands except for the eight-pointed star: the Seal of Solomon. It lit up, pulsing deep red, like an open vein. She looked at Raif and he held out his own arm, with its identical, glowing star.

"We're standing on the entrance," Nalia said. "Everyone step away. I don't know how this is going to open or what's beneath the sand."

The jinn moved back, leaving just Nalia and Raif in the center of the star. She looked at Raif, but he shook his head.

"I'm fine right here," he said.

The moon was high above them and as Nalia slipped her jade dagger out of the leather holster at her waist, Malek couldn't help but think they were about to make a sacrifice to an ancient and terrible deity.

Nalia whispered over the dagger, then held her palm above the sand. She slid the blade over her skin, quick and deep, her face calm. As her blood hit the ground, the dune began to cave in on itself, the black circle becoming a gaping hole, a mouth starved. Nalia tried to roll away as the dune shifted, but there was no time. Raif grabbed hold of her as they toppled into the hole, swept up in a whirlpool of sand. Malek's feet flew out from under him as the ground gave way and his shout was lost in the roar of the deluge as it pulled him down, faster and faster. He tried to grab hold of something to slow his fall, but there was only sand, bodies slamming into his, and terrorized screams. *Chiaan* of every color swirled above him as the jinn attempted to evanesce, but the sand whisked the magic away.

"Nalia!" he shouted, but his cries were lost in the Sahara's skin.

He hit the ground, hard, and a stream of Arabic curses flew from his mouth. It was pitch black, and the sliver of moon that had been in the sky disappeared as the dune rebuilt itself over the entrance.

"Fire and blood!" he heard nearby.

"Zanari?" he said.

"Oh great, the *pardjinn* survived," the irritable jinni muttered.

"Immortal, remember?" Malek said.

"Raif?" Nalia. Of course he'd be the first one she'd want to find.

"I'm here." Raif groaned. "Phara, I hope you're good at setting broken ribs," he called into the darkness.

"It's my specialty," said the healer's voice, a bit farther away.

"And Nalia, let me take a look at your hand. It'll get infected if I don't heal it."

"I don't suppose any of you thought to bring a flashlight," Malek said.

An orb of glowing light appeared in the palm of each jinni's hand.

"Bright enough for you?" Raif asked with a smirk. *Little shit.*

"Er, right," Malek said. "Now what?"

Zanari pointed to a towering statue of a man seated atop a horse a few feet away. "Maybe he knows."

Malek gaped at the statue, a legend come to life. "I wouldn't be surprised if we found Aladdin's lamp while we're down here," he said.

The jinn glanced at him, confused.

"Magic carpets?" he tried.

"I think the *pardjinn* hit his head on the way down," Zanari said.

Malek gave up. If this place was anything like it was in *The Arabian Nights*, they'd find out soon enough what the cave had in store for them. He looked at their little group—it was unlikely all of them would see the light of day again.

He had no doubt Raif's fellow jinn would back up him and his sister when they got to the ring. The last thing the Dhoma wanted was another human Master King. He didn't mind getting his hands dirty, but Malek hoped the cave would kill them before he had to.

Nalia hugged the darkness, watching as the others began inspecting the brass horseman. She desperately needed to be alone, to take in all that had just happened. The sphere of *chiaan* in Nalia's hands cast violet shadows on the rocky walls beneath the dune and bathed her skin in its familiar, tingling sensation. It pulsed inside her, a river that raced through her veins, more power than she'd ever felt in her life. It seemed the gods had been listening to her prayers, after all.

She could still taste the lightning.

"Nalia. What do you think?" Malek was motioning her toward the statue.

She moved closer and read the inscription at its base. *For whosoever wishes to gaze upon the City of Brass, he need only offer me his hand and I will guide him thence.*

"In *The Arabian Nights*, the horseman leads the travelers into the City of Brass," Malek shook his head. "I can't believe this is actually here."

Nalia released the ball of light in her hand so that it lay suspended in the air above her as she walked slowly around the statue. On the tip of the horseman's middle right finger there was a tiny eight-pointed star.

"Here's what we're looking for," she said, pointing to the star. The others drew closer. "This is the Seal of Solomon. Antharoe carved the seal throughout the cave beneath the City of Brass to guide us. Well, not *us*. Whatever Aisouri deemed it necessary to retrieve the ring." Nalia narrowed her eyes at Malek. "Or whichever Aisouri was *forced* to retrieve the ring."

Malek nodded to Raif. "Seems to me there's a lot of ways to *force* an Aisouri to do something you want."

"Enough," Zanari said. "Gods, this is going to be a long trip."

"This is all we have?" said a low voice to Nalia's left. Anso. In the darkness of the cave, her face had an almost ghoulish aspect, her skin stretched taut over the bones. "A few stars carved by a dead jinni? A map—now that's helpful. Stars? Ridiculous."

"The stars *are* the map," Nalia said. "There are eight of them—one for each of the points on Solomon's Sigil. When we find the eighth star, we find the sigil."

"How are we going to get through a city covered in sand?" asked Phara.

"There are passages under the dune leading to it," Nalia said. "We just have to find the right one. I'm guessing this guy will help us." She pointed to the brass statue. "And then the cave is below that. *Vasalo celique.*" *Follow the stars.*

The wound on her hand was still raw from opening the cave's entrance, so she passed her dagger to Raif and held out her other palm. "Please?" she asked.

As he took her hand, Nalia felt the rush of his *chiaan* and their eyes locked. For a moment they were the only two people in the cave. She looked away from him, afraid of the feeling creeping into her face. She focused on Zanari's words: *What the two of you have—it's reckless. How many people need to suffer before you see that?*

He turned her hand over, and gently ran his fingers over her palm. The dagger's blade stung as it cut through her skin and when Raif let go, she pressed her bloodied palm against the horseman's cold bronze hand. *For whosoever wishes to gaze upon the City of Brass, he need only offer me his hand and I will guide him thence.* The statue's eyes snapped open, eyes of pure fire that stared at nothing, and the horse reared its legs. Nalia darted to the side, narrowly missing the horse's hooves.

The horseman's hand pointed to the right. Then, just as

suddenly as it had come to life, its eyes closed and the horseman was still once more.

"Well, I'd say that was pretty clear," Malek said.

"Ready?" Raif asked Nalia, after she'd rubbed some of Phara's cream onto her palm. He put his hand on her arm and she tried to ignore the joy that simple touch gave her.

Nalia gently shrugged off his hand and nodded. "Yes. No time like the present."

She looked away from the hurt and confusion that flashed in his eyes. It cut her more deeply than her jade dagger ever could.

Nalia led the way as the group headed in the direction the horseman had pointed, walking for what felt like hours on an ancient cobblestone road. A wall of sand stood to their right and an endless wall of black obsidian on their left, the top of which was covered by the underside of the dune. Every hour or so they would come upon an ornate gate carved into the wall, but no matter what magic Nalia tried, the gate wouldn't open.

"Remarkable," Malek said, trailing his fingers along the stone. "Just like in the story. They're locked from the inside. There's no getting into the city through them."

Finally Nalia saw two pillars of flame in the distance. As she drew closer, she noticed that they were made not of fire, but brass that glowed with an otherworldly light. They stood on either side of an ornate gate, carved with a motif similar to those she'd seen in Marrakech: flowers and ancient script twisted together.

As they neared, the gates opened with a soft *whoosh*. "That was easy," Nalia muttered.

Malek laughed with delight. "Welcome to the City of Brass."

ZANARI LOOKED DOWN WHAT ONCE MUST HAVE BEEN the city's main street. In the light emanating from the pillars behind her, she could make out arcaded porticos made of mud brick the color of bruised peaches that flanked either side of a dusty cobblestone road. Long-dead vines hung over balconies where desert flowers had once bloomed. A large building with columns and a domed roof made of gold—a palace or temple— stood at the end of the road. It was a maze, an ancient puzzle. And over all of it, a solid dome of sand.

"It's like a *bisahm*," she said, pointing up at the improbable sand sky. It shouldn't be there, suspended above them. It was hard to breathe, knowing Earth's largest desert was lying on top of them.

"Well, at least the Ifrit will have no idea we're down here," Raif said.

Noqril made his way up to Zanari, standing closer than was necessary. He wrinkled his nose at the flecks of shimmering rock the flaming pillars brought out of the sky's sand. "You're sure the thing's not going to cave in and bury us alive?" he asked.

"It's a little late to ask that question, brother," Zanari said. She moved closer to Raif. "How are we going to find a ring *here*?" she asked him. "Or these godsdamned stars? They could be anywhere."

He ran a hand through his hair. "I have no idea. Where do you suggest we start?"

"Stairways?" Nalia and Zanari said at the same time. She hadn't even noticed Nalia standing there, her face a mess of shadows in the light from their *chiaan* and the bronze pillars.

Zanari bit off her smile. She'd meant it when she'd told Nalia she could never forgive her for Kir's murder. And if Nalia didn't have a talk with Raif soon and end things with him, she wouldn't forgive her for that, either. Zanari wanted her brother back, not this lovesick boy who ran headlong into death at the slightest provocation.

Up ahead, Phara was pushing open the door of one of the small shops that lined the main street. Zanari hurried to catch up with the other jinni—anything to be away from Nalia and Raif and the confusion they caused her.

"Find something?" Zanari asked.

Phara looked up. "Honestly, I was just curious."

"Need some company?"

Phara's answering smile made Zanari turn warm inside, as though she'd just gulped half a bottle of *savri.*

"Sure," Phara said. "I hear you're quite the warrior, so you must promise to defend me if there are ghouls inside."

Zanari laughed. "Who told you that?"

"Nalia," Phara answered. "She said you fought the Ifrit beside her in Marrakech and that you helped her kill a *s'arawq*."

Zanari frowned. "Oh." That had been one of the proudest moments of her life, keeping up with a Ghan Aisouri.

Phara was looking at Zanari like she wanted to keep looking. No one ever looked at her like that. She'd seen plenty of jinn look at *Raif* like that. Male jinn with pretty lips, female jinn with doe eyes—they'd only ever seen her brother. And if they'd paid any attention to her, it was only to get closer to Raif. No one had ever just wanted Zanari.

But Phara . . . she was *only seeing Zanari.*

Which was totally weird and unnerving and somehow made Zanari want to run away and get closer to Phara at the same time.

Fire and blood. Zanari looked at the ceiling. The door. The window. Finally, Phara caught Zanari's eyes with her golden ones.

"So?"

"So what?" Zanari managed.

"Will you protect me?" Phara blushed, a lovely pink that crept up her cheeks.

Zanari took out the scimitar strapped to her back. Protect. Yes. She could do that. "Absolutely."

Phara pushed open the door and shone her golden *chiaan* into the tiny room.

"It seems to be some kind of . . . home store," Zanari said.

The shelves were lined with earthenware jugs and simply

designed plates and bowls. Everything was covered in a fine layer of dust.

"Humans are so . . . I mean how do they do it?" Zanari said. "Their lives are so short, they can't manifest anything, they have no *chiaan*. Can you imagine, having to *buy* plates and bowls?"

"It's true that their time and abilities are limited," Phara agreed. "But think about what they've managed to do without *chiaan*. The knowledge they have, the skills. Have you ever tried to drive an automobile?"

Zanari shook her head. "I've only been on Earth a few weeks."

"Well, it's hard, trust me. You can't make them do what you want, like with a camel. Well, actually, camels are stubborn as all hells but at least you can scold them. With automobiles, there are so many controls and *other* automobiles and humans in them and . . . You should have seen me trying to drive in Tangier. Gods, I was awful!"

Zanari's eyes slid over to where Phara stood near a shelf of vases. She was lovely, all gentle curves, elegant in her healer's robes.

"The sooner I can leave this realm, the better," Zanari said. Every minute spent on Earth was a minute that her land plunged further into chaos and suffering, a minute where she questioned ever returning to her ravaged land. The guilt over wanting to abandon Arjinna was a thorny, thrashing thing inside her.

"You don't like Earth?" Phara was genuinely surprised.

Zanari tilted her head to the side, thinking. Most of her time in the human realm had been spent tracking a cannibal intent on eating Nalia and any other jinni he could get his hands on. Not the best introduction to another realm. And yet somehow, it had taken hold of her imagination.

"I'm not sure what I think of Earth," Zanari said. "I haven't exactly been sightseeing."

"It's a wonderful place," Phara said. "And humans aren't so bad, once you get used to them."

"But wouldn't you rather be in Arjinna?" Zanari asked. "To be in your own land and dance under the Three Widows during harvest time?"

"I've never been to Arjinna."

Zanari nearly dropped the delicate bowl she was holding. "*What?* Not once?"

Phara shook her head. "I was born in the desert among the Dhoma, as was my mother before me, and her mother before her."

"Phara, that's just . . . *wrong*. Oh my gods, you've never seen the Water Temple of Lathor? The Infinite Lake? The Qaf Mountains? *Are you serious?*"

Phara laughed. The sound was like toasting wine glasses. She smiled, sly. "Maybe when you win the revolution, you can show me these things."

"I'd love to." She looked away before she did something stupid, like kiss Phara's full, pink lips. Her eye caught an arch at the back of the store. "Should we see what's in there?"

"I was afraid you were going to say that."

"Where's your sense of adventure?"

"I'm a healer, remember? My idea of an adventure is gathering herbs for my poultices."

"Well, allow me to broaden your horizons." Zanari moved

forward, one hand holding a glowing ball of *chiaan*, the other gripping her scimitar.

She edged through a decaying wooden doorframe, Phara close behind. Zanari raised the light in her hand as they got deeper into the pitch-black room. First, it was just shadows and a musty scent and then . . . and then the room became a crypt. The ball of light in Zanari's hand faltered as fear surged through her, cold and hot and *gods*. A fully clothed skeleton sat in a wooden chair, clutching a blanket. The bones had a macabre gleam in the flickering jade light of Zanari's *chiaan*. Phara dug her fingernails into Zanari's arm.

"I'm not sure about this whole broadening-my-horizons thing," Phara said.

"Yeah, this wasn't really what I had in mind."

Zanari moved closer to the long-dead corpse and reached out a finger to move back the blanket the skeleton's bones were curled around. When she saw what was underneath, she jerked away, her face pale. Wrapped in its decaying folds was a much smaller skeleton.

"Oh my gods," Phara said, noticing the infant's remains. "The poor thing." She looked around the room. "Zanari . . . I think . . . I think they must have starved to death."

"That is a really awful way to go." That was one thing jinn never had to worry about—even the lowliest Djan could produce food.

"Manifesting that sandstorm to cover an occupied city was pretty low, even for the Ghan Aisouri," Zanari said, when they'd returned to the main room. "I knew she'd probably magicked the dune, but *gods*, all these people . . ."

Phara leaned against a table in the center of the small store. "Are you saying that this Ghan Aisouri—Antharoe—are you saying that she buried the humans in this city alive and left my ancestors here *on purpose?*"

"Antharoe did the expedient thing. It would have taken too much effort to evacuate the city. She might not have known about the bottles of jinn, but if she did, I doubt she looked very hard for them." Zanari wiped a finger in the table's dust. "Just another day in the life of the Ghan Aisouri."

Phara took in a shuddering breath. "It's starting to make more and more sense, why my family stayed on Earth for so long."

Zanari frowned. "Sometimes . . . sometimes I wonder why we stay. What we're fighting for. It's been so bad for so long." She looked up. "Part of me feels like we should just get as many jinn out of Arjinna as we can. Come here and . . start over."

Phara shook her head. "The way your eyes light up when you talk about the Water Temple of Lathor and dancing under the moons—that's what you're fighting for. You'd never be happy here."

Zanari wasn't so sure.

The door pushed open and they both jumped. "Hey, we've been looking for you two," Raif said. "You okay?"

Zanari nodded. "Other than finding corpses."

"Yeah. Didn't realize we were in a graveyard." A shadow passed over Raif's eyes and he looked old and tired and too much like their father. He cleared his throat.

"We're gonna set up camp and get some rest," he said. "Better

"Good point," Zanari said.

He headed back to the cluster of jinn standing on the main road. As Zanari moved to follow him, Phara grabbed her hand. The healer's *chiaan* felt like a gentle desert breeze. The confusion, hurt, and frustration inside Zanari faded until all that was left was a deep peace.

Gods, that's nice.

"I—" Phara stopped, blushing. "There's a *sadr* that my mother used to say whenever I was discouraged. I don't know if you're religious, but . . . well. It helped me. Still does."

Zanari wasn't religious. But at the moment she wanted to be.

"I try to honor the gods," Zanari said, careful. Hesitant. Among jinn, this topic was eggshells—things that break if you held them too tightly. "But it feels like they don't listen anymore. Like maybe they never did." Zanari sighed. She didn't have the words for these thoughts, these feelings. This wasn't the sort of thing the *tavrai* talked about. Dthar Djan'Urbi's scimitar-wielding daughter didn't have the sweet vocabulary of a Dhoma healer raised in the peace of a sun-kissed desert.

"I don't mean to offend," she finished. Healers, Zanari knew, were very devout. They had to be, in order to work their magic.

"Truth doesn't offend. You're speaking your heart—there's nothing wrong with that, Zanari." Phara interlaced her fingers with Zanari's long, thin ones.

"I'd like to hear it," Zanari whispered. "The *sadr*."

The *sadrs* came from the jinn holy book, the *Sadranishta*, hundreds of prayers to the gods. Zanari knew some of them, the ones the traveling priests had said around Djan fires after a day's work in the fields. Like the others in her caste, she'd never been able to read the holy book. Even after she'd been taught the language of letters, the words were too ancient for her newly educated mind to comprehend and, besides, the few copies that existed were locked away in the temples and palace.

Phara spoke, her voice soft with memory. *"You cannot have the moon without the night. Its light needs the darkness to kiss. Who else can hold it but the shadows? What else can make it shine?"*

The words slipped inside Zanari and filled her to the brim with something warm and sweet and good. They were nectar. Phara leaned close, her voice scarcely above a whisper. "The revolution is Arjinna's moon, no? If you leave, what will be left? Only darkness."

Her lips, just inches away from Zanari's, seemed to catch the slivers of light that slipped in through the shop's dusty window-panes.

"This is getting complicated," Zanari said, her eyes on those lips.

"The whole world is complicated. Maybe this moment—the present—is the only thing that makes sense."

"Zan, what in all hells is taking so—" Raif pushed through the door, then stopped when he saw how close they were standing, his eyes going wide. "I'll . . . um . . . yeah."

He grinned, then scurried out. Phara giggled. "I was wondering what it took to surprise the leader of the Arjinnan revolution."

Zanari thought of the look in Raif's eyes when he told her

that Nalia had killed Kir. "He doesn't like surprises, that's for sure," she said.

"But some surprises are good," Phara said softly, a hopeful look in her eye.

Zanari smiled. "Yeah. Some surprises are good."

She'd thought that when something like this happened to her—whatever *this* was—that it would be fireworks and magic and all-consuming want. Like it had been for Raif and Nalia. But *this* was a slow-moving river on a hot summer's day, bees lazily buzzing, the feel of warm grass beneath her fingers.

Not exactly something Zanari had expected to find on her search for Solomon's sigil.

Raif took up the rear of their small party, his eyes scanning the deserted streets of the city, Nalia by his side. It'd only been a few hours since her transformation in the lightning storm, and the enormity of what had happened to her seemed to be taking its toll. He could feel her exhaustion, the need to stop moving. The others were ahead, checking one of the vacant buildings to see if it was a suitable resting place for the night. The city was filled with skeletons, and no one wanted to sleep with the dead. Zanari had told him her theory about Antharoe leaving the humans in the City of Brass to die and he couldn't help but agree—he'd thought as much that first night with the Dhoma. The city had been magically preserved, that much was clear. No natural sandstorm made domes above the cities it ravaged.

Nalia stopped, hands on her hips as she looked around, her eyes full of sorrow. "I can't believe she'd let them die."

Raif turned, confused. "Who? What are you talking about?" "Antharoe."

"It makes sense," he said gently. "Other than the Dhoma, the jinn have never been friendly with humans. Maybe Antharoe felt it was a just punishment. Samar said this city was built by jinn under Solomon's control and that as soon as they'd completed building the city, they disappeared."

"The jinn in the bottles?"

Raif nodded. "I can picture Antharoe, looking at this human city built by jinn slaves. I almost understand why she did it."

You've become the monsters you're fighting. Maybe Jordif was right.

"Nothing could ever justify this." She swept her hand over the city. "All these people—*children,* even. I can't believe Antharoe was my hero growing up." Nalia turned to him, her eyes anxious. "Her blood runs in my veins."

He brushed her cheek with the back of his finger. "Hey," he said. "You're nothing like her."

She stepped away from him. "I am, a little."

He sighed. "Maybe a little. But only in good ways—your determination, your refusal to give up. Your power. That's all."

Nalia looked at him then, *really* looked at him, her heart laid bare. "Welcome back," he murmured.

He pulled her into a nearby alcove and, rather than let go of her hand, as she was trying to make him do, he held her palm against his lips. He gasped as her *chiaan* surged into his skin.

He could feel her, finally, he could feel Nalia's *chiaan* flowing into him, rich and spicy, achingly familiar yet more searing than before, infused with lightning. It latched onto him like a drug, intoxicating.

Raif pressed his fingers against her lips and her eyes fluttered as his *chiaan* seeped into her skin. He smiled as he took her face in his hands and gave her the kiss he'd been dreaming about since before she woke up, since the moment he'd left the *riad* in Marakech. Nalia melted against him, her lips matching the urgency of his own.

She tasted like a heady wine, and he wanted more more more. Her arms wrapped around him and pulled him against her and he didn't care who heard them, didn't care who saw, he needed to be as close as possible to her.

Then, without warning, she shoved him away, her palm pressing against his heart.

The rush of cold air brought him back to himself, and Raif stumbled, groping in the darkness. In the rusty orange light from the pillar by the main gate he saw the misery in Nalia's face, the way she touched her lips like they were something rare and precious.

"Raif, we can't. This has to stop."

He could hardly control his breath, hardly think with her *chiaan* inside him, the smell of her all over him.

"Is this about Kir? You think I'll change my mind, decide we can't be together, after all?"

She shook her head.

He took a step toward her, but she pressed herself against the wall, as if she could somehow dissolve into the stone. Away from him. Which didn't make any sense. Their connection, the way their bodies responded to one another—she wanted him as badly as he wanted her. It was undeniable. So what was going on?

"I don't understand," he said.

Her eyes were bright, too big for her thin face. They filled and she angrily brushed at the tears.

"Love is a weakness," she said softly. "It's one of the first things I was taught as a Ghan Aisouri. I used to hear my mother say that and think I was special because I had this wonderful secret—I knew how to love. But she was right."

"No she wasn't." He took a step forward. "Nal, you're exhausted. You're not thinking straight, okay? I should have given you space, I just . . ." He stared at the ground, hands on his hips. "I miss you so godsdamned much."

"It's not about being tired or needing space," she said. "Raif, Bashil *died* because I loved him. Calar used my brother to get to me. And even before that, I was willing to sell out the entire jinn race so that I could free my brother from Ithkar."

The ring. Guilt stabbed him as Raif remembered how cruel he'd been to her, refusing to help free Nalia from her bottle until she agreed to take him to the sigil. At the time, he hadn't known about Bashil, but that wasn't the point.

"Love can be a strength, too," he said. "It's saved your life twice in the past few weeks."

Raif, calling Nalia back from the godlands after Haran. And Malek—keeping her alive in the Sahara. He knew the *pardjinn* would have saved her with or without that wish.

"And almost killed you," she said. "How many times have you risked your life and the revolution for me? If Calar finds out how we feel about each other, I guarantee she will use that. And everything you've been working for will suffer. We're hurting Arjinna by being together. You know that. We have to stop."

He remembered Malek's words on the *Sun Chaser*: *She's the best weapon in your arsenal.*

"You're wrong, Nalia. The realm only stands to gain if you're alive. I'd be a fool to let the Ifrit kill you. You hate them as much as I do; having you on the revolution's side is worth any sacrifice I make," he said. "Besides," he added with a small smile, "I've already tried to stop loving you. I can't. I *won't*."

"You'll have to learn." Nalia slipped past him, out of the alcove, and back onto the main street.

"Nalia." She stopped. He knew how hard this was for her, saw it in the tightness of her shoulders, her clenched fists. "You're the bravest person I know. But you're being a coward right now."

Nalia whirled around. "You weren't there when he died," she said, her voice shaking. "I refuse—*I refuse* to watch Calar take you away from me. I refuse to wash your dead body and sit by your side all night as your skin gets cold, knowing you will never smile again. I refuse to burn you, to taste your ashes on the wind." She was yelling now, tears streaming down her face, *chiaan* sparking from her fingertips.

He stayed where he was, still. Silent. For a few breaths they just stood there, staring at one another. When he finally spoke, his voice was quiet.

"Do you want to know the first thing I said to you, when I

saw you lying in the tent, not waking up? With no *chiaan* and knowing what had happened to you, what happened to Bashil?"

"Raif, don't," she begged.

"I said, 'I love you and I will never leave you again.' And if that's weak, then fine. I'm the weakest godsdamn jinni in the world. Push me away all you want, Nalia. I'm not going anywhere."

AS NALIA ENTERED WHAT MUST HAVE BEEN A PALACE IN the City of Brass, light spilled out of its main chamber. As she walked through the wide double doors, she came upon the Dhoma, deep in conversation. The Ifrit among them had lit several torches and placed them in the braziers hanging on the Roman columns that graced the wide throne room. Light flickered over the carved stone and reached up to the domed ceiling, where the shadows were thickest.

"Is everything all right?" she asked Samar as she took in their grim expressions.

"This is an odd question to ask in our situation, no?" he said, not unkindly.

She smiled. "I suppose so." It felt like nothing was all right, anywhere. "Did you find any bottles?"

"No," he said heavily. "And we have no idea where to start. We are not here for the sigil, so your Aisouri markings are of no help to us. We might have to go our own way."

"You do what you want, brother," Raif said, coming up behind Nalia, "but I wouldn't want to go through this cave without as much protection as possible. Who knows what's down here."

"Raif's right," Nalia said, careful not to look at him. "Of course you're welcome to do as you wish, but the bottles may be as difficult to uncover as the ring. They could be anywhere. And Malek has a theory that they'll need the seal to open them, anyway."

Samar's expression darkened. "You know this for sure?"

Nalia shrugged helplessly. "From here on out, we don't know anything for certain. But if we go our separate ways, we may never find one another again."

"In *The Arabian Nights*—" Malek began.

"Just a human story," Zanari said. "Gods!"

"The horseman was here, wasn't he?" Malek said, glaring. "As I was saying, in *The Arabian Nights*, there's a story: 'The Fisherman and the Ifrit.' The bottle the Ifrit is contained in is pulled up from the sea. My guess is the bottles you're looking for are in some body of water. People lived here. They had to drink, fish, grow food. Their water source would be close."

"Why are you helping us?" asked Umbek, the huge Marid.

"Keep your friends close and your enemies closer," Malek said. He shoved his hands in his pockets. "I play a long game."

The Dhoma looked at one another. "Fine," Samar said. "We will stay with you until we find this water the *pardjinn* speaks of. If we are unable to open the bottles without the ring, we'll continue the rest of the journey with you, as well."

"In the meantime," Zanari said, manifesting a small mattress, "I say we get some shut-eye."

It didn't take long for Nalia and the others to manifest their own mattresses and blankets. Nalia lay on the mat she'd manifested and turned to the wall—it was the closest she could get to being alone. She couldn't even begin to process everything that had happened on top of the dune. Wasn't sure she wanted to. It had been a baptism of light, a refining that had changed her in some fundamental way she didn't yet understand. She closed her eyes and tried to sleep, but she could feel the death of this place, a dark energy as a result of Antharoe's mass murder. Death seemed to follow Nalia and her race everywhere they went. Maybe the coup had been a blessing in disguise. Maybe the worlds were better off without the Ghan Aisouri.

Nalia reached out a hand and a plume of purple smoke rose above her palm. She stared at Bashil's image for a long time, the quick smile, the laughing golden eyes. Finally, her own eyes grew heavy and then she was drifting, away from the cave, from Earth, from everything. Sleep overtook her and the smoke on her palm slipped away.

Nalia dreamed of the sigil.

So close, she could feel its heartbeat, somewhere deep under the earth below her. She was swimming in a lake of fire, her arms twin flames that reached reached reached—

A cackle.

Nalia's eyes snapped open. Something soft and black brushed against her cheek.

Hissssssssss.

She tried to move but her body felt as though it were encased in cement. Only her eyes were capable of motion. And, gods, she wished they weren't.

Another cackle.

A form cloaked in darkness crouched over Zanari, whispering in her ear. Zanari moaned. From where Nalia lay, the thing beside Raif's sister looked like a person dressed in black rags with pasty skin and long, stringy black hair.

Nalia tried to scream, but it lodged somewhere deep in her throat, the creature somehow muzzling her. Her *chiaan* thrashed beneath her skin, caged. Clawing her from the inside out.

The witchlike thing beside Zanari looked up, its entire face covered in hair that hung to halfway down its torso, its eyes a milky white. Yellow teeth gleamed through the strands. It smiled at Nalia.

Hissssssssss.

Nalia closed her eyes and found the lightning within, the animal part of her that had taken a bite out of the sky. The scream inside her tore itself free and echoed around the cave, awakening the others. She threw her body up and it felt like breaking out of the bottle all over again, as invisible chains fell off of Nalia's body. The nightmare in their midst stared at her, wide-eyed, and scurried backward as the slumbering jinn shot out of sleep.

Nalia thrust her hands before her and a torrent of *chiaan* blazed toward the intruder, narrowly missing its head. She sprinted toward Zanari as the monster shot forward and pressed the palm of its hand to the girl's forehead before skittering away.

Raif's sister jumped up, a blood-curdling scream spilling from her lips. She hit at her body as she cried out and stamped her feet on the floor.

"Get them off, get them *off!*" she yelled, her eyes wild with fear.

Nalia barreled toward the creature as Phara scrambled to Zanari's side.

"Zanari, there's nothing on you—it was just a dream," Phara was saying, but Zanari was hysterical, the room echoing with her terrorized cries.

"Please, *please*, oh gods!" Zanari shrieked.

The room was in confusion, *chiaan* going in every direction. Nalia ducked as a stray dagger of sapphire *chiaan* cut past her.

"What's wrong with her?" Raif asked Phara, panicked. He caught Nalia's eye and she pointed toward the thing sprinting across the stone floors.

As Zanari screamed one word—*scorpions*—Nalia lunged, but Zanari's tormentor was quick and slipped out of her grasp. "Godsdammit!" Nalia pounded her fist against the stone floor. She heard a soft cackle just beyond a grate set low into the stone wall and she sent daggers of *chiaan* through, though she knew the thing was beyond her reach.

Zanari's screams abruptly cut off. Nalia turned. Raif's sister now lay slumped against Phara, silent, her eyes closed. Her body glowed with Phara's golden *chiaan* and the healer was giving directions to Raif as he pulled tonics out of her medicine bag.

"Are you okay?" Malek was looking down at Nalia, concerned. She was still on the floor, sitting in front of the grate.

"I'm fine. That thing got away, though." She looked at the grate again, then gasped as her eyes took in its shape. "*Vasalo celique.*"

The grate's metal had been worked into an eight-pointed star.

"What a helpful little monster that was," Malek said.

Nalia moved closer. She beamed her *chiaan* into the cavern below, but all she could see was a rocky path and the smooth walls of an underground cave.

"Too bad that thing is down there as well," she said.

Malek shrugged. "It's a cave in the middle of the Sahara, containing one of the world's biggest secrets—I'd say that creature was only a taste of things to come."

Nalia shivered. She'd had enough of monsters.

She crossed to where the other jinn crowded around Raif's sister. Her eyes were closed, her breathing fast, as though she were running. Phara held her cradled in her arms, smoothing Zanari's braids. Every now and then she would lean down and whisper softly in the other girl's ear.

"Is she going to be all right?" Nalia asked as Raif turned to her.

He ran a hand over his face, his eyes heavy with exhaustion. "We won't know until she wakes up. She kept screaming that scorpions were all over her, stinging her. But we haven't seen a single one."

Nalia nodded. "The thing cast some sort of spell over her. I wasn't able to get to it in time. It . . . it touched me. I woke up, but something about its touch paralyzed me. I couldn't move."

"Well, *that,*" Umbek said, pointing to where Noqril lay slumped near the room's entrance, "makes a lot more sense now."

"Fire and blood," Samar said. "Phara, have you seen something like this before?"

She shook her head. "Let me take care of Zanari, then I'll work on Noqril."

"What did it look like?" asked Anso.

Nalia described the pasty skin, the long black hair.

"Haraja," Malek said, coming up from behind her.

"What?" Nalia looked at him.

Anso nodded. "This is most certainly Haraja's work. I have never seen her, but I have heard the stories."

"Explain," Raif said, his voice betraying his impatience.

"According to Moroccan legend," Malek said, "there is a jinni named Haraja. One of her descriptions is just as Nalia said—the black hair over the face. She can appear in other forms as well. Her specialty is inflicting madness or instilling fear in her victims."

"To what end?" Nalia said.

Malek shrugged. "Who knows? She has a knack for homing in on the thing you fear most and using that to drive you insane."

"Fear is power," Nalia whispered. How many times had she heard that in the palace? And it was true. The serfs had feared the Ghan Aisouri and it had only made them more powerful. She had feared Calar and so Calar had had power.

Raif glanced at her. "Haraja feeds off our fear?"

"That is correct," Anso said. "The energy of our fear makes her stronger. But we are powerless against her once she has whispered her words in our ears and touched us."

Phara's lip trembled. "I know of no cure for madness, but I'll try everything. I . . . I'll think of something."

Raif blanched and Nalia slipped her hand into his, unthinking. Comforting him was instinct. "Is Zanari so deathly afraid of scorpions?" she asked him softly.

"More than anything. She was bit by a particularly nasty one as a child and was ill for months. Gods . . . so she thinks . . . I mean, Zan thinks that *right now* she's covered in . . . ?"

Samar frowned. "Who can say? When madness inflicts our brethren we say it's Haraja, but we've never had such . . . proof. She seems at peace with this medicine."

"It won't last long," Phara said.

Anso reached for Zanari's hand. "May I?" she asked Phara. The healer nodded.

"What's she doing?" Raif asked, his voice sharp.

"Anso has an unusual gift," Phara said. "The opposite of mine, but just as powerful."

"The opposite—wait, she can *make* people sick?" Raif asked.

"Very," Phara said.

Anso's skeletal frame and sallow skin suddenly made sense. The jinni herself wasn't sick, but she carried sickness inside her all the time. Nalia had never heard of such power. It was more than a little frightening.

Malek stared. "Are you saying you have a biological weapon at your disposal?"

Anso glared at him. "That is not how I look at it. We don't use our gifts for ill. I protect my people when I need to, that is all." She looked at Raif. "I am not going to hurt your sister. I just want to see the nature of what ails her. The shape of it."

She held Zanari's hand, eyes closed. After a moment, Anso

stood. "I've never seen anything like this. I tried to . . . to take it on myself but it's too individualized. It's all in her mind. I can't go in there. I'm so sorry."

Phara paled. "But I . . . I don't what else to do!" She looked at Zanari's face, frantic. "The stories can't be true, they can't."

"What stories?" Raif said, his voice growing increasingly tight.

"They say if Haraja whispers in your ear, you will be mad forever. Until you . . ." Phara bit her lip and looked away.

"Until you kill yourself just to make it end," Malek finished.

"You mean that when Zan wakes up, she'll still think there are scorpions all over her?" Nalia asked.

As if in response, Zanari moaned in her sleep and started weakly brushing at her clothing.

"Phara, there has to be *something* you can do," Nalia said. The healer leaned over Zanari, and her tears covered the other jinni's face.

Malek cleared his throat. "I can't believe I'm saying this . . ." He frowned. "I think I can help."

"You want to hypersuade her," Nalia said. It was actually quite brilliant. All he had to do was tell Zanari she wasn't covered in scorpions and she'd be healed. Theoretically, anyway.

Raif moved in front of Zanari. "The last time you used your power on my sister, you made her put a gun to her head. I'm not letting you anywhere near her."

"Fine," Malek said. "Let your little bitch of a sister die. I certainly don't care." He turned on his heel and stalked off.

Nalia glanced at Raif. "I think it'll work. I've seen what he can do—"

"We'll find another way," Raif said.

"There *is* no other way." Phara looked up at them. "We need the *pardjinn* or we'll have to kill Zanari ourselves, just to put her out of her misery."

Raif blanched. He crouched down, gripping Zanari's hand.

"He could say anything," Raif said. "*Anything.*"

"Anything is better than what's in her head right now, brother," Samar said.

Zanari whimpered and Raif hesitated, then looked at Nalia, nodding.

She took off after Malek, catching up with him at the top of the stone stairway outside the building. The only light came from the distant bronze pillars at the gate. The City of Brass lay before them, a ghostly tomb.

Malek glanced up when she neared, unsurprised. He was already smoking a cigarette, the air filling with its heavy clove scent.

"Help her," she said.

"Not in the mood anymore. Offer's off the table."

Nalia grabbed the cigarette and ground it under her foot. "Well, *get in the mood.*"

"You've cast me as your villain, Nalia. I'm merely playing my role." He raised his dark eyebrows. "Perhaps I should add an evil laugh to make it more believable?"

"Why do you do this?" she yelled. Her voice echoed off the stones.

He looked at her, surprised. "Do what?"

"Every time I think you might actually have a shred of

decency, you say something like that."

Malek stepped closer, his eyes flashing. "If your lover had kept his mouth shut, we wouldn't be having this conversation. He wants his sister to go mad and kill herself, fine by me. One less person in my way."

"So this is about Raif, not Zanari," she said, shaking her head. "You have a power that can save a jinni's life and yet you won't use it because her brother loves me."

Love?" Now Malek laughed, low and cruel. He played his part so well. "Darling, what you two have is a crush, nothing more. You've known that hotheaded fool for a few *weeks*. I won't deny you your fun, but don't let it get out of hand—I don't care for sloppy seconds."

Nalia slapped him. The sting of her skin hitting his felt good. Anger coursed through her, stronger now, as if the lightning had ignited some hidden spark. He took a step back, considering her.

"I suppose that was a bit out of line," he said.

"I will never forgive you if you let her die, Malek."

"When have you ever forgiven me for anything?" he asked softly.

"I guess you'll never know."

Nalia stalked back toward the palace's wide double doors. She knew he'd follow. Oh, he'd wait. Light another cigarette. Lord his power over them. But Malek could never bear to see her back turned to him. And that, Nalia knew, was what would save Zanari's life.

MALEK STOOD OUTSIDE THE BUILDING, FINISHING HIS cigarette. He almost felt at home in this wasted city, with its skulls and secrets, the despair buried deep below the surface of the desert.

Nalia was starting to sound like his brother; that disappointment in her eyes was too damn familiar.

"Why do you do this, brother?" Amir is staring at the corpses around the conference-room table, his face ashen. Malek had put a bullet in the head of each member of the board after hypersuading them to sit still.

"They tried to cheat me. To take away my fortune. They had to be eliminated." Malek frowns as he picks at a bloodstain on his cuff. He holds it up for Amir to see. "Prada. Eight hundred

dollars down the drain."

Amir backs away, toward the door. "You've gone too far, Malek. Too far. I can't do this anymore."

"Do what? Cover every time someone in this family takes action?" He pointed at the dead men, his voice rising. "Do you know what they see when they look at me? A piece of brown trash, a Saudi they want to screw, a boy they think they're better than."

Amir shook his head. "No, they don't. This is all in your head. It's this pardjinn chip on your shoulder, thinking everyone is out to get you. Our father didn't give a damn, it's true, and he made our lives a lot harder than they needed to be. But this"—he gestures at the bodies slumped over the polished table—"doesn't make what he did to us go away. It doesn't matter how much power you have, Mal. This is what matters." He points to the wedding ring on his finger. "Family. Love."

Malek waves him away. "Go home to your pretty wife, then. I'll clean up."

There is a pause, then—

"I want you to stay away from us," Amir says quietly.

"You're joking."

Amir's eyes, softer than his but the same onyx shade, stare into Malek's. "When we were little, you used to protect me. From our uncles, our cousins, the whole world. Now? I need to protect my wife and son—from you. You're putting us in danger. And I don't want Tariq to revere his uncle Malek, who murders humans without a second thought, who manipulates and lies and steals and cheats."

"Everything I do has been for this family!" Malek roars. "To give us a position, pride. Protection."

Amir shakes his head. "If that's what you need to tell yourself to sleep at night, brother." He turns to go.

"You want to know why I do things like this?" Malek says.

Amir stops, his hand on the door handle. "Why, Malek?" His voice is strained. Malek's brother is tired of playing this game. "Why do you torture these humans? Tell me why."

"Because someday, he's going to hear of me. Our father. And he won't be able to contain his curiosity. He will come, gloating. And I will kill him, Amir. I will kill him."

Amir looks at his brother for a long moment. Then he opens the door and softly closes it behind him.

Malek will never see him again.

Malek closed his eyes. *Family. Love.* Those are the things Amir had said mattered. Turned out they mattered to him, too. How would things be different, if Amir were still alive? If he could have a beer with his brother and tell him he loved someone who refused to love him back? What advice would Amir have given? In those few blissful moments by the pool back in Los Angeles, when he'd really believed that Nalia wanted to be with him as much as he wanted to be with her, it had been as though the entire world had broken open for Malek. God, what a fool he'd been. His face burned even now, remembering how he'd allowed himself to imagine . . . everything. A whole lifetime with her by his side and all it meant to share his life—*really* share his life—with someone. He'd even caught himself wondering about children. *Children.* Laughable stupidity.

But.

Malek hadn't become the ruler of Earth in everything but name by accident. His ability to hypersuade was a power that involved more than simply telling people what to do and convincing them they wanted to do it. Like any jinni, he traded in desire. He couldn't grant wishes, no, but he could *see* what people wanted. His job was to make them not want it—or want it so badly they'd do anything to get it. And Nalia wanted him. He knew that. It was a tiny part of her—infinitesimal. But it was there. Unlike with his clients and victims, he wouldn't abuse that want. He would cultivate it. A seed he would water until it grew and bloomed into something he could prune. *No.* No more pruning. He'd let it run wild, free.

Malek threw down his cigarette and walked back into the building. He could hear Zanari's moans, louder. Pitiful. When he walked into the room, the jinn turned.

He caught Raif's eye and the little prick walked up to him, his body stiff. "Please help my sister."

"What will you give me in return?" Malek asked. *Life is business*, he'd once told his brother. Everything is a negotiation.

"What do you want?"

"The ring."

Raif's fists clenched and Malek threw back his head and laughed. "No, that wouldn't be very sporting, would it?" Malek said. He looked over to where Zanari still lay with her head in the healer's lap.

"Tell you what?" Malek leaned against a pillar, milking this for everything it was worth. "You just stand right there. Don't move a muscle until I say. And we have a deal."

Raif narrowed his eyes. "This is obviously a trick."

"No trick. It'll take just a few moments, but I don't want you interfering."

"If you hurt my sister—"

Malek raised his hand. "On my honor—"

"You *have* no honor."

Malek smiled. "Well, you have me there. A deal, then?"

"I need a little more to go on," Raif said.

"Ah, you have some business savvy after all." He turned to Nalia. "This involves you, too, my dear. Might as well join us."

Nalia walked over to where they stood just outside the circle of jinn. Her violet eyes shot daggers at him.

"This is my offer—my *only* offer, so take it or leave it. Nalia, I want you to kiss me. Kiss me like you mean it. Right here, right now."

It was a foolish gamble, Malek knew, but maybe if Raif himself could see the connection Nalia shared with him, it'd drive at least a slight wedge between them. Malek knew that if he could just latch his *chiaan* onto Nalia's, she wouldn't be able to hide their connection. He'd felt how powerless she could be against it and he needed Raif to see that, too.

Malek wanted a fighting chance at her heart. He'd play dirty, break the rules—he didn't care. He wanted to stay in the game and this was the only way he knew how.

"Absolutely not," Raif said.

Nalia looked at him. "I can speak for myself."

Malek snorted. "*Absolutely not?* You'd rather your sister die after being tortured by imaginary scorpions than see Nalia give me one kiss?"

"You're a bastard, you know that?" Raif said.

"I *am*, actually, that's quite accurate. Don't even know my father's name." A bitter smile slashed across his face. "I suppose your reluctance to agree to my terms is simply because you're just the slightest bit afraid you'll see that Nalia's time in my, shall we say, *employ*, was not all work and no play?"

"If you were the last living creature in any realm in the universe I would *never* want you," Nalia said, her voice shaking with anger.

"Darling, we know that's not true." He leveled his eyes at her. "I've shared a bed with you. You're a good liar, I'll grant you that. But not that good."

"Nalia . . ." Raif's voice trailed off and he looked at her, waiting. She turned to Malek. "I kiss you—"

"Like you mean it," he interjected.

Nalia rolled her eyes. "Like I mean it, and you will help Zanari right away, right after?"

"Of course. I'm a man of my word. Well"—he smiled, devilish—"in this case."

Before either of the men could say anything, Nalia stepped forward and pressed her lips to Malek's. They were soft and she smelled like amber, just as he remembered. He stepped away.

"Nalia. I thought we had an agreement," he said.

"I kissed you!"

"*Like you mean it*."

Raif growled as Malek laughed softly and crooked his finger toward Nalia. It was all the more fun with their audience. The

Dhoma watched them with poorly concealed interest.

"Let's try again, shall we?"

"I hate you," she said.

"I love your pillow talk," Malek murmured.

She grabbed his face with both hands and stared into his eyes.

He let himself get lost in her and as he pulled her closer, Malek pushed his *chiaan* into her skin. Her eyes widened and he smiled, soft. He forgot about Raif, about the jinn who stared at them, about Zanari. He'd have her now, in front of all of them, if she'd let him. Nalia's lips parted and she kissed him. Slow, soft. He opened her mouth and tasted her, felt her gasp as his tongue touched hers. His hands slipped down her back and she bit his lower lip, tugging gently. He moaned against her. Her kiss unmade him. Remade him.

Nalia stepped back and the lack of her was cold and empty and wrong. He stared at her, his eyes a bright crimson, drunk on her *chiaan* and the feel of her skin against his.

"Time to hold up your side of the bargain," she said. Then she swept past them, out of the room.

Raif stared after her, gutted.

Malek took off his jacket and rolled up his sleeves. "Let's see about this sister of yours, shall we?"

Raif stood nearby while Malek hypersuaded Zanari. He'd never felt so impotent in his life. Phara's fingers were holding back his sister's eyelids so that Malek's magic would work. Zanari seemed unaware of her surroundings, lost in the misery in her mind.

"There are no scorpions on your body," Malek purred as he stared into Zanari's glazed eyes. "There never were. It was a bad dream and you will never have it again."

It took less than one minute. When he'd finished, Malek stood and dusted his hands.

"I've done my good deed for the day," he said. "I suggest we all get some rest. Put this little interruption of sleep behind us."

"That's one messed-up *pardjinn*," Anso said after Malek sauntered over to the corner he slept in. All of the jinn had refused to manifest a mattress for him, but the *skag* lay on the stone floor as though it were a king's bed.

Raif nodded. "Yeah."

Samar motioned for Raif to follow him over to a quiet section of the room.

"My friend, do not let him get to you. Her kiss meant nothing, anyone could see that."

"I'm not so sure."

Any fool could see the heat between them. Gods, when she'd bitten his *lip* . . .

The Dhoma leader lay a heavy hand on Raif's shoulder. "Talk to her. She must be feeling very unhappy right now, no?"

How many times would Nalia have to use her body to get something she needed from Malek? And how many times would Raif's pride keep him from comforting her afterward?

"You're right."

He'd let her down after she'd stolen the bottle, allowed himself to dwell on what had happened between her and Malek. It had cut Nalia to the core. Here he was, doing it again, just hours after she'd nearly died on the dune.

Idiot.

He grabbed a torch off the wall and went in search of her. Nalia was deep in the recesses of the building, huddled against a crumbling stone column. The mosaic floor at her feet was inlaid with mother of pearl that caught the fire's light and held it. She was tracing it with her finger, but as he came near, she looked up, her eyes glassy.

Raif set the torch in a brazier and sat on the floor opposite her.

"I'm sorry he's such a *skag.*"

She tried to smile. "Not your fault."

It looked like you wanted him was what he longed to say. But he didn't.

"Zanari?" she asked.

"Good as new."

"Thank gods."

Their eyes met and Nalia looked down, hesitating.

"What?" he asked softly.

"I want to do something really selfish." She raised her eyes, and the feeling in them tempered the misery that was eating him up. "Something . . . wrong in light of our recent conversation."

She crawled across the space between them and slipped onto his lap, her legs straddling him. He drew in a sharp breath and she placed a finger against his lips.

"I don't want the taste of him in my mouth. I don't want him to be the last person I ever kiss." Nalia wrapped her arms around his neck and pressed her body closer. "What you saw when I was with Malek . . . I was imagining you. It was the only way I could kiss him as if I cared. I was kissing *you*. That's what you saw."

"It . . ." He coughed. "Did look pretty . . . intense." And he believed her because he could feel how much she wanted him right now, could feel the love she was trying to deny them both.

"Can I kiss you?" she asked, her lips inches from his own. "Even though we can't be together? Even though it will be the last time?"

He reached up and tucked a small strand of hair behind her ear. "It won't be the last time, *rohilfa*. Not if I can help it."

He closed his mouth over hers and Nalia's *chiaan* poured into him, somehow ragingly powerful and sweet at the same time. He hated that Malek had tasted her lips, that his tongue had been in her mouth. He kissed her again and again, his lips covering her face, her neck, the soft skin just above her breasts. His name became a whispered gasp as his hands moved over her body and slipped under her clothes. She pulled off his shirt and pressed her lips to his heart. He felt her tears drip down his chest and he tightened his arms around her.

"I'm here," he murmured. "I'm not going anywhere."

"I wish you could promise that."

But he couldn't.

Later, they walked back, her hand in his. As they reached the entrance to the room their party had commandeered for the night, she stopped. He knew what she was going to say: that this couldn't happen again, that it was wrong for them to love each other. Selfish. Dangerous.

Raif brought her hand to his lips. "You'll change your mind." He let go and walked away. He didn't turn around—he knew she was watching.

31

THE WALLS OF THE SUBTERRANEAN CAVERN GLISTENED as the jinn's *chiaan* swept over it. The rock was a swirl of color, a river of stone frozen in motion. The rainbow of light emanating from their hands dispelled some of the cave's gloom, but the darkness beyond their reach hovered, waiting to consume them. It was cold and damp, the air heavy with a musty, mineral scent—a grave. The constant *drip drip drip* of beads of water falling from the honeycomb ceiling onto the rocks below threatened to drive Malek insane. He didn't like to think about how far below the Earth's surface they were. Malek wasn't prone to fear, but the idea of being buried alive did not appeal to him. He turned as Raif stepped through the grate.

"You the last of us?" he asked.

Raif nodded. As soon as he jumped down onto the rocky

path, there was a rumble, as though a thousand tanks were suddenly driving through the City of Brass. Dust rained down from the cavern's roof. Malek and Raif looked at one another, their enmity suspended for one brief moment.

"Run!" Raif shouted.

They sprinted down the path toward the others, but just as soon as the cascade of rock started, it stopped.

"What was that?" Samar asked.

Malek returned to the grate, struggling to catch his breath. For a minute there, he'd had a horrible vision of being forever buried under a pile of rubble, the amulet denying him the mercy of death. The other side of the metal was covered by rocks, the entrance into the city obscured.

"My guess is that Antharoe created some kind of safety valve," he said when he'd rejoined the others. "We can't go back the way we came. It sounded like the whole city fell apart out there. The only way out is through."

Nalia nodded. "That makes sense. She wouldn't want us to be able to retrace our steps, to return here with others if we can't find the sigil the first time."

It cheered Malek to no end that the journey held innumerable ways for Raif to meet his demise. He felt the old ruthlessness returning, as if that stint in the desert with Nalia had simply been a head cold that had taken Malek out of the game for a while. Seeing Saranya had shaken him up, it was true. No one likes to be reminded that he's killed his own brother. But here, far away from his sister-in-law's eyes and closer to the sigil than ever, he forced the cold inside him to grow.

They walked for hours down the natural path. The rock flowed beside them, sinuous as a naked sleeping body. Deep blue stone swirled into rosy peach, turning the cave's wall into a canvas. Crystals of every color grew from the ground like wild-flowers, shimmering beneath the *chiaan* and the harsh glare of the flashlight Nalia had manifested for Malek. They passed under a natural arch and entered an enormous cavern, its ceiling reaching far above them. Stalactites hung from its domelike roof, and its floor was covered in a maze of thick, sinister stalagmites that reached up, their tips nearly touching the daggers that hung from above. From where Malek stood, the structures resembled a monster's gaping jaws.

"Well, this looks delightful," he said.

Nalia raised her hands, her palms glowing violet, beaming her light across the rocky expanse. Malek couldn't help but rest his eyes on her lovely profile, sharper now with her short hair. This all would have been so much easier if he'd gotten a male jinni, or one that looked like a hag.

"See any stars?" Zanari asked.

Nalia shook her head. "I think we have to sort our way through this mess. I just hope Antharoe doesn't have any surprises for us."

Umbek directed his sapphire *chiaan* over the rocks, staring doubtfully at the narrow paths weaving between them, likely wondering if his big frame would be able to get past some of the trickier sections. "I thought the whole point of the stars was to *help* future Aisouri find this thing," he said to Nalia. "Seems to me like your ancestor was hoping to kill whoever came looking for the ring."

"Seems that way to me, too," she said. "Gods, I wish we could see the other side."

The light from their *chiaan* cast as many shadows as it banished, which made the rocks all the more menacing. No matter what, Malek would have to go through this thing the old-fashioned way, but the jinn would've been able to evanesce across if they could picture where they were going.

"I have a feeling this is going to be unpleasant," Anso muttered.

Nobody moved.

Malek clapped his hands. "No time like the present."

He stepped past the group of reluctant jinn and strode into the forest of rock. His heart beat just a little too fast—he couldn't die, of course, but Malek didn't relish the thought of one of those stalactites goring him.

He turned. "Coming?" he said to no one in particular. He caught Zanari's eye and she looked away.

I shouldn't have saved her, he thought. After he'd hypersuaded away her scorpion illusion, Zanari hadn't so much as thanked him. *Since you used your power to try to kill me, I'd say we're even,* she'd said. All Malek had done was make sure there was one more person to fight him when it came time to get the ring. Weak—that was what he was. All Nalia had to do was threaten to never forgive him and he'd come crawling after her.

Malek turned and strode past the trunks of rock that rose

from the cave's floor, ignoring the fear that clawed his insides. Samar and Noqril assumed their *fawzel* forms and floated in the air above Malek, skirting the stalactites high above his head. The others followed, *chiaan* bouncing in the air, lighting their way. The rocks looked eerie in the jinn's light, as though they were traipsing through the skeleton of a primordial beast.

A *whoosh.*

Cold air slicing just past his head.

Then rock, biting into the ground from above.

He looked up just in time to dodge the needle point of a falling stalactite. The jinn screamed as the thin columns of rock became the jaws of a monster gnashing its teeth. Up, down, up, down. The cave floor tilted, forcing Malek to brace himself against the stalagmites on the ground. To his horror, he saw new rock pushing through the cave floor, breaking up what few pathways the deadly labyrinth contained. He hurled himself out of the way as a stalagmite's point burst from beneath his feet and pushed toward the cave's roof.

The jinn stumbled blindly though the gauntlet, narrowly avoiding the stone knives that moved in tandem all around them. He looked at the faces he could make out in the half light, searching for Nalia. He saw a flash of violet *chiaan*, just to his left. She was helping Phara, who'd fallen to the ground, turning the rock around her into dust. Nalia leaped aside as a falling stalactite carved a hole in the place where she'd been standing. She turned, as if sensing his gaze.

"Duck," she called.

"What?"

Nalia pointed to a spear of rock sailing through the air, not bothering to do more than that. He jumped to the side and it stabbed the ground. He looked toward Nalia, but she had already moved forward, darting around the gnashing teeth with graceful leaps.

It took the longest twenty minutes of Malek's life to get through the rest of the gauntlet unscathed. By the time he reached the other side, sweat was pouring off him and his arms were covered in scrapes from flying shards of rock. Phara attended to the jinn. Several had deep gashes in their skin or dust in their eyes. Once the last jinni stepped safely to the other side, the rocks closed like a clenched jaw, barring any attempt to go back the way they'd come.

Nalia ran her glowing hands over the walls, the ceiling, the floor. She shook her head. "I don't see it."

"I'd use my *voiqhif*," Zanari said, "but it doesn't seem to work in the cave."

This was news. Malek didn't know if that was a good or bad thing. He certainly would have liked to know what waited for them on Earth. He wondered if Calar knew what they were doing. She had to—no doubt she would have tortured it out of every jinni in that Dhoma camp by now.

They seemed to be at a dead end, nothing but a few feet of rock on all sides and a small pool of water lying in an alcove beneath a collection of tiny stalactites. It reminded Malek of the architectural models he'd once inspected for a hotel he owned in Dubai. The pool spanned several feet, but the space between the water and the shelf of rock above it was hardly large enough for someone to sit beneath.

"Magnificent," Malek whispered as he drew nearer to the pool. It was a large, shallow puddle, accumulated over thousands of years through the constant drip of water from the sweating rocks above it. The water was so pure that the surface of the pool perfectly reflected the stalactites so that it seemed as though the daggerlike rocks were in the pool, rather than above it. A mirror image so real it was hard to believe it was simply a trick of the light, an optical illusion.

"*Oh*," Nalia breathed as she drew near the water. She stared at it, transfixed. He moved the flashlight's beam slowly over the pool, then stopped at the cluster in its center.

"Nalia," he said. "Look."

The stalactites formed a perfect, eight-pointed star.

"We found it," Nalia called over her shoulder as she pulled her dagger from its sheath and crawled into the shallow water.

"Watch your head, *hayati*," Malek said as he angled the flashlight so that she could see the stars better.

Nalia sliced her palm and smeared thick, red drops of blood over the symbol. Without warning, the bottom of the pond gave way and Nalia shrieked as she fell through the stone. Seconds later, there was a splash far below them. Malek moved forward, hesitant, unsure what the wisest course of action would be. Raif charged past him and dove headfirst through the hole.

There was a shout and then a peal of laughter. Nalia's laughter. Malek suddenly realized he'd never heard her laugh. Not once in all the years they'd been together.

"Raif? Are you okay?" Zanari called, leaning over the hole.

Malek couldn't help but notice Raif's sister didn't seem concerned about Nalia. He'd noticed the slights since their time in the Dhoma camp and wondered if Nalia had, too. Didn't Zanari know that she was only alive because Nalia had fought for her? If it hadn't been for Nalia, Malek would have happily let the jinni suffer Haraja's madness.

"Well?" Malek yelled into the hole, impatient. "What do you see?"

Zanari ignored him as she beamed her hand into the darkness. In the jade light of her *chiaan*, Malek could make out Raif and Nalia treading water in what looked like an underground lake.

"We're fine," Raif called. His voice echoed. "I hope you all know how to swim."

32

ZANARI TWISTED HER BRAIDS INTO A CROWN AROUND her head, then lay back against the water, floating. The water was cold, but it numbed her skin and, best of all, there weren't any scorpions. She stared at the slabs of rock that covered the ceiling and walls of the cavern. This rock was different from the other caverns, a luminescent silver that shimmered whenever she swept her *chiaan* across it. The sounds of the jinn's voices echoed in the cave as they searched for bottles on the lake's bed. The desert water was salty, wonderful for floating, but terrible for diving. In order to reach the lake's floor, they'd had to tie weights to their ankles. It was slow, exhausting work, and Zanari was giving herself a much needed break.

Not one bottle had been found, and the joy of possibility was quickly turning to surly frustration.

A beam of golden *chaan* moved toward her and Zanari pushed herself into a standing position, treading water. Phara.

"Come with me," she whispered, grabbing Zanari's hand.

Phara led her around a tiny bend in the lake, out of sight of the others. The clear turquoise water was shallow here and Zanari's bare feet touched down on the soft mud. She sighed as her body connected to the earth. She could never get enough of her element's energy.

"How are you?" Phara asked.

"After nearly being cut in half by a thousand rocks, I'd say I'm doing pretty well."

"You know what I'm talking about," Phara said quietly. "No more . . . scorpions?"

Zanari shook her head. "No, thank the gods." She hesitated, not even sure she wanted the answer to the question sitting on her tongue. "It won't come back, will it—the hallucination or whatever was happening to me?"

"I hope not. Anso seems to think you'll be fine. She said she couldn't detect any disease inside you."

It'd been horrible, what Haraja had done to her. Zanari could still feel the sting of the scorpions, still hear their claws cutting at the air as they tried to gain purchase on her skin. Phara reached out a tentative hand, then traced Zanari's jaw. Zanari opened like a flower under the healer's light, delicate touch. Her eyes filled with tears and Phara leaned in and brushed them away, her touch like butterfly's wings.

"It's over," she murmured. "You're okay."

Zanari shook her head. "It's . . . not that," she said.

"What?"

"I've been fighting for most of my life." She looked up at the glittering ceiling. Waited for the tears to stop before continuing. Zanari wasn't used to confessional conversations or having someone other than her brother give a damn about what she had to say. "I grew up in a war zone. I'm surrounded by soldiers every minute of every day. But being with you . . . you're like the first deep breath I've gotten to take in a long time." She looked down, guilty. "The scorpions . . . they were kind of it for me, you know? I just can't take any more. Part of me doesn't want to go back to Arjinna." She took in a shuddering breath. "Like, a big part. Does that make me a horrible person?"

Phara shook her head. "No, of course not. You could never be a horrible person." She ran her fingers down Zanari's arms, then gripped her hands. Zanari shivered as Phara's *chiaan* melded with her own. Again, there was that inexplicable sense of tranquility. "We're not meant to live like this—fighting, running, hiding." Phara brought her lips close to Zanari's. "*This* is what we're meant for."

Kissing Phara was like running through the fields in spring, barefoot, with the sun playing on her face. Zanari's *chiaan* was melting, singing, dancing, and it felt so good to finally be *wanted*. It was temporary, she knew. When they got out of that cave, Zanari would go back to Arjinna and Phara would stay on Earth. The thought threatened to crush her.

All the more reason to make it count. She pressed closer to Phara, her thoughts falling away as the healer's *chiaan* took over.

Later, when they returned to the beach, Noqril looked up from where he was roasting fish. A sly grin spread across his face.

"Ladies," he said, with a pointed look at Zanari's messy hair.

Zanari threw him a contemptuous glance before joining her brother by the fire. He sat by himself, a short distance from the glum Dhoma who spoke in quiet voices.

"What's next?" she asked, falling down to the sand beside him.

"After we eat and take a bit of a rest, we'll follow that tributary," Raif said, pointing to where the lake became a fast moving river.

Zanari could hear the distant roar of rapids.

"We're swimming it?" she asked, beaming her *chiaan* in the direction Raif had pointed. The shore stopped a few feet before where the lake disappeared inside a tunnel.

"Got to. See what's over the arch?"

A large star had been carved into the silver rock just above the tunnel.

"Not to mention that it's more water—there could be bottles down there," he added.

The water in this cavern was one thing—it was calm and Zanari could see the bottom when she lit the surface with her *chiaan*. But trying to navigate violent water with unknown depths in a pitch-black cave?

"Perhaps there's an alternate route?" she said.

Raif laughed. "Not even if you could wish for it, sister."

Phara frowned at the water as she settled down beside Zanari.

"Is it possible the *pardjinn* is wrong? Maybe the bottles aren't in the water, after all. They could be hidden anywhere."

Zanari glanced at where the slaver stood removed from the others, gazing at Nalia as she helped Noqril prepare the fish.

"His guess is as good as any," Zanari said. "Besides, I haven't seen any other particularly good hiding spots."

The Dhoma had said there would be upward of two thousand jinn trapped in the cave. So where were they?

"No matter where the bottles are hidden, we're all in this together if the only way to open the bottles is with the ring," Raif said. "I can't believe how long this is taking. By the time we get the sigil, the godsdamned war will be over."

Zanari rubbed his back. "You're doing the best you can, little brother."

He was right, though; she didn't think the *tavrai* would be able to hold out against an Ifrit offensive indefinitely. Their mother, Zanari knew, was worried sick—about them and about the prospects for the revolution. But there was nothing to be done for it.

"Samar has agreed to help me take Malek down," Raif said quietly. "When the time is right."

"How?" she said.

"We have an invisible jinni, a disease maker, two *fawzel*, and one of the strongest jinn on Earth," Phara said, nodding over at Umbek. "The Dhoma can handle one *pardjinn*."

"But you're forgetting something," Zanari said. She jutted her chin toward Nalia. "Her."

"I don't understand," Phara said. "We're on *her* side."

"Anyone who tries to interfere with Nalia's ability to grant

Malek's wish will feel the full might of Ghan Aisouri power," Zanari said. "She'll have no choice but to do whatever it takes to keep him protected."

"Zan's right," Raif said. "We wouldn't stand a chance. Which is why we're waiting to make our move. Nalia only agreed to take Malek to the *location* of the sigil. After that, she's on our side." Raif leaned back on his hands, his eyes flicking to Nalia. "You saw what happened on the dune. She's more than capable of handling Malek."

"She's pretty good at killing people, too," Zanari said, her voice sharp. She glanced at Raif. "Or have you forgotten?"

"Zanari," he said quietly, "not now."

"When's a good time to talk about this, then? Because it's like you've *forgotten*—"

"Zanari." Raif glared at her, his eyes flashing. "Drop. It."

"Better come get your grub," Noqril called. "Couple more minutes on the fire and these fish will be black as Calar's heart."

Raif swept past Zanari and she stared at the lake, fuming. Phara placed her hand on Zanari's shoulder. "It does no good, you know."

"What?"

Zanari threw a rock at the lake's surface. She watched as the ripples moved further and further toward the water's edge. It was like the Ghan Aisouri. All the pain in her life seemed to stem from that one point.

"Holding on to the hurt." Phara glanced at Nalia. "Her heart is pure, Zan. What she did for you—"

"Did for me? What are you talking about?"

Phara's eyes widened. "I thought Raif told you."

Zanari shook her head.

"Malek required . . . payment from Nalia. He wouldn't hyper-suade you otherwise."

Zanari's stomach turned. "What kind of payment?"

"He made her kiss him—*really* kiss him—in front of Raif. In front of everyone."

"Gods, he's despicable." It could have been worse, she knew, but Zanari had to admit that she hadn't done much to make Nalia want to help her. "That was . . . kind of her." She frowned. "Still doesn't mean I want her anywhere near my brother."

"Would you deny Raif the one happiness he has?"

"*Happiness*? All Nalia's done since she's met him is put his life in danger and break his heart!"

"I suspect you're oversimplifying," Phara said.

It didn't matter that Nalia had told Raif to leave LA and go to the cave without her. How she'd practically begged Zanari to get Raif out of Marrakech. Yes, she'd wanted him to survive and had been willing to face Haran and the entire Ifrit army on her own. But her brother never listened to Nalia. That was the problem. Even when Nalia was good to Raif, she was bad for him.

"She's not one of us," Zanari said, stubborn.

Phara pressed her lips to Zanari's hair, then stood. "Neither am I."

"I didn't mean—"

But Phara was already walking toward the fire.

If Papa could see us now, she thought. Raif, in love with a Ghan Aisouri, and Zanari kissing a Dhoma in secluded lagoons.

If they made it back to Arjinna alive, the Djan'Urbi kids would have a lot of explaining to do.

Nalia stood by the arch bearing the third star. They couldn't put it off any longer. It was time to see what new horrors awaited them. Noqril whistled as he peered into the tunnel's gaping mouth. "Can't say I'm looking forward to that."

"Maybe the Marid and I should go ahead and check it out?" Nalia suggested. Samar and Umbek were the only other jinn in the group who wouldn't be harmed by rapids or unexpected whirlpools.

"I go where Samar goes," Noqril said.

Anso stepped forward. "As do I. We should not separate. It may be far too easy to never find our way out again."

"As you wish," Nalia said.

She beamed her *chiaan* into the darkened entrance. All she could see was more tunnel, more water. Black rock, black water. Gods knew what was beneath its surface. She hoped Haraja couldn't swim.

Nalia threw a silent prayer to Lathor, then pushed into the tunnel. The water moved swiftly, pulling her body down a serpentine path. Below her, she could see Samar and Umbek's bright blue *chiaan* searching the water for more brass bottles. There was the faint crimson glow of Noqril's *chiaan*, the Djan emerald of Raif and Zanari, the gold of Phara and Anso. Malek floated in the middle, surrounded by the light he couldn't produce.

Their *chiaan* did little to dispel the darkness, but Nalia savored the water's cool energy as it seeped into her. The gauntlet had been exhausting, terrifying. This was almost fun, the water pulling them along faster than they ever could have walked. Yes, she could do this for a few hours. This was her very own Lethe.

Until the water turned on them.

There was a rumble, slow at first and then a deafening roar. It took Nalia a moment, but then she suddenly realized what it was: the cavern behind them was closing, pushing them faster toward the rapids she could hear further down the river. The tunnel echoed with the panicked screams of the jinn, the darkness overtaking them as they lost their connection to their *chiaan*.

"Marid!" Nalia yelled, "grab hold of someone!"

Umbek and Samar cut through the water, their sapphire light blazing as they sped toward the flailing limbs of their companions. Nalia swept her *chiaan* over the water's surface, searching for Raif. She caught him several feet away from her, struggling against the water's power. Nalia screamed his name, but he couldn't hear her, not over the deafening roar of the rapids.

She started toward him but the water smacked her against the tunnel wall, and bright pinpricks of light flashed across her vision as her head hit the rock. Nalia pushed under the water, letting the rapids rumble over her until her *chiaan* swept away the pain in her head. It was tempting to lose herself in the folds of cool liquid, but she couldn't dissolve into the river, not now, not if she was going to help anyone. Nalia flooded the water with violet light. No Raif. She caught Malek, struggling underwater, the current pulling him down. She shot toward him and wrapped her hands around his waist, hauling him to the surface. He gasped and spluttered.

"Thank—" he started, but she was already swimming away.

He wasn't the one she wanted to save.

Nalia tried to calm the water, to tame it, but she was too disoriented, everything moving too fast from behind, the water angry and charging and hungry. The roar she'd thought were rapids grew louder and Nalia steeled herself, waiting for the chaos, but when her *chiaan* lit up the tunnel, her stomach lurched.

Oh gods.

A waterfall.

"Raif!" she screamed. "Zanari!"

No answer. Just screams that suddenly fell away as the jinn tumbled over the ledge, and the sound of water pummeling rock and flesh.

Louder, louder, no time.

Nalia dissolved into the water just as the river pitched her into the falls. She was the water, a cascade, shredded ribbons and spray and power. If she could just stay here, falling forever . . .

She was the foam at the bottom of the falls now, light as air, then she burst through the rolling water, back in her body. The black surface of the lake they'd been thrown into glittered with the light of the jinn's *chiaan*. Emerald—just one.

Just one.

Was it Raif or Zanari? A whistle pierced the din of the waterfall: two high tones, one low. A second later an answering whistle came. She remembered Zanari doing that in Marrakech, when they'd lost track of Raif in the medina.

Alive—they were both alive.

"Nal?" a voice called out to her. *Raif.* Where was he? Nalia could barely hear him over the roar of the falls.

"I'm here," she said, her voice breaking as she finally saw him across the lake.

He started moving toward her, then jumped and began kicking frantically at the water. Nalia swam toward him with fast, sure strokes.

"Something grabbed my leg," he said, when she reached him.

"What was it?"

"I couldn't see, but I swear to the gods it was a hand or . . . something."

Nalia's blood went cold. "A fish. I'm sure it was just a fish."

There was a shout at the other end of the cavern and a burst of blue light. "The bottles!" Samar crowed in delight. "They're here!"

Raif jumped again, pointing his *chiaan* into the water. "There!"

Nalia shone her light into the blackness below her. All she could make out was the end of a thick fishtail. She opened her mouth to say as much to Raif, when the entire cavern echoed with a hideous screeching, like a choir of bats.

Raif immediately relaxed and a soft smile played on his face.

"Gods, that's lovely."

"Lovely?"

He nodded. "Like a dream." He pushed toward the rock in the center of the lake, quick and purposeful. Nalia pressed her hands against her ears and whirled around.

"Fire and blood, what in all hells is that?" Zanari yelled over the din.

First Raif, then Samar, Umbek, Malek, and Noqril swam toward the rock, their eyes glazed and faces plastered with dazed smiles. Nalia had never seen Malek so happy—he was positively radiant. There was a splash to Nalia's right and she turned, defensive, her hands brimming with *chiaan*.

Nothing.

Then a body rose out of the water near the rock. It appeared human, its naked back turned, the spine curving beneath wet skin. She could just make out the shimmer of fleshy scales below its waist. The creature slowly turned around. Nalia's breath caught, her eyes riveted to the horror. A feminine torso rose to a long, sinuous neck and bald head that glowed like the surface of the moon. Its flesh was so pale it was nearly translucent and it shimmered in the flickering light of Nalia's violet *chiaan*. Above the naked torso and large, pear-shaped breasts was a face like a ravaged clown. The lips cut into the skin in a permanent, crazed smile from ear to ear, revealing the jagged teeth of a shark set in double rows along the top and bottom of the mouth. Red capillaries snaked past the lips, as though the creature had just feasted on raw, bloody flesh. But the eyes were what made Nalia go cold: a soft doe brown, beautiful except for a wicked, intelligent gleam.

Phara, Anso, and Zanari's expressions mirrored Nalia's own: sudden understanding coupled with horror.

"*Si'lah!*" Anso screamed. Sirens that feasted on the flesh of male prey.

Nalia shot toward Raif, infusing the water around him with her *chiaan*. A *si'lah* was cutting through the lake toward him, fast and sleek. Nalia was only a few feet away when her body crumpled in pain. The wish had other plans for her.

Malek. The wish would make her save him first, the magic somehow sensing he was in danger. Zanari hurtled through the water toward her brother while Nalia changed direction, to where Malek trod water, entranced by another of the hideous creatures. It beckoned to him with a webbed hand. The *si'lah* reached out a long, spindly arm but Nalia crashed into Malek, pushing him off course. The creature couldn't kill Nalia's former master—the amulet protected him from that—but she would render him unrecognizable.

"Stop!" Malek thrashed against her and the *si'lah* hissed at Nalia, its mouth opening and closing like a fish.

The creature lunged itself at her, and Nalia let go of Malek just as the *si'lah*'s tail smacked into her skull. Nalia slammed into the dark lake, the light around her dimming as she struggled to remain conscious. She sank into the water like a stone, and her *chiaan* shifted, allowing her Marid side to take over so that she could breathe. The darkness under the surface began to glow with an eerie red light, like plumes of blood. The *si'lah* glided toward her with astounding speed, its spiked tail slicing through the water. Nalia kicked toward the surface, but the weeds at the bottom of the lake shot toward her and began curling around her wrists and ankles, binding her to the muddy floor.

This was how the *si'lahs* killed their victims, drowning them before they feasted. Nalia willed her body to dissolve into the water. Seconds later, she was a jinni-shaped current, no longer flesh. The *si'lah* keened, an underwater cry of rage. Nalia pushed at the creature, spinning it into confusion. Its webbed hands grasped at the parts of Nalia it could sense, but they could gain no purchase. Nalia swam faster, an outline in the water, nothing more. When she neared the sharp rocks that surrounded the cave, her body took on its usual form. The *si'lah* reached for her and Nalia threw herself onto the rocky shore, grabbing the webbed hands and pulling with all her strength. The fish flapped against the rock, desperate to return to the water. Nalia thrust her knee against the *si'lah*'s breastbone, and dug her fingernails into its cold flesh.

She held on, her muscles straining against the creature's powerful tail, which reared back and slammed into her, again and again, nearly knocking her unconscious once more. The cavern filled with the shouts of the other female jinn as they grappled with their own *si'lahs*, and Nalia spared a quick glance to her left, her eyes searching for Raif. He was alone, treading water, bemused. Zanari had her arms around his attacker's neck and they thrashed about, wrestling in the dark lake. Nalia had to hurry; Zanari wasn't a Marid, she wouldn't be able to survive the *si'lah*'s attempts to drown her.

Webbed hands reached for her throat, cutting off her air, and Nalia choked as the *si'lah* gasped her own death rattle, the gills in her neck finally closing. The light in the brown eyes dimmed and the webbed hands fell from Nalia's neck. The *si'lah*'s dead eyes stared at the cavern's roof. Nalia sank against the rock, breathing hard.

A strangled cry in the center of the lake sent Nalia back into the water. She dove deep, to where a *si'lah* had dragged Zanari toward the sandy floor. Raif's sister struggled, her mouth open, her movements slowing as the oxygen left her body.

Nalia grabbed the *si'lah's* neck and squeezed. Instantly, it let go of Zanari and Nalia threw it against a rock jutting from the lake bed. She closed her eyes and made sure fish met rock, over and over, until there was no more struggle.

Nalia let go and pushed through the crimson water, grabbing Raif's sister before she shot to the surface. The cave no longer echoed with the sound of *si'lahs*, and the men were coming out of their daze, shouting to one another. She lay Zanari onto the flat edge of the rock in the center of the water. Zanari's lips were blue, her skin as pale as sugarberries.

There was no time. Nalia leaned down and breathed into Raif's sister, filling her with air and *chiaan*.

"Please," Nalia cried, when she felt the jinni's cold skin and the stillness of her chest.

It was no longer Zanari below her but Bashil. Her brother bleeding, his eyes terrified, the breath leaving him in agonized gasps.

"Please don't die, don't die," she sobbed. "Phara!" she screamed.

The healer looked up from where he crouched over Umbek. Blood poured from a gash in his neck. Raif was on the beach with the other males, his head in his hands. At Nalia's scream, he looked up and charged back into the water.

No time. No time.

Chiaan and air and pressing against Zanari's chest. Again,

again, again. She felt Zanari flicker to life. Her eyelids fluttered.

Chiaan and air and *chiaan* and air and—

Zanari coughed, spewing water.

Nalia cried out, her words a tangle of every curse word she knew in Kada and Arabic. She helped Zanari sit up, holding her as she regained her breath. Zanari heaved, gasping for air. She looked at Nalia, her eyes wide, terrified.

"You're okay now," Nalia said.

Raif slid onto the rock and as soon as he got to Zanari's side, Nalia transferred her to his arms.

Raif cradled his sister, his eyes full of worry. When her breathing became normal, he helped her settle against the rock. "Bet you wish you'd gone through the portal when I told you to, huh?" he said.

Zanari laughed weakly. "Don't be so smug, you little *skag.*"

He laughed and they spoke in quiet murmurs. Nalia looked away, her hand immediately straying to the zippered pocket where she kept Bashil's worry stone. She pressed her thumb against it, imagining his little fingers holding it in the prison camp.

Seeing Raif and Zanari ripped open the hole in her chest. Killing things was so much easier. She wanted to do more of that. Zanari reached out and gripped Nalia's hand. She looked up, startled.

"Thank you, sister," Zanari said.

Sister.

Nalia nodded. "Of course."

The adrenaline of the fight and the love between the Djan'Urbis was threatening to overwhelm her. She moved to stand, but

Zanari held on. "All that stuff I said . . . and you still saved me?"

Raif's eyebrows drew together and he watched them, silent. She knew Zanari would explain if she wanted to.

Nalia smiled, soft. "At the palace, I was taught how to save lives as much as I was taught to take them. The only difference now is that I can choose to save who I want. Your life will always be worth saving to me, Zanari. Always."

Nalia squeezed Zanari's hand, then left to join the others on the shore.

UMBEK WAS DEAD.

Raif stared at the Marid's massive body where it lay on the beach beside the roaring fire that would consume it. The lake glimmered with shards of tangerine flame. Umbek's face was frozen in a grimace of pain, but the Dhoma had covered the horrible gash from the teeth of the *si'lah* that had killed him and surrounded his body with shells taken from the lake's beach.

The ceremony was short. The words of the dead were chanted as the flesh burned in smokeless fire. Nalia stared at the flames with haunted eyes and Raif thought guiltily of how he'd been absent when she'd sent Bashil to the godlands. Her shoulders slumped and her body seemed to cave in on itself. Her lips formed her brother's name.

Raif moved quietly toward her, and Nalia didn't flinch or

push him away when he stood behind her and gently took her hands. She leaned against him and Raif wondered if she could feel his heartbeat speed up as their *chiaan* connected. She flowed into him and he into her and he relished this hard-won intimacy, this breath of her soul inside him. They stood like that for the rest of the ceremony, his lips whispering words of comfort in her ear.

When the fire went out, she held his hand to her cheek for a moment, then let go. He watched her as she walked to the shore to join Samar, now the only Marid in their group. The *si'lahs* were dead, but the bottles they'd been protecting littered the lake's floor. In the light of the jinn's *chiaan*, they glimmered like nuggets of gold. Nalia had been pressed into service, as the job was too big for Samar alone. She waded into the water, then disappeared under its surface.

Zanari came to stand beside him. "I'm sorry, little brother."

"For what?"

"For being such a *skag* about Nalia." Zanari looked up at him, contrite. "She saved my life. Twice. Both our lives, really. Phara says I have to let it go. What she did, I don't know if I can, but . . . I want to. I'll try, anyway."

He sighed. "Zan. I haven't forgotten what she did to Kir. And I don't want to dishonor his memory. But I know Nalia's heart. I truly believe she'd been forced to kill him." He ran a hand through his hair. It was growing long, falling past his ears, and there was dark stubble on his face. "I love her, Zan. I've tried not to, you know I have. But I do."

Love is a weakness.

"I know. I'm just scared," she whispered. "When we get home, you have a revolution to lead, soldiers who are looking to you to keep them alive. But I feel like . . . the whole world could explode, and you with it, but as long as Nalia was okay, you wouldn't care." Zanari glanced at him, her jade eyes dark. "And I'm not up for burning my brother's body anytime soon."

He wanted to deny it, had to deny it. Couldn't. Instead, he pulled her toward the fish that Noqril was roasting in a fire pit. "Glad you're still here, Zan. Don't know what I'd do without you."

"Don't forget that."

He glanced at her, confused. "How could I?"

"I'm a good fighter, Raif. And with my *voiqhif*, I'm more valuable than any of your *tavrai*, and yet you shut me out of every fight."

"Zan, you're a great soldier, I agree. I'm just . . . I'm trying to keep you safe. When I go on raids, I never know who's coming home, who's going to make it out alive."

She ruffled his hair. "I'm just saying . . . when we get home, I don't want to be on the sidelines anymore. The *tavrai* chose you to lead, I get that. But the blood of Dthar Djan'Urbi runs in my veins just as much as yours."

"Wait . . . Are you saying you wish our roles were reversed?"

Because he'd be more than happy to hand over the reins. The thought surprised him, but it was true. Raif felt done and he'd hardly even started.

Zanari looked toward the lake. Nalia was dragging a net filled with bottles to the shore and Anso was running out to help her.

"I don't know." She shook her head. "No. But you made Shirin your second."

"Aw, Zan. She's my second because she's one of the best fighters I've ever met. And the guys are scared shitless of her. Me too, if you want to know the truth."

Shirin. That was going to be a complication when he got home. He wondered what Nalia would think of her, this jinni who'd been by his side day and night, helping him plan his war for years. He had a feeling the two of them wouldn't hit it off; his second was ruthless and crass, the opposite of Nalia in so many ways. He wasn't worried about jealousy. Shirin would get over him, and quick. Probably already had—she'd think Raif had lost his edge and that would be enough to curdle her affection for him. He'd be lucky if he didn't have a mutiny on his hands.

"I agree that Shirin is a good choice for a second. But she doesn't watch your back enough. She's as crazy as you are out there when you're fighting," Zanari said. "Things can't be the same when we go home. I feel like everything's changed. Don't you?"

He watched Nalia dive back into the water, her limbs becoming translucent. "Yeah." He raised his eyebrows. "Speaking of changes . . . you and Phara, huh?"

Zanari blushed. "Yeah. Maybe. I don't know." She laughed, shaking her head a little. "The world goes quiet when she's around, you know? Like I can just . . . breathe. For once."

"That's nice."

"Yeah. But it can't last."

"Why not?"

"She's Dhoma. I'm Arjinnan."

Raif nodded. "I think that's what the humans call a long-distance relationship. Doesn't sound very fun."

"Not so much." Zanari hit his hip with hers. "The *tavrai* are going to have a fit when we come home and they see you with a Ghan Aisouri."

She was trying to keep the worry out of her voice, Raif knew, but he could hear it anyway. *Fit* was an understatement.

He groaned. "Fire and blood."

"Literally."

He laughed, though it wasn't at all funny. "You know what we need right now? A bottle of *savri*—or at least something that tastes like it."

"You manifesting?" He nodded and she smiled. "Then lead the way, little brother."

They walked through the cave for several days without seeing a single star. As the days dragged on, Raif could feel his anxiety grow. Each time they finally made camp for the night meant another day in Arjinna that the *tavrai* had been slaughtered by the Ifrit. And though there'd been no sign of Haraja since that first night, Raif knew it was only a matter of time before the monster struck. He often felt a presence in that darkness, menacing and hungry.

"She's somewhere in here," Samar warned. "She's just biding her time."

This made sleep nearly impossible. They slept in shifts, but because of Haraja's unique ability to paralyze her victims, there was no telling how successful a guard would be. Noqril and Nalia were two of their strongest jinn, and Haraja had managed to paralyze both of them on that first night in the City of Brass.

The underground labyrinth seemed to go on and on, with no end. As their party moved through the cave, the rocks behind them fell, making retracing their steps an impossibility. There was only one way out and if they didn't find it, they would remain trapped beneath the Sahara until they died.

The one bright spot on the journey was that every time they reached a body of water, they found more brass bottles, the metal somehow protected from the effects of the salt water. They gleamed as if they'd just been fashioned, Solomon's seal glittering over the opening. Each of the jinn carried dozens in small packs Nalia had manifested so that their party went from seven to hundreds, nearly thousands. Now that they knew for certain that the sigil was needed to free the jinn inside the bottles, Raif felt a little more confident about his chances against Malek—and Nalia, if it came to that. If Malek got the sigil first, they'd all be as trapped as the Dhoma's ancestors. Failing to get the ring in his hand wasn't an option.

The air turned cold the deeper they went into the cave, and the jinn manifested thick coats made of sheep's wool. The only reason Nalia manifested one for Malek was because his constant complaints about the cold had become unbearable. When they spoke, their breath hung in the air, like white evanescence. The Dhoma were miserable. Though the Sahara could get quite cold at night, it was nothing like the deep arctic chill that lived in the cave. And still, no star.

Raif lost track of time. He wasn't sure how long they'd been in the cave and, without the aid of the sun, it was impossible to know how much time had passed. There was no day and night; they stopped when they were too exhausted to go on, sleeping as little as possible. Just when Raif was on the verge of despair, convinced he would never go home and that entering this cave was the biggest mistake of his life, he saw the star.

He'd been lobbing a ball of *chiaan* up and down, bored out of his mind, and as he glanced up to catch it, Raif noticed a strange grouping of stalactites. He fell back, curious. They stood suspended over the cave floor, the rock dripping toward him like candle wax. The stone was different, too—a deep red that stood out from the marble of the dark tunnel. Raif lay on the ground, reaching both his hands toward the stalactites. They glowed with the emerald light of his *chiaan*.

"Little brother," Zanari called, "I hate to say it, but it's not nap time yet."

He laughed, triumphant. "I found it!" The group rushed to him, hope on their faces for the first time in days. "You have to lie down to see it," he said.

"Good eye," Nalia said as she stared at the eight-pointed star on the ceiling. "Give me a boost?"

"Nothing else I'd rather do." He gave her a wicked grin. She bit back a smile. Nalia was still keeping her distance, but it was as he suspected: she just needed time. More and more he'd noticed her watching him and finding excuses to be near.

It was the same ritual, her blood and the star opening onto yet another cavern. A blast of frigid air greeted them, far colder than what they'd been walking through for days, and a steep slope made of ice was all he could see of the entrance. The jinn stared, but Malek stepped forward.

"Manifest shoes with metal spikes at the bottom and walking sticks," he said. "It's what humans use in conditions like this."

He was right. The shoes enabled them to move up the perilous slope. Eventually it evened out to a plateau that overlooked a glacial cave, all ice and water.

"I wonder what we'll see next: the Abominable Snowman?" Malek said, frowning at the scene before them.

"The what?" Raif said.

Nalia smiled. "Human thing. A snow monster."

When they settled down to sleep that night in a cavern coated entirely with ice, Raif risked lying beside Nalia. They'd manifested platforms to sleep on, but it was still freezing. Fires were no good: they only caused the ice to melt and drip all over them.

"Raif . . ." she whispered, her tone admonishing, but weak. Little by little he was wearing down her resolve to keep him at arm's length.

"I won't touch you, I promise," he said. He turned so that his back was to her and smiled at her answering sigh of frustration. He envied Zanari and Phara, curled against one another under the same thick blanket.

Raif had just drifted off to sleep when the screaming started. He sat up, disoriented, and reached for Nalia,

"Phara," she said, already wide awake. He wondered if she'd been able to sleep at all. She grabbed her jade dagger and ran to where the healer lay on the ground, pushing at the air. Her breath came out in ragged gasps, as though she were being suffocated.

Zanari was shouting for help, her hands moving helplessly over Phara's writhing form. The other jinn spread out, their eyes peeled for Haraja. There was no doubt she was behind this. Raif scoured the cavern, but there was no sign of the monster, just Anso and Samar lying paralyzed on the floor, where they'd been on watch.

Raif crossed to where Malek calmly lay under a pile of furs. He reached under the blankets and hauled him to his feet by his shirtfront.

"Help her, you bastard," Raif growled.

"Not the most diplomatic, are we?" Malek pushed Raif off him with surprising force.

Raif pointed to Phara. "Do you not see how much pain she's in?"

Malek's eyes slid slowly to where Phara was covering her face and choking. Suddenly, Nalia was beside them.

"What do you want this time, Malek?" she asked, her voice cold.

His eyes flicked to her. "Nothing."

Malek moved past them, toward Phara. Raif sighed. "I can't get a read on this guy."

"He's insane," Nalia said. "That's all you need to know."

Malek was kneeling on the floor. "This only works if she opens her eyes," he was telling Zanari. "And I need to know what she thinks is happening."

Zanari nodded, her hands shaking as she tried to hold down Phara's body. "Phara, tell me what's wrong. Please," she begged.

Raif felt a pang of recognition at Zanari's panic. He was the same when Nalia was in danger.

"Can't breathe, pressing . . ." Phara was wheezing, clutching at her neck.

"I'm here, Phara, I'm here." Zanari's voice broke. "Open your eyes."

But Phara wouldn't. She squeezed her eyes shut tight and her body began to convulse, her breath stopping altogether. Malek drew back a hand and slapped Phara across the face. Zanari shouted, but Phara's eyes snapped open.

"Look at me," Malek said, his tone of voice suddenly soft and coaxing. His eyes turned crimson and the pupils dilated, pulsing like coals.

Phara stared into them, her eyes glazing over as she took one long, hard-fought breath.

"You can breathe," he said. "You are not suffocating. You had a bad dream and now you're going to wake up. Wake up."

Phara shuddered and her eyes cleared. She looked around, confused. She saw Zanari and immediately relaxed.

"Haraja?" Phara asked in a quiet voice.

Zanari nodded as she stroked Phara's long, dark hair. "Yeah. You're okay now."

Phara took a deep breath and exhaled. She took another, then another.

Malek stood, waving away Phara's thanks. He walked out of the ice cavern they'd chosen to sleep in without another word.

Nalia touched Raif's arm.

"I'm going to talk to him," she said.

His jaw twitched, the jealousy returning. Malek's ability to persuade extended far beyond his dark power, Raif knew that. "Don't forget what he is just because he did one nice thing—which I had to force him to do, by the way."

She rolled her eyes. "Raif, I'm just trying to find a way to get through this cave. What happens if Haraja attacks you next? I need to know he'll help you."

A sad smile played on Raif's lips. *"Rohifsa,* he'd never help me. You know that."

"If I asked him . . ."

Malek would do almost anything for Nalia, but he wanted that ring more than her good opinion.

Raif shook his head. "Never gonna happen." He leaned down and kissed her forehead before she had a chance to pull away. "Good luck, anyway."

IT WAS EASY TO FIND MALEK. NALIA JUST HAD TO FOL-
low the scent of his clove cigarette. He stood near a towering
blue-green glacier, resting a hand against the ice. Pensive.

"Thank you for what you did in there," she said.

He turned, then blew a lungful of smoke away from her face.

"I did it for you."

"I know," she said softly.

Malek threw his cigarette down, grinding it underfoot as he
rubbed his temples. Nalia remembered how every fireplace in his
mansion had blazed, even during the hot Los Angeles summers.
The cold must have been driving him mad.

"Are you unwell?" she asked.

"I'm fine," he said.

"Your eye twitches when you lie."

The corner of his mouth turned up. Though he was a *pard-jinn*, Malek still had to replenish his *chiaan* after hypersuasion. Nalia reached out a hand.

"Give me your lighter."

She brought the flame to the palm of her hand and as her *chiaan* latched onto it, the fire spiked, its warmth filling her. Malek hesitated for a moment, then rested his bare hand on the flame. He sighed, as though he were having his first sip of a long-awaited glass of absinthe.

Nalia pushed the fire onto his palm, their hands briefly grazing. His eyes met hers and she turned away. She pressed her hands against the ice to extinguish her flame.

"You don't have to be a slave to your Ifrit side," she said as Malek stared at the flame in his hand. "Why don't you try doing things because they're the right thing to do? Because they're good. Gods, Malek, the things you could do with your gift!"

"Gift." He snorted. "Curse, you mean."

"No. *Gift.* Imagine. Convincing a would-be murderer to lay down his weapon. Telling a tyrant to give up his power. You'd have just as much control of the world. You'd just be running it differently."

His eyes fastened on hers, flickering in and out with tongues of flame. This was the battle he fought within himself all day, every day. She knew that now.

"It must be exhausting," she continued. "Fighting the darkness in you." For the first time, she was realizing the strain Malek was under. How hard it was for him to keep the rage of the fire inside him at bay.

"What do you know of it?" he said, bitter.

"Because that darkness is inside me, too."

How many times had she wanted to hurt, to kill, to lash out in anger? How many times had the darkness in Malek pulled her to him, despite her hatred and disgust of the *pardjinn* who'd bought her?

He stared at her. "So I wasn't imagining it—our connection?"

"I don't love you, Malek," she said.

"But you've *wanted* me." His eyes gleamed. "That's a start."

She shook her head. "No."

"Yes," he said gently. He drew closer and she felt the pull, hated it. He was the dark corner at an illicit gathering, honey on the tip of her tongue, a wild call in the middle of the night. If she gave in, he would obliterate her. For one brief, terrible moment, she wondered what it would be like to accept his poisoned love.

"We have all the time in the world to build on this, *hayati*. With the ring, you can rule by my side, we——"

She stumbled back, before he could touch her. Before she could feel that heat on her skin.

"Stop it," she hissed. "I'm not something you can claim. I am a living, breathing, feeling *person*. Yes, some sick part of me reacts to you in ways I hate. But that jinni in there?" She pointed to the cavern. "When he touches me, I feel whole. I've never wanted someone so much in my life. Do you see the difference? I would kill you the first chance I get and *die for Raif* the second he needed me to. You are *nothing* to me but a wishmaker who has made my life hell."

Hurt lashed across his face. "Spare me your high and mighty speeches, Nalia. You're not telling me anything I don't already know."

"Obviously this whole conversation was a mistake," she said. "I came out here because I saw what you did with Phara and it made me think that if someone just saw the good in you—"

Malek laughed, his face cruel and hard. "The *good in me?* You beautiful little fool. You want to know how good I am?" His eyes were fully crimson now and he slowly unbuttoned his shirt.

"You're not my master anymore," she said, staring at the deliberate way his fingers slid the buttons out of their holes. Violet *chiaan* spilled from her fingertips. "Touch me and you'll wish to the gods you hadn't."

He pulled the shirt off, silent. Draega's Amulet gleamed on his bronze chest, a complex series of knots seared into his skin.

"Ask me what I gave for this."

Nalia went cold, not sure she wanted to know anymore. Malek's eyes sparked.

"Ask me!" he shouted.

"What did you give in exchange for the amulet?"

The air was heavy, weighted down by their past.

"My brother." As soon as Malek said the words his shoulders sagged and the light went out of his eyes. "I gave the gods Amir." Nalia blinked. It took a moment for his words to make sense, to tear wider the hole Bashil's loss had ripped in her heart.

Malek raised his chin as understanding dawned in her eyes. "Don't ever make the mistake of thinking I'm good," he said. Nalia threw her hands against Malek's chest, her palms burning with *chiaan*, pummeling the amulet, trying to rip out his heart. He kept his arms at his sides, welcoming her rage.

"How *could you*?" she screamed. "He was your brother! Your godsdamned brother! He had a wife, *a son*."

The cave echoed with her cries and she hated him hated him hated him. Nalia aimed a barrage of *chiaan* at Malek, but her hands were shaking so much that it flew over his head and hit the glacier behind him. It burst apart, throwing shards of ice everywhere. She didn't move, didn't flinch as needle-sharp slivers of ice cut into her skin, grazed her face. Then there were strong hands on her arms and Zanari was pulling her away.

"Sister, I want to kill him as much as you do, but you know you can't. Come on. Don't waste your breath."

"Your *brother*," Nalia screamed as Zanari dragged her to the other end of the cave. Her voice ricocheted off the rock, but he was silent, watching her. "You piece of shit!"

And then she was sobbing because he'd killed *her* brother, too. By buying Nalia, by not setting her free.

"I could have saved him," she cried. "But you wouldn't set me free. And now he's dead, he's dead and never coming back, you bastard."

Something in her snapped and her hands flew toward Malek, her fingers like claws. Her *chiaan* landed square on his chest and Malek's body flew up and hit the icy ceiling with a sickening crack before falling face first into the frigid water between floating chunks of ice. She stared at his unmoving form, spent.

Nalia swayed, suddenly dizzy. The wish didn't like *that*. She gasped as that age-old summoning pain cut into her and then she was laughing and she couldn't stop *oh gods wasn't it so fucked up wasn't it so fucked up?*

There were murmured voices behind her and then there was Raif and she was in his arms. He carried her back to the cavern without a backward glance, then held her against him as she plummeted into sleep, clutching Bashil's worry stone to her heart.

THE ICE INSIDE MALEK WAS CRACKING. THE TERRIFYING emptiness he'd carried with him for three years threatened to obliterate him. For the first time in decades he considered death a happy alternative to his existence.

He followed the jinn, hardly aware of the jagged spikes of ice that jutted out of the cave's floor like oversized crystals. They cut across the paths that wove between looming glaciers, hopping from one island of ice to the next, then pushing through tunnels of snow. Bend. Duck. Bend. Crawl. He did it all, but he wasn't there, not really. The decades of his life were visiting him, an endless stream of ghosts. He ran his fingers along the smooth ice walls that swelled over the rock. Remembering.

Amir stands in the middle of the ice hotel, his eyes wide.

"How is this even possible without jinn magic?" he says.

"Pretty magnificent, isn't it?" Malek smiles, a little smug.

"It is. Thank you, brother."

"It's our birthday," Malek says. "Have to do something out of the ordinary to celebrate."

Amir hands him an envelope. "Happy birthday."

Malek takes it. "A gift card?" He smirks. "You shouldn't have."

"Shut up and open it."

He slides a thin finger underneath the seal and takes out the blurry image. He stares at the tiny figure in its center. He can make out the head, the body curled into itself. Malek's hand shakes just a little. It means more than he thought it would.

Amir claps a hand on his shoulder. "Ready to be an uncle?"

Malek waited until the jinn were a good distance away, then ducked behind a glacier and gave in to the silent sob that had been building within him. He shut off his flashlight and let the cave consume him as he slid to the ground, his body shaking, and drew his knees to his forehead. The tears froze before they had a chance to fall down his cheeks. If he loosened his arms right now, he'd shatter into a million pieces, shards of ice the others could crush under their feet.

It was goddamn terrible timing to start feeling again. First Nalia, now Amir.

I'm sabotaging myself. If he didn't keep it together, the sigil was as good as Raif's.

"Malek!" Raif, close by. Emerald *chiaan* danced along the

frozen walls. "Where in all hells are you?"

He heard the crunch of Raif's boots on the icy floor and his muttered curses.

Malek hurriedly wiped his eyes, then shot up, drawing the old Malek around him, hiding. "Can't a man have a moment to himself?" he snapped as he stepped into Raif's line of sight.

"No," Raif said, already turning around. "Let's go."

Malek could kill him. Right now, with no one else around. He gripped the flashlight in his hand. One good blow to the back of the head was all it would really take.

Amir's voice, then Nalia's: *Why do you do this?*

He hesitated, then gripped the flashlight harder. Before Malek could move, a burst of *chiaan* sent him flying back. Raif stood over him, his hands glowing.

"The thing about being evil, Malek, is that you lose the element of surprise," he said, grabbing the flashlight from where it had fallen to the floor. "I can play dirty, too, you know." He began walking away, leaving Malek alone in the darkness.

Malek groaned as he sat up. "Enjoy living while you can," he said. "Because I promise you, I won't be keeping you around once I have the ring." Even to his own ears, the words felt hollow, rote.

"You're delusional." Raif stopped and turned around. His eyes were hard, belying his youth. "This is what will happen: I will get the ring because I'm a jinni and you are not. Because nobody here is on your side. It's a pity I can't kill you, but I almost like it that way. While you're here on Earth, with nothing left to live for, Nalia and I will be in Arjinna. We will grow old together. We will never speak of you. To her, you will be nothing more than the scars around her wrist and a bad taste in her mouth."

"A nice fairy tale, boy." A small, cold smile played on Malek's lips. "But that's all it is—a fantasy. Even if you get the sigil, you'll never grow old. Fearless heroes of doomed revolutions rarely do."

Malek brushed past Raif before the boy could see the terror that had taken hold of him at the thought of never seeing Nalia again. Malek wondered if he could bear it. He'd rather her scorn, her hatred, than nothing.

"Why's the sigil so important to you?" Raif called. His *chiaan* lit the path the others had taken, a bright, springtime green that clashed with the frozen wasteland the cave had become.

Malek stopped. He hadn't been expecting that. Saranya's words came to him, just as damning as they'd been the first time she'd said them: *Did it ever occur to you, Malek, that you can live forever and yet you have nothing to live for?*

"Because it's all that's left."

The look on his father's face as the bastard died—that was what Malek had to look forward to. He'd summon the jinni that had ruined his mother's life, that had created a monster like Malek. He'd inform his father that he would be stoned to death, just as the men in Malek's family had threatened to do to Malek's mother when she had two children out of wedlock.

He didn't wait to hear what Raif said. He stalked through the frozen tunnel, dimly lit by Raif's *chiaan* as the boy followed, to where the other jinn stood near Nalia on the bank of a frozen lake. She looked up as Malek neared, but his eyes slid away before they could meet hers. One look at Nalia would shatter him. He was far too unhinged now, unsure of what he'd do next. Cry like a child, no doubt. The tears had burned.

"How many more bottles are we looking for?" Zanari asked no one in particular.

"We have eighteen hundred and fifty," Anso said. "And we know for a fact that two thousand jinn disappeared after the City of Brass was built."

"Are you ready?" Samar asked Nalia, coming to stand beside her.

"Yes," she said.

Nalia knelt next to the lake and set her hand against the thick slab of ice that covered the water. It cracked in two almost immediately, creating a large entrance to the dark, frigid world below. She stood and glanced at Samar.

"I'm not looking forward to this," Samar said.

She grimaced. "Nor I."

Nalia handed her coat to Zanari and stepped to the edge of the hole. Malek had seen the Marid gather the bottles several times now, but it never ceased to amaze him how their forms could become water and yet, when they stepped out of the lakes, they'd be fully clothed and not one hair on their head would be wet. He supposed it was similar to the magic of evanescence.

Samar gestured to Nalia with a grin. "Ladies first."

She rolled her eyes and jumped in, letting out a very un-Nalia-like screech as her body hit the water. She disappeared under the surface and, seconds later, her head popped up.

"Fire and blood," she said, gasping. She picked up a wayward chunk of ice and threw it out of the hole. "Get your ass in here, brother."

Zanari laughed. "Boy am I glad to be a Djan right about now." Samar closed his eyes and jumped. Several expletives passed through his lips before he remained under the surface long enough to gather bottles.

Every few minutes one of them would come to the surface and deposit bottles onto the ice, then slip back into the arctic water. The others counted them before placing the vessels safely in the bags they all carried. It was nearly two hours before Nalia and Samar were through.

"Zanari, can you manifest us some tea?" Nalia asked.

"I'm on it, sister," Zanari said.

Nalia's lips were blue and she'd barely got the words past her chattering teeth. It was hard not to go to her, give her the Ifrit heat that lived inside him. Malek doubted very much that Nalia would ever suffer his touch again and so he stayed where he was, on the outskirts of the group.

Raif manifested a thick blanket and wrapped it around Nalia's shoulders. She clutched at it with a murmured thanks, but deftly dodged his arms. Malek wondered what that was about, but only dimly. He'd forfeited the game: even if he had the sigil, Nalia would never be his. In fact, he'd order her as far away from him as possible.

"Two thousand!" Anso yelled.

Nalia clutched her cup of tea. "We got all of them?"

Anso nodded, beaming. "I doubt there are any more, but we should still keep an eye out, just in case."

The Dhoma whooped and hollered, sounding out a tribal cry. They embraced one another and Noqril grabbed Nalia, spinning her around. Her tea flew out of her hand, but she threw back her head and laughed. Somehow, their victory had become hers, as well.

Malek turned and walked away from the celebration. He fished a headlamp out of the small rucksack he'd brought into the cave with him and walked until he could no longer hear their joy. This was his place, hugging the shadows, making the next move. The ice rippled overhead, as though he were just beneath the surface of a frozen sea. White turned to blue, then green. Mesmerizing.

There was a fork in the path.

Two roads diverged in a wood . . .

Short, dark tunnels and, he quickly realized, dead ends, both of them. Except. He drew closer to the wall at the end of the tunnel on his right. The rock jutted out of it, like thick, knotty pieces of coral, each knot twisting to a point. Eight points. He took another look at the peach rock, then stepped back to confirm what he had seen.

The sixth star.

Raif passed through the entrance at the end of the tunnel where Malek had found the star. His whole body was numb with cold after days in the ice cavern and he sighed gratefully as the temperature warmed considerably.

"Six down, two to go," Zanari said. "Almost there, little brother. Almost there."

He nodded. "We can't find that godsdamned ring soon enough." What was happening in Arjinna? He wished he could contact his mother, but *hahm'alah* didn't work in the cave. Of course. Antharoe wouldn't have wanted anyone outside to know how to get in. *Hold on. Just a little longer.* Maybe if he thought the words hard enough, his *tavrai* would feel them.

As soon as the last jinni stepped through the passageway, the cave crumbled behind them and the ice disappeared. Raif looked at the rock formation before him, groaning.

"We'll never find this next star," he muttered.

It was like being in the middle of a beehive. The cavern they were now in branched out into countless passages in all directions, each one accessible through a small arch. The arches were layered so that from the floor to the cave's roof, it seemed as though there were hundreds of windows looking down at them. He craned his neck. He could scarcely see the stalactites that hung from above.

For the next several hours, the cavern was full of multicolored strands of evanescence as the jinn flitted from one cavern entrance to the next, marking each one they checked with pieces of glowing chalk. Some were no deeper than a few feet, only big enough for a child to lie down in. Others were entrances to long tunnels that led to dead ends or starless caverns. There were nearly a thousand arches to explore in all and it was slow, mind-numbing work.

Raif kicked at the wall of one particularly frustrating passage, cursing. He heard a low chuckle nearby. Raif whirled around, the hair on his neck standing on end. *Haraja.*

"Throwing a tantrum, brother?" said a familiar voice.

Raif let out a breath. "Noqril. Has anyone ever told you it's unspeakably rude to be invisible without giving fair warning?"

"Yes." Noqril's form materialized before him. "But warning people takes all the fun out of it." The Ifrit leaned against the wall, grinning. "Besides, you wouldn't want me to tell Malek of my impending invisibility when the time comes to help you get the sigil, now would you?"

"Not unless you want him to put that ring on and make you his slave," Raif said.

Noqril followed Raif back to the main cavern. "I don't understand what you're so worried about. Between me and the other Dhoma, the *pardjinn* doesn't stand a chance."

"Let's just say he has an uncanny way of getting what he wants," Raif said.

When he emerged in the airy central cavern, most of the others had given up their searching as well.

"We'll look no more today," Samar manifested a bottle of wine and held it up with a flourish. "We need to celebrate recovering all the bottles. It's not *savri*, but—"

"—it'll do," finished Anso. The common refrain among jinn.

"I like the way you think, brother," Raif said.

Noqril manifested a campfire with his Ifrit energy while the others set about preparing food. Malek sat outside the warmth of the circle, lying on his back and gazing into the darkness of the cavern's ceiling. Raif wondered what the *pardjinn* was plotting. Two more stars. Raif would find out soon enough.

Nalia was still combing through the tunnels, but she joined

the group once the jinn were settled around the fire and the bottle was making its rounds. There was an empty space beside him, but she chose to sit as far away as possible, on the other side of the fire. Raif knew Nalia would come back to him when she was ready. He would wait as long as it took, hundreds of years if need be.

But it was hard.

He caught her watching him from across the dancing flames. He smiled a little and she bit her lip and looked away. He took a large swig from the bottle before passing it on.

As the night wore on, Raif felt himself becoming more withdrawn, brooding as he stared at the flames. *You'll never grow old,* Malek had said. *Fearless heroes of doomed revolutions rarely do.*

Raif felt the truth of those words, much as he didn't want to. He'd fight like hell to stay alive as long as he could, but Raif couldn't guarantee a future with Nalia. Even if he got the sigil, it didn't make him invincible. There were far too many jinn who wanted to see him dead. And if he put that ring on, it'd be a different kind of death. Nalia might not ever forgive him for it. And Raif wasn't sure he'd be able to forgive himself. Could he bind every jinni in Arjinna to his will, even if it was for the greater good?

Noqril manifested a *zhifir*, a traditional jinn instrument that sounded like a cross between a violin and sitar. The sound it made as he played was rich and mournful, a beautiful rush of sound that Raif never would have thought the vexing Ifrit capable of.

The song was familiar, an ancient melody known to all jinn. It was home wrapped in weeping notes. Each time Noqril swept the bow across the strings, the responding note seemed to draw deep from the well of longing within Raif. He had been gone too long from Arjinna. He wanted a glimpse of the dawn sun glinting off the snow-capped tops of the Qaf Mountains and to bathe in the moonlight of the Three Widows. Yet without Nalia, it'd be meaningless. Without the ring, it'd be impossible.

Samar turned to Raif. "Why do you fight, Raif Djan'Urbi?"

The question caught him off guard. He should have an answer—a good one. The right one. But nothing came to his lips.

"I don't know anymore," he said, surprised.

Nalia stood and moved away from the fire, slipping into one of the long tunnel passages. Raif's eyes followed her.

"That," Samar said, pointing to Nalia, "is what you fight for. Caring for your realm, your people—that will only get you so far. Victory comes when you fight to save the ones you love. You will stop at nothing for them. It's a good strategy, no?"

Raif remembered the last conversation he'd had with Dthar Djan'Urbi, on the sand dunes beside the Arjinnan Sea the day before his father died. For all his powerful rhetoric and the fierceness with which he fought in battle, Raif's father had said he fought because he wanted his family to be free, because he could no longer bear seeing Shaitan overlords whip and demean his wife and children. His father hadn't died for the revolution—he'd died for his family. And lived for them. Nalia was wrong: Love wasn't a weakness. It was love that had given the serfs a voice for the first time in thousands of years. It was love that had returned their dignity.

Raif clapped Samar on the back. "Thank you, brother."

"I'm just telling you what I see."

As Raif moved toward the tunnel Nalia had disappeared into, he could hear Noqril begin a new song, a field worker's tune Raif knew by heart. He remembered singing it as a little boy, when he was still a serf who'd had to labor on his overlord's land. He could see the scarred backs of the male jinn, shirtless and dripping with sweat as they swung their scythes. He whispered the words as his pace quickened.

I love you as the earth loves rain
Without you I will die

THE TUNNEL WAS A WIDE-OPEN MOUTH AND NALIA LET it swallow her.

The darkness was a comfort and a shield. Here, no one would see what she knew must be written so plainly on her face: she'd never wanted anyone or anything more than Raif Djan'Urbi. When he looked at her, she lost all sense of herself, of time and space and everything under the sun because he *was* her sun. The only light in her life, the only thing that could fight the endless night inside her.

Nalia stayed in the darkness just inside the tunnel, listening, but Noqril's next song had only made the feeling building inside her worse. It was a favorite of hers, one that caused her *chiaan* to rush faster through her veins. She remembered late summer nights sitting on her balcony, when everyone in the palace was asleep except for the servants. In the heat of an Arjinnan midnight, they would convene in the garden, playing music and singing in soft, rich voices. This song, and others. How many hours had she spent in the bottle, humming that very tune? Sometimes, it was the only thing that kept her sane.

The last notes of the song faded as Nalia moved deeper into the tunnel. It was too much, this sudden longing for home that filled her, this need for Raif and Arjinna, as though the two were somehow one and the same.

She kept reaching for the fury, the desire to kill Calar, because the ache in her hurt less when she thought about the vengeance due her. But the rage wasn't there like she thought it would be. Revenge is what she wanted, what Bashil deserved. And yet all Nalia felt was an overwhelming grief: for Bashil, for the land, for all the people of Arjinna, and for the slaves on the dark caravan.

In the darkness of the tunnel, in that place without light or hope, Nalia realized that she didn't want to fight. She wanted to build. To plant and grow and nurture. She wanted long, uneventful days. She wanted time. But to get any of those things, she'd have to fight and fight hard.

And she wasn't sure how much fight was left in her.

So she walked. As far away as she could, as fast as she could. Nalia didn't know where she was going, didn't care. All she knew was that she couldn't sit across the fire from Raif any longer or hear songs that made her blood cry with homesickness.

Raif. Oh gods, Raif.

She was so close to giving in to him. And she couldn't.

What the two of you have—it's reckless.

This was a fact. Irrefutable.

But he wasn't making it easy. Every chance he got, Raif reminded her in some way that she was never far from his mind—a whispered kindness, a light touch on her arm, eyes that never looked away. Nalia's fingertips slid along the rough rock and her mind conjured his laborer's hands, how they were surprisingly gentle when he touched her and how his *chiaan* whispered to her own.

Reckless.

Hadn't she been reckless when she set Calar free in the palace dungeon all those years ago? Reckless mercy turned into the ruin of her realm.

Nalia's hand fell from the rock. These thoughts were pointless, little tortures she came to again and again. Nalia didn't deserve Raif, not after what she'd done to Kir. Not after her very existence had snuffed out Bashil's short life.

She pushed on through the darkness, as though physical distance from Raif could somehow erase him, little by little, from her heart. Up ahead, the tunnel widened and as she rounded a corner, she stopped, her breath catching as a faint aquamarine glow emanated from further along the passage. She curled her fingers into her palms, extinguishing her *chiaan*, then she slid her dagger into her hand and crept closer, hugging the wall. Her skin prickled as she imagined stumbling into Haraja's lair or some other as yet unseen monster.

The light pulsed, growing brighter the closer she got. Now Nalia could see that the tunnel opened up into a small cavern.

She raised a hand, ready to beam her *chiaan* at anything that came toward her. She pointed her dagger outward, and its jade tip caught the light. Then she lunged forward.

Nalia gasped, her hands falling to her sides, any thought of foes completely forgotten in the face of the incandescent beauty before her. The entire ceiling and walls of the cavern were covered with glowworms, thousands of them. They looked like sea-green fireflies or the phosphorescence that floated in the Pacific at night. A small pool of water took up most of the cavern, reflecting the ethereal light of the creatures. The water was pristine, so clear that she could see the pool's sandstone bottom. A low, rocky ledge covered with thick tufts of moss ringed the pool. It glimmered, verdant.

This was a place the gods had touched.

Nalia kicked off her thick hiking boots and pulled off her socks. She stepped onto the moss and let the soft cloud of vegetation caress her tired feet. The energy of the plants and stone grounded her, as though Earth were holding her in the palm of its hand.

"If you had three wishes, what would you choose?"

She turned, startled. Raif stood a few feet away, leaning against the rocky wall of the cavern's entrance. She didn't know how long he'd been standing there.

"I've never thought about it," she said, recovering. She looked away from him, her heart pressing, pressing, bursting. It wanted free. As though it knew it belonged in his hands.

Nalia dipped a toe in the water. It was warm, like a bath. "Everything I would wish for is impossible—the dead to come back to life, the coup to never have happened. For Malek to know nothing of the sigil." She sighed. "Wishes are for humans."

"Then what is left for the jinn?"

Nalia gazed at the glowworms' impossible beauty. "Hope," she whispered, turning to him.

He smiled, a secret hiding somewhere inside him. "Hope," he repeated. "And what are your three hopes?" he asked.

"For the war to end. For Calar to die. For . . ." Her eyes slid to his, purple to green, heart to heart. "For you."

Raif walked toward her, slowly. "That would be a waste of a third hope. I'm already yours."

He placed his hands on her arms and drew her to him. Nalia's body obeyed, even though her mind screamed at it to stop.

Selfish, reckless, selfish selfish selfish.

"Nalia, I know you think by keeping me away that you're somehow protecting me or punishing yourself or saving the realm. But when we're not together, when things are unwell between us . . . I'm lost. Utterly. It's all I can think about, all I care about. That's no way to command soldiers and win a revolution. You have to agree, it's not a very good strategy."

"Then I'm a distraction, something that keeps you from—"

"That's not at all what I'm saying and you know it."

The cave's glow licked his skin and she wanted to taste him, to feel the salty sizzle of Raif's *chiaan* against her tongue.

Nalia closed her eyes. Took a breath. "But what about Kir? How can you still want me after what I did? To everyone."

"Because you're a part of me." He ran a hand through her

short hair. "Because you were a child, forced to do a terrible thing." His fingers trailed across her jaw. "Because I love you."

"Raif . . ." Her voice, a weak protest. The only thing that made sense was the feel of his *chiaan* slipping into her, twisting with her own until there was no Nalia, no Raif. Only *Us. We. Our.*

"I want us to belong to each other," he said softly. "Not like you belonged to Malek—it doesn't have to be like that. You can belong to a person without them owning you. Does that make sense, *rohifsa?*"

The words were a final piece to a puzzle she'd been trying to put together all her life. *Belong.* Yes. She wanted to belong to him. And he to her.

Nalia fell into him, a wave crashing upon a shore. Raif pulled her down onto the thick carpet of moss, cradling her in his arms.

"Do you remember what I told you, in the glass house in Los Angeles?" he asked.

Malek's conservatory, the night she killed Haran. The night Raif had told Nalia he had to be with her. She blushed.

"Yes."

I intend on kissing every inch of you the first chance I get.

His hand reached for the zipper on her sweater. As he pulled it down, Raif gave a soft laugh. "This is a funny little human invention, isn't it?"

That was all it took to banish any lingering uncertainty inside her: Raif's laughter, the moment somehow more intimate than everything that had gone before it. Nalia reached for his shirt, her eyes on his.

Love was Raif's breath, hot against her skin. His fingers exploring, his lips burning, his tongue, tasting her, all of her.

Love was an explosion, falling up in an exhilarating burst, emerald and violet *chiaan* swirling around naked skin, moss against a bare back, and sweet, slick sweat.

Love was a gasp and a moan. It was an arched back and fingers gripping shoulders and a whispered *more more more.*

Love was a waking dream and truth.

It was freedom.

Raif held Nalia's hand as they floated in the pool beneath the glowworms. His body buzzed with the feel of her *chiaan* inside him. Every now and then she would look at him and smile and he wondered if it were possible to feel any happier without dying from it.

"I'm never leaving this cavern," he declared.

She laughed. "You'd miss the sun. And fresh air. And *widr* trees."

"Not as much as I'd miss this."

He hated that they'd have to go back.

"What about Zanari?" Nalia said.

"She can visit us when she wants to."

"Well, she might be busy with Phara . . ."

Raif smiled. "So you've noticed."

"*Everybody* has noticed. I think it's wonderful. Zanari deserves to be happy."

He nodded. "I've never seen Zan so relaxed. Keeps her off my back, too, which is nice."

Nalia gripped his arm. "*Raif.*"

"What, it's true. She's always nagging me about something—"

"No. *Look.*"

Her finger pointed above them, at the glowworms. The creatures were moving slowly and the light from their bodies swirled across the cavern's roof. Then they stopped.

They had assumed the shape of an eight-pointed star.

"How did Antharoe manage *that?*" he said. The seventh star—only one more to go.

"Beautiful magic." Nalia said, clearly delighted. "She must have spelled the whole cavern somehow."

"*Gods.*"

Nalia kissed his cheek and slipped out of the pool, her limbs graceful as ever. Even with the scar that began at her hip and ended at her belly button, a result of her brush with death while fighting Haran, she was perfect. Nalia caught him looking and blushed, but she didn't try to cover herself.

"We should tell the others about the star," she said.

"Mmmm," was all he said.

She raised an eyebrow. "You might want to get dressed before they come looking for us."

"Everyone's asleep by now. They won't be up for hours."

"Two of us disappear and no one's going to be worried?" she asked.

Raif sighed and swam a few lazy strokes toward the ledge,

then pulled himself up onto the moss. He leaned forward and kissed her collarbone. She caught his face in her hands and pressed her lips to his.

"I love you," she said. "No matter what happens."

The side of his mouth turned up. "That's foreboding."

"You know what I mean." Nalia craned her neck to look at the star above them. "I wonder how long they stay in their star form?"

She went quiet and he took her hand and squeezed it. "What's wrong?"

"It's stupid, really. It's just . . . my whole life I've looked up to Antharoe. The stories of her adventures, her strength in fighting, her magical abilities." She pointed to the ceiling. "I mean, how could she do this *and* kill all those people in the City of Brass?"

"I told you before, you're nothing like her, *rohifsa*, I promise." He kissed her forehead and drew her to his side. "Now, let's go tell everyone they don't need to look in any more of those gods-damned caverns."

They heard the screaming long before they reached the others. When they burst out of the tunnel, the first thing Raif saw was Malek. The *pardjinn* was clutching at his head and his cries were an anguished stream of Arabic.

"Haraja," Zanari said, when they ran up to her.

Nalia stared at her former master, a strangled gasp escaping her lips.

Raif felt no such horror. He fell to his knees and kissed the earth as he whispered a prayer of thanks to Tirgan, his patron god.

"Little brother," Zanari said, "are you thinking what I'm thinking?"

Raif nodded. "I could kiss Haraja right now."

"Well, I wouldn't go that far," she said.

Malek Alzahabi had been doomed to a lifetime of incurable madness. One that, because of his own greed, he would have to endure until the day he chose to take his own life. If the only cure for Haraja's madness was hypersuasion, then the *pardjinn* was screwed. He couldn't very well hypersuade himself.

Nalia gripped Phara's arm. "Do you have any idea what he thinks is happening?"

"He keeps screaming your name," she said. Nalia blanched.

Tears had begun streaming down Malek's face and Raif watched, disgusted. Furious. His own greatest fear was harm coming to Nalia and it seemed so wrong that he should share that with Malek.

Nalia moved toward Malek, but Raif grabbed her hand, stopping her. "Don't. He deserves this. Whatever Haraja has slipped into his mind . . . it doesn't begin to punish him for what he did to you."

"But he's so . . . so . . ." Nalia trembled.

"He put you in a bottle for months, Nal," Raif said. "He refused to free you, even when you told him about . . ."

But he wouldn't say Bashil's name. It would cut her open, hearing it said aloud.

Malek fell to his knees and began laughing hysterically. Phara rushed to him, her medical bag at hand. He looked up, his eyes clearing momentarily as he looked beyond Phara to where Nalia stood.

"*Hayati?*" he whispered, grabbing for her.

"Get off her, *skag*," Raif growled.

Malek didn't seem to hear him. He stared at Nalia and a look of pure horror spread across his face. He grabbed at the air with his hands, screaming Nalia's name again and again. Phara pulled a powder out of her bag and poured some onto her palm, then blew it in Malek's face. He swayed from left to right, then fell onto his back in a dead sleep. The cavern was silent, but Raif could still feel the echo of Malek's cries.

"You're too kind," Raif said to Phara.

She returned the powder to her bag. "I can't watch someone suffer."

Raif glanced at the jinn gathered around them. "Nalia and I found the next star. I know none of us will sleep tonight, but a little rest won't do us any harm. Should we stay here or press on?"

Samar frowned, considering. "I think it would be wise to rest. Everyone is tired from searching the caverns. If we do encounter Haraja again, I want to make sure we're strong enough to fight her. She's never attacked twice in one night."

With Haraja on the loose and the only cure for her madness currently incapacitated, sleep seemed like a death wish, but Raif nodded. It'd been a long day.

"All right," Raif said. "Everyone who can manage to stay awake, keep your eyes open."

The Dhoma nodded their assent and, after a few last backward glances toward Malek, returned to their makeshift beds.

Raif clapped Samar on the back. "You want first or second watch?" he asked.

"First," Samar said. "It'll be a while before sleep comes to me this night."

Raif nodded. "Wake me when it's my turn."

He left the Dhoma leader at his post and began setting up a pallet for him and Nalia near the fire, as far away as possible from Malek. Zanari gave him a curious look and when he smiled, his sister gave him a thumbs-up. Nalia was drinking a cup of wine, her hand shaking slightly. There was nothing he could say. Malek Alzahabi would never get his pity. And he certainly didn't deserve Nalia's.

Raif stole behind her and pressed his lips against her shoulder.

"C'mon. You need to rest."

He manifested several thick blankets and kicked off his shoes before crawling under them. Nalia set her jade dagger within reach before settling against him.

He pulled her close and whispered, "Just so you know, you're never sleeping alone again."

"What if I steal all the blankets?" she teased.

"Then I'll manifest more."

Across the cavern, Malek cried out. Nalia buried her head against Raif's chest and he wrapped his arms around her.

"Tell me our story again," she whispered.

"Our story?"

"When I was asleep for so long, you told me about our future. Tell me again."

He looked down at her. "You heard me?"

She nodded. "You brought me back again, I think."

"We'll always bring each other back," Raif said. He played

with the short strands of her hair as he spoke. "After the war is over," he began, "we'll have a house and some land. We'll make love in our field under the Three Widows, as much as we want, whenever we want. Our two children will look exactly like you . . ."

Soon, Nalia's breath became deep and even. He kept telling her their story. He would tell it to her until it was no longer a story. Raif could almost see the moonlight on her bare skin and smell the wildflowers that would grow around their home.

A SMALL PART OF MALEK WASN'T SURE IF WHAT WAS happening was really happening.

Every now and then, the prison cell would shiver and he'd see another place: the cave where he thought he'd been, Nalia's face, the Dhoma. But all of that would disappear in a second. A mirage. Maybe he'd dreamed it all—taking Nalia from this cell after Calar killed her brother, running with her through the streets of Marrakech, saving her life in the sandstorm.

Maybe *this*, right now, this horror movie, was reality.

"You thought you could get away from me so quickly?" Calar said.

She was not talking to Malek.

Nalia sat in an iron chair, her hands tied roughly to the chair's back. He could smell her flesh, slowly burning as it made contact with the metal. Nalia mumbled something, but Malek couldn't hear her.

Calar produced a whip and lashed Nalia across the chest and she cried out, an agonized growl.

"You'll kill her!" he screamed. Malek reached for the whip, but he couldn't move. It was as if he were encased in cement.

Calar glanced at him and her bloodred lips turned up. "That's the point."

She ran a finger along Nalia's cheek in mock tenderness. Nalia's hair was matted with blood and one side of her face was purple, nearly the same shade as her eyes. A red line had appeared over the chest of the thin chemise she was wearing.

"Please," Malek begged as blood began to drip from Nalia's lips. "I'll do anything. Anything, I swear, just let her go. Please."

"You have nothing to give me, *pardjinn*," Calar said.

"I do," he whispered. Some part of him had known it would always come to this. "I can give you the sigil. Solomon's sigil for Nalia's life."

The room disappeared. Then: a pair of jade eyes. Rock everywhere. An endless dark he couldn't see his way out of.

Zanari leaned closer to Malek.

"What's he saying?" she said to Noqril.

"Hell if I know." The jinni roughly set Malek down on the floor and poured a canteen of water over his face, then held it out to Nalia.

She touched her hand to a drop of water on the outer rim of the canteen, then held her finger over the opening. Her hand turned violet with *chiaan* and then a stream of water issued from her palm. As soon as the canteen bubbled over, she closed her fist. He began chugging the water.

"Noqril, I believe the words you're looking for are *thank you*," Zanari said.

Noqril grunted, then threw back his head and drank until the canteen was empty.

"What can you do?" Zanari said. "A brute is a brute."

Nalia smiled and, once again, Zanari felt grateful to no longer be consumed by that anger that had driven a wedge between them. Raif was right: Nalia's heart was good. How many people had Zanari been forced to kill? They were all victims of this endless war.

Malek's body suddenly became rigid and he jerked as though he were trying to free himself from imaginary bonds. His arms were flat at his sides, two wooden boards.

"I can give you the sigil," he gasped. "Solomon's sigil for Nalia's life."

Nalia stared at her former master, a hand over her lips.

"Phara, he's waking," Zanari called. She reached out and clasped Nalia's free hand. "Sister, it isn't real. None of it is."

"I know," Nalia said. "But whatever's happening to Malek must be excruciating. He'd never give up the sigil."

"Whatever's happening in his mind is happening to the *you* in his mind. He's fine." Zanari frowned. "As usual."

Malek's eyelids fluttered and Zanari got a glimpse of his onyx eyes just before Phara blew her powder in his face again. Immediately, he slumped back into a fitful sleep.

It had been a challenge getting Malek through the glowworm star in the roof of the cavern Nalia and Raif had discovered. They'd had to devise a pulley system to transport Malek's body, and then there had been a long walk down a tunnel black as coal. All the while Malek had screamed and thrashed.

"Gods, I hope we don't have to deal with this for too much longer," Zanari said.

"One more star." Nalia's voice betrayed her exhaustion. She wiped a hand over her face. It glistened with sweat. In the past few hours the tunnels had become unbearably hot, and steam floated along the passage, stifling them.

Phara hugged herself and worried lines cut into her face. Her eyes glazed over with a faraway look that Zanari had come to recognize. She knew Phara was thinking about her family and the other Dhoma outside the cave. It was so frustrating, not being able to use her *voiqhif*. If Antharoe hadn't spelled the cave, Zanari could have told Phara what had happened to the Dhoma they'd left behind in seconds.

Maybe it's better this way.

They'd entered the cave just as the Dhoma were being attacked by the Ifrit. Calar's army wasn't known for its mercy. Zanari had heard Phara and the other Dhoma listing all the possible outcomes of the attack, none of them very good. Zanari knew how distressed they were; it was what she and Raif had been living with since they'd abandoned the *tavrai* to come to Earth in search of the sigil.

Raif jogged over to them from the front of the column. "The tunnel opens up into a large cavern. I'm hoping we can rest there for the night. I'll take him if you want," he said to Noqril, nodding his head toward Malek.

"Fine by me." Noqril walked away, whistling a human song Zanari had heard in Marrakech.

Raif grunted as he picked up Malek and threw him unceremoniously over his shoulder.

"Bet you didn't know this was how you were going to fulfill Malek's wish, did you, sister?" Zanari said to Nalia.

Nalia shook her head. "Tell me about it."

They trudged through what remained of the dark tunnel, but the cavern proved to be even more miserable than the enclosed space they'd just come out of. It felt as if they'd hit a wall of solid heat.

The landscape of this cavern was nothing like the one that had come before it. It was a huge landmass, with what looked like a mountain on her left followed by a forest of stalagmites. The ceiling was impossibly high. So high that the cavern had its own weather system. Thick clouds masked the roof of the cave, which was at least a thousand feet above them. Gusts of wind whipped the air and whistled against the rock like a crazed banshee.

Raif was just leaning down to drop Malek on the ground when a low rumble began under their feet.

Zanari swayed and grabbed onto Phara. "What was *that*?"

"Fire and blood," Anso cursed as she pointed to the mountain Zanari had noticed when they'd entered the cavern. Only it wasn't a mountain.

Nalia threw her hands against the base of the volcano as the rumbling intensified. She looked at the jinn, her eyes filled with panic.

"Run!" she screamed.

The top of the volcano exploded, sending a geyser of crimson lava into the sky. Zanari was desperate to evanesce, but the smoke spilling from the volcano's top made it impossible to see even a few feet in front of her.

Nalia raised her hands above her and violet *chiaan* shot up to meet the lava just as it began its downward journey to the cave's floor.

"Nalia!" Raif yelled as the lava threatened to rain down on her. Malek fell from his shoulders, hitting the ground with a thud. The *pardjinn* groaned.

"Go, Raif. *Go*," Nalia yelled. She kicked her bag of brass bottles to him. "Keep the bottles from melting. *Go*."

"I'm not leaving without you," he said.

"Raif, she's part Ifrit—the fire can't hurt her," Zanari said. The roar of the erupting volcano was deafening. She grabbed Phara's hand and pulled the healer toward Raif. "Pick up the *pardjinn* and let's get out of here!"

"I can't hold it much longer," Nalia shouted. The lava was a slow-moving wave, hungry for the cave's floor and the jinn on it.

Noqril moved to help her, but Nalia shook her head. "It's too strong," she said. "Help the others—they'll need an Ifrit on hand."

He glanced at the volcano and then moved away. "I'll find a place for us to go."

Raif wavered and Zanari punched him in the arm, as hard

as she could. "If you don't move, this fire will kill you and you'll never see her again."

He nodded, once, and grabbed Malek. Nalia chanced a look at him. "I'll be okay."

Phara's hand trembled and Zanari turned to her. "Nalia will get us through this. She always does."

Zanari pulled Phara along, following Raif as he sprinted through the thick gray smoke. As they entered the stalagmite forest, the lava spilled down the face of the volcano and covered Nalia completely, Nalia flailed, her mouth open in a scream, and then she went under and didn't come up again. Zanari's heart stopped and she prayed to all the gods that Nalia knew what she was doing, that she'd be able to survive a lake of fire.

"Oh gods," Phara cried. "Is she . . . ?"

"I don't know," Zanari gasped. "We have to keep going." A molten river surged toward them with unbelievable speed.

Please gods, please gods . . .

They wove through the stalagmites, flying over the rock below their feet.

She could see Raif's back, not too far ahead of her. The other jinn were clustered on a high ledge just beyond where her brother ran for his life.

"We're almost there," Zanari cried. "We can evanesce!" Now that she had a destination, there was no need to run.

Phara tripped and Zanari felt a sharp tug on her arm and she heard, then felt, her shoulder joint pop as it got pulled out of its socket. They both screamed as Phara fell to the floor. The lava had become a rapids and it was only a few feet away. Phara motioned for Zanari to leave her.

"It's broken." She pointed to her ankle. "I can't—"

Zanari reached down and pulled Phara up with her good arm, screaming as white-hot pain ripped through her injured shoulder. Her arms shook, her legs were made of rubber, and the lava's spray singed the thin material of her shirt, peppering her back with burning arrows of fire. Zanari pushed on at a crawl and her muscles burned and she couldn't, no she *had to*—she stumbled forward and they crashed to the floor.

"Go, you stupid girl, go!" Phara was sobbing, but Zanari shook her head and wrapped her arms around the healer. She'd never make it.

We're going to die, she thought. Surprised. She'd really thought she had more time.

The lava was inches away now. She gripped Phara and they stared death in the face. Zanari blinked. It was looking right back at them. The lava seemed to stop, as though an arm were holding it back. Zanari's eyes widened as she made out the faintest hint of Nalia's features in the flames. Then Noqril and Raif were there, pulling Zanari and Phara into clouds of evanescence. Seconds later, they were standing on the ledge overlooking the lake, gripping one another as a heavy wind gusted past the rock face.

The part of the lava that was Nalia dove forward and all Zanari could see was a boiling river of fire blocking their only exit from the cavern.

Nalia was gone.

THE FIRE DIDN'T WANT HER TO GO.

Nalia struggled to pull herself out of the flames, but the lava held on to her like a long-lost lover, its heat so much more powerful than the oceans and lakes she had morphed into.

She wasn't sure she wanted to leave its burning embrace.

Nothing and no one could hurt her here. It felt good to give into the darkness, to the fury and rage that had been boiling within her all her life. *Yes*, the fire seemed to *say, you are home.*

Nalia's body licked up the sides of the cavern and she destroyed, burned, annihilated. After a lifetime of keeping her Ifrit nature in check, she gave into the gorging delight of destruction. She was heat and flame, she was the terror in the night.

But almost as quickly as she settled into this new sensation, the wish was upon her and her body writhed, an inferno of pain, fire lacerating every part of her until all she wanted was to get out, to grant and grant and grant.

The wish, the wish.

It didn't matter if Malek was out of his mind. She still had to grant his wish. The magic wouldn't let her get out of her obligation that easily. Nalia writhed in the wish's grasp over her *chiaan* as her body began to shift from flame to flesh. The force of the lava threw her onto a low rocky ledge then pooled below her in a shallow bed of rock, her bare skin resting in a molten puddle. The sides of the rock were just high enough to stop the lava's flow and it rushed by her, a river of fire.

Nalia glanced around in desperation for the others, but the smoke was too thick to see through. There were only the gray plumes of acrid air and the red glow of the burning lava below. Had she hurt any of them when the fire took over her body? She wondered if this was what it was like for Malek, trying to keep the siren song of the fire at bay. Nalia heard a shout, but it was lost in the din of the volcano's sporadic erruptions.

Raif.

He had to be alive, he *had* to. She reached up, pulling at the air until gusts of sulphuric wind swirled around her head like a lasso. She threw her arm across her body, tossing the wind so that it scattered the gray clouds of volcanic smoke. Not twenty feet in front her, she saw Raif standing on a ledge with the others. His hair was damp with sweat and his cheeks bright red. He was looking below him, his face full of worry.

Nalia cupped her hands around her mouth and shouted. "Raif."

He turned toward her, his face breaking out in a huge grin. Nalia closed her eyes, picturing the ledge. Her body curled into the cloud of violet, amber-scented evanescence that enveloped her. In seconds, she was standing beside him. Raif didn't say a word, just pulled her against him and hugged her so hard she thought he might break a rib.

"I'm okay," she whispered. He gripped her tighter.

"I'd really like to know if there's anything she *can't* do," Anso said, to no one in particular.

Nalia pulled away from Raif—she'd forgotten about the other jinn entirely. The cave offered no privacy. It was a wonder that she and Raif had found that glowworm cavern and that no one had come in search of them. It was likely the last chance they'd have for a while to be alone.

"Is everyone all right?" Nalia said.

Zanari nodded. "More or less."

Phara sat beside her, pale. "I'll be fine," she said, when Nalia looked at the bandage wrapped around her ankle. "With my tonics, this thing'll be good as new in a few hours."

"What now?" Samar asked.

"I say we build another *Sun Chaser*," Nalia said. "But this time, we'll call it the *Star Chaser*."

Just one more star to go. *Home*, Nalia thought. She was so close.

Samar nodded, his eyes on the lake of fire below. "Seems like sailing is the only way we'll get out of this cavern." He turned to the Ifrit beside him. "Noqril?"

With the help of the other jinn, Noqril and Samar manifested a sailboat big enough to fit all of them and spelled to withstand the lava's heat. It somewhat resembled the gondolas of Venice, where Nalia had once vacationed with Malek. Despite how temporary it would be, the boat was elegant: narrow enough to navigate the tiny canals between the stalagmites, with ornate prows in the front and back and a large, eight-pointed star etched into the boat's floor.

In seconds, they were aboard. Only Malek and Raif remained on the ledge. Nalia manifested a ladder and Raif threw Malek over his shoulder, then began his descent. As he drew closer, she could see his muscles straining as he gripped the rungs.

"You're almost there," she called.

At the sound of her voice, Malek's eyes fluttered open and he began to rave. His body thrashed and Raif cried out as his hand slipped on a rung. Malek fell off his shoulder and into the boat with a crash. Nalia rushed to him. A trickle of blood ran from a cut on his forehead, but he seemed otherwise uninjured.

Raif cursed as he leaped into the boat. "Godsdamn *par-djinn*."

"I could fry an egg on my ass it's so hot in here," Noqril said, as he took up the rower's position at the back of the boat. He held a long pole in his hands made of the same spelled material as the boat, and looked every bit the Venetian gondolier. "Let's get out of this sauna."

Nalia and Raif settled onto one of the cushioned benches Samar had manifested on the sides of the boat. She ran her hands over the miracle of his unburned skin, dripping with sweat from the cavern's heat.

Raif rested his forehead against hers. "I can't handle you

almost dying every day. Let's get the ring and go home. Sound like a plan?"

It would be just as easy for them to die on the battlefield, but Nalia decided not to point that out.

"Sounds like a great plan."

"Maybe I can find someone else to lead the revolution," he said. "It'll be hard to command from the bed we're never going to leave."

She knew he was only joking, but Nalia wished it could be true. "Is it silly to hope your story about us could happen?" she whispered.

It seemed unlikely that after the revolution, she and Raif could run off and live a quiet life in the Arjinnan countryside.

Raif opened his mouth to respond, but Malek suddenly began shouting again, his voice ragged. "The sigil," he cried. "Take it. Just . . . don't hurt her anymore. *Please*. I'm . . . begging you."

Nalia turned toward Malek. Would he really do that for her?

"Ignore him, *rohifsa*," Raif said as she watched Malek writhe on the floor of the boat.

But she couldn't. Because for once he was actually doing the right thing. Even though it wasn't real, *he* thought it was. At that moment, Malek was giving up everything for her.

But she was the only one who seemed to notice.

"Lover boy," Noqril called to Raif. "Your turn."

Raif brushed his thumb against the tip of his nose. Noqril smirked at the rude gesture and held out the pole.

While Raif navigated the twists and turns of the cavern,

Nalia kept an eye on Malek. It hurt her to see him suffer, and the hurting made her angry. He deserved this, didn't he? *He killed his own brother*, she thought. It didn't matter how many times Malek saved her life or told her he loved her. There was nothing he could possibly do that could make up for the wrong he'd brought into the lives of every person he'd touched.

And yet Nalia's hand reached out of its own accord and brushed Malek's blood-matted hair off his forehead. Malek sighed at her touch.

"*Hayati,*" he whispered.

She pulled her hand away. She'd never understand this connection to her former master. Even now, his *chiaan* pulled at her. It was confusing and a little sick-making.

"He was the first man who ever loved you. Or tried to, anyway," Raif said softly. She hadn't realized he was watching her.

She turned, stricken. "Raif—"

He shook his head. "I understand, Nal."

"*I* don't."

"I know you don't love him," Raif said. "But he saved your life more than once and that counts for something, I have *tavrai* I can't stand, but we've bled for each other and you never forget that."

Nalia rubbed her fingers over the scars on her wrists. If Raif could forgive her for killing his best friend, maybe she could begin to forgive Malek for what he'd done to her. Maybe. Forgiveness: it was the hardest thing in all the worlds.

Nalia reached down and gripped Malek's hand. She sent her

chiaan into his skin and he took a shuddering breath, then smiled softly before falling into a peaceful slumber.

It wasn't long before they were able to step out of the boat and onto dry land. The orange light from the lava pulsed against the cave walls. *One more star,* Nalia reminded herself. They were almost there. She scanned the rock, but there was no visible eighth star. She knew Antharoe wouldn't have made it that easy. The area was empty, save for eight tunnels leading away from the plateau where they'd docked the *Star Chaser.*

"Sometimes you just want to see a good old-fashioned street sign," Nalia said, frowning at the dark entrances to the tunnels. "I really miss GPS."

Raif looked at her. "What?"

"Human thing."

Noqril and Samar manifested a stretcher and laid Malek onto it. Anso stood near Phara and Zanari. All three of them looked exhausted as they stared at the tunnels, eyes dim.

Raif turned to Nalia. "Which one strikes your fancy?"

Eight dark arteries, each connected to the heart of their search.

Now that she was so close, Nalia found herself wanting time to stand still a little. She'd been so intent on finding the ring that she hadn't allowed herself to think about the vow to the gods she was breaking. How would they punish her this time? She reached inside her pocket, her thumb on Bashil's worry stone. Could she really do this? Wasn't death preferable to insulting the gods?

The wish took hold of her and Nalia gasped as needles of pain shot through her veins, stinging her blood. It seemed to know when her commitment to fulfilling the wish wavered.

Raif grabbed her before she could fall to the floor. "The wish?" he asked.

Nalia nodded and the pain subsided as she focused her intention back on retrieving the ring. "I'm about to offend the gods," she said. "Best keep your distance."

"That's like telling me not to breathe." He kissed her forehead. "I don't think they care what we do. I don't think they care at all."

Nalia placed her fingers on his lips. "Don't. Other than you . . . they're all I have."

He nodded. "Fair enough."

She pointed to the third tunnel. "This one. Three was Bashil's favorite number." She needed him now, his sense of adventure, that curiosity that never dimmed.

Raif took her hand. "Good choice."

Nalia could feel the peace that coursed through his *chiaan*. Now that Malek was in no state to fight him for the ring and they were nearly to its location, Raif was relaxed, hopeful. She hadn't realized how much tension he'd been holding inside him until some of it was gone.

Malek had begun to rave again and Phara hurried over to Nalia. "I don't have any more of that powder. I'm afraid we'll just have to . . . deal with him."

"It's okay," Nalia said. "He doesn't know what's happening, anyway."

They left the light of the lava's fire behind and forged through the darkness. The tunnel echoed with Malek's screams. He begged an invisible Calar for mercy. He told the Nalia in his vision to stay alive. The powder seemed to finally have left his system when he recognized Raif. Nalia was careful to stay in the shadows. She had no idea how Malek would react if he saw her.

"Raif! Where the devil have you been?" Malek snapped. "Calar has Nalia. There's no time to explain. We have to help her." He grabbed Raif's arm, shaking him. "Do you hear me? She's going to die!"

Raif pushed him off. "No she's not."

Malek swung at him, an off-center punch. Raif easily dodged aside.

"Calar's right over there!" Malek shouted, pointing at the wall next to him. "God, she's got a whip out now . . ." Malek's eyes widened and then he screamed.

Nalia quickened her pace. Her *chiaan* had begun reflecting off of bright stones just up ahead.

"Raif. I think we're nearly there," she said.

Raif turned to Samar and Noqril. "Keep a good hold on him."

Nalia stepped out of the tunnel onto a wide ledge. She threw her *chiaan* in the air so that a ball of violet light hovered above her, casting its glow over the whole cavern. They were in a circular chamber that climbed to dizzying heights, a stone cathedral made entirely of amethysts. The precious stones jutted out from the rock, various shades of purple mixed with clear white crystal. The royal jewel was a calling card—there was no doubt that this was Antharoe's work. The ledge Nalia was standing on encircled the whole cavern, a threshold for the entrances to the eight tunnels that presumably led back the way they had come.

Then Nalia looked down.

The center of the chamber was a chasm, so deep it seemed to lead to the center of the Earth. In the middle of the chasm, a single cone-shaped rock jutted up from the darkness below as though it were suspended in midair, an island with a flat top upon which a stone altar covered with markings sat. It was too far away for Nalia to make out the details, but as she cast her light further she could see that something lay on top of the altar: something small and golden. It seemed to catch and hold her *chiaan* as it hovered above it.

Solomon's sigil.

Behind her, one of the Dhoma whispered its Moroccan name, *"Khatem l-hekma."*

Raif stood beside her. *"Rohifsa,* I have a feeling it's not going to be as easy as evanescing over to that rock."

"I know. I just . . . gods . . . " Her eyes glistened. "After this, we can go home." With any luck, this endless journey would be over. *By this time tomorrow* . . . Was it possible? Could she be in Arjinna that soon?

"Yeah, but . . ." Raif's hands trembled a little and she could feel the agitation in his *chiaan,* irregular spikes of energy that flitted in the air around him. "Let's see what the cave's price is first, okay?" He was eyeing the ring warily, not with the satisfaction she'd expected.

Nalia smiled. "Don't tell me you've come all this way just to turn around."

As if on cue, there was the now familiar rumble of rock as the tunnels leading into the cavern collapsed. The sound of every exit being cut off had become all too familiar.

"Considering it's impossible to turn around in this place, no." Raif took her hands. "I just want you in one piece when this is all over."

Behind her, Noqril whistled. "Holy gods and monsters, it really *exists*." He stared at the altar in the center of the chasm. "Solomon's godsdamned sigil."

He and Samar each held one of Malek's arms. He'd become subdued almost as soon as they brought him into the cavern. Now he blinked, his eyes opening as though he'd just come out of a trance.

"What the fuck is going on?" he said. His voice was hoarse from all the hours of screaming.

Nalia turned. "Malek?"

His eyes were clear and there was no hint of the madness that had been lurking in them since Haraja had whispered in his ear, and yet he seemed dazed, uncertain. He struggled against Samar and Noqril, and Nalia felt that tug in her stomach again—the wish.

"You have to let him go," she said, the misery plain in her voice. "Or else I'll have to make you."

"You've brought him to the location," Zanari said. "You've fulfilled your obligation, sister."

Nalia shook her head as the pain in her stomach radiated through her. She pointed to the rock in the middle of the chasm. "That's the location," she said.

The thought of Raif and Malek fighting for the ring on that tiny stretch of rock made her blood run cold.

She turned to Raif. "It must be the wish. It knows I can't truly grant it unless he's aware of his surroundings. It's somehow . . . cured him. I don't know. I'm sorry."

Wish magic had never been an exact science. It was an enigma even the greatest mages had yet to truly understand. The only thing Nalia could hope for was that her hand moved more quickly than Malek's. If she could somehow grab the ring first . . . another stab of pain in her stomach: the wish, it seemed, would not let her plot against Malek until she'd granted it.

"It's all right," Raif said quietly. "Let's just get this over with."

He flexed his fingers as Samar and Noqril released their hold on Malek. Nalia noted the look that passed between Raif and Samar. She could imagine the *chiaan* that ran through her *rohifsa*, just waiting to burst through his skin to take Malek down.

Malek stumbled toward her. "I'm dreaming. Right? This is a dream. Don't let her wake me up, Nalia. Just let me stay here with you. Maybe she killed us both? But she can't kill me. I don't know. It's been—"

"You're not dreaming, Malek," she said.

The pain in her abdomen receded as Malek moved toward her, free of his Dhoma guards. He staggered forward and wrapped his arms around Nalia. He smelled awful—sweat and fear, the body of a tortured, grieving man. He smelled human.

"I thought I'd lost you," he said. "The things she was doing to you . . ." He kissed her hair. "*Hayati,*" he whispered. "*Hayati.*"

Nalia pulled away. "It wasn't real."

Malek stared at her, a starved man. Whatever Haraja had done had broken him. The Malek Alzahabi who ruled Earth in Armani was gone. He gazed around him. His eyes landed on the rock in the center of the chasm. "Is that . . . ?"

"Yes," Nalia said quietly.

She walked forward, toward the place where the ledge they stood on dropped off into the black hole surrounding the sigil. She reached out a hand and as her fingers brushed the space above it, she felt the impenetrable barrier she'd been expecting. She looked up. There, in a patch of her *chiaan*'s light, she saw a stain in the air, like oil on water.

"Antharoe put a *bisahm* around the sigil," she said, pointing to where her *chiaan* glinted off the protective shield. No jinni would be able to evanesce past it.

Raif shook his head. "Why would she use a *bisahm*? Isn't the ring here so that a Ghan Aisouri could find it if she needed to?" Nalia pointed to the star carved into the rock at her feet. "But you're forgetting: there's an eighth star."

THE STAR, JUST A BREATH FROM THE ENDLESS DEPTH OF the chasm below. Elegant text surrounded its elaborate points, and Nalia slowly walked the length of the rock's lip, studying each character.

"What language is that?" Anso asked.

"Ancient Kada," Nalia said.

"I'm guessing your fancy tutors at the palace taught you that, eh?" said Noqril.

"Yes." For a moment she was a child again, sitting at the long *widr* table in the center of the palace library.

The wood is polished to a sheen and the air smells of old paper and sealing wax. Balls of light hang suspended above Nalia as she copies out the swirling script. Her penmanship is perfect, calligraphy elevated to an art form. Ink stains her skin. Nalia is ten summers old and she wonders why these long hours in the drafty old room matter. She cares little for this dead language, spoken only by ghosts.

Nalia knelt down and brushed her fingers across the words, her lips moving as her memory struggled to access the long-forgotten language. It had been over three years since she'd held the leather-bound tomes of the palace library in her hands, years since she'd had to copy down words such as these onto parchment.

ejër: blood

Ü æ: passage

She read them again. And again. Each time the meaning sank deeper, a stone thrown into a bottomless well. *Blood Passage.* A sacrifice.

Nalia could feel the others behind her, and the weight of their expectation lay heavy on her thin shoulders. Her eyes filled with tears as she stared across the chasm at the ring. She reached into her pocket and gripped Bashil's worry stone. Had he held it before he died, too, when he was alone in the cell in Marrakech, waiting for Calar to kill him?

"Nalia?" Raif's voice was soft in her ear and the feel and sound and smell of him lashed her heart.

I will love you forever, she thought. *In the godlands, for all time.*

Nalia swallowed her tears, then turned to the waiting jinn. She wanted to do this on her own terms. The Ghan Aisouri way.

"In Arjinna's oldest days," she said, "there was a practice called the Blood Passage. It was our people's way of honoring the gods. This was before civilization. Before temples and priests. We were just tribes scattered across the land, warring. Nomads. All we knew was that we had power from nature and that someone had given it to us. We wanted to please the gods and we thought the best way to do so would be to offer up our most precious resource—one another. A life, given to the gods to appease them, or offered in exchange for an answered prayer. Our ancestors believed the life of the sacrificed jinni would provide a passage to the gods, that the blood would open up a doorway to our desires."

"So someone has to die, is that what you're saying?" Malek said.

Nalia now understood how love could be strength.

"Yes," she said.

Malek turned to the jinn. "I don't suppose anyone here wants to make a noble sacrifice?"

Raif suddenly understood what Nalia was about to do.

"No!" He lurched toward her, but she took a step back, the heel of her boot flush with the edge of the rock. The smallest touch would send her over.

"Nalia . . ." Raif's voice was a strangled whisper. "Don't do this."

"Get away from me, Raif."

He went absolutely still, his eyes warring with hers.

"I mean it," she said. When he didn't move, she dangled one foot over the chasm and he leaped back.

"Okay, Nal. Okay. Just. Okay." He held out his hands. "Wait. Please. Not like this, *rohifsa*. Please. Not like this."

Her eyes begged him to understand, but he couldn't. Wouldn't.

I could lose everything right now, he thought. Nalia, the revolution . . . his mind. This was his greatest fear, right here. Haraja couldn't have done a better job of creating it for him.

He turned to Malek, his eyes still on Nalia. "Do something, you fucking *skag!*"

Malek was watching Nalia, his expression unreadable. His eyes flicked to the sigil. To Nalia. Back to the sigil.

Raif shoved him. "If you love her, make this stop."

Malek turned to him, his eyes red-rimmed, feverish. "I can't undo the wish. It's impossible."

Nalia knelt down and slid the knife over her palm, then pressed it to the star at her feet. The *bisahm* began to shimmer until it looked as though the whole cavern were covered by a sky of silk.

Now, Raif thought.

He lunged forward and grabbed Nalia's arm. She cried out as he pulled her away from the cliff's edge and they tumbled to the ground. His elbow smashed against the stone, but he ignored the white-hot pain and held on to Nalia.

"You're not killing yourself," he growled.

"Raif. Please. Don't make this harder." She brought her hands to his cheeks and her lips covered his face. Her tears, his tears, the blood from her wound on her hand all mixing together.

"Nalia, please," he begged. He heard a sob behind him and

turned—Zanari, her hands over her mouth, eyes streaming.

"That life you told me about," Nalia said, "with the field, the house, the children . . ." He could feel her leaving, even as he gripped her arms. "You're going to have it. For both of us."

"I can't. Nalia . . ." He kept whispering her name, to remind her, maybe, of the girl who'd always refused to give up.

She wiped his cheeks with the backs of her fingers and he closed his eyes and held her against him. Saw her descend the staircase at Malek's house the night they met. He'd never told her how she'd taken his breath away. He'd hated her then, but it hadn't mattered. He saw her, fierce and lovely, battling Haran, becoming a tidal wave. He saw the lightning strike her, felt her shudder beneath him as they made love in the glowworm cave.

Raif opened his eyes and stared into her violet ones. The last Ghan Aisouri. A daughter of the gods. There was a reason she'd been the only royal to survive—he knew that now. Nalia was the true leader of the revolution. Maybe even the true leader of Arjinna. Raif brought his lips to hers one last time.

"Long live the empress," he whispered.

Raif sprang up and bolted toward the cliff's edge. Nalia screamed, a gut-wrenching wail, but he didn't stop. The revolution would be fine. Nalia would live. For the first time in years, he had real hope.

Raif grinned as his hand broke through the *bisahm*, and his blood surged with the same rush he felt when he led his *tavrai* in battles against the Ifrit. The chasm opened for him, hungry, and he spread out his arms, welcoming death like an old friend.

Malek had never been able to see her cry.

He sprinted toward the cliff's edge and grabbed the back of Raif's shirt just as the boy's body started to go over. With a strength he didn't know he possessed, Malek threw him several feet away from the chasm. Raif landed on his side and looked back at Malek, confusion, then sudden understanding, dawning in his eyes.

As much as he detested Raif, Malek had seen what Bashil's death had done to Nalia's spirit. He couldn't bear for that to happen again.

"You always underestimated me," Malek said, when he turned to Nalia. She was staring at him, her lovely mouth slightly open, eyes glistening.

He pulled her to him and pressed his lips against hers. She wasn't his. Never would be. This would have to be enough. For once she rushed into him, and he drank her *chiaan*, drank until he was full. He felt something like love—maybe not love, but something like it, something warm and sad and rich—flow from her to him and it was enough, more than enough.

He pulled away. "Do you remember what *hayati* means?"

"My life," she whispered.

"Exactly."

He reached into his pocket and pulled out the lapis lazuli necklace that she'd thrown at his feet all those weeks ago. The necklace was so much more than a pendant. It was the best parts of himself, and Malek wanted her to have those. He took her hand in his and dropped the delicate chain onto her palm, his eyes locked on hers. For the first time in his life, Malek Alzahabi was at peace.

"Third time's a charm," he said.

Malek turned away from her and dove into the chasm.

"What do you think happens when we die?" Amir asks.

He and Malek are sitting under a pomegranate tree, hiding from their cousins. Their knees are skinned from crawling around and their hands sticky from the candies they stole when everyone was distracted with grief. One of their uncles has died.

Only Malek knows why.

"I'm not sure," Malek says. "The Imam says we'll go to heaven. But I think he's a liar." He looks over at Amir to see if he's shocked.

"Is not!" Amir says. He squints at Malek. The sun is high and it beats down, relentless. "Is he?"

Malek shrugs. "You think Allah loves us? We're cursed. Like demons."

"Bismillah," Amir says, pointing his finger at Malek as though it's a magic wand. Malek clutches his stomach for a moment, but the pain passes quickly.

"See?" Amir says, smirking. "If you were evil, the bismillah would make you go away. But you're still here."

Malek grunts. What does it matter? He's damned anyway. Boys who murder their uncles don't go to heaven, he's pretty sure of that. Even if those boys have a good reason.

The call to prayer breaks the silence: Allahu Akbar. Allahu

Akbar. Allahu Akbar. Allahu Akbar.

The boys stand up and start making their way back to the family home. Malek shuffles his feet through the yellow dust. His leather sandals make a shushing sound.

"What do you think it feels like to die?" Amir asks. He kicks the stones in their path and Malek watches them roll away.

A shadow passes overhead and Malek looks up. A heron soars above them and cries out to its flock.

"Like flying."

"MALEK!"

Nalia's voice slapped at the air, the only sound in the vast cavern. The others seemed to be holding their breath, Raif included. After what felt like minutes, there was an almost indiscernible thud far below them. Raif thought he'd imagined it until a bright, golden light filled the room, soaking into the amethyst walls. Eight bridges appeared from the tunnel entrances surrounding the cavern.

The Blood Passage had been paid.

Nalia covered her mouth and sank to her knees. The hands holding Raif let go and he rushed to her. She fell against him and together they watched as the bridges of light became more solid. The sigil was so close and Malek was gone—the ring was as good as his. Raif held Nalia to him, dazed. *Long live the empress.* Had he really said that? The certainty he'd felt just before he'd planned to die echoed in him now: *Nalia* as the leader of Arjinna's revolution, by divine right. *This changes everything*, he thought.

"I suggest we get the sigil before these bridges disappear," Noqril said, looming over them.

Raif helped Nalia stand and they walked to the nearest pathway to the sigil. The bridges seemed to be made of sunlight. He could see dust motes moving through them.

Nalia stared at the darkness pooling below. Something like grief had settled in her eyes. "Why did he do it? He was so close . . ."

It had been difficult for Raif to watch them together. There was no doubt Nalia had felt something for her master. And yet, jealousy seemed petty.

"He loved you," Raif said. "In a fucked-up kind of way, but still. How could he not?"

Nalia reached for his hand. "I don't want you to think—"

"Shhhh," he said. "It's over. We're together. That's all that matters." He lifted her hand and kissed the crescent scar on her wrist, the mirror image of the one on his own wrist. He stared at it for a long moment, remembering everything that had brought them here.

"Raif?" she said softly. "What's wrong?"

His mind was racing, jumping from one thought to the next, the revelation he'd had moments ago trumping his desire for the sigil: the *tavrai* would execute him, his mother would disown him, he was a disgrace to his father's memory. And, oh gods, Zanari. Would she stand by him if he bent the knee and called Nalia his empress?

"Nothing," he said. He squeezed her hand.

"Malek owed you big time, Nalia," Zanari said as she joined them, her voice uncharacteristically gentle. "I won't speak ill of the dead, but there's a lot more I could say."

Nalia nodded. "We better get what we came for and get out. It's time to go home."

Their journey wouldn't be over until they were standing on Arjinnan soil. *First the ring, then home.* They were so close.

"Agreed," Phara said, as she looked over the ledge. "I don't know about the rest of you, but I'm ready to get out of here."

Raif felt Zanari stiffen slightly beside him and he wondered what his sister and her lover had decided to do once they'd left the cave. He promised himself he'd talk to her about it later.

"Doesn't seem very reliable," Raif said, staring at the bridge.

"I'm assuming evanescing won't work. Or manifesting our own bridge. That'd be too easy."

"I'm afraid to try," Nalia said. "Gods know what protections Antharoe put in place."

Raif tugged on Nalia's hand. "Ready?"

"Maybe we shouldn't cross together. Let me go first, just in case——"

"Together," he said firmly.

Raif placed one foot on the bridge. He'd half expected his boot to slip through, but the bridge was solid, however ethereal it appeared to be. They made their way across slowly, with Raif in the lead. He was careful not to look down, all too aware of the dark beneath them and the terrible price that had been paid.

"We're going to have some pretty great stories to tell our grandkids someday," he said, forcing his voice to be light.

"Pretty confident I can put up with you for that long?"

"Oh yeah."

Nalia laughed and some of the tension spilled away. His heartbeat quickened as they neared the freestanding rock. For a moment, Raif wanted to turn back. The sigil would change Arjinna—but would it be for better or worse?

You've come this far, brother, he said to himself.

Nalia stopped. "Raif."

He turned his head slightly. "Yeah?"

"What would happen if we didn't take it?"

The sigil was only a few feet away. He couldn't see it clearly yet, but the carved white marble of the altar shone as though it had just been crafted by a master.

"It would be the end. The Ifrit would have Arjinna. Maybe forever."

"What if I killed Calar? Could you win then—without the ring?"

This time he turned all the way around. "Nalia—"

"Whether or not we get this ring, I'm killing her. What she did to Bashil—" Her voice shook and the pain in her echoed in him. "This ring scares me, Raif. It's an evil thing. I just . . ."

Raif crossed his arms, thinking. He couldn't believe he was second-guessing this, but the terror in Nalia's eyes and the confusion he felt over what had happened inside him on the ledge gave him pause. A Ghan Aisouri who could swallow lightning and become lava was a considerable weapon to have at his disposal. At *their* disposal. He caught sight of Samar, waiting at the end of the bridge.

"Even if I changed my mind," he said, "we made a promise to the Dhoma."

Nalia's face fell. "What if we freed the jinn from their bottles now and—"

"What's going on?" Samar called.

Raif waved a hand. "We're fine. Almost there!" He looked back at Nalia. *Rohifsa—*"

"I know, I know. Let's get this over with."

He took her hand. Her *chiaan* felt jittery. It was so unlike Nalia to be afraid.

Moments later, they were stepping onto the rock. The others cheered, but Raif barely heard them. In the center of the altar, atop a mother-of-pearl mosaic of an eight-pointed star, sat Solomon's sigil.

Raif sucked in his breath. "I can't believe it's actually here. Part of me thought it wouldn't be."

The gold on the side of the ring was worked in intricate detail and in its center was a large oval stone, a pale canary diamond. In the center of the diamond was an eight-pointed star that glimmered with its own light. He could feel the power emanating from it. The ring was heavy looking, masculine. Meant for a king to wear.

"We're going to win this war, Nalia," he breathed.

Nalia clutched his arm. "Raif. Look at me."

She was shaking, her eyes full of terror. He'd never seen her so afraid, not even when she thought she was going to die.

"Promise me you'll never wear the ring," she begged. "No matter what. Promise me."

Raif hesitated. He wasn't one for making promises he had no intention of keeping. He was still trying to figure out what his role in everything was. He needed time and they didn't have that right now.

"*Raif.*"

He placed his hands on either side of her face. "Nalia, I swear to all the gods, I swear on my love for you, I swear on *everything:* I will not put this ring on—unless there is no other option." She paled and he drew closer. "I know that's not what you want to hear. Do you trust me?"

Nalia rested her hands on his chest. "You—yes. The ring . . ." She shook her head. "No."

Raif pressed his lips against her forehead. "Well, I'll take what I can get." He moved closer to the altar. "Before I pick it up, do these words say I'll be killed on the spot if I touch the ring?"

He pointed to the ancient Kada scrawled all over the altar's marble. Nalia shook her head. "No. Just old *sadr's* praising the gods and warning of the sigil's power. Go ahead."

Raif reached out, fingers trembling, and took the ring from where it had sat for three thousand years. The stone glowed and a beam of golden light shot out of the diamond as a rumble filled the cavern. The ring dimmed as the sound in the cavern grew louder and Raif went still, half expecting the rock they stood on to topple over. He blinked as a blinding shaft of light streamed down from above. Raif shaded his eyes as he gazed upward. There was now an opening in the cavern's roof through which sunlight—*real sunlight*—poured into the chamber. After being underground so long, it was almost painful to look at.

The others cried out, joyful, but Nalia was silent, her head tilted back and eyes closed. Silent tears dripped down her cheeks. Raif took a leather string from his pocket and slipped the ring onto it, then stepped behind Nalia.

"It's safest with you," he said as he placed the makeshift necklace around her neck. If anyone could protect the ring, it was Nalia. She shivered as the metal touched her skin. Raif tied the knot twice, then pressed his lips against her neck.

She turned around. "We've come a long way from fighting in Malek's garage," she said.

He laughed. "Yes we have."

His arm began to burn and he cursed, looking down at his skin. Nalia sucked in her breath at the same time, a small gasp of pain.

"Our tattoos," she said. Nalia held up her arm. The eight-pointed star had disappeared, leaving behind a faint scar of its outline. So had his.

"When is your ancestor gonna be done fucking with us?" he muttered.

"Raif?" He turned at the sound of Zanari's panicked voice.

"Apparently never," Nalia said.

The bridge they'd crossed was disappearing. Raif turned in a circle, desperately hoping the other bridges had remained solid, but they, too, were nothing more than swiftly disappearing lines of light above the chasm.

"If Antharoe weren't already dead," Nalia said, "I could kill her right about now."

THEY WERE STRANDED.

Nalia sat on the floor, leaning against the altar that had held Solomon's sigil. The ring felt heavy around her neck. She was sorely tempted to throw it into the chasm.

"Try to get some sleep, Nal," Raif said. "I seriously doubt Haraja can get us here and there's nothing more we can do tonight."

He was right. They'd spent hours attempting to figure out how to get back to the others. Evanescing across the chasm had been the obvious choice, but when Nalia tried, her smoke stayed by her feet and her body remained solid. The only way out was up, but evanescing through the hole at the top of the cavern was also impossible. As was manifesting anything. For the first time in the cave, they couldn't manifest food, water—anything they needed to stay alive or escape. They could still access their *chiaan*, but there wasn't much good it did them, other than provide a light source. Nalia wasn't surprised. The whole cave had been protected by magic so sophisticated, she couldn't begin to imagine how it worked. Antharoe had left them an exit, but no way to reach it. Her very last effort to keep the ring hidden. Not for the first time, Nalia wondered why Antharoe hadn't simply destroyed the sigil. She clearly didn't want anyone to have the godsdamned thing.

Home seemed farther away than ever.

Nalia's voice was hoarse from shouting across the chasm and her bones weary from the volcano and those endless minutes staring into the darkness below, waiting to die. But her heart wouldn't let her sleep.

"Raif," she began.

"Yeah?"

"I have to say the prayers for him."

There was a long silence, and the confusion and grief and shame she felt inside her seemed to jolt the air.

"Malek doesn't deserve them," he said quietly. "And, besides, they'll do his soul no good, not without a burning."

For so long Nalia had wanted Malek to die a painful death. Now she hoped it had been fast and that his last memory was of the kiss she had let him take before he jumped.

Her hand strayed to the lapis lazuli necklace around her neck, that little bit of home Malek had given her, and she let herself mourn him.

Because nobody else would. Because, gods help her, she *did* mourn him. It didn't make sense. Things like this rarely did.

"I have to, Raif."

When he looked at her, his eyes were kind and seemed to understand, at least a little. He kissed the palm of her hand, relenting.

Nalia stood and crossed to the other side of the altar, the only private part of the rock they were marooned on. She placed her palms on the earth and whispered the prayer of the dead. The words were too familiar. Gods, she'd said them so many times in the past few weeks. The past few *years*.

Then she accessed the lightning inside her. Before, she'd had to find a fire source to ignite her Ifrit power. Not so anymore. Fire tore through Nalia's fingers and she cast it down into the pit. It roared and blazed, a dragon free of its restraints. Solomon's rock became an island in a sea of flames. She heard the jinn across the chasm scream and Raif call out to them, but she ignored it all. She prayed to Ravnir, god of fire, that he would take this dead half-child of his to the godlands so that Malek could see his brother and find the peace that had eluded him on Earth. He didn't deserve it, Raif was right. But Nalia wanted Malek to have it, anyway. She wasn't really sure why.

When the flames died down, she returned to Raif's side.

"How can you forgive him?"

Nalia took his hand. "I don't think I have, not completely anyway. I'm not really sure what forgiveness feels like. But he died for me." Her throat tightened and she scooted down so that her head rested on Raif's lap.

He wrapped his arms around her and as she drifted off to

sleep, Nalia realized that this was her first night as a truly free jinni.

She was no longer on the dark caravan.

The dream began as it always did, right in the middle of hell.

Ghan Aisouri blood is everywhere. Thick pools of it soak into Nalia's clothes, coat her lips, drip into her ears. Her blood, their blood.

But tonight something is different. Instead of lying beneath a pile of her sisters, Nalia stands against the wall. This is not real, not what happened, and she knows this, knows she is dreaming.

There are no Ifrit soldiers in the cellar with them. No Haran. Bullet holes are torn into the wall all around her. She doesn't feel any pain. Why can't she feel any pain?

The empress lies at her feet. Her eyes are closed. Her chest is crimson and wet. And still. The light from the torches on the walls licks the glimmering stones on the Amethyst Crown. It has fallen off the empress's head. Nalia picks it up. It's warm.

"Put it on."

Nalia jumps, her spirit nearly flying from her skin. She knows this voice. She looks down.

The empress's eyes are open, violet and searing, and yet her chest does not move with breath and her skin is pale and lifeless.

"Put it on, Nalia Aisouri'Taifyeh. It is yours."

"No," Nalia whispers. "You're the empress. Not me. Please, not me."

"Wadj kef, child. You do not have a choice." Obey the blood. "Hala l'aeik." It is the will of the gods.

Nalia raises the crown above her head as she stares at the bodies of the Ghan Aisouri.

"I can't," she says.

She feels a rush of chiaan and her hands press down and she cries out as her body, as her very soul, feels the weight of a kingdom.

The Ghan Aisouri who was once the ruler of Nalia's race sighs. As her eyes close, she whispers, "Long live the empress."

42

ZANARI LAY ON HER BACK, HER EYES WIDE OPEN, PHARA asleep beside her. Their cure for Haraja's malice was lying dead at the bottom of the chasm. Zanari wouldn't close her eyes again until she was standing outside the cursed cave. But as much as she longed for sleep and fresh air and an end to the muzzle the cave had put on her *voiqhif*, a small part of Zanari dreaded going aboveground. The days searching for the sigil had been night-marish or just plain exhausting, but they'd also been a reprieve from the war, from the loneliness that had stalked Zanari all her days. Returning to the earth's surface meant that the loneliness would return, too, worse now because she knew what it meant to have someone look at her the way Phara did. Zanari didn't know how she'd say good-bye.

Her eyes grew heavy and she rubbed them, focusing on the

moonlight that shone through the small opening in the cavern's ceiling. Bright enough to see Haraja if she were going to make another appearance. Even from so far below ground, Zanari could see the stars covering the night sky like a decadent blanket. She didn't care that they weren't green like Arjinna's; right then, they were perfect. Her eyes blurred . . . dimmed . . . closed.

At the sound of falling rock, Zanari's eyes snapped open. She turned her head slightly, scanning the ledge. It was lighter in the cave now: dawn. She silently cursed herself: gods, how could she have *slept*?

Zanari tensed, her eyes darting everywhere, careful not to move lest she attract the intruder's attention. Then, so small she very nearly missed it, Zanari noticed a figure crawling up the rock face from the depths of the chasm, moving swiftly toward the ledge where Zanari and the other jinn rested. For one wild moment, Zanari thought it was Malek, somehow alive after all, but then the figure scurried through a patch of moonlight—she'd seen that curtain of dark, greasy hair before: Haraja. A jolt of fear cut through her, but Zanari ignored it. She had to attack before the monster was able to cast her paralyzing spell. To Zanari's left, Samar peered into the darkness. She caught his eye and he nodded.

Zanari leaped to her feet and sent a stream of *chiaan* at the creature while Samar charged forward, a scimitar in his hand. Haraja screeched as Zanari's magic found its mark and the sound of her cry echoed off the stone walls. It wasn't enough to kill the little beast, though. In one quick movement, Haraja hoisted herself onto the ledge.

The sleeping jinn sprang to their feet at the sound of the

commotion. Phara was standing beside Zanari in a moment, yellow *chiaan* zipping along the length of the ledge. A blast of violet and emerald *chiaan* came from the rock where Raif and Nalia were stranded. They stood side by side, tracking Haraja's lightning-fast movement.

Anso stepped forward. "Allow me," she said.

She held out her hands and a sickly puff of chartreuse smoke billowed from her fingertips. The disease-maker leaned forward and gently blew on the deadly cloud. It sped toward Haraja and as the smoke made contact, the monster let out an ear-splitting wail. She was close enough for Zanari to see the lesions that bubbled over her translucent skin. In a matter of seconds they were oozing pus and blood. Haraja clawed at her face as the skin began to split.

"Leprosy," Anso said, a hint of pride in her voice. "Advanced stage. It won't be long now."

"*Gods*," Zanari said.

Phara looked away. Zanari knew how hard it was for her to see sickness, even if it was in a creature like Haraja. She pulled the healer to her and Phara buried her face in Zanari's neck, her body trembling.

It didn't take long for the creature to die.

"That is some power you have, Anso," Zanari said.

The other jinni nodded. "It's rarely useful, but it does the job when it needs to."

"Does it only work on one person at a time?" Zanari asked.

Anso tilted her head to the side, considering. "I don't know. I've never had cause to make a whole group of people ill."

Zanari remembered what Malek had called her—a biological weapon. The revolution could certainly use one of those.

"Is everyone okay?" Nalia called across the cavern.

"Yes," Samar shouted. "And you?"

Raif waved a hand. "We're fine."

Noqril walked over to where Haraja's corpse lay. It was now nothing more than swaths of skin covering bones. He kicked the creature's remains into the chasm.

Phara sighed. "That one has no sense of decency."

Zanari kept quiet. As much as she disliked the Ifrit Dhoma they'd had to spend the past several days with, she would have done the same thing.

She stared back to her makeshift bed; now that Haraja was dead, she'd sleep like a baby. Zanari happened to look across the chasm before she closed her eyes, to check once more on her brother as she had countless times since he'd nearly made himself the Blood Passage. She blinked, then stared as a ladder appeared just above the altar. It seemed to be made of sunlight, each rung growing in substance as it climbed from the altar to the opening in the roof. The human call to prayer sounded outside the cavern and as the worshipper's voice rose to the heavens, so did the ladder.

Prayer is better than sleep, sang the muezzin somewhere above the cave.

Nalia stared at the golden ladder, speechless. It was as if the gods had truly heard the constant, silent prayer that had been on repeat ever since they'd found the ring.

Please let us go home, she'd begged. *Please.*

"Why didn't we see this before?" Raif asked.

"*We rise to greet the sun and climb the heights of the self.*" Nalia said softly. The words that were chanted every morning by the Ghan Aisouri before their dawn *Sha'a Rho* exercises were more ancient than she'd thought.

"I've got to hand it to her," Nalia said. "My ancestor did everything she could to keep this ring down here. This is the ultimate guilt trip."

It was as if Antharoe were standing with her in the cave, reminding Nalia of her promise to the gods. Reminding her that the ring could only be used by someone who had reached their very fullest potential—*the heights of the self*—and would do well by the responsibility.

Raif took her hand. "If the gods loved anyone, *rohifsa,* they have loved you. They've put you through hell, yes, but they want you to live, not spend the rest of your life in this cave. You're not breaking your vow to them by taking this ring; you're fulfilling your promise to serve your realm. Now climb."

And she did.

Nalia gripped the rungs which, like the bridge, were solid despite their translucence. Still, she didn't trust them. About halfway up she looked down at Raif, now just a speck on a rock.

"Let me manifest a real rope for you when I get out of here," she called down. "I don't want this thing to disappear on you."

He waved to show he'd understood and Nalia turned back to

the dawn sun that grew brighter the higher she climbed. Its rays splashed across the amethyst walls of the cave, surrounding Nalia in glittering violet light. She couldn't look down, didn't want to see how far the fall would be if she slipped. It was terrifying, the height, the knowledge that she had to trust a somewhat psychotic, dead ancestor to get her out of the cave alive. Then: a breeze—wind flowing into the cave, carrying the scent of the awakening earth, of outside, of freedom. She was almost there, so close. Her master was dead at the bottom of the chasm, everyone she loved was still trapped inside, but Nalia was rising, higher and higher.

The last rung.

Nalia pulled herself out of the darkness, and into the light.

43

THEY WERE IN THE DRÂA VALLEY IN THE MIDDLE OF A palm forest, hundreds of miles from the *Erg Al-Barq*, where Nalia had channeled the lightning. The fanlike trees grew in every direction, as far as Nalia could see. A stream gurgled nearby. Succulent dates hung off the branches and lush vegetation grew at her feet. It felt as thought she'd risen from hell and entered the Garden of Eden.

Zanari was the last jinni to leave the cave. She hauled up the rope ladder Nalia had manifested, then bent down and kissed the earth before crossing to where Nalia stood in the shade of a palm. Zanari clapped her on the back, beaming. "You're officially a free jinni. How does it feel?"

Nalia took in their surroundings, her heart a collage of emotions. So much had happened in the cave, more than any of them could ever have anticipated. "Good," she said. "But it'll feel even better once I kill Calar."

"How about tonight?" Zanari asked, her eyes mischievous.

Nalia grinned. "Works for me."

The hole that opened into the cavern began to close. The ground shook as the earth crumbled in on itself, concealing the world beneath its surface. Nalia turned away, thinking of Malek's body lying in the cave's depths, with only Haraja's remains for company. She hoped her fire had released him. She couldn't bear the thought of him trapped down there, his ghost forever seeking a way out.

And suddenly it was too much: Malek, the ring, and everything that had come before. It threatened to suffocate her, all this loss and power.

"I need a minute," she said to Raif. "Come find me after you contact your mother."

Now that they were out of the cave, Raif would be able to see how the *tavrai* were doing. Zanari was already sitting in a circle of earth, using her *voiqhif* to track the Ifrit. He nodded and rested a hand on her arm before joining the others.

Nalia walked, then ran, blindly, weaving between palm trees and shrubbery. She didn't know where she was going, just needed to be alone, gods it had been so long since she'd been *alone*. She halted at the bank of a river lined with fragrant palms, staring.

Bashil shrieks as a school of rosefish shoot between his legs. He loses his balance in the river and falls in, then looks up at Nalia, shocked.

She laughs with her mouth open, tasting the sky. Then she pulls him up so that the water is once again around his knees. The air is warm, the sun hot on their backs.

"You'll never catch one if you're scared of them, gharoof."

She bends down and sets her hands a breath above the water. She is Marid now, using her power with the water to coax the fish back.

Bashil stares, mesmerized, at the churning river that has gone suddenly still beneath his sister's palms. "How can you do that?"

She smiles. "Purple eyes, remember?"

He reaches out, one tiny hand on her back for balance while the other skims the surface of the water.

The memory cut deep and, once again, Nalia saw the *chiaan* spill out of her brother's dead body, his spirit evanescing. Nalia wanted to crumple to the ground, to rage at the gods, to go to sleep and never wake up. Before the lightning, before the dream last night, maybe she would have. But the dead empress's words rang in her head like the solemn toll of a bell:

Long live the empress.

Raif had said the very same thing to her, just before he nearly died to save Nalia's life. They hadn't talked about it, but the memory lingered, ever present. Why would the leader of the Arjinnan revolution have those be his last words?

Nalia could still feel the weight of the crown on her head, a phantom circlet of amethysts worn by the Ghan Aisouri for centuries, even by Antharoe herself. In the dream, she'd had no choice—the crown had had a will of its own, forcing itself upon her. Though Nalia couldn't explain how or why, she knew something had been set in motion, something vast and far beyond her control. The Nalia Aisouri'Taifyeh who had walked into the cave was not the same one who climbed out of it.

Empress. *Empress.*

No.

Never.

What was she thinking? The last thing the jinn wanted was another empress. And it was the last thing *Nalia* ever wanted to be. It was laughable, the idea of her sitting on the throne. A sad, sick joke that after throwing her realm into ruin she would be the last one standing.

Nalia slipped off her clothing and waded into the river. The water was too cold, but she didn't care. It felt good to bathe in sun-dappled water, to feel the wind on her face. There wasn't a human in sight, but there was life everywhere: birds called to one another and small animals rustled through the grass on the riverbank. It had been so deathly quiet in the cave, the only creatures inside it intent on killing them. Nalia drank the air in sips, then gulps, the memory of the cave's closeness all too fresh in her mind. It had reminded her of all those times that Malek had put her in the bottle. Not being able to evanesce from the tomb-like cave, trying not to panic at the thought of a whole desert lying on top of her . . .

There was the sound of stomping through the brush and then Raif's voice, calling her name.

"Nalia?"

She hoisted herself out of the water, but instead of putting on the gray mourning rags she'd worn in the cave, she manifested a simple purple tunic, black leggings, and knee-high black boots. She wasn't ready for Ghan Aisouri leathers yet, but the *sawala* she'd worn in the palace as her everyday uniform would do. As she got closer to going home, she could feel the realm reclaiming her, bit by bit.

Home. The word wrapped around Nalia and she went still, basking in it. *Home.* She could go right now. *Right now.* She was a free jinni, all her obligations fulfilled. She grasped Solomon's sigil with her fingers. What would it be like to return to Arjinna, with the lightning inside her and the sigil around her neck?

"Nal?"

She turned. Raif was striding through the palm forest, his face lined with worry. He stopped when he saw her by the river, the worry dissipating a bit as he took in her wet hair and new clothes.

"Ready to go home?" he asked softly.

His eyes were red from lack of sleep and the thick stubble on his face was practically a beard. In the light of day, she could see how much he looked like his father. It was strange to be in love with a boy that so resembled the man she'd been taught to hate.

"I've been waiting for three years," Nalia said. "Yes, I'm ready." But was she? Her stomach twisted at the thought of the *tavrai*. Would they accept her, or reject her on sight? She frowned.

"It'll be okay," Raif said, as if he'd heard her thought. But his voice was strained.

Nalia nodded. "I know." That was a lie and they both knew it. "How's your mother? The *tavrai*?"

Raif looked away. "I don't know," he said, his voice barely above a whisper.

"She . . . she didn't answer when you—"

"No."

Gods, please don't let her be dead. But it was the only explanation for *hahm'alah* not working—unless Raif's mother was unconscious or ill, as Bashil had been before Calar. . . .

Nalia wrapped her arms around him, trembling. "Don't give up hope yet," she whispered.

When would it ever stop?

Raif's arms stayed at his side as his forehead dropped to her shoulder. She gripped him tighter, as though she could somehow hold him together, this broken boy who'd lost so much already. After a few moments he straightened up and stepped away. He'd been a soldier nearly all his life. Loss—even one this monumental—was something he'd been trained to accept.

"We should go," he said. "The Dhoma are anxious to see their families."

As he started back into the palm forest, Nalia grasped his hand. "Hey." He turned around. "When we get home, Calar won't know what hit her."

His eyes settled on the ring around her neck and Nalia stepped closer. "Once she knows you have the ring, she'll have to stand down," she said. "And if she doesn't, then I'll make her. I'm more than happy to do that. We won't need to use it, Raif."

"Actually, I thought of something that might work even better," he said.

She raised her eyebrows. "I'm listening."

"There are two *thousand* jinn in those bottles, right?"

"Assuming they've all survived, yes."

His eyes sparked and he got that devil-may-care look that she'd fallen for. "That's an army."

Nalia sucked in her breath. "You want them to fight for the revolution."

He nodded. "And with Anso's powers—you saw what she did to Haraja—and the *fawzel* for spying, Noqril's invisibility . . . and with you, of course . . . Nal, we could really win this thing. The ring notwithstanding."

"Raif, these jinn won't want anything to do with Arjinna," Nalia said gently. "*Dhoma* means 'the forgotten,' remember? The Aisouri—everyone—abandoned them. The last thing they're going to want to do after nearly three thousand years trapped in a bottle is fight a war they don't care about."

"But look at it this way: if we win the war, then all the Dhoma have a peaceful homeland to return to," he said. "They won't have to be stuck on Earth, living in the middle of a desert. They wouldn't be fighting for us; they'd be fighting for themselves."

"And what happens when the Dhoma in the bottle see this ring?" Nalia held up the sigil. The diamond glittered in the sunlight, throwing flecks of gold across Raif's skin. "Do you think they're going to trust anyone who thinks this is an acceptable weapon to fight with?"

"What about Samar and the Dhoma in the camp?" he said, ignoring her question. "Let's say the jinn in the bottles are too weak to fight right away. Samar and his people aren't."

Nalia sighed. "He's already said that the revolution isn't his war. We can't force them to fight."

Raif's eyes flicked to the ring and Nalia pushed it under her tunic. "*Raif. We can't force them,*" she repeated.

All Raif would have to do was slip the ring on his finger and he'd have every jinni on Earth under his command. The thought was terrifying, even if she did trust him.

He shook his head. "I know. I would never make them." He leaned against a palm tree, his arms crossed. "If the Dhoma want to stay on Earth, fine. It's a free realm. But if they want to be welcomed back in Arjinna, then they need to fight, too. They've remained on the sidelines long enough."

"It is not for you to decide who is and who is not welcome in Arjinna," Nalia said. "I agree with you that they should fight. But they're our people just as much as Zanari or the *tavrai*." As she spoke, she felt something within stir, a slumbering part of herself that was finally awakening. "If the Dhoma decide they want to come home, we won't turn them away."

Raif looked at her for a long moment, then inclined his head, relenting. "When you talk like that," he said softly, "you sound like an empress, you know."

That's because I am one. The thought startled Nalia and she pushed it away. *Hala l'aeik,* the dead empress had said the night before: *It is the will of the gods.*

No, she thought. *I make my own destiny.* But she wasn't so sure anymore.

"Yesterday," Nalia began, hesitant, "what you said to me before . . . before you were nearly the Blood Passage . . . I've been trying to figure it out. I don't understand."

The wind swept through the palms and the sound was like hundreds of silk gowns spinning on the palace's dance floor.

"I can't explain it," Raif said, his voice suddenly strained. "I've been thinking about it ever since."

"Me too," she said, quiet. *Tread softly*, she thought, as Raif pushed off from the tree and began pacing. She'd never seen him so agitated. "If you don't want to talk about it now——"

"No, we should." He sighed. "I had this sudden, I don't know, *clarity*. It was so obvious that you, that you're . . ." He glanced at her, his eyes confused . . . scared. "I used to hate the idea of you wearing the Amethyst Crown. But sometimes I think . . ." He stopped, turned away from her. "Gods, listen to me. The *tavrai* would string me up if they heard me talking like this."

"Come." She tugged on his hand, pushing away the disappointment that threatened to overtake her. This was a conversation for later, after they'd rested and eaten. "The others are waiting for us."

What had she been expecting him to say? What had she *wanted* him to say?

When they entered the clearing above the cavern, the Dhoma were deep in discussion.

"It's bound to be extremely disorienting at first," Samar was saying. "We must do everything we can to help the jinn once they evanesce from their bottles. Phara." He turned to the healer. "You might have a lot of work to do. I'm not sure how being in those bottles for so long will have affected our ancestors."

"I'm up for it," she said.

As Nalia and Raif joined the circle, Noqril clapped his hands.

"Well, the lovers have finally joined us. Now we can all go home."

Nalia shivered at the sound of the word. *Home.*

She was almost there.

Don't think about her.

Raif wouldn't grieve his mother. Not yet. *First the ring, then home.* There'd be time to mourn later, if the gods had truly taken her from them. He needed his focus now more than ever. Grief was how you made mistakes, how you fell into traps. He needed to be ready for Calar.

Raif held on to Nalia's hand as they evanesced to the Dhoma camp. It was the first time she'd been able to evanesce since losing her *chiaan*. He knew she'd be fine, but he wasn't taking any chances. He wondered, as he held her hand in his, how much longer he'd be allowed to do this. If she really was the empress, what did that mean for him? For them?

The air filled with the smoke of every caste. In seconds they were standing on Dhoma land.

Or what was left of it.

Raif stared. The desert floor was littered with all that remained of the camp: a lone shoe, a broken sitar, a crushed lamp. The air smelled like Ithkar—fire and death. In the distance, he could see the blue of the lake, little more than a pond now that there weren't any Marid to ensure its continued existence.

It was hard to believe how final the carnage was.

Nalia's hand slipped out of his as she fell to the sandy dune they'd evanesced onto. "Because of us," she whispered to herself.

He remembered the first words she'd said to him, after she'd woken up in Phara's tent: *You should have let me die.*

There was nothing he could say that would assuage her guilt. Though it wasn't Nalia's fault, the camp had been ransacked because they'd harbored the last living Ghan Aisouri and the leader of the revolution. If anything, Raif was to blame. He'd brought her here, made a deal with the Dhoma. Raif placed a hand on her shoulder and she gripped it, leaning into him.

All around him, their Dhoma companions grieved. Anso and Phara clung to one another, weeping. Samar and Noqril cursed as they walked the perimeter of the camp, searching for something—anything—to tell them what had happened. Sunlight skimmed the dunes and the wind gusted the fine sand into the air. It was as if the desert had consumed the camp.

"Captured or killed?" Zanari said quietly, coming to stand beside him.

"My guess is captured," Raif said. "Otherwise, the Ifrit would have left the bodies here."

The Ifrit never burned their victims, preferring to let them wander as ghosts for eternity rather than giving them peace in the godlands.

"All those people . . ." Nalia said. "Gods, so many children."

"I'll see what I can find out," Zanari said, her voice flat.

Raif squeezed her shoulder, and she rested her hand on his before walking across the dune's ridge. She settled onto the sand, gathering it around her for more energy. Raif hoped having a task would hold her together for the time being.

"My sister will be able to tell you what she can see," Raif said to Samar when the Dhoma leader returned from his inspection of the area where the camp had once stood. "I'm so sorry, brother."

Samar nodded. "There is, I think, much to discuss. And several bottles to open." He seemed to have aged in the past few minutes; the lines in his weathered face had carved deeper into his skin, his Marid eyes heavy with despair.

Raif exchanged a glance with Nalia. He knew she would never abandon these people. It killed him to wait even a second to go home, to find out whether his mother was dead or alive, but did he have a choice? He thought of Samar's wife, Yezhud, and he nodded as he gripped the Dhoma's shoulder. It was going to be a long night.

"You're not alone," Raif said.

"Thank you, my friend."

Friend. Yes, somehow that was what they'd become to one another. It was hard to believe Raif had been Samar's prisoner not that long ago.

Samar turned to the rest of the group. "Let's manifest what we need to camp for tonight, and then we shall see what we can do about getting our people back. And if they are . . . gone forever . . . we will avenge them. Every last one."

A true leader of his people, Raif thought, admiring. Calm under pressure, gracious, fearless. *Like Nalia,* he couldn't help but think. Despite their differences, Samar was a good jinni, one Raif wanted on his side and in the fight.

While the Dhoma began manifesting tents and supplies, Raif

waited on the dune with Nalia as Zanari traveled the lines that led to the Dhoma. After a few minutes, she opened her eyes, dazed.

"They're in Ithkar," she said. "I don't know how many survived the battle here or the journey. All I can see is smoke from the volcanoes and . . . and the prison camp."

Nalia went still. Bashil—of course. The brutality of the Ithkar camp was infamous. Raif had been surprised a child had survived it for as long as Bashil did. He imagined the Dhoma, injured from battling the Ifrit, reeling from being taken to the realm they'd shunned for so long.

What a horrible way to see Arjinna for the first time, Raif thought.

"I'll tell Samar," he said heavily.

To his surprise, the Dhoma leader smiled. When he noticed Raif's confusion he simply said, "Where there is life, there is hope."

Raif left Samar to his work and joined Nalia at the far edge of the makeshift camp, where she was manifesting their tent. Despite the horror the afternoon had brought, he couldn't help but feel grateful for the sight of the temporary home he'd share with Nalia. They'd never been alone, not like that. He caught her eye and she smiled. He didn't say a word—didn't have to.

They joined the others around a small fire in the center of their circle of tents. It was a far cry from the joyous gathering of musicians, singers, and dancers that he remembered from his time in the Dhoma camp. They were just settling down to a simple meal of bread and stew that they'd manifested when a screech in the air made Raif look up. The sight took some of the weight off his shoulders. The *fauzel* had escaped the Ifrit. They'd have more answers, maybe a few scraps of hope to share.

The ebony birds circled the camp once, then swooped toward the earth in a swirl of evanescence. The Dhoma ran to their brethren. There was a shout of joy as Samar caught sight of his *fauzel* wife, Yezhud. Raif's eyes smarted as he watched their reunion. He'd felt the same way when Nalia had survived the lightning, and again when she'd made it through the volcano's fire unscathed. And then once more, when Malek became the Blood Passage.

"So they're not all dead?" Noqril said as he and the other Dhoma made their way back to the fire.

Yezhud's eyes filled with sadness. "Many are—we fought before we surrendered. The council members are in the godlands. I burned the bodies myself."

"All of them are gone?" Nalia asked, stricken.

"They took their own lives," one of the *fauzel* said. "We couldn't risk Calar reading their minds. They were the only Dhoma other than us who knew about the sigil. We needed to keep it that way, no?"

Raif sighed heavily. Nalia was right: this ring brought nothing but suffering.

"After burning the camp, the Ifrit rounded everyone up and starred walking into the desert," Yezhud continued. "Then they went through the portal and . . ." She shook her head. "We didn't dare follow until you'd returned."

Yezhud's eyes fell on Nalia, and the *fauzel* made no effort to disguise her hatred. Raif remembered how she'd yelled at Nalia on the *Sun Chaser*.

"It's not her fault, Yezhud," Raif said, careful to keep his voice even. "The Ifrit are your enemy, not us."

"It's okay," Nalia said. She stepped toward Yezhud. *"Hif la'azi vi,"* she whispered. *My heart breaks for you.*

Yezhud's eyes filled with tears and she nodded.

Raif cleared his throat. "We want to do everything we can to help you. That being said, I must return to my soldiers. I've been away from them far too long. My hope is that you'll come with us and that we'll fight our common enemy together. With the ring and the power in our small group assembled here, I know we can be victorious."

"And what if we don't want to fight your war?" Anso said.

Nalia spoke before Raif could. "Then you don't need to. I will help you free the Dhoma. I pledge my blood." She turned to Raif. "And I know the *tavrai* will, too."

The silence was tense, filled with unspoken accusations, weighed down by the catastrophic loss.

"It is pointless to fight about this. We couldn't go to Arjinna even if we wanted to," Yezhud said.

"What do you mean?" Raif's question came out as a bark.

Yezhud looked at him across the fire. "The Ifrit have closed the portal."

ZANARI SPRANG TO HER FEET, AS THOUGH BEING UPRIGHT could somehow make her understand Yezhud's words better. Nalia made a choking sound and Zanari caught a brief glimpse of the agony on her face before Nalia pressed her head against her knees and covered it with her arms. Her body shook with silent sobs. Raif stared at the fire, dazed.

"That's impossible," Zanari said. "The portal has never been closed. *Never*."

She turned to Raif. He'd managed to put an arm around Nalia and pull her against him, but his face was expressionless. "Raif. Tell them."

He looked up at her. It was as if someone had sucked all the life out of him.

"A portal is simply a door," said one of the *fawzel*, his voice cold. "This one has been shut and locked from the inside. We've tried—it's impossible to get through. But go over there, see for yourself."

"I will." In seconds she was evanescing. Through the clouds of jade smoke, she noticed Phara watching her. The healer's expression was unreadable.

Zanari felt the weightlessness that always came with evanescing. Her body lost its form and she was spinning around, faster and faster until the earth became a blur, just swirls of color. Those few mindless seconds between the Dhoma camp and the portal were a sliver of peace, where Zanari had no thought, no consciousness; she simply existed, like a ray of light or a breath of air.

If the portal was truly closed, she'd have to evanesce again and again and again, just to avoid thinking about what it meant to never go home. To never see the Three Widows or drink from the River Sorrow. To never know her mother's fate or have a chance to say good-bye to the *tavrai* Zanari had bled with for years.

She landed directly in front of where the portal should have been. Though it was night, there was a full moon and the desert was bright as day. The entrance that had once been cut into the air was gone. The only evidence of the border between the worlds was a lone tree from which a rotting corpse hung.

Jordif.

Zanari covered her nose, trying to block out the powerful stench of the body as she reached her arm through the place where the portal should be. All she could feel was the desert air.

This wasn't a closed door. It was a closed universe. It was as if Arjinna didn't exist.

She felt a shift in energy and when she turned, Phara was walking toward her out of a cloud of golden evanescence. She wrapped her arms around Zanari.

"I'm so sorry," Phara whispered.

Zanari trembled against her. "It's gone. There's no other way home. What if they never open it again?"

Phara hugged her tighter. "They will. They love human weapons too much—it's the only way the Ifrit have been able to maintain their power. They'll have to come back eventually."

"That could be hundreds of years! By then your family and everyone I know will be—"

"Don't say it," Phara whispered. "Saying it makes it seem true. And it's not. We're going to save them." Phara kissed the top of her head, then pulled away. "Come. Your brother needs you."

When they touched down at the Dhoma camp, Nalia and Raif looked up as one.

"It's gone," Zanari whispered.

Raif stood up. Turned around as though he were looking for something. Sat back down. He gripped his hair with his hands.

The one bright spot in all of this: their mother wasn't necessarily dead. The portal's closure made any contact with Arjinna impossible.

Nalia straightened. "There's another way."

Raif's head snapped up. "What?"

"The Eye," she said.

"Nalia . . . that's . . . *suicide*," Zanari stared at her. "I know we need to get home, but, you know—*we need to get home.*"

The Eye of Iblis: the Devil's Eye. It was a swath of desert land shared by Arjinna and Earth, the only physical point at which the two realms met without the aid of a magical portal. The Eye was a land of utter darkness, like being inside a sealed box of horrors. The gods had abandoned the land or maybe they had never been there. On the Arjinnan side, an ancient gate made of solid, spelled iron stood where the Eye began, thick and high and impenetrable. From the top of the Qaf Mountains, Zanari had once seen how the light in the sky gradually disappeared as soon as it hit the gate, fading into the inky darkness that covered the Eye at all times. No moon, sun, or stars shone above that land. No fresh wind blew through it, and rain never fell onto its parched soil. Total sensory deprivation.

"It's only suicide if you intend to die," Nalia said. "And I don't." She looked around the fire, her eyes blazing. "Calar has taken enough from me. From all of us. I'll die before she bars me from my land."

Zanari winced slightly at the possessive: *my.* The more time she spent around Nalia, the more Zanari felt like she was in the presence of royalty. It wasn't anything Nalia was consciously doing; Zanari was pretty sure of that. It was almost as if Malek's death had unlocked something inside Nalia, something that was answering an ancient call. She wondered if Raif felt it, too. He hadn't been himself since that last cavern, but there'd been no time to ask him about it.

Samar leaned forward. "The human myths say that Muhammed visited the Qaf Mountains once to try to convert the jinn to Islam. They say he journeyed through the Eye to get there—a land without light. Their legends say that it would take a human four months to travel through this darkness, but surely it wouldn't take us as long."

Nalia shook her head. "When Antharoe went through the Eye—"

"Gods, not Antharoe again," Noqril said. "Hasn't your Ghan Aisouri given us enough trouble already?"

"Let her talk," Zanari growled.

"As I was saying," Nalia continued, "when Antharoe traveled through the Eye, she didn't do it alone." She glanced at Zanari. "Do you know the story?"

Zanari was already shaking her head. "Don't even think about it, Nalia. I know what you're going to say."

"*Antharoe and the Blind Seer*." Nalia leaned forward, her eyes on Zanari. Her words tumbled together in her excitement. "She had a jinni with her who had your *voiqhif*. Zanari, you found me when you were in Arjinna. You kept track of Haran while he roamed the whole Earth. You're far more powerful than you give yourself credit for."

"First," Zanari said, "we don't know how much of this legend is true. Second, my *voiqhif* is hardly reliable. I mean, what if I end up getting us stranded in the middle of the Eye? We'd just be wandering around in complete darkness until we died. You really want to risk all of our lives for the *slight* chance I can get us to Arjinna?"

"Yes," Nalia said. "Because I believe in you. And because Calar won't open that portal again. Not for a long time, anyway."

"To keep you out, of course," Yezhud spat. "You said so yourself, she doesn't want anyone challenging her for the throne." She glared at Nalia. "We were fine until you came along. Safe and at peace. Now our people are gone—dead or enslaved because of you, because we saved your life."

Raif stood and when he spoke his voice was cold as steel. "You will stop speaking—*now*." His fingers sparked with *chiaan*. "Or I will give you sufficient motivation."

Samar angled his body in front of Yezhud. "Are we going to do this, brother?"

"I won't have her speaking to Nalia that way."

"Raif—" Nalia began.

He turned to her. "You've punished yourself enough, Nal. This isn't your fault."

"My brother's right," Zanari said. "This is exactly what Calar does. She makes people so afraid, so desperate, that they'll give up their own family members to save their skin."

"She isn't our family?" Yezhud said.

"But I *am* your empress."

Nalia gasped as soon as the words left her mouth, her fingers flying to her lips, as though she could somehow shove them back in. Zanari stared at her, then glanced at Raif. His eyes were wide.

"I'm sorry," Nalia whispered. "I don't know where that came from." She looked around her, dazed. "*Shalinta. Forgive me.*"

Nalia sprinted into the darkness. Raif started after her, but Zanari grabbed his arm. "Let her go," she said. "Just . . . first things first."

Gods, Zanari thought, *if Nalia wants the throne we might as well give up right now. Or help her.* Because one thing was for certain: whatever side Nalia was on would be victorious.

Raif looked to where Nalia had gone, then turned back to his sister. "You were right—I've never given you enough credit. No one has. You can lead us through the Eye."

Raif's eyes pleaded with her, eyes she'd never been able to say no to. Eyes full of a feverish, desperate hope. Zanari couldn't bear to take that away from him. They'd come so far.

Zanari eyed the jinn assembled around the fire. "I will do everything in my power to help us cross. I won't lie—it's incredibly dangerous. In Antharoe's stories, ghouls live in the Eye and gods know what else. And there's nothing there to draw power from. We can bring elements with us, but we'll have to use them sparingly."

Zanari turned to Anso. "With your power, Anso, we might actually be able to defeat them. What you did to Haraja—maybe you can do that on a bigger scale." She smiled. "It'd be good practice before we face the Ifrit army, anyway."

Anso nodded. "I could try."

"We won't make it across without an army," Raif said.

"Where are we going to find an *army*?" said Noqril.

Raif had already told Zanari about his plans. Before the Dhoma had been captured, she'd thought they'd never agree to helping them fight. But now, they had no choice.

"There's our army," Raif said, pointing to the pile of bottles they'd brought up from the cave.

"You can't be serious," Yezhud said, but Samar's eyes were on the bottles, thoughtful.

"You said these jinn were being punished for rebelling against Solomon, correct?" Raif said.

Samar nodded. "Yes. And we have reason to believe they were soldiers—their leader had been forced to command a jinn army on behalf of Solomon, to fight the Master King's wars. In my family, the story is that all of these jinn were under this jinn leader's command and had agreed to rise up against Solomon." Samar glanced at the bottles again, his eyes dark. "But they could not fight against the power of the ring."

"We don't know what shape they're in, of course," Raif said, "but right now it looks like we have two thousand trained soldiers who, I'm guessing, might be more than a little happy to let off some aggression. If I were them, I'd be pretty upset after being forced into a bottle for three thousand years. A fight might be just what they need."

Samar looked at the Dhoma and, one by one, they turned their hands so that their palms faced up. He stood and crossed to Raif, then held out his hand.

"We will help you across the Eye, Raif Djan'Urbi. In exchange, you and your *tavrai* must help us free the Dhoma who have been imprisoned in Ithkar. You will have to ask the jinn in the bottles yourself about joining your army. I cannot speak for them but I, for one, simply want to free my people. I'll fight with you against the Ifrit until my people are rescued and the portal is open."

Zanari knew it wasn't quite the agreement Raif was hoping for, but it was the best he could get.

Raif shook the Dhoma leader's hand. "Deal."

NALIA SAT ATOP ONE OF THE DUNES BORDERING THE camp. The Sahara lay before her, calm and silver in the light of the full moon. Its immensity was comforting. She liked being a tiny speck on the surface of its vast, ever-changing skin. The desert reminded her that the universe was bigger than she was, bigger than portals and Calar and dead masters and murdered brothers.

She lay on her back and closed her eyes, her fingers automatically straying to Bashil's worry stone. It was cold out here, far away from the warmth of the Dhoma fire, but there was no wind and she'd manifested a thick shawl to cover her *sawala*. The tunic and leggings were comfortable, yet elegant. No more clothes from Earth for her; she wanted to feel like a jinni again, not a slave to human wishmakers.

The problem was, Nalia didn't know what that meant

anymore. Being suddenly free after years of exile and slavery was disorienting. She had become so used to being the Nalia Earth had forced her to be that she had no idea who she *really* was. The girl she'd been before the coup had died in that cellar with the other Ghan Aisouri. The slave who'd been desperate to free her brother had burned with his body. The stoic warrior who'd fought her way to Solomon's sigil was no longer under the compulsion of a wish or a promise. And now . . . .

Nalia kept hearing herself say those awful words to Yezhud: *I am your empress.*

Where had that come from? It'd been as if someone had stolen Nalia's voice and spoken for her. There'd been no thrill of power when the words left her mouth: just a calm certainty, a rightness. But how could asserting her claim to the throne feel right when Nalia had no desire to rule Arjinna? The Amethyst Crown held no allure for her. She agreed with Raif—Arjinna was better served being ruled by its jinn. To her, the palace was nothing more than a graveyard now.

She dreaded returning to the tent she shared with Raif. How could she explain what she'd said by the fire if she didn't even understand it herself? He hated the royal family. He believed the monarchy was evil and had spent his whole life fighting against such consolidated power. How could he trust that she wasn't a threat to his revolution after what she'd said? It didn't matter that the words *long live the empress* had slipped past his lips—neither of them would live very long if he said them when anyone else was around.

The tavrai would string me up if they heard me talking like this.

Nalia sat up, suddenly, desperately anxious. She had to talk to him. They'd been through so much—she couldn't bear him being upset with her. Or leaving her. He was all she had.

When Nalia reached the tent, a sigh of relief escaped her lips. A dim light streamed from underneath the flap: he'd decided to stay. She suddenly felt silly for doubting Raif. He'd been willing to die for her—he certainly wasn't going to leave her after one ill-advised comment. Nalia ducked inside, then pulled the flap shut behind her. They'd been in a hurry, and the tent was small, with nothing more than a few thick rugs strewn on the floor and a mattress in one corner, covered with heavy blankets. It was all newly manifested, but it felt like home. Maybe because it was theirs and blocked out the rest of the world.

Raif was sitting on a rug, shirtless, squinting at a small mirror. A single lamp hung from the center of the tent, casting a rose-tinted glow over their few possessions. His face was covered in shaving cream and he held a razor blade in his hand. He looked up when she came in.

"Hey," he said. His voice was soft, guarded.

Nalia sat across from him, folding her legs underneath her so that she rested on her knees.

He gestured toward his face. "I tried doing it the old-fashioned way, but I can never manifest a perfect shave."

"Do you want help?"

"Please." He handed her the blade.

She rinsed it in the bowl of water beside his knee and leaned toward him. He smelled like summer and sandalwood. Nalia ran the blade along his cheek, holding her breath as Raif's eyes watched her. His energy made her blood heat and she knew she should be thinking about what she'd said by the fire, but he was so close and they were alone, finally alone. She was too full of want and need and the feeling she always got in her stomach whenever he was around. The silence felt dangerous and she wasn't sure if it was in a good way.

"You look like your father with this beard," she said.

"That's why I'm shaving it off."

Nalia glanced at him, furrowing her brow.

"I'm not him," Raif said. "And I don't want people at home to see me and think I'll be the leader he was. I would only disappoint. Especially now," he added.

What did he mean by that? She was afraid to ask.

"You're very good at what you do, Raif." Nalia smiled softly. "You certainly terrified Yezhud."

He grunted and she continued her path across his face: shave, rinse, shave, rinse. Outside, a wind picked up and the grains of sand brushing the sides of the tent sounded like the soft patter of rain. She could hear the other jinn in the camp moving about—quiet conversation, the clatter of dishware. Inside the tent, there was only the scrape of the razor against Raif's skin, the sound of his breath.

"Nalia." She looked up. "Tell me what happened out there."

His voice was gentle, concerned.

"I don't know," she said. She dipped the blade in the water and set it over the bowl, then manifested a towel. "Something . . . came over me. I don't understand what happened or why it happened. It wasn't me and yet for the first time in my life I felt like I was real. Does that make sense?"

He ran a callused finger across her jaw. "Yes and no. Mostly yes."

She began wiping the shaving cream off his skin.

"I've been a fool, Nal." She opened her mouth to speak, but he pressed a finger against her lips. "Just listen to me for a second. You are the most powerful jinni alive and as much as I hate it, according to our ancient laws you *are* the heir to the throne. It was stupid of me to think you could be one of the *tavrai* or that it would somehow be easy for you to reject the crown."

"Raif, I don't want to be empress—"

"But you are," he said. The sadness in his eyes was like a knife thrust between her ribs.

She rested her forehead against his chest and he smoothed the short locks of her hair as he continued.

"I didn't really understand before. All I knew of the Ghan Aisouri was their cruelty," Raif said. "But I know *you*." He lifted her chin with his finger. "I've seen how your power can be used for the highest good. I know your heart. And I can't deny that the gods have given you all this power for a reason. Maybe it's not to rule, but it's for something bigger than you and I, that much is obvious."

"Right now, I only know two things for certain," she said. "I love you. That's one. The other is that I'm going to do everything in my power to make sure Calar is destroyed. Other than that . . ." She shrugged. "I just want that house near the Forest of Sighs you dreamed up for us. Not a palace or a throne."

This was the truth of her, as she knew it now. Nalia reached up and let her fingers graze the smooth surface of his cheeks. He leaned into her touch.

"When we were stranded at Solomon's altar, I watched you all night," he said. "Couldn't sleep."

He reached out and brushed his finger across Solomon's sigil, where it lay against her skin.

"You were talking in your sleep," he said. She tensed, the memory of that last night in Marrakech still painfully clear. He must have noticed the worry in her eyes because he shook his head. "Not about Kir. You were arguing with the dead empress of Arjinna."

Once again, she saw the empress's eyes opening, felt the weight of the Amethyst Crown upon her head.

"It was just a dream," Nalia said. "I have nightmares all the time. It was about the coup and . . . it was just a dream." Her voice was laced with desperation.

"Nalia." He grasped her hands, kissed them. "When my father died, nobody asked me if I wanted to take his place. Did I ever tell you that?"

She shook her head.

"I was fifteen. The *tavrai* voted that very night. My father had only been dead for a matter of hours and suddenly I was leading hundreds of jinn—most of them far older than me—in a war we were obviously losing." He shook his head. "I cried myself to sleep that night. You're the only person who knows that."

"Raif, we're fighting for the same thing. I promise. I don't want the throne. I *don't.*"

But something had made her say those words to Yezhud—a part of Nalia believed she was the empress already. *Wadj kef*, the empress had said in her dream. *Obey the blood.*

"I know." Raif placed his palm against her heart, warm and protective. "But not everyone is going to see it that way. What you said tonight—"

"I didn't mean it!"

He sighed. "I don't know if you have a choice in the matter. The gods have a way of controlling things where you're concerned."

"Maybe an empress doesn't have to sit on a throne or wear a crown," she said. "Maybe she can just love her land and her people and fight like hell for them. Maybe that's enough."

"Well, you certainly fought for them tonight. We're going, by the way. To the Eye."

"The jinn inside the bottles, too?"

"Hopefully. We're freeing them tomorrow and then I'll make our request known. We'll see how willing they are to go to the Eye after being stuck inside an equally dark bottle."

"What about the other jinn on Earth? The ones not on the dark caravan. They could fight, too."

She thought of Malek's sister-in-law, Saranya, and the jinn she'd spent so many nights with at Habibi. *Saranya.* Would she want to know that Malek had finally done something good? Probably not. Nothing could erase murdering his own brother.

"I thought of that, but there's just no time," Raif said. "Once we get the portal open again, I can come back and recruit."

Nalia nodded. "That makes sense." She suddenly smiled,

struck by a thought. "Your mother——"

He nodded. "Yeah. Zan said with the portal closed, *habma'alah* is impossible. So . . . good news. Kind of."

"Definitely good news."

Outside, she could hear the faint sound of Noqril's *zhifr*. It reminded her of that night over a month ago when she and Raif had danced at Habibi and, later, when Raif had followed her to the glowworm cave. He caught her eye and she was almost certain he was remembering the same thing: the heat of the dance, discovering each other's *chiaan* for the first time. Becoming one under a glowing underground sky. Nalia crawled into Raif's lap and brought her lips to his neck.

"I want my last nights on Earth to be the only thing I remember about it."

He sucked in his breath as her lips grazed his earlobe. "I think we can manage that."

Raif wrapped his arms around her waist and stood, carrying Nalia over to the bed. They tumbled onto it and she pressed her mouth to his, hungry. The wind picked up outside and Nalia shivered as it found its way through the flap. Raif pulled back the covers and they slid underneath the blankets.

"Whoa," he said, looking down at the sheets. "What's this?"

"Silk." She blushed. "I wanted it to be nice."

"Ah, so *this* is what it's like to spend a night with the empress," he said with a wicked smile. "A lowly Djan like me . . ."

"Shut up," she said, hitting him. He laughed and pulled her closer.

They peeled off the layers between them and in the warmth

and comfort of their little tent, Earth became a place of joy and discovery.

"Empress or no, I choose you," Raif whispered. "Every time, Nalia. I choose you."

Nalia would never be able to forget being a slave. She'd never forget Malek's cruel affection or the loss of Leilan. And she'd never, ever get over Bashil.

But Raif's kisses and the feel of him against her was a world reborn and she wanted to live there forever.

EARLY-MORNING LIGHT FOUND ITS WAY INTO THE TENT, stealing the night.

Raif opened his eyes and in that first waking moment, life was perfect. Nalia was asleep in his arms, alive. The sigil hung from her neck, pressed between them. Malek was dead.

Then he remembered what the day would bring: convincing two thousand jinn to join the revolution and possibly die on the journey there.

Raif gently disentangled himself from Nalia and slipped out of bed. He pulled on his uniform: black tunic and drawstring pants, white armband. It was time to start looking like a soldier again. As he rolled up his sleeves, he glanced down at the scar shaped like an eight-pointed star, all that remained of the tattoo on his forearm. For him, it represented Nalia as much as the sigil.

He pressed his fingers against it. Raif didn't expect anything, but there was a wisp of magic still left inside his skin. Instead of the hologram image that had once appeared of *Erg Al-Barq*, the lightning dune above the cave, all he could see was a swath of Sahara under a calm morning sky. It hovered in the half-light of the tent, a shimmering mirage. The City of Brass, the cave, Haraja—all of it—might as well have been wiped off the face of the earth. The image faded and when he tried to call it up again, nothing happened.

There was a rustle of sheets and a soft sigh. He turned around. Nalia was sitting up, watching him. One look at her and Raif dropped his head into his hands.

"Oh my gods, there is nothing sexier than you wearing only the most powerful magical object in the worlds," he groaned, turning away from her. "Put some clothes on before I make us embarrassingly late for breakfast."

Nalia stood and crossed the space between them. She wrapped her arms around his waist and pressed her lips to the back of his neck. "Good morning to you, too," she whispered.

"Now you've done it," he growled.

They were embarrassingly late for breakfast.

When they arrived at the communal fire, Zanari took one look at him and shook her head. "Late night, little brother?"

"Don't start with me, Zan," he said. He glanced at Phara.

"Two can play that game."

She reddened. "Right."

Off to the side stood a long table laden with row upon row of brass bottles. *My soldiers, gods willing,* he thought. For a moment, he let himself picture it: walking through the Gate of the Silent Seers, with thousands of jinn behind him and Nalia by his side, the sigil around her neck.

It'd be a miracle if they made it that far.

The *fawzel* circled overhead while the remaining Dhoma manifested yet another table to hold all the bottles.

Samar looked up as Raif approached. "*Jahal'alund,*" he said. Raif returned the greeting as he looked over the bottles. Each one had a small eight-pointed star pressed into its lead stopper.

"The *fawzel* just returned from the portal's location," Samar said. "It remains closed."

Raif nodded. "I wasn't expecting anything different." He looked up at the shape-shifting jinn. The morning sun shone on their ebony feathers and the colorful stripes on their breasts. Every now and then, they would call out to one another in their curious bird tongue.

"Do you and the other *fawzel* stay in your bird form often?" he asked.

"Usually, no. We only shift when we're patrolling or fighting," Samar said. "I wanted to make sure we're uninterrupted this morning, so they're keeping watch for us."

Nalia came up and handed Raif a mug of maté tea. He took a sip of the earthy brew. "Just think," he said. "Soon, we might be drinking real Arjinnan tea."

"It's hard to imagine," Nalia said softly.

It was one of the worst things about Earth, that strange magic that prevented the jinn from manifesting anything from Arjinna. Items from the jinn realm had to be physically transported through the portal, which meant the portal's closure had effectively halted all trade between the two worlds—good for ending the dark caravan, bad for any jinni who wanted a bottle of *savri* or a decent cup of tea.

Nalia gestured to the bottles. "Shall we begin?"

Samar bowed slightly. "Please."

She manifested a small table with a flick of her wrist and set her mug of tea on top of it. Raif shook his head. To have so much power—it would have taken him at least a minute to draw on his *chiaan* and visualize the table before manifesting it. Nalia had done it in the span of a breath, her attention directed on the bottles rather than the table.

She took the leather chain off her neck and held Solomon's sigil out to him. "Wake your army, *tavrai*."

He reached for the ring, his fingers buzzing with *chiaan*: his, Nalia's. Her violet eyes were bright, the thrill he felt reflected in them.

The bottle flew out of his hand and crimson smoke spilled from its top.

Raif picked up the first bottle and pressed the seal on the ring against the star set into the lead.

"*Our* army," he said.

"Nalia," Raif murmured. "Just in case . . ."

Violet *chiaan* sparked at her fingertips. "I'll be ready," she said.

The evanescence cleared and an Ifrit jinni stood a few feet away. He was dressed in rags and his hair was long and unkempt. Huge scars circled his wrists where iron shackles had once braceleted them. His eyes landed on the ring in Raif's hand and he began to shake uncontrollably. The jinni fell to the ground, prostrating,

"There is no god but the God of Solomon, his prophet. Prophet of God, do not kill me, for I shall never disobey you again in word or deed! I'll do anything, Master of all. Please, I beg of you—do not return me to my prison!"

Samar rushed forward. "Brother, rise. Solomon is long dead. You have nothing to fear. You're among friends."

The jinni slowly raised his head. His eyes slid from right to left, then he jumped up with surprising speed.

"Then I will give you the courtesy of choosing your own death," the Ifrit said.

"Why would you kill us?" Raif said, incredulous. "We *saved* you."

The Ifrit moved forward, his red eyes gleaming. "For a hundred years, I waited in the bottle, praying for rescue. I told myself that whoever freed me, I would give him wealth enough for a lifetime. But no one came." He took another step closer. "For the next hundred years, I vowed that I would find every treasure on Earth and give it to my rescuer. And yet no one came. I waited four hundred more years. Three wishes—that's what I would give whoever let me out of my prison. Finally, I promised myself that I would kill whoever opened the bottle, for I've had enough of masters."

He raised his hands, but before he could make good on his threat, a rush of violet *chiaan* engulfed him.

"No!" Samar yelled, but whatever else he was going to say died on his lips as he saw the transformation that was taking place in the swirl of *chiaan* Nalia had raised around the jinni.

His hair gleamed and fashioned itself into one long braid. His rags disappeared and were replaced with the same black tunic and pants that Raif and his revolutionaries wore. His skin glowed, clean of three thousand years of imprisonment. As her *chiaan* fell away, the Ifrit stared at them, blinking. He looked down at his clothing, his skin. Then he met Nalia's eyes and his own filled with tears.

"Forgive me," he whispered.

"There is nothing to forgive," Nalia said. She crossed to the Ifrit and held him up as he sobbed.

Raif remembered the words she'd said to him the night before: *Maybe an empress doesn't have to sit on a throne or wear a crown. Maybe she can just love her land and her people and fight like hell for them. Maybe that's enough.*

The people will love her, he thought. His first response to the Ifrit had been anger, yet Nalia had seen through the jinni's posturing and looked into his heart.

The jinni attempted a bow. "I am Touma."

Nalia placed a hand over her heart in return. "Nalia."

He looked into her eyes. "Ghan Aisouri," he breathed.

She shook her head. "Just a jinni like you, Touma. We're all the same here."

Phara gently took Touma's elbow. "Let's get that *chiaan* replenished, shall we?" She gestured toward the fire, and the jinni's eyes lit up. "Gods forgive me for my blasphemy," he said. He appealed to the jinn around him. "I denounced them because my refusal to accept Solomon's God and to rebel against him is what sent me into the bottle in the first place."

"Tell us your story, brother," Samar said. He motioned toward the fire. "Most of us here are Dhoma, like you. We understand."

The jinni's eyes widened. "Some of our people survived the Master King?"

Samar nodded. "Those who didn't rebel were freed after Solomon died. They settled near the place where you were imprisoned."

"The City of Brass," Touma said.

"More or less," Raif agreed. "It's much changed. We have a lot to discuss." He directed Touma's attention to the hundreds of bottles on the table. "But first, I'm sure you'd like to catch up with some old friends."

The jinni burst into fresh tears.

It took the entire day to free the jinn. By sunset, the sand was littered with empty brass bottles. Touma's tumultuous re-entry into the world made it obvious they needed a more gentle transition for the imprisoned jinn. Touma refused to leave Nalia's side, so grateful was he for her kindness. She finally put him to work as the official emissary. A system quickly developed: Raif would open the bottle, Touma would greet his old comrade and ease his fears, and Nalia would hand the jinni off to Phara for healing treatments and immersion in their element in order to replenish their *chiaan*.

It wasn't long before the camp became loud and boisterous. The Dhoma spent the better part of the day manifesting food, clothing, and shelter for their ancestors. Laughter and stories were traded over fires where succulent meats roasted. Some of the Dhoma who hadn't been captured by the Ifrit in the raid met their great-grandparents and other relatives for the first time. Raif had never seen such joy. The jinn who played music manifested their instruments, and as night descended, the air filled with song. Jinn covered the desert for as far as Raif's eyes could see.

He sat on one of the low dunes surrounding the camp, watching. Raif longed for his own reunion with his mother and the *tavrai*. But first he had to find a way to convince these jinn to go into the darkness of the Eye with him and fight for Arjinna. Judging by the festive atmosphere of the camp, he expected a fair amount of resistance to the idea. A part of him felt guilty for asking them to give up the stars so soon—and possibly their lives. But the longer they waited, the more *tavrai* died at the hands of the Ifrit. He sighed and rubbed his temples, exhausted. He wasn't at all ready to take on Calar.

Raif felt Nalia before he saw her, an energy that called to his. She stood beside him and gazed at the jinn. "I guess the Eye will have to wait a few days," she said.

He sighed. "It's starting to look like it. What's that?" he asked, gesturing to the small bag that dangled from her wrist.

A look of embarrassment crossed her face, something he hadn't seen on Nalia before.

"It's a tonic Phara made for me. You know, since last night . . . we, uh . . ."

"Ah. I suppose it would be difficult for you to fight Calar while pregnant."

"Oh, *gods*," she said, burying her face in his shoulder.

Raif wrapped an arm around her and laughed softly. They sat there for a while, content.

"Did you meet their leader?" he asked quietly. He nodded

toward a Shaitan who held court at a nearby fire.

"Not yet. Do you think you'll have trouble getting him on your side?"

Raif had only spoken to him briefly, a short conversation full of wary sizing up, each of them trying to determine the strength of the other's character. The jinni's name was Tazlim, but his jinn called him Taz. He was young, like Raif, but their ages on Earth meant little. The bottle may have arrested Taz's age, but his lengthy prison sentence made him Raif's senior by far.

Raif sighed. "I haven't had a real chance to talk with him. I'm not sure what he's about."

"It's his first night free of his bottle in thousands of years," Nalia said. "If I were him, the last thing I'd want to do is discuss several ways in which I could die. Give him some space. I'm sure he'll come around. Who can resist Raif Djan'Urbi?"

He rolled his eyes. "Plenty of people, I assure you." He intertwined his fingers with hers. "Mind working on him for me?"

"What makes you think I'll have better luck with him?"

Touma had been singing her praises all day and the story of Nalia's survival of the coup and years of slavery had spread like wildfire through the camp.

"Just a hunch," he said.

"I'll try." She brushed her lips against his cheek and headed in Taz's direction.

Raif watched her for a moment, then trudged through the camp, waving at the newly freed jinn who called out to him. He located the tent Zanari shared with Phara. A light shone inside, but the flap was closed.

"Zan?" he called.

"Come in," she said.

Zanari was seated on a thick cushion in the center of the room, surrounded by a circle of earth glowing with *chiaan*.

"How's it going?" he asked.

Her eyes were heavy, lined with dark circles that hadn't been there in the morning.

"It's . . . going," she said.

"That bad, huh?" Raif sat across from her. "Tell me how I can help."

"I found it," she whispered.

His eyes lit up. "Zan, that's great!"

But Zanari's expression was troubled. "Are you sure you want to do this, little brother?"

"We don't have a choice."

"I was afraid you'd say that." She looked at her hands. They trembled. "It's the most terrifying place I've ever been, Raif. There's nothing there. I mean *nothing*. It's like hanging out in Haran's soul."

"Zan, we *have* to do this."

"Stop saying *have to*," she snapped.

Raif stared at her. "I only meant—"

"Say *want to*. Because we have a choice, little brother. We're here. We're alive. I don't know if that will be the case tomorrow." Her voice shook and she drew her arms around her knees. "It's like being in one of those boxes the humans put their dead in. There's no *chiaan*. No light. The air is . . . dead. No wind. I put my hands on the ground and the earth gave me nothing. It was dry, not like sand, like ashes."

Raif went cold. Zanari was the one person he'd always been able to count on. But maybe being on Earth had changed that.

"Are you backing out?" he asked.

Part of him wanted her to. The evil, selfish part. He'd grab Nalia and run. Make love every night and never think of Arjinna again.

"No," she said. "But I wish to the gods I could."

"Tell me," Taz said as he wiped grease from the evening meal off his hands, "how does an empress find her way to the Dhoma?"

There it was again: *empress.*

Nalia sat back on her hands. "It's a long story."

"I've got time."

He was handsome, pretty in that Shaitan way. Princely: almond eyes, bronze skin, delicate features. And yet the leader of the rebellion against Solomon was like Raif in many ways. There was a stubbornness in his eyes that all his years in captivity hadn't been able to erase. He held himself with the tenseness of a soldier, as though he expected to be attacked at any moment, but knew he would defeat whoever attempted to harm him.

"A trade," she said. "Your story first, and then I'll tell you mine."

"You're used to getting your way, aren't you, Ghan Aisouri?"

"Nalia," she said. "And, no, I rarely get my way."

"No doubt you do with Raif Djan'Urbi." Taz's Shaitan eyes

met hers, a challenge, but of what she didn't know.

"Raif's my *rohifsa*," she said softly. "It isn't about getting my way or not getting my way with him."

Taz cocked his head to the side. "A royal with a Djan peasant? Times *have* changed in Arjinna."

Something flashed in his eyes, a secret hurt. Nalia recognized it and wondered at the source of the wound.

"Not in Arjinna," Nalia said. "We've made our own rules here on Earth. That's what Raif's fighting for."

"And you?"

The weight of the crown. The empress's dead eyes looking up at her.

"I was a slave on the dark caravan for years and have only just been freed. Other than the Djan'Urbis, I've lost everyone I love. What am I fighting for?" She hugged her knees to her chest. "*Life.* The right to go home. Same as you, no?"

Taz nodded and cast thoughtful eyes on the fire. "I left Arjinna just before I was enslaved by Solomon. My father was an overlord and I couldn't bear the way he treated his serfs. He sent me to the border wars—he thought making me kill Ifrit would turn me into a real jinni. Instead I fell in love with a fellow soldier. He was a Djan, same as your Raif." He shook his head, as though he could make a memory fall out. "Anyway, my father and I fought. Horrible things were said. Me to him, him to me." He studied his hands. "I've thought of that last conversation with him so many times. I wish . . ." He sighed. "Anyway, my *rohifsa* and I came here—ran away. We thought it was romantic. An adventure. But then Solomon and his ring turned us into serfs

468

and I lost . . . more than my freedom." That flash of pain again, just for an instant. He glanced at where the sigil lay around Nalia's neck. "You should destroy it."

"I know."

He raised his eyebrows. "But . . ."

She said nothing. She shouldn't have said anything at all. Talking to this Dhoma was a mistake.

"Ah," he said. "Your *rohifsa*."

"He hopes it will drive Calar and the Ifrit from Arjinna." Even to her ears, Nalia could hear how defensive of Raif she was.

"But you think otherwise."

This is not going well, she thought.

"I think there are many ways to fight our enemy," she said.

"The ring is one of them. You and your jinn are another."

He smiled. "I was wondering when you'd get around to this." Nalia leaned forward. "You said you hated how your father treated the serfs. I felt the same way when I was a Ghan Aisouri. They made me do . . . terrible things. Even if I lived as long as you have, I could never forgive myself for the pain I caused. I'm trying to make things right. Better. With us, you have a chance to change all those things that made you leave Arjinna. You can go home: we have a way even though the portal's closed. And you can help free the Dhoma who've been captured. What would you do instead, Tazlim? *Ya ghaer bhin fa'arim.*"

It was a scrap of ancient poetry, beloved by the Shaitan.

"*My land, a whisper on the wind,*" he quoted. His eyes misted and he looked away. "I can see why Raif sent you over here."

She opened her mouth to protest, but he held up a hand.

"It's hard to resist a beautiful, learned jinni with passion for the oppressed. But tell me, Nalia Aisouri'Taifyeh, what will you do when the Amethyst Crown is no longer upon Calar's head?"

"Return to Earth." No matter what role she played in Arjinna's future, this was nonnegotiable.

His eyes widened. "You're full of surprises, aren't you?"

"I plan to free the slaves on the dark caravan, not sit on a throne." She smiled. "When that's done I want to be a farmer's wife."

A fantasy, that last part. Still, it was true. It was what she wanted.

Taz threw his head back and laughed. "You don't like having power, then?" He brought a clay mug of wine up to his lips. He offered it to Nalia first, but she shook her head.

"I rule myself," she said. "And no one else."

He looked at her for a long moment, a searching gaze that took the measure of her. "Tell me your story," he said softly.

Nalia stared with the afternoon in the dungeon with Calar, before Nalia knew the prisoner she was freeing was actually the Ifrit leader. She described the coup, the slave auction where the human wishmakers stared at her body and bid on her. She told him of Malek and the bottle and trying to take him to her bed. Losing Leilan to Haran's fiendish appetite, and her night in the shadow lands of death. Bashil, dying in her arms, and that long, grief-filled sleep in the Dhoma camp. The terror of losing her *chiaan*, the burn of the lightning as it split her wide open. The *si'lah*s and the other horrors of the cave. Malek falling into the chasm. It took less than an hour to narrate three years of terror and grief.

Taz pressed his hand to his heart. *"Hif la'azi vi,* My Empress."

My heart breaks for you.

"Don't call me that," she whispered.

"I said I opposed the way my father and the Aisouri treated the serfs—*not* that I opposed royal rule," Taz said. "I don't want a Master King ruling over me, as Solomon was. But you know the history of our land as well as I do. Before the Aisouri took power, we were just warring tribes. Uncivilized. Do you really think the jinn today will fare much better? And what of the Ifrit who follow Calar? If they're anything like they were three thousand summers ago, I doubt very much you want them crawling over your land."

"Our land. And that's not for me to decide. Arjinnans want to be free, they want—"

"A leader. Look at your Raif. He leads them, does he not? Will *he* wear the Amethyst Crown?"

"Raif isn't a dictator. He doesn't want—" Nalia shook her head. "You don't understand him. He's good, through and through. It's not power he wants: it's freedom. Ruling is just another kind of shackle. Besides, if he really wanted to rule, he wouldn't have risked his life so many times for me."

"Then you have answered my question."

"What do you mean?" she snapped.

"You told me how Raif stayed to help you fight Haran. How he jumped into the chasm before you could sacrifice your life for your master's third wish. He would have died if your master hadn't saved him. These are the actions of a subject who values his empress's life above his own."

The truth of what Taz was saying hit her hard. But Nalia

didn't want it to be the truth. "You're wrong. He did those things because he loves me."

"Yes, he does. But you, I think, are empress of his heart in more ways than one. He just might not yet know that yet."

Taz stood and bowed. "My army is yours, My Empress. We will fight for you."

He turned and walked away, toward the tent that had been manifested for him. Nalia wrapped her arms around her chest.

What have I done?

ZANARI GAZED ACROSS THE SEA OF BODIES THAT COV-
ered the Sahara from her vantage point atop a mountainous dune.
Most of the jinn in the bottles had agreed to join them in the Eye.
They were calling themselves the Brass Army, and their ranks
glimmered in the early-morning light, where their chests bore
witness to their imprisonment in the form of brass pins, melted
down from the bottles that had trapped them. Zanari had seen
a few of the pins already: the sign of the Djan—a *widr* tree; the
cresting wave of the Marid; the flame of the Ifrit; a swirl of wind
for the Shaitan. All four castes, wearing the same uniform. This,
in and of itself, was a victory.

Those who had refused to join their ranks were unwell. Their
haunted expressions told the story of what their time in the bottle
had cost them. Phara, along with Samar's wife, Yezhud, and most

of the *fauzel*, would be staying behind to care for the jinn whose spirits had been shattered by their enslavement, and prepare the camp for the return of her people.

"So this is it? I just . . . leave and you stay?" Zanari had said the night before.

Phara had smiled, sad, but certain. "Yes, I think so." She rested her forehead against Zanari's. "But I will miss you. And pray to the gods for your safety every night."

It hadn't been a surprise. Zanari knew that Phara was Dhoma through and through. She had no love for Arjinna, no desire to be there. And though Zanari could see herself making a life on Earth, she missed her land. More than that, she couldn't abandon her brother.

Zanari didn't know what it meant, that she'd been able to make the choice to leave Phara. When Raif and Nalia thought they had to be apart, it was the end of the world for them. What they shared wasn't just love: it was a partnership that would shake the very foundations of the realm. Someday, jinn would sing songs about them around campfires.

Zanari and Phara didn't have that, but maybe love didn't always look that way.

She closed her eyes and raised her face to the sun, savoring these last few moments of light and fresh air. Phara wasn't the only thing she'd be leaving behind when she and the army crossed into the Eye.

Raif came to stand beside her, a low whistle escaping from between his lips. "I want to see the look on Calar's face when this walks through the Gate of the Silent Seers."

She opened her eyes. "You can say that again, brother."

The Brass Army stood as one. Female and male, they all wore the black uniform of the revolution and their brass pins, but there was one other addition to the uniform—something that worried Zanari to no end. Where she and Raif wore the white armband of the *tavrai*, the Brass soldiers wore a braided one with white and purple fabric twisted together: the white of the revolution and the violet of Nalia's royal line.

"And those armbands?" she asked softly. "What do you think of those?"

Raif sighed. "Nalia wants the people of Arjinna to decide for themselves who will lead them, but Tazlim was very clear that his jinn are fighting for her to take the throne. These armbands were a compromise, trust me."

"And . . . how do you feel about this?"

He hesitated. "I don't know."

"You don't know," she repeated. Fear bloomed inside Zanari as the words sank in. So she hadn't been imagining the change in her brother since that moment in the cave when he'd nearly died for Nalia. He'd been silently wrestling with something, she knew, but Zanari had no idea it was something this big.

"I know everything you're going to say, Zan. I can't talk about it. Not right now."

She held her brother's eyes for a long moment, then finally nodded. This was a conversation that belonged to an entire night, with a bottle of *savri*. The problem was, that night wasn't happening until *after* the *tavrai* saw those armbands.

"The *tavrai* . . ." she began.

"I know, Zan. Trust me, I know." He rested a hand on her shoulder. "Phara?"

Zanari sighed. "It's over."

He gave her a thoughtful look. "I wouldn't be so sure." Then, unexpectedly, Raif wrapped his arms around her. "I love you, Zan. Whatever happens in the Eye, I just . . . I want you to know that."

She hugged him tight, then pushed him away, the side of her mouth turning up. "Don't go soft on me, little brother."

It took a surprisingly short time to assemble the jinn. They wiped all traces of their presence in the desert. If Calar had spies, they didn't want to tip their hand that they'd raised an army.

"So you're the sister," Taz said, coming up to Zanari.

She nodded, unsmiling. "Yep. I'm the sister." She was getting so tired of that role.

"Also known as the Incredibly Talented Seer?" Taz raised an eyebrow and when he did, his face lost some of its perfect beauty. It made her warm to him, just a little.

A small smile sneaked onto Zanari's face. "Now you're just trying to get on my good side."

Taz nodded in mock solemnity. "You're the one who'll see the ghouls coming—I plan to stick quite close to you for the next . . . however long we'll be roaming impenetrable darkness."

"I have a personal bubble," she said. Nalia had taught her that human expression after one too many of Noqril's advances.

"I like bubbles."

Zanari rolled her eyes and he laughed. For a jinni who'd been imprisoned in a bottle for thousands of years, Taz was remarkably well adjusted.

"So, how exactly does this work?" he continued.

Zanari pointed to where Nalia and the other Djan stood at intervals around the large circle of jinn, their hands pressed to the earth.

"The Djan are creating a circle around all of us," Zanari said. "In order to access my *voiqhif* to the extent we'll need it today, the more power the better. The circle also has to remain strong enough so that we can evanesce as a group."

Taz whistled. "We're all going to evanesce at the same time based on your vision of the Eye—can that even be done?"

Zanari nodded. "It's been done before. Just . . . on a smaller scale."

A much smaller scale, she thought. Antharoe and her blind seer hadn't made their way across the Eye dragging over two thousand jinn.

Zanari noticed a puff of violet smoke shoot up on the other side of the circle and in seconds, Nalia had evanesced beside them.

"We're ready," Nalia said.

Zanari settled onto the sand and placed her fingertips on the outer rim of the circle. It glowed bright green.

Touma, the first jinni who had been freed of his bottle, rushed up to Nalia, bowing low before her.

"My Empress—"

Nalia held up her hand. "Touma, *please.* Nalia, just Nalia, okay?"

Zanari bit her lip, watching them. How had this empress thing gotten so out of hand, so quickly?

Touma rose from his bow. "Please let me be of assistance to

you on the journey. Anything you need." His eyes glistened with tears. "Taz told us of the terrors you've endured. When I think of you losing nearly everyone you love . . . "

Great, fat tears began falling down the Ifrit's face.

"Oh, gods, not again," Zanari said. "Nalia, control your pet."

Nalia glared at Zanari, exasperated, then manifested a handkerchief. "Why don't you stay nearby, Touma? Your presence is a . . . comfort to me."

"Oh, yes, My Emp— " He coughed. "Er, Nalia. I'd be most honored."

Raif watched the exchange, frowning.

"Okay, little brother, do your thing," Zanari said.

He manifested two ladders and climbed to the top of one.

Taz began to climb the one beside him. "Wish me luck?" he said, looking back at Zanari.

"Luck," Zanari said. As Taz began ascending the ladder, she turned to Nalia. "I hate to admit it, but I kinda like him."

"I like him, too," Nalia said. "I think. But I don't know if I trust him."

"I hear you on that, sister," Zanari agreed.

Raif began speaking to the assembled jinn, his voice magically amplified. Despite the size of the crowd, it was silent. "Brothers and sisters. Today we are going home. To Arjinna. To the land that is ours and ours alone."

The Dhoma cheered.

"The journey will be dangerous," Raif continued. "And anyone who does not wish to undertake it may feel free to leave this circle."

None of the jinn moved.

"Good," Raif said, after a moment. "I admire your courage and pray the gods will bless you for it. *Jahal'alund.*"

His speech lacked the intimacy he had with the *tavrai*. This wasn't Raif's army—not yet, anyway. Zanari wasn't surprised. His *tavrai* fell in love with her brother on the battlefield, not off it. He was no politician. Give him a fight, though, and there was no one better to lead.

Raif turned to Taz and nodded.

"Fellow slaves of the Master King—you are slaves *no more!*" the Shaitan commander called.

The jinn responded with a roar. The sound gave Zanari goose bumps. It reminded her of her father, cheering on the *tavrai* just hours before he died in the second uprising.

"And you have one person to thank for your freedom," Taz said. "One person who knows what it's like to be imprisoned in a bottle with no hope of escape. Her royal blood paid the price for our freedom. We give her ours in exchange." Taz gestured to where Nalia stood beside Zanari, shrinking into the ground.

"Fire and blood, what's he doing?" Nalia growled.

"I take back the part where I said I liked him," Zanari said.

"We pledge our blood to you, Nalia Aisouri'Taifyeh, rightful Empress of Arjinna, Keeper of the Amethyst Crown, and heir to the throne."

The jinn were silent, each one immediately going to their knees.

Taz descended the ladder and bowed before Nalia, one knee on the desert floor.

"Stop it," Nalia hissed. "I don't want this!"

"*They* need this," Taz said. "If you ask jinn to die, they need to know *why*. And for *who*." He stood and reached out a hand. "Speak to your people."

Nalia looked up to where Raif stood. His jaw was tight and he gave her a slight nod. She ignored Taz's hand and pulled herself up the ladder.

Zanari couldn't hear what Nalia whispered to Raif when she joined him, but she saw his hand reach back to caress her spine and knew his anger wasn't at the jinni beside him, but at Taz.

"Please," Nalia said to the jinn. "Rise."

Zanari couldn't help it—something about seeing Nalia up there, hearing her speak—it made *her* want to bend the knee.

What have we done?

"I do not want you to fight for me," Nalia called. "Fight for yourselves and your families. Fight for freedom and the right to live the life you want. Spill your blood for an Arjinna where there are no shackles and bottles and masters. The revolution is inside all of us." She turned to Raif. "*Kajastriya vidim.*"

"Light to the revolution," Zanari whispered to herself. Her eyelids slid down and she began searching for the Eye.

The Eye of Iblis, the Devil's Eye, a place without the gods. In some cultures, they might even call it *hell*. The jinn didn't believe in hell as the humans did. For them, Hell was a place where the gods refused to go. It was an absence of all that was good and beautiful. An absence of life and the things that made it worth living. This was the world without the gods.

Zanari pushed deep into her mind, no longer aware of her

surroundings. She could feel the energy of the circle pulsing through her fingertips as she traveled the lines of her *voiqhif*, rushing past the twists and turns of the universe. A child's laugh, a sunny beach, buildings that touched the sky. Faces, faces, so many and the world so big and so much and—

Nothing.

There, in the corner of her mind, a place hollowed out of time and space. Silent. Dark. Without form or color, without anything.

Zanari pressed closer, until she could see the darkness before her, a gaping mouth. She stepped inside. This was it. She concentrated on the exact sensation of erasure, of absence.

Then she willed her body to evanesce.

Zanari could feel them now, Raif and Nalia and Anso, Samar, Noqril, Taz, Touma, and the thousands of strands of *chiaan* that made up the Brass Army. They pressed close to her and as her body began to break apart into specks of jade evanescence that hurtled across the earth, Zanari melted into the energy around her, pieces of her mixing with pieces of all the jinn until she began to lose all sense of herself. They were one, the fierce desire for home pulsing through these broken hearts, a communal wish to reclaim what had been stolen from them. Zanari cried out, holding on to the image of nothingness, the sense of deletion.

Finally, stillness.

Zanari opened her eyes to oblivion. "We're here."

The darkness swallowed them whole.

Pronunciation Guide

Jinni: JEE-nee
Jinn: JIN

JINN CASTES

Shaitan: shy-TAN
Djan: JAN
Ifrit: if-REET
Marid: muh-RID
Aisouri: ass-or-EE

CHARACTERS

Amir: ah-MEER
Anso: AN-so
Bashil: bah-SHEEL
Calar: cuh-LAHR
Dthar: d-THAR
Haraja: hah-RAH-ja
Haran: huh-RAHN
Jordif: JOR-diff

Leilan: lay-LAHN
Malek: MAL-ick
Nalia: NAH-lee-uh
Noqril: no-KREEL
Phara: FARE-ah
Raif: RAFE
Samar: sah-MAR
Saranya: sah-RAN-yah
Tazlim: TAZ-leem
Touma: TOO-mah
Umbek: OOM-bek
Yezhud: YEH-zhood
Zanari: zah-NAHR-ee

Glossary

bisahm (bee-ZAH-m) A magical shield used to cover an area in order to prevent jinn from evanescing into it.

chiaan (chee-AHN) The magical energy force that all jinn possess.

Dhoma (DOH-ma) The Forgotten—a desert tribe of jinn on Earth. The jinn are from all different castes and reside in the Sahara.

evanesce / evanescence This is the same word in English, but used differently. When jinn travel by smoke, they evanesce. The smoke itself is called evanescence.

fawzel (faw-ZEL) Jinn who shape-shift, usually from human to bird form.

gaujuri (gow-JER-ee) A hallucinogenic drug used in Arjinna.

gharoof (gah-ROOF) A term of endearment for children. Translates as "little rabbit."

hahm'alah (HAHM-ah-lah) The magic of true names, whereby jinn can contact one another psychically.

jai (j-EYE) A term of endearment used among family members; a *suffix, as in Nalia-jai.*

Kada (KAH-dah) *The jinn language.*

keftuhm (KEF-toom) *Blood waste. A term referring to male off-spring of the Ghan Aisouri.*

ludeen (loo-DEEN) *Tavrai homes in the Forest of Sighs; jinn tree houses.*

niba (NEE-bah) *The jinn currency.*

pardjinn (PAR-jin) *Someone who is half jinn, half human; seen as abomination by the jinn.*

rohifsa (roe-HEEF-sah) *Jinn word for "soul mate" that translates as "song of my heart."*

sadr (s-AHD-r) *Arjinnan prayers in the jinn holy book, comparable to the Christian psalms.*

Sadranishta (s-AHD-r-ahn-EESH-tah) *Jinn holy book.*

salfit (SAL-feet) *A derogatory term used by the lower castes when referring to Shaitan and Ghan Aisouri jinn, who mostly reside in the mountains. Literal translation: "goat fucker."*

s'arawq (s-AR-ah-wok) *Arjinnan monsters; half cobra, half scorpion.*

savri (SAH-vree) *The favorite drink of the jinn, a spicy wine with hints of cardamom.*

sawala (sah-WALL-ah) *Traditional Arjinnan clothing consisting of pants and a long tunic. Worn by both males and females.*

Sha'a Rho (SHAH-ah-ROE) *Ghan Aisouri martial art, with similarities to yoga, tai chi, and kung fu.*

si'lah (SEE-lah) *Cannibalistic sirens found in underground water sources in Morocco.*

skag (SKAG) *Insult used for any caste, male or female. Loosely* translates as "motherfucker."

tavrai (tuh-VR-EYE) *Form of address used for members of the jinn resistance, similar to "comrade."*

voiqhif (v-wah-KEEF) *A psychic power similar to remote viewing. Very rare among the jinn.*

widr (wi-DEER) *An Arjinnan tree, similar to a weeping willow. Has silver leaves.*

zhifir (zh-if-EER) *An Arjinnan fiddle.*

EXPRESSIONS IN KADA

Batai vita sonouq. (buh-TAI VEE-ta soh-NOOK) *My home is yours. Used when visitors come to one's home.*

Faqua celique. (FAH-kwah seh-LEEK) *Only the stars know. Used when the future is uncertain.*

Ghar lahim. (GHAR la-HEEM) *Nice to meet you.*

Hala l'aeik. (HAH-la l-EK) *It is the will of the gods.*

Hala mashinita. (HAH-la mah-shi-NEET-ah) *Gods save me.*

Hala shalinta. (HAH-la SH-ah-lin-tah) *Gods forgive me.*

Hif la'azi vi. (HIF la-AH-zee vee) *My heart breaks for you. Used as a condolence.*

Jahal'alund. (JUH-hahl-uh-loond) *Gods be with you. Typical jinn greeting.*

Kajastriya vidim. (kuh-JAH-stree-yuh vih-DEEM) *Light to the revolution. Expression used among jinn revolutionaries, as a toast or battle call.*

Ma'aj yaqifla. (mah-AHJ yah-KEEF-lah) *I wash my hands of it.*

Shundai. (shoon-DIE) *Thank you.*

Vasalo celique. (VAH-sa-lo suh-LEEK) *Follow the stars.*

Wadj kef. (WAH-DJ KEF) *Obey the blood.*

ARABIC PHRASES

Alhamdulilah. (al-HAHM-doo-lee-lah) *Thank God.*

Bismillah (BIZ-meel-ah) *Islamic phrase, "In the name of God" —
often used colloquially before travel, for protection, and to ward
off evil spirits.*

habibi (ha-BEEB-ee) *darling.*

hayati (hai-YAH-tee) *my life: used as a term of endearment.*

Khatem l-hekma (kah-TEM l-EK-ma) *Ring of wisdom (Moroccan
term referring to King Solomon's sigil).*

Salam aleikum (sah-LAH-m ah-LIKE-koom) *Greeting in Arabic-
speaking countries. Translates as "Peace be unto you."*

Ya Allah! (YAH ah-LAH) *Oh, my God!*

Yalla habibi! (YAH-la ha-BEEB-ee) *Let's go, darling! Used among
friends and strangers.*

ACKNOWLEDGMENTS

This is a book about siblings, so I must first thank mine for all their love, support, and crazy-making ways: Meghan Demetrios, Jake Dowell, and Luke Dowell. I would fight a Calar for you.

Another round of thanks to the absolutely fantastic team at Balzer + Bray and HarperCollins: you have made this whole experience great, great fun. Next, to the B+B+B trifecta: Balzer, Bray, and Bowen. Donna Bray, brilliant editor and tireless cheerleader; Alessandra Balzer, reader of blush-inducing scenes; and finally my agent, Brenda Bowen (and everyone at Sanford Greenburger) for making dreams reality. A kiss across the pond to my UK editor, Kirsten Armstrong, and to the team at Random House UK.

My betas, for letting me know what I could get away with and what needed to be cut: Kathryn Gaglione, Sarah and Brandon Roberts, Jamie Christensen, Elena McVicar, and Megan

Gallagher. My Allies: if ever I need an army, I know you're standing by with the VCFA family. And, as always, Leslie Caulfield, Jennifer Ann Mann, and Shari Becker, my writing sisterhood of awesome. Unending thanks to Zach, ever my *rohifsa* (TS&TM&EO), and all my family and friends who continue to cheer me on. Love to Becky Stradwick, Megan Shepherd, and Sarah J. Maas.

Finally, to my readers, my Blogger Caravan, and all the bloggers out there who have shown so much enthusiasm and support for my characters and their stories: *shundai*.

Special Thanks to the
BLOGGER CARAVAN

Supernatural Snark

The Silver Words

Lili's Reflections

The Unofficial Addiction Book Fan Club

A Reading Nurse

Safari Poet

What Sarah Read

Book Whales

Swoony Boys Podcast

Book Lover's Life

Crossroad Reviews

Curling Up with a Good Book

Addicted Readers

Such a Novel Idea

The Eater of Books

YA Fanatic

[Fiktjshun]

Alexa Loves Books

Hello, Chelly

The Book Rat

Great Imaginations

Adventures of a Book Junkie

The Best Books Ever

Michelle and Leslie's Book Picks

Book Chic Club

Bewitched Bookworms

Forever Bookish

Falling for YA

That Artsy Reader Girl

The Quirky Reader

The NerdHerd Reads

A Glass of Wine

Turn the page for an excerpt from

FREEDOM'S SLAVE

BOOK THREE

of the

DARK CARAVAN CYCLE

BOTTLES.

They were the only illumination in the pitch-black room. Hundreds of them, filled with jinn of every caste. Clear bottles, pulsing with the light of their prisoners' magic. Emerald, sapphire, gold, ruby: the jinn energy swirled inside, trapped.

They covered the shelves that had been carved into the lapis lazuli wall behind the throne, just one of many changes Calar had made to the palace. She had taken to calling them her court. When faced with a decision, Calar would smile, brilliant in her cold beauty, and say, *Why don't we ask my court?* She'd caress a bottle or two, speak to the miserable jinni inside it. *What do you think I should do?*

From where Kesmir now stood, hidden in the shadows, he could just make out the shapes of the naked bodies stuffed into the vessels. A curved spine, head on knees, eyes closed in order to block out what was happening. It was a small miracle Calar had decided not to line the bottles with iron, the sick-making element that would have killed most of the jinn by now. She claimed she was being merciful by allowing them to keep their *chidan*, but Kesmir knew the truth: she liked seeing them in pain. Liked making them watch what she did from the throne. It was no fun if they were dead.

Several bottles were so tiny, they could have rested in Kesmir's palm. Others were grotesque—tall, but incredibly thin, so that the jinn inside had no choice but to stand with their arms raised above their heads. There were bottles that were so squat, they resembled discs more than vessels, and the jinn inside these looked like contortionists, their limbs held at painful, impossible angles.

They hadn't noticed Kesmir yet. He couldn't bear to see their accusing eyes. He might as well have put them in there himself. He'd often considered setting them free, but there was little good that would do. Calar would just kill them all, then find some horribly inventive way to punish her disobedient lover.

It was already too late for the prisoners whose bottles no longer emanated light. The corpses inside were slowly decaying, their spirits finally free of the bottles' confines. He'd tried to get Calar to take the dead jinn away, but she wouldn't.

They're a message, she'd said, *to anyone who dares to defy me.*

Just last night, Kesmir had been present when an Ifrit peasant begged that Calar spare his daughter's life. Begged on his knees, forehead touching the mosaic floor in deference. Sweaty skin against tiles that curled into elegant geometric stars and vines. Kesmir had been standing in his usual spot: three steps to Calar's left. The Royal Consort, His Wretchedness Kesmir Ifri'Lhas. *Royal Whore, more like,* he thought.

He faced the great hall as the sun streamed through the latticework windows and climbed the carved pillars covered with ancient Kada scrollwork—prayers to the gods for the safekeeping of the Aisouri who were long dead. The high, vaulted ceilings were covered in mother-of-pearl mosaics made to look like the sky at dawn, when the Aisouri had once trained in their ancient martial art, *Sha'a Rho*. It was the most magnificent place Kes had ever been.

Yet in the three years since taking up residence in the palace, Calar had turned it into a slaughterhouse. The throne room stank of dark magic, fear, and blood. This day would be no exception.

"Why should I spare a traitor's life?" Calar had said. She spoke in a wine-drenched drawl, more interested in the *savri* in her hand than the agonized father at her feet.

She was toying with him. Kesmir had already seen what Calar had done to the jinni's daughter—this false hope she was dangling before him was nothing more than the amusement of a bored tyrant. He shuddered and Calar's eyes flicked to his. He gave her a small smile, the cruel one they used in their games. Only he didn't want to play the games anymore. She returned the smile and Kesmir relaxed: she hadn't noticed his revulsion.

Gods, when had that happened—*revulsion?* Not so long ago his sole purpose in life had been to love her, and love her well.

"Not a traitor, My Empress. No," the jinni had said. "A silly child in love. The boy's a Djan, yes, but not a *tavrai*. I swear it. He is still a serf—please, you can ask his overlord. My daughter is a good Ifrit."

"What would you tell your daughter right now, if she could hear you?" Calar had said, her voice going soft.

This, Kesmir knew, was her favorite part.

The Ifrit began to cry. "I . . . I'd tell her I love her and that I will find a . . . a good Ifrit boy for her. No more Djan. A . . . a soldier from My Empress's army, perhaps."

Calar smiled, false benevolence. She gestured to one of the bottles behind her. Inside, an Ifrit girl's mouth was open in a silent scream, palms against the glass. Her face was bruised, lips swollen and bleeding. Like the other jinn in the bottles, she was naked. The bottle was just big enough for her to sit on her knees, her arms covering her breasts, a useless attempt at modesty. Her eyes were full of terror and shame.

The old jinni looked past Calar. Even now, Kesmir could still hear that father's precise howl of pain. It echoed in his heart and would not let him sleep at night. Not that he would have, anyway.

A sound near a far corner of the room brought Kesmir out of the memory. He gripped his scimitar, waiting. A figure in a dark cloak strode toward him, wearing a wooden mask that disguised the jinni's features—a peasant mask from the harvest celebrations, this one depicting a fox. Necessary precautions when you were trying to overthrow an empress who could read minds.

"I heard a phoenix cry tonight," the jinni said. A male this time.

Kesmir drew closer, his hand still gripping his scimitar. "I'm surprised it still has tears," he answered, voice soft.

It was a different jinni each time, but the same code. Kesmir suspected the jinni behind the mask was a Shaitan—he had the soft cadence of the jinn aristocracy, the perfect diction only the wealthy could afford to have.

"We've found someone who can help you," the jinni said.

"There are many jinn who offer to 'help' me."

The jinni slowly lifted his index finger to the side of his mask and gently tapped twice near his temple. "This kind of help, General," he said, his voice soft.

Impossible. It was too much to hope for. And yet, what this jinni presumed to offer was what Kesmir's whole plan hinged on: the first step on the path to wresting his lover's hold on Arjinna was for Kes to control his own mind, build a wall between his thoughts and her own. It would be pointless for Kesmir to overthrow Calar until he knew how to keep her in the dark, to protect his mind from being ravaged until he begged for death. Reading his mind was a pastime of hers. It used to be a way for Calar to be closer to him, but not anymore. Her mind was a weapon pointed at him as often as not. He couldn't influence her anymore, couldn't hope that her tyranny was just a phase. If he didn't depose her, someone else would. And, unlike him, they would kill her. Fool that he was, Kesmir still had hope that once she no longer had power, Calar would return to herself, to the girl she'd been when she'd rescued him long ago.

"I don't have time to waste—you've put us both at risk by setting up this meeting," Kesmir now said to the jinni before him. Disappointment tinged his voice—he couldn't hide the desolation of yet another hope dashed. "Calar killed every Aisouri trainer during the coup. There is no one left with that knowledge."

Gryphons, Shaitan warriors—anyone who knew how to protect the mind had been burned in the massive cauldron that now sat before the palace.

"That is what you were supposed to think," the jinni said evenly. He took off his mask, revealing a gaunt face with too-large golden eyes and a mess of burn scars covering nearly every inch of his skin. Even so, Kesmir recognized him.

"You're dead," he said, taking an involuntary step back. "I saw Calar set you on fire, saw her kick you off the cliff."

"My daughter is the last living Ghan Aisouri," Baron Ajwar Shai'Dzar said. His eyes glimmered in the wan light of the bottles. "Did you really think there was no one who wanted to keep me alive long enough for me to see my child on the throne your imposter empress has claimed?"

"Your daughter is barred from Arjinna. The portal—"

"The gods will find a way," Ajwar said. "She is their eyes, their voice, their sword in the darkness."

Before Kesmir could say another word, the baron pressed a golden whistle into Kesmir's hand. "Blow this from the top of Mount Zhiqui when the sun rises."

Without another word, Nalia Aisouri'Taifyeh's father evanesced. Golden smoke swirled around him and then he was gone, leaving behind nothing but wisps of honeyed evanescence and the whistle in Kesmir's palm.

He'd seen them on the Aisouri, when Kesmir and the others had fastened the ropes around the dead royals' necks before hanging them from the palace gate where they remained to this day.

It was how they'd contacted their gryphons.

Kesmir's eyes fell on the throne. The Ghan Aisouri dais had been replaced by one made of pure volcanic rock, a massive thing with hard edges and evil spirals that spilled around it like a demon's halo. Its smooth surface reflected the light of the bottles, and Calar's dark energy hung about it like a shroud.

His mind settled on his own daughter. What had the gods planned for *her*, this child of luckless love?

Calar wouldn't understand what Kes was doing, but it didn't matter: she'd left him no choice. The jinni who'd taken him in after he'd lost everything, who had shown him tenderness and a loyal, fierce love that brought down a kingdom, was still inside her, lurking in some forgotten corner of Calar's heart. But if he didn't act quickly, the best parts of Calar would be gone, stamped out by her increasing dependence on dark magic, her obsessive need to kill Nalia, whether or not the portal was closed.

Kesmir was trying to overthrow the jinni he'd once loved more than anything in the worlds not because he wanted to destroy Calar, but because it was the only way to save her.